Right Target

jay gee heath

ISBN: 0999245406
ISBN Ebook 978-0-9992454-1-5

ISBN Print Book 9780999245408
Library of Congress Control Number: 2017916367
Jay Gee Heath, Naples, FL

Also by jay gee heath

Romantic mystery
Right Talents
Right Skills
Right Dreams

Mystery with romance
Right Response
Right Target

Anthology of Tiger's Adventures in the Everglades
as told by T F Gato, a cat with attitude

Dedication

Sam

Acknowledgement

Again, thank you for your help

Janet Benjamins
Jo Anne Sullivan
Jean Smith
Lisa Wroble

I also want to acknowledge here that I have stretched the truth in the interests of telling the story. The FBI does not hire outside specialists, they have their own wine experts. (But, I guess they made an exception for Robin.)

He was gone when Robin woke. She felt the sheets. No warm spot. She let herself hope for a second that he was in the bathroom, but if so, he'd been in there a long time. In the dark. He wasn't in the kitchen making coffee either, because why would he make coffee at four in the morning? The house was quiet. Too still. It felt empty.

He had warned her; he never spent the night. But she hadn't thought he meant her. He loved her. "You love me," she whispered. "I know you do." She rubbed her hand down her face. "He loves me," she told the darkness.

He had never actually said the words, but all his actions, the attention he'd lavished on her, the thoughtful gifts, the tender endearments, spoke of love and Robin had fallen hard and fast. He'd made it easy for her. And, because she loved him, she'd thought he loved her. How could he not?

What happens now? Would he call her? Should she call him?

She sat up. An emergency. There could have been an emergency. Yes, he'd had an emergency.

But no phone had rung. Maybe he had it on vibrate. That gave her hope. He'd call. He would. And explain with a laugh why he left.

Maybe he left a note in the kitchen.

That was it. There would be a note in the kitchen. Afraid to hope, she climbed out of bed and turned on the lights. She put on a robe because she was naked and uncomfortable.

She wasn't really surprised, though, when she didn't find a note. She sank down on a stool at the counter and looking out the dark window saw her reflection. She told it, "But I'm different. I'm not one of his pickups. Not me. David loves me."

Her reflection, mussed hair and all, didn't say anything.

He was gone.

She felt a tear slide down. Wiped it. She wasn't going to allow herself to cry. Tomorrow she would ...what? Wait for him to call?

If he didn't, what would she say when she saw him again? Because she would see him again. They worked many of the same events. What would she say? How was she supposed to act?

Friday

When he hadn't called, she'd sunk low enough to call him. It hadn't been easy. She didn't have his cell number; his calls to her simply displayed as *Florida call*. He either didn't have a home phone or it was unlisted. In the end, she'd tried the security firm he worked for. He wasn't in and they wouldn't give her his number. Probably not the first woman to call him at work, she decided and left her number and a message for him to call her. God, she'd felt like an idiot. It was so high school.

And now, there he was, sitting by the desk across the room. Robin didn't falter when she saw him, and she didn't curl her lip. Or snarl. Instead, she composed her face into the bland, politely interested expression she had perfected for her work. She and Sally were here on business. Her company Fine Wines Fine Foods organized dinner parties, events, and fundraisers around wines and they were here for one last meeting with their client Brad Carlisle, one of their most difficult clients. True to form, Carlisle remained seated, not giving them the courtesy of a welcome, but he made a vague gesture to David. "My security will sit in on our meeting."

She was not quite ready to look at David; afraid her true feelings might show, she glanced around the room. The maid had called it a library, but it was more of a study with a modern theme of glass and metal which was probably considered elegant, but which felt bare and cold. The one glass-covered bookshelf made it a library.

She placed her briefcase on the desk, ignoring Carlisle's rudeness and said, "I'm acquainted with Mr. Ramirez." Too well acquainted. She waved a hand toward him, nodding to the petite redheaded woman behind her. "Sally Ramone, this is David Ramirez. Mr. Ramirez works for Discreet Security Protection. Sally is my partner and Fine Wines' chef." Robin dared a quick look. Solid, medium height, dark hair, square face, eyes of blue. She was too far away to see the silver flecks in the blue.

David stood. "Robin, Mrs. Ramone."

Taking immediate offense Carlisle said, "Mr. Ramirez doesn't just work for the firm; he is the owner."

"Oh." Robin hadn't known. "I'm sorry, I wasn't aware." And she should have been. She should have known.

"Part owner." David's correction earned him an angry glare from Carlisle.

Robin busied herself with files in her briefcase to avoid looking at Carlisle or David. "We don't need security today. This is a simple review of the arrangements for your fundraiser."

"I want him here," Carlisle said.

"You want him to check the table and seating arrangements?"

"I want him in on all phases of the dinner and auction: the schedule, the wines, the menu, table placements, wine stewards, and servers, everything." His pompous attitude reflected his physical shape, a man slightly below average height, wide, soft, and puffy. And a blowhard.

Robin withheld a sigh and shrugged. Carlisle had insisted on this last meeting before the event tomorrow night, and she had acquiesced, in part because her company liked to keep the client happy, even one as irritating as Carlisle. She dared another glance at David and her stomach knotted; she looked quickly away.

"He's welcome to sit in," she said and opened a file folder. "Table arrangement and seating plans." She opened another folder. "Menu: appetizers, main course, dessert."

Carlisle held up his hand interrupting her. "Your dessert is unacceptable. It's too boring. I've selected a more exotic flaming chocolate cherries jubilee. With cognac which I had to order."

"Mr. Carlisle, per our contract, no changes will be made at this late date." She kept her tone firm. He rated near the worst of her clients. He micro-managed with questions and complaints, continually finding fault, constantly making changes; as soon as an item was settled, he changed his mind. But now the plans were finalized. Robin might allow Carlisle to make a minimal change today, but nothing that would affect her timeline or bottom-line. Fine Wines' contract was explicit.

Sally had completed the frozen desserts and all the supplies were purchased. The glassware and serving platters were bundled and ready for delivery tomorrow.

"While you and Sally review the menu items, I'll look at the wines," Robin said. Never before had she let a customer order the wines, but when Carlisle had insisted, she'd given in. She'd been distracted at the time, distracted by David Ramirez. But lust hadn't made her completely stupid. She'd added a rider to the contract. Carlisle could order the wines and pay her company a premium for the privilege. Robin would verify the purchase before the event and Carlisle would pay for any exceptions. That's why she had come with Sally today. To inspect the wines.

"They're in my cellar. Don't concern yourself."

"I'm here to verify the wines are here in the amounts specified; I'll do that while you and Sally review the plans."

He ignored Robin's statement. "I expect Mr. Ramirez will have changes for your floor plans. I want our guests to be safe while they're in my home."

She wasn't sure how the floor plans could affect guest safety. "We have always worked closely with security firms and with Discreet Security Protection. Mr. Ramirez is welcome to review the plans and suggest changes." She might agree to changes; it would depend on what they were.

David said, "I'll also need a list of your employees."

"Your firm already has that," she said keeping her eyes on her briefcase.

"Updated list."

"There have been no changes in our employees. Fine Wines has little turnover." She picked up her purse. "Mr. Carlisle, while you confirm the schedule and general layout, I'll check the wines."

"I purchased everything we agreed upon, including the cognac for my dessert."

She ignored the intended rebuke. "I'm sorry, but our contract specifically states no changes are allowed this close to the event. It also states which wines will be served, the exact number of bottles, and that I inventory the wine today. If you can have someone show me the way, please."

His excuses and delays worried her and she decided which of her suppliers could deliver what she needed if the proper wines were not in the wine cellar. The fundraiser and meal were built around specific wines; there could be no changes. "Now."

Disgruntled, Carlisle called the maid, and as Robin turned to head out he said, "Mr. Ramirez will accompany you. He's responsible for the wines."

She stopped, her heart skipped a beat. "It's not necessary, Mr. Carlisle. I'm not going to steal any wine."

"I hired security and I want him to go with you." He waved them off.

The maid led them down the hall. His closeness made her uncomfortable, but he leaned over and whispered, "Sorry about Carlisle. He's a moron, but right now he's my boss."

She relaxed a little. Business, they'd talk business. "Mine too. The customer is always right." Keep it professional. But while she tried to think about work, her gut, she was going to call it her gut, wanted to remember his touch. The problem was his scent. Clean, sharp, male. It brought back memories; memories she intended to ignore. She wasn't going there; couldn't afford to go there. She tried not to breathe near him and slowed to let him move ahead.

The maid left them alone at the wine cellar, a ten-by-twelve interior room off the kitchen. Built-in wine racks lined three walls, three racks to a wall. Each rack was six feet high with a storage drawer along the base. Space for two thousand bottles, though it wasn't a third full. Cases of wine were stacked in a double row against the racks on the back wall.

Her event wines were in the front row. Curious, she peeked at the back row: cases of a sorry red, the type of overpriced wine Carlisle would pick, and an under-aged cognac, for the flaming dessert. She wasn't surprised by his choices.

"We need to talk, Robin. About us," David said.

"No. We don't." She turned to her wines and counted cases out loud.

He was silent a moment, then asked, "What are you counting?"

"Tomorrow night's three selections, four dinner wines, eight dessert, and six champagne." Pointing out each as she named it, she breathed a sigh of relief. They were all here. Nervous, she chattered on. "A very fine champagne for the guests as they arrive, a sought-after red dinner wine for the main course, and an ice wine. A truly wonderful dessert ice. The whole event was planned around this ice wine." She could almost taste the ice—a honey nectar, thick on her tongue. She was looking forward to serving it. And sampling it. Couldn't help the smile of anticipation.

"What's an ice wine?"

She replied without looking at him. "Grapes are left on the vine until a frost and then they're harvested. It's a very risky undertaking. A gamble…" She stopped in her monolog. Something was wrong. She looked again. Something had caught her eye. What was it?

"Hmm." She looked back and forth, up and down, and there it was. "The label," she said to herself and walked over to give it a closer look. "Strange."

The label was crooked on the ice wine. Of course, it could happen. It shouldn't, but it could. The corner of another label was visible beneath it. A different label from a different winery. They had re-boxed it? No way.

"That's not right," she muttered. The case was in the bottom row. She turned to David. "I need to open this case. Could you move the top ones? I need to see inside this box."

He carried the top two cases to the middle of the room and put them into one stack. "What's wrong? The label is crooked? Is that unusual?"

"Maybe. Maybe not."

She was already using her box cutter to open the top. Pulling out a bottle, she looked at it, put the bottle back, then looked at three more. She covered her eyes with her palms and then wiped both hands down the side of her face. She stared at the label. It just wasn't possible. No one could be this stupid. She pulled out another bottle and examined the label. It was a fake and not even a good fake. The design was off center, the colors wrong.

"Shit. Shit. Shit. Shit. I knew it. I knew it. Don't ever trust a customer to buy the wine. Especially don't trust Brad Carlisle."

"Want to clue me in?"

She'd forgotten he was there. "Counterfeit. Phony. Fake wines are common in China, but I haven't heard of it here. I need to look at all of the dessert wines. All the cases."

"Because the label is crooked?" He frowned, disbelieving.

She gave him a long look. Almost mimicked him; thought better of it, but she couldn't keep the derision from her voice. So what? He hadn't kept it out of his. "No, David, not merely because the label is crooked. The label for this ice is on top of a label of a different vintner. The labels on the bottles have the design off center and the paper color is wrong, as is the design color. But the real indication is the bottle itself. This particular ice wine, in this particular year, should be in a green-brownish bottle with a long neck and obvious shoulders, not this clear glass, sloped, bottle." She held the bottle up for him and then put it back, pulling out another. "I'm sure we'll find subtler indications later. I need to check each case."

It didn't take long. The bottles in all eight cases were forged. Then, resigned, she studied the stacked cases. "The champagne, too. And the wine. I'm going to have to check all of them."

With the champagne, the forger had done a professional job. She picked up a green bottle with a colorful label, stroked it, but shook her head in disgust. "I love this champagne. And it's popular with my customers too."

"Okay. What's wrong with the champagne?" This time he sounded interested. She gave him a quick glance.

"Again, the shape is wrong. She hefted the bottle, so he could see. "I think he, the counterfeiter, peeled the label off a cheap champagne and pasted on his own fake label. The capsule looks fine and I'm guessing the cork and wire hood are original. It's hard to bottle your own champagne, easier to print a label. This label is good, except for the colors. The colors on the real champagne are vibrant, iridescent, engraved, and gilded. Beautiful. A shimmering red and gold. Gives a hint of the taste." She paused, running through her reasoning.

"Yes. He used a cheap bottle of champagne, slightly different size and color. Washed off the label, replaced it with one he printed on the computer and voila, he has forged a one hundred fifty dollar bottle of champagne." She checked all the cases. "Six cases, six bottles per case, thirty-six bottles, one fifty a bottle. About fifty-four hundred dollars. Maybe he spent fifty, sixty dollars for the cheap stuff. Nice little profit. This dull, dingy label probably reflects the liquid inside."

She moved on to the reds, opening a box. "This red is a newer vintage of Conti, a very popular wine. A year or so back, a counterfeiting ring sold hundreds of fake Conti. Of course, those were much older and more valuable, but it looks like someone has done it on a smaller scale with this later vintage." She opened the rest of the boxes. "Three cases are obviously fake, the other? I'm not sure. This wine sells for about seventy dollars a bottle, four cases, twelve bottles in each case, forty-eight bottles." She closed her eyes, but was too angry to do the math. "You figure it out. And the ices? They cost around a hundred dollars a bottle."

Disgusted, she had David restack the cases. Bogus, all but the one case which she wasn't sure about. She couldn't be sure what was in any bottle. She looked at the cases stacked behind hers, hopefully. The sorry red Carlisle had chosen was more expensive than her selection and wouldn't pair with the meal. A decent champagne, twice as expensive as the one she had chosen, and a dessert which was not an ice. Plus, the overpriced cognac. If they were even real. She wasn't going to check. They weren't her problem.

"What now?" David asked.

"I don't know. I won't serve any of these. No way to know what's in the bottles without testing. Colored water would be the safest, but it could be any combination of ingredients. Some might be deadly. We're going to have to call the police. Let's go tell Carlisle the bad news."

Carlisle didn't take the news well. He argued with her. "I didn't buy fakes."

"The wines are counterfeit. You can't serve them; you don't know what's in those bottles.

"You're not calling anyone."

"We cannot use that wine. We need to report the counterfeiting."

"You will use the other wines I purchased."

"No. Those wines will not pair with the food. Your guests are expecting to sample unique wines. Besides, if you purchased them all from the same supplier, their authenticity is in doubt."

He stood. "You're fired."

"You can fire me. That means no fundraiser. And I'll still report it." Fortunately, she had been paid in full to date with a small balance due after the event.

He tried to look down at her, but he was too short. He glowered. "You work for me. You will do as I say."

Did he forget he had just fired her?

David spoke up. "We have to report it, Mr. Carlisle. My firm won't guard fake wine. I'll make the call for you; I have a contact in law enforcement." He walked to the corner of the room.

Robin said, "The authorities will probably confiscate everything you purchased. Do you want to cancel the benefit? Or do you want me to find replacement wines?"

Carlisle glared, but he didn't have a choice. He'd lose face if he cancelled. "Order the wines."

"I'll place the order with my supplier. It will be market price, plus. And my distributor will charge extra for immediate delivery. Payable today. No discounts. I'll use my own judgment if I need to make substitutions." She waited. She wasn't sure which way he would jump.

"Go ahead. Go ahead. Get it done." He was almost too angry to speak. At her? For finding the fakes? Or at his supplier?

She went to the opposite corner of the room to call her distributor and, after considerable discussion, was able to find the champagne and dinner wine but had to replace the ice-wine with two substitutions, both of which would pair with the desserts. Delivery was promised to her warehouse tomorrow. She wasn't going to have them shipped to Carlisle's and chance they would become mixed with the fakes. She'd bring them to the event herself—after she checked each box and every bottle.

"The two dessert wines can be presented as a special honor for your guests. It will be good public relations," she told Carlisle and handed him her point-of-sale tablet which he reluctantly signed for the full price.

David walked back, putting away his phone. "An agent will be here within twenty minutes. We are to wait. Not call anybody."

Carlisle reached for his phone and David touched his arm.

"I'm calling my supplier," Carlisle said.

David shook his head. "If you notify him of the forgeries, you may find yourself an accessory after the fact."

Robin thought David made that up, but Carlisle put down his phone.

"We do nothing until the agents get here," David repeated.

Carlisle poured himself a scotch and went back to his desk. He didn't offer anyone else a drink.

Robin and Sally moved to a chair grouping across the room to wait and David followed and sat with them. Robin busied herself fingering her cell; she didn't want to talk to David.

Sally broke a long silence. "Who did you call?" she asked him.

The question seemed to make him uncomfortable because he hesitated a moment before answering. "I called a guy in security. He said he'd call the FBI, they have jurisdiction. He knows a guy."

"Why FBI?"

Robin answered for him. "Because counterfeiting can cross state lines and wine labelling is a federal regulation."

"Oh."

After another long silence, Robin decided she had a question. "I didn't know you owned the security firm." How come you didn't tell me?

A small grimace to go with the firm jaw. "My brother does. He found a niche. Match up cops who need work with people who need security." He shrugged. "I help him sometimes."

Sally asked, "But you're part owner?"

He looked a little sheepish. She was surprised at how well she could read his expressions. "Yeah. Silent partner, mostly grunt."

She closed her eyes a moment. Part owner. And he hadn't told her. Not when they'd met at a Fine Wines event. He'd introduced himself as security. She'd replied, wine steward with the caterers. They'd found they had a lot in common and had gravitated toward each other after that. Laughed and talked. He was the rugged type she liked. His blue eyes, indigo-blue faceted with silver, shimmered when he laughed. They'd never talked shop, never talked about work, friends or family. She'd never even asked if he was married, but since he'd picked up a woman at every event, she'd assumed he was single.

Maybe they would have talked family, friends, business, work, eventually; when the new wore off. But it never did. She'd been wrapped up in the fantasy of the romance and her glands really had taken over.

She pulled herself back to the present to hear Sally say, "Fine Wines is a niche business, also. Robin started it, then brought me on when she decided to add snacks and meals. We became partners and changed the name to Fine Wines Fine Foods."

Robin stopped her from saying more. "Did you finish the walk-through?" she asked and Sally rolled her eyes. "He still wants to change things and I expect he will. Except maybe for the security requirements. The tables and layouts will be different when we get here tomorrow night. It's a good thing we have the food truck and will be bringing everything, otherwise his kitchen staff would be cooking to his order."

Sally explained to David. "We purchased a mobile food truck for storage and transport. Now we can cook or reheat the meals in our own facilities. We keep cold foods cold, frozen foods frozen, warm foods warm, and chill the wines and champagnes. It makes us totally independent."

The maid showed in two men, dressed like twins in dark suits, white shirts, dark blue ties, and black wrap-around sunglasses. Both about six feet tall, around thirty, close-cropped hair, one blond, the other dark. Why did she think typical FBI? She didn't even know what the type was. When they removed their sunglasses, she saw the dark-haired man had a scar across his right brow and cheek, at the edge of his eye. It gave her a shudder. He introduced himself as Agent Tucker, FBI. The other, the blonde, Agent Stan Caruso, smiled at her with a predatory glint in his blue eyes and held her hand too long. He did the same with Sally. Robin resisted the urge to wipe her hand on her pants.

Tucker pulled a notebook out of his pocket. "A David Ramirez reported you have some counterfeit wines?" He looked around.

Carlisle motioned to David. "My security operative insisted we call you. I'm not sure the wines are fake."

"I called John Southern; he called you," David said.

"You found the wines?"

"Ms. Garman. She says the wines are fake."

He sounded like he was supporting her, not placing blame.

Agent Tucker looked at her and she could see the doubt which he didn't try to hide. She knew he was already chalking this visit up as a waste of time, but she'd been insulted by better men.

"You think the wine is fake? You know enough about wine to be able to recognize a fake?" he asked.

"Yes."

The agent took a deep breath. "Can I see the wine please?"

"I'm going to call my supplier," Carlisle declared.

"Let us look at the wines first. If they're not fake, you don't need to worry about calling. If they are, we don't want him forewarned. Can we see the wines? Now, please."

"She'll take you." He motioned to Robin and leaned back in his chair nursing his scotch.

"Stan, get the information we need for our report while I check the wines. Lead the way, Ms. Garman." He motioned Robin ahead.

David fell in behind them.

When they reached the cellar Tucker said, "Tell me what makes you think the wines are fake. In terms a novice can understand. I'm a lover of fine wine but not an authority."

"The label on that box is crooked, the corner is loose. It caught my eye." She pointed.

He raised his eyebrow at her then walked over and stooped down to give the label a closer look. "Okay, but that could have happened during delivery."

"Doubt it, and it wouldn't explain the different label underneath."

He whistled. "Good catch." He put on a pair of gloves and gently pulled the corner of the label away from the box.

He talked to himself as he opened the case of ices. No, not talking to himself. He was using his cell to record his steps and comments. "Case of ice wine, opened." He snapped a picture of the label on the carton then of the label on one of the bottles. She watched him make a Google search and compare what he found. He looked at her with surprise and she gave him a sweet smile.

He continued talking into his cell. "Should be green/brown glass, but it's clear. The label is straight, but the design is off center. Appears to be slightly off color. No back label." He examined three bottles and then turned to her. "How many cases are counterfeit like this?"

"All the dessert." She pointed to those boxes. "And all of the champagne are fake. Three of the dinner wines are bogus, the other, I don't know.

"Did you touch the bottles?"

"I sure did."

"How about you Mr. Ramirez?"

"I touched all the cases. No reason for me to handle any bottles."

Tucker seemed to realize he still had his cell in his hand. "Okay if I record this?"

Robin snorted. David nodded.

Tucker looked in a few of the cases, pulled out a sampling of bottles. She couldn't hear what he was saying into his cell. Finally, he asked her, "Can you tell me the problems with these?"

She gave him points; he had acknowledged there was a problem. "The color is slightly paler than it should be."

Tucker nodded, frowning. "Okay. Where did you learn about wines?"

"I have been a Sommelier for twelve years and am a member of the North American Sommelier Association." If he knew anything about wines, he would know she was an expert.

"I apologize," he said. "I jumped to a conclusion. Chauvinist conclusion. I don't generally do that and my wife will give me grief when she hears about it."

"Apology accepted. I'm used to the attitude, though I don't generally get apologies. Thank you." She smiled. "And I won't tell your wife."

"I will. She'll enjoy ragging on me." He put out his hand. "It's nice to meet you."

She shook it. He might be a pretty good guy after all.

"What are you two talking about?" David asked.

Tucker explained. "The lady is a Certified Sommelier. Our expert hasn't even reached that level. What about that back row?" he asked her.

"Don't know. I didn't check. Those are not for my event."

"We will." He headed out of the cellar. "Let's go back. Do you see a lot of fake wines?"

"No, actually, these are the first."

When they entered the library, Carlisle was arguing with Agent Caruso.

"The wines are fake," Tucker said. "The ones we looked at anyhow." He referred to his cell and named them. "We'll need the shipping orders on those."

"Can't be fake. I've been buying from this guy for a year. Nothing's wrong with the wines. That woman is crazy."

"No, she's not," Tucker said. "She knows wines and those wines downstairs are bogus. The purchase orders, please."

Reluctantly Carlisle opened a drawer and pulled out a form. Tucker gave it a quick glance before handing it to Robin. She read it and looked up at Carlisle with surprise.

"You paid a fraction of what these wines are worth; weren't you a little bit suspicious?"

"No, my dealer always cuts his prices for me. I'm a good customer." He puffed up.

So the supplier didn't make as much as she'd figured. She went back to the purchase order, and her mouth dropped open. "You bought a case of 1945 Château Mouton, RC? This is one of the most faked wines in the world. There are more counterfeit bottles than real. And there is no such thing as a case. Is this in your cellar?"

When Carlisle didn't answer her, Tucker repeated the question with all the authority of law enforcement, "Is this case in your cellar?"

"No. My dealer is bringing it this afternoon."

"Have you paid for it?"

"I'm paying him when he delivers it. I'm not dumb. I wouldn't pay without having the wine in my possession."

Robin snorted. "Do you have any idea how much a single bottle of 1945 Chateau Mouton Rothschild with the *R.C. Mg* would be worth?" she asked. "It would probably bring close to one hundred thousand dollars and you think you can buy a case for ten thousand?"

"What's a shatomutton whatever?" David asked.

"A legend. One of the finest wines ever produced." Robin's voice was breathy. "Ambrosia. Or so I've been told anyway. The Chateau reserved about 2,000 bottles for itself; which is what the 'RC' on the label means. 'Reserve du Chateau'. I've never even seen a bottle."

"I have," Tucker said. "We have one confiscated."

Robin's eyes lit up, but Tucker added, "Evidence. Sorry. Locked up." He pivoted back to Carlisle. "This guy is coming this afternoon?"

"At two. To drop off my wine and pick up his money."

"We're going to be here. You're going to pay him and we're going to arrest him."

"I'm not paying for fake wine."

Tucker stared him down, pulled out his cell. "We'll work it out." He turned his back on Carlisle and issued orders to whomever answered the phone. When he turned back he found Sally in front of him.

"May we leave? We have a full schedule today," she asked him.

"Sure. You guys can go. Don't tell anyone what's happening here." He gave them a stern look. "Is that understood?"

They made affirmative motions.

"No one else knows about it do they?"

"Yes," Robin said. "I had to tell my distributor why I needed the rush order on replacement wines. He promised to keep it private."

"My friend at the FBI, the one who called you," David said, "he knows."

"Right. I'll call him. No one else?" he asked again.

They shook their heads and he waved them off with one more admonition of silence.

As soon as they were alone in the car, Sally's said, "That's the guy. The one you liked. Isn't he? The one you were dating."

Robin took a deep breath. "Yes."

"He's a hunk."

"Yeah."

Sally said, "He backed you up tonight."

Backed her up? Or just followed the law? It amounted to the same thing. She looked down at her hands clasped in her lap. "I'll remind you; he dumped me. After he bedded me." Robin had confided she had a beau and had told Sally when he'd abandoned her.

"Bastard," Sally said.

"Yes. He is. I'm still dealing with it. Can we not talk about it?" She leaned her head back in the seat and shut her eyes with a sigh.

It had been a whirlwind courtship. He hadn't come on too strong. He was smart, funny, not handsome, but terribly, mouthwateringly male. Lithe, but muscled. She could look him in the eyes in her heels. Add in the attention and affection he had showered on her and she was completely snowed. They did all the tourist things. Strolled through the craft shops; not the shop where she sold her beaded jewelry. He'd bought her a small etched plaque, *Why is the Merlot all gone?*, because it had startled a laugh out of her. At Shark Valley they'd rode the tram, climbed the tower and lunched at the Miccosukee Indian restaurant. He'd bought the frog legs and let her try one. Tasted like chicken.

Another day, it was Everglades City and the tour boat ride, lunch at the Oar House, grouper sandwiches. He'd made her sit on the stuffed alligator. Then it was the casino. Loud, noisy—neither of them liked it. She didn't gamble because she always lost. He wasn't interested. They stopped at Corkscrew Swamp Sanctuary on the way back and savored the quiet and beauty.

They'd listened to the Philharmonic orchestra and had a quiet dinner on the waterfront.

She'd thought it was real though some part of her must have recognized it was just sex. A short-term affair

And today he wanted to talk. Maybe she should have listened. Maybe, if he attended the Fine Wines event tonight, she would listen. She shook herself. No. Not going back.

**

When she spotted him that night, leaning against the wall, her lip did curl—just for an instant. Then she smiled and gave him a slight nod and managed to stay busy and avoid him most of the night. She was packing up when she sensed him behind her; his aftershave, soap, whatever it was, gave him away. It also had a direct line to her gut.

He was frowning when she turned around. "Are you avoiding me?"

She squared her shoulders and looked him in the eye. She could do this. She'd practiced.

"Yes."

"Why?"

"Because."

"Because why?"

She studied him a long moment trying to remember all the things she'd planned to say to him, but his anger confused her. Why was he angry? Wasn't she the one who should be angry?

"Because I know I'm supposed to act like nothing unusual happened between us, and I can't. So, I'm avoiding you." This morning at Carlisle's she'd been working. There had been people around. This morning she'd been able to act normal.

"What?" he said as if her statement had confused him.

"One. More. Time." She ground out the words. "I'm uncomfortable and embarrassed. I've been out of the dating game a long time. And I never did the casual sex, one-night stand thing."

"We're friends. We had sex. What's the big problem? We're still friends."

"No, David. We are not friends. We were friends. Then you courted me and made me fall in love with you. We made love. At least I thought we were making love. You left. I'm avoiding you because I can't pretend it didn't mean anything."

"Of course it meant something. We're friends. Sex didn't change that."

She dipped a shoulder. "It did for me."

"It shouldn't. We're good together. We're still friends."

She wanted to reach out, touch him, wrap herself around him. But she held firm. "We were. Past tense." It hurt to be near him.

"We still need to work together."

Only through tomorrow night, then I'm done. "As business associates, not friends."

A guest asked her about the wine allowing her to turn away from him. The next time she saw him he was in a corner talking to a blonde. Well, what had she imagined? She'd turned him down. Couldn't expect him to go home alone. He never had. Good thing he was part owner because he seldom worked a whole night and frequently left early with the blonde of the evening. She'd asked him about it, back when they were just friends. If he took them home. And he'd told her, *No, I never take them home; I go home with them. I never spend the night.*

Saturday

She was lying in bed, in that luxurious in-between zone, not asleep, not quite awake basking in the erotic warmth, the sensual tingles of his hands on her when the phone jerked her out of the memories. She groaned, took a deep steadying breath, then rolled over and reached for her cell.

"Yes?"

"We have to talk."

It took her a moment, her dream still vivid. "David?"

"Yes. We have to talk."

Again? Hadn't they talked last night? Must be what triggered her dream; she could still feel his hands.

She thought about hanging up. That would be childish, but still she was tempted. What if he was calling to tell her he had been a fool? To tell her he loved her? She could picture him. All male and determined. The blue eyes that melted her heart. The mouth that wanted to kiss her. His lips, they had done marvelous things to her in her dream. She sat up.

"What do we have to talk about?"

"Carlisle wants us to go over your schedule again."

Work. He wanted to talk work. Not love. Business. Besides, he'd left with the bimbo last night. Annoyance replaced her bittersweet memories and she closed her eyes and took a silent breath and gave herself an order to act like an adult.

"Carlisle is going to drive me crazy."

"Tell me about it, but he is the client and he wants me to go over the schedule and staff with you one more time. How about I come over to your place?"

"No." She didn't even think, spit it out. She didn't want him in her house. Near her. Near her bedroom. She didn't trust him near her. Didn't trust herself with him near her. "I'm still in bed." Why had she said that?

"Then it's a perfect time for me to come over."

"No, David, we're business associates." She hung up, her hand shaking. She was angry. At him. At herself for wanting him. He'll call back, she thought. I'd better have some type of adult explanation.

He called with an apology. "Robin, I'm sorry. Won't happen again. But we still need to meet."

"Give me a minute." She was still angry. Where? Not here. She really didn't want him here. Not the office. "Meet me at the donut shop on Fifth in half an hour." That should work.

"OK." He hung up.

She showered the anger off. Hot. Then cold. Then hot. There was a lot of anger. At herself, for believing he loved her. At him, for misleading her. At herself, for hoping still. That was the worst part. The hope. Well fuck it. She laughed at herself. Good choice of words. She dressed casually, jeans and a tee shirt. No makeup. She seldom wore make up, no reason to start today. She grabbed her purse and headed for the donut shop.

He was waiting at their table out front. She had forgotten. Their place, their table. Damn. He was watching her from behind his sunglasses. Well two could play that game; today she'd remembered her own. He was drinking coffee and had a bagel in front of him. Another cup was sitting on the table with an apple fritter. Her favorite. Damn. He was smooth.

"I ordered you coffee and your favorite donut."

She didn't say anything. Couldn't. She was working on her poker face. Love, hate, and self-disgust were warring inside her.

"Our first date."

She froze half seated, glad for the sunglasses. She could feel the tears try to well in her eyes. She blinked them away. "I'm done. Call

Sally. Talk with her." She stood and started to walk away, but he was quick and grabbed her arm.

"I'm sorry. Again. I promise to keep it all business, if you'll sit down."

She shook off his arm and sat.

"What is it Carlisle wants us to go over?" She didn't touch the coffee or the fritter.

"The timing for champagne, dinner, dessert. Which employees you'll assign to what areas. Where they'll be stationed."

"You have all that."

"I know. Carlisle wants to be sure there are no changes."

"There are no changes."

David hesitated. "He wants me to be present when the wines are delivered."

She frowned. "Why?"

"Who knows? Told me to double check the inventory. Carlisle's paying. We work for him. I do what he wants."

She didn't have much choice and what did it matter? Simply some more Carlisle micro-management. "Noon. At Fine Wines. I will be touching each bottle, so the delivery will take time. My supplier understands and will wait. Anything else?"

"Yeah. Eat your fritter."

"No thank you. From now on, any dealings you have with my firm, call Sally." She stood.

"Robin."

"What?"

"I'm sorry."

"Yeah, so you said."

"No." He stood, took off his glasses. "I'm sorry we can't be friends."

She studied his face, saw the remorse. Because he hurt her? Or because she was avoiding him?

"Yeah. Me too, David. Me too." She turned and left. *Me too.* She'd get over it. Time heals a broken heart. Maybe she hadn't really fallen in love. Maybe it had been so long since she had looked at a man she had forgotten the difference between love and lust. Maybe. Maybe. But she knew what love was. No one mistook this feeling.

Time would help. Once she got through Carlisle's dinner she'd never see him again. Next week Fine Wines would be launching its wine university and she would begin a new phase in her life as wine tutor. Back when David had romanced her, she'd toyed with the idea of putting her future on hold. Now she was glad she hadn't. Teaching people about fine wines was the distraction she needed to begin the healing process.

She didn't go straight to her new office but took a detour to admire the two large comfortable classrooms, the wine tasting room, and the ultra-modern kitchen with seating for twelve students for the cooking classes. She sighed in satisfaction. Fine Wines was expanding, moving into a new niche, wine education and appreciation. At events she'd found people wanted to know more about the wines and there was never enough time to go into detail; her series of four two-hour classes would cover wines from planting, to growing, harvesting, bottling, and tasting.

Sally's classes paired meals and their preparation with fine wines; that's what the kitchen was for.

The school opened next week, and classes were full with a waiting list.

Robin sat at her desk and let her mind drift to the first time David had asked her out. It had surprised her. Tempted her. But he'd already chatted up his chosen blonde conquest, so what did that mean? He'd take the bimbo home. Leave her bed to take Robin out? Ugh.

She'd said, "No. Busy," and walked away to circle the room. Do her job. She must have become a challenge because their relationship changed. A barely perceptible change. They still worked together, but now he was more attentive, in the way of a man interested in a woman. Watching her, listening when she spoke with guests. He hadn't neglected his duties, but he always seemed to be close.

He talked to her more. Feeling her out, she saw now. He'd played her. She'd let him. What did that say about her? His attention excited her, and she was pleased because she wasn't stacked or blond, but average build, average height, average brown hair, lighter brown eyes. She snorted. She sure fit his empty-headed bimbo role. She'd believed he really liked her. He'd been so thoughtful. So loving.

Deep down had she known? Had her heart hoped her gut was wrong, because it wasn't her gut which let him into her bed. It was lust and love mixed together. Oh, maybe one corner of her mind said watch it, this is too good. But the warning never reached her heart or the part of her which longed for a man.

"Idiot," she said and began entering the final figures from last night. She had to use multiple programs, opening and closing each separately. One for food and supplies. Another for employees and payroll. Still another to order wines. She worked until Jimmy her supplier arrived on schedule with David right behind him. She introduced the two men then led the way to the food truck. "Sorry about this, Jimmy," she said.

"I understand. Hard to believe Carlisle had fake wine. You know Robin, none of this makes any sense."

"I know, Jimmy. I can't figure it out. The labels were so bad, I don't see how anyone could hope to pass them off." She shook her head.

"Do you suppose someone wanted to make Carlisle look foolish? He's kind of a pr— um, a jerk," Jimmy said.

"Could be, I suppose, if the supplier knew there were wine buffs invited. But those buffs would know I was catering and the mud would splatter on me too. It's a real stupid counterfeiter."

"Why do you say the counterfeiter is stupid?" David asked.

Robin answered. "The wine and ice substitutes were sloppy and amateurish. Anyone with a little wine knowledge would notice. The champagnes might pass a quick visual inspection; the guy actually did a pretty fair job with both the bottle and label, except for the vibrant colors and the engraving." She shrugged. "Stupid because we'd never have served those bottles."

She opened another case. "The red is a popular fine wine. Most of the people at the fundraiser would have a bottle at home. We leave two or three bottles of wine on every table after we pour the first glass and the patrons would know immediately the wine was a knockoff. The reds were incredibly bad forgeries. The forger didn't even try to make them look real."

She shook her head. "Besides, I told you, there's no way my people would have served them. My crew knows wines." She moved to another case. "It doesn't feel personal. Just stupid."

"You have a lot of wait staff. Would they really recognize the fakes?" David asked.

"Fine Wines Fine Foods is a wine caterer and our stewards are knowledgeable, so yes, they would have noticed. The only thing which might make sense would be if the supplier thought Carlisle would keep the wines in his cellar. But surely Carlisle bragged about his fundraiser." She shook her head again. "Not my problem, thank God. Let's finish here."

They moved the ices and champagnes into the chiller to start cooling. Both she and Jimmy had coats. She hadn't thought to tell David to bring one. Meanness? No. She hadn't been thinking. "There's a jacket on the back of the door into the washroom," she told him.

"I'm okay."

"We'll wait for you. This will take a while." He shrugged and went for the jacket.

Twenty minutes later they were done. "That's it. Everything is okay," Robin said.

"Knew it would be. My people are all trustworthy."

"I know, but we had to do it. I'll sign the paperwork and add ten percent for your time."

"You're being more than fair. Always good working with you, Robin. Going to miss you. Hope Rome will be as easy."

"He will be. You'll like him, maybe even more than me."

Jimmy gave her a salute and drove off.

"What was that all about? Why is he going to miss you?" David asked.

"Sally and Rome will be managing the party and event side of the company beginning at close of business today. I'm heading our new sub-division, the wine school. We're giving classes on fine wines and pairing wines with fine foods. I'm teaching the wine classes. I'll still be around as advisor and attending a few events, since some clients insist."

"How long have you known this?"

"It's been in the works for about a year."

He was silent for a long time. "And you didn't think to mention this to me?"

"It doesn't affect security."

"It might have affected you and me."

"There is no you and me. There never was any you and me. Remember? Mr. It-is-only- sex; I don't spend the night."

"You should have told me."

About switching her responsibilities in her own business? "Neither of us discussed what we did for a living, so any change in my position was immaterial."

She didn't want to talk about 'them'. "What do you want to do with the wine? We can lock the truck."

"I'll have one of our men stay with it. Who is Rome?"

"Sally's husband. We brought him in about three years ago as a sommelier. We've been training him to take over. You've seen him at the other events." Rome and Sally had fallen in love and married. The thought made her frown. She'd believed she'd found that happiness with David. Silly girl.

"Which one of you is working tonight?"

"Both of us. Carlisle insisted and we made him pay for it." She said that with a little smile until she remembered she was talking to David. "I have paperwork." She held up the delivery papers. "You can wait here for your man." She turned and left, dropped the forms in accounting, stopped in to let Sally know the wines were set, and headed for her new office where she sat and gazed unseeing out the window.

A small part of her was a little teary-eyed about saying goodbye to her duties as a sommelier, but a larger part was excited about the future. She shook off the self-pity and double-checked the plans for Carlisle's event.

**

The guests were loud, and boisterous, and splurging. Each item in the silent auction had multiple bids. Of course, there were minor glitches which Fine Wines glossed over. Glitches made because Carlisle had changed the seating arrangements and placed a bottle of his cognac on each table. She'd heard him taking credit for choosing the wine and champagne and boasting he had demanded she supply the pair of dessert ices.

She'd managed to avoid David and was feeling pretty smug, until she turned and nearly bumped into him standing behind her. When he reached out to steady her; his hand burned her arm.

"David. I didn't realize you were here."

"Really? You've been avoiding me all night. Again. I finally figured the only way I'd get to talk to you would be if I came up behind you."

She shrugged.

"Pretty dress. Nice necklace."

She gave him a real smile, touching the low neckline, feeling the silk. A special design from May's Vintage Clothing. Her hand moved to the beaded necklace, her own creation. She stroked the center stone. "Thank you. My going away presents to myself." Why had she told him that? She shut her eyes. When she opened them she saw Monica standing behind him.

Monica glowed. "Robin, you promised to introduce me to this handsome man."

She hadn't. Now what should she do? Introduce David the player? He never left any of the events alone; he always went home with some woman. And now, blond, bosomy Monica wanted to meet *Mr. always-leaves-events-with a buxom bimbo.*

She made the introduction, but since she didn't know Monica's last name, she didn't bother with David's and she wondered if they would bother to tell each other. "David, meet Monica, Monica meet David."

David gave her a strange look and then smiled at Monica. When they seemed to forget she was there, she edged around them. She wasn't going to cry. That would be pitiful. He wanted to be friends and friends helped friends with introductions, didn't they?

She stopped by a table to answer questions about the ice wines, grateful for the distraction. "Yes, ice wine is made from frozen grapes. Different rules apply in different countries, but for it to be a real ice the grapes must be left to freeze on the vine. In the U.S. if the grapes are frozen after harvest there must be a disclaimer on the bottle."

To another question she agreed, "Yes, you really can taste the difference." To another she explained, "In parts of Canada the VQA—the Vintners Quality Alliance—governs the picking. The grapes must be picked at minus eight to minus ten degrees."

She loved serving the ice wines, customers were excited about the taste, the rarity, and the gamble vintners took leaving grapes on the vine to freeze. For some reason, the two ice wines loosened checkbooks and wallets. Rome had noticed and she knew it would be factored into the next fund raiser.

Mixed in were questions about the dessert itself. She nodded; this was why they'd set up the education division, because of the interest and the questions. "Yes, the actual dessert should always be less sweet then the ice, which is why Fine Wines chose the toffee pudding. Yes, I believe the pudding is made from dates. It is amazing isn't it? Did you also sample the chocolate mousse cup?"

Midway through dessert, she noticed Monica slip upstairs to the main house. Then she saw David follow her. Oh, an assignation in the owner's bedroom? That was pretty blatant. This was the first time he followed the bimbo to the bedroom area.

She happened to be looking in that direction about a half hour later when David came back into the room. Huh. She could be honest with herself; she'd been wondering how long they would take and had kept one eye on the door. Their eyes met for a second and then he stepped quickly to the side, turning away, as Monica came back in. He followed her out the front door a minute later. Going back to her place? They'd missed dessert to get their early start on a short night.

Not my business, she thought and went back to work.

Sunday

Before opening her front door, she peeked through the peephole. David? She looked down at herself, blue pajamas with bunnies, blue bunny slippers. Silly, maybe, but decent. So what? She pulled the door open far enough to face him, but with her body braced behind it. "What are you doing here, David?"

"I want to talk to you."

She didn't roll her eyes. "I told you. We don't have anything to talk about."

He thrust some papers into her hand. "Look at these."

She glanced down and saw a picture of Monica. "I introduced you. I know what she looks like."

"Next picture," he ordered.

"I don't understand," she said as she looked through the photos.

"Those are her mug shots. After, I arrested her last night. Things aren't always what they appear." He rubbed his jaw. "I wasn't going home with those women."

He left with them. Didn't go home with them? Curious, she opened the door wide. "Maybe you should come in and explain." She motioned him to the living room.

"I'm a cop. I've been working undercover as a security guard. We were after a jewel thief working parties catered in private homes."

One more thing she didn't know. She interrupted. "You're not part owner of Discreet Security Protection?"

"No. I mean yes. I am part owner. My brother runs the business. I help with funding and send him cops who want extra work."

She nodded, waiting.

"The description we had of the thief, was blond and, um…" He looked embarrassed.

"Buxom? Built?" Robin helped.

"Yes. I approached the appropriate blondes and determined if they had an invitation. If not, it was a simple matter to find out who the woman came with. If she was alone, then we ran her name and I escorted her off the premises. Up until last night, all we had were dead ends.

"You introduced me to Monica and she admitted slyly she'd crashed the event. I stayed close while my men ran her name. She excused herself to use the ladies room and I followed her and watched as she went directly to the library and opened the safe. She grabbed the jewelry and cash and shoved it into a holster-like bag she had strapped to her inner thigh. I recorded the whole thing. My men arrested her when she went out the front door."

He paused.

"We had enough for a warrant and searched her place where we found a number of pieces from earlier robberies. She's not answering any questions; she's lawyered up, but we're guessing she worked alone and used the newspaper society section for event schedules. It was a pretty profitable gig, but she should have stopped while she was ahead."

Robin remembered how she'd felt last night and studied her bunny slippers. "When you both disappeared upstairs, I thought…. Well I misjudged."

"Yes. I know what you thought you saw last night."

That sounded a little like a rebuke. "I drew my conclusion based on an impression you worked very hard to convey."

"I know. I'm sorry. I had to mislead you. I came over today because I wanted you to know the truth."

She searched his face. "You really were not going home with the bim—um, blondes?"

"No. I never even left with them."

"And your maxims? You never bring a woman home." She couldn't say the other one, *never stay the night*. "Were they true?"

He stopped and swallowed, his turn to look down. "That was the truth. I never bring a woman home. Never spend the night."

And he'd proved it with her.

"I want you to know," he said. "When we, um, you and I, um, became friends. You were different. Special. I never set out to hurt you." He paused. His voice was quieter as he added, "You believe me?"

She saw it was important to him. Didn't understand why he would care what she thought; they weren't involved anymore. Why would he need her to believe him? The only difference his confession made was at least she wasn't one of many.

"Yes. I believe you thought I was special." Maybe she had been special when it began. She had felt special. He'd said all the right things, made all the right moves. A touch on her shoulder to point something out, leaving a warm spot. Or his hand on the small of her back to guide her. Their first kiss was on the Naples Pier at sundown. He'd asked first. By then she was ready to beg him to kiss her. It was sweet and gentle. The second though, the second kiss, made her melt and turned her insides to mush.

She waited, but he didn't seem to have more to say. She looked down at the photos again. "It's shameful, but I really want to gloat at the mug shots."

He laughed.

"What happens to her now?"

"She has some outstanding warrants. One is federal. Whoever gets her, she'll go to jail."

Another long silence.

She asked him the question she would have asked a long time ago if she hadn't had fairy dust in her eyes. She wanted to know. "Are you married?"

"Once. Seems like a long time ago. Ended bad. Divorced."

"Children?"

"No. How about you?" he asked.

"I was married. To a really good man. He died."

"I'm sorry."

"It was a long time ago, but thank you."

He hesitated. "I have to get back to work. Can I come back?"

She stuck her tongue between her lips, but shrugged her shoulder, not sure how she felt.

"Can we can be friends?" he asked.

She looked down. "Maybe. I don't know yet. What you did today? Coming here." She motioned with her hand at the pictures. "This helped." She didn't feel so used.

He stopped with his hand on the door. "Can I call you?"

She paused, deciding. Could she be friends? She still wasn't sure. But, he seemed desperate for her to agree. "Yes, call. No promises."

He looked relieved, maybe she'd been right about desperate.

"Okay, thanks. I'll call tomorrow." He stood there, and then seemed to rouse himself. "Gotta go. I'll call. In the morning." And he left.

She watched through the peep hole as he stepped into his car and drove off. Then she turned and leaned against the door. She wasn't sure she could be friends. But maybe an affair? A little passion. Some excitement. Certainly more satisfying than pining for him. It would be good for her.

**

David caught himself whistling as he left her bungalow. He felt light, relieved. He laughed. He'd been annoyed when she'd told him about the wine school and he wasn't sure why. What did he care? Why did he want to know? He'd had his time with her. That should have been enough. Always had been. He didn't do repeats. Once he'd slept with them, it was over.

But Robin? His attraction to her had been unusual right from the start. She wasn't blond or built, the type he normally liked. His height, long brown hair. She wasn't beautiful. Average, maybe. But somehow she was different. Three dimensional, rather than a paper cutout. Laughing, alive, vibrant.

She wasn't his usual type, but he made it a point to seek her out and found her fun to talk to; easy to be with, sweet, friendly. Asking someone like her out? That wasn't his usual pattern. But he'd wanted time alone, uninterrupted by people and work responsibilities. She hadn't made it easy for him, but something about her pulled, made him want to be near her. He liked the way she made him feel, happy wanting to smile. But she scared him, too. Deep down scared him. If he got too close, he'd be snared. Near her, he didn't worry, like an addict he enjoyed her closeness. Away from her, he became more objective, and he feared her attraction.

She was giving him another chance. They would be friends. She was the first woman he wanted to spend time with, the first he wanted to be with. She was smart and savvy. A hard worker. He enjoyed her company, her gentleness and smile. Her laugh. It was intoxicating. It was just like her to admit to some shame and enjoyment over the arrest photos.

He was going to win back her trust. It might take time, but he'd do it. Because she was under his skin. He'd made a mistake before. He should've kept it friendly. Those few weeks with her had been the best he could remember in a long time. Carefree. She was easy to be with. He wasn't always on guard as he had been with his ex. Robin always saw the good, the positive; never looked for hidden motives. He shouldn't have kissed her, but he'd wanted her so much he could taste it. He shouldn't have let it end up in bed.

Once they were friends again, he'd court her. He knew her weak spots. He'd romanced her into bed once, he could do it again. God she'd been fantastic. Shy to begin with and then a passionate lover. He had forced himself to leave. He'd almost stayed. He'd wanted to, but he hadn't greeted the dawn in a woman's bed in years. They got ideas if you did that. If he was gone, they understood. He didn't have to listen to begging, wailing. The women knew going into it he'd be gone. He was a little ashamed because he might have led her on. Led her to think she was special. She was different. She was special. He'd made a mistake walking out. He was going to win her back. It might take time, but he'd do it. Because she was under his skin.

He could live with this woman.

He wiped the silly smile off his face. Where had that thought come from? He wasn't getting tied down to any one woman. No matter how happy she made him feel. He'd gone to her because, as his friend, she needed to know about Monica. That was all.

And he'd been relieved when she said he could call, but already he wasn't sure he would. The sex had been great, sure, but he liked his life exactly the way it was. She had him so mixed up. When he was with her, he felt like he was on a high, drunk.

But now? He wasn't sure he should see her again. And tomorrow? How would he feel tomorrow?

Monday

Robin needn't have worried about renewing their friendship, David didn't call. Still, she had done the high school girl thing of looking at her cell every few minutes, shaking it to make sure it worked, checking for missed calls. There hadn't been any. She was angry at herself again for believing.

She didn't try to call him, but used her energy to clean the house top to bottom, a task she had started Sunday. She found dust in the kitchen drawers along with crumbs. Wiped the cobwebs off the ceilings and the walls and the dust from behind the pictures. How did dust cling to a vertical surface? She pulled out every piece of furniture and cleaned behind and under it. More dust, along with dead spiders and bug parts. Ugh. She wasn't a bad housekeeper, merely a disinterested one.

The phone rang and she mentally slapped herself; disgusted, because her heart beat faster, still hoping it was David. Caller ID told her, Florida call. That wasn't helpful. Her tentative *Hello?* brought a response from Agent Tucker asking if she would come to his office in the morning and meet with their wine expert, Agent Johnson, to discuss the fake wines. He added a bribe. "I'll make you a deal. Help us out and you can see Carlisle's fake '45 Château Mouton."

David wasn't the only one who could make her heart beat faster. "It's a deal. If you also tell me what happened after we left Mr. Carlisle's."

There was a long pause on the other end of the line. "You drive a hard bargain, but I think we can share. We confiscated all the cased wines and arrested his supplier who is now in jail."

"Thank you. Can I see your real Mouton?"

"No. That's locked up. But you can see and touch Carlisle's."

That would have to be enough. "Okay, tomorrow at ten. Where?"

"At my office."

"Where is your office?" She rolled her eyes.

"Tamiami Trail North." He gave her the address.

She was almost giddy, the Château Mouton. Okay, a copy. But still. She did a little dance and decided she had done enough work today and her house was clean and she was restless, she decided to hit the beach and walk off her energy. Besides, she was having problems with the dolphin design she wanted for the beaded necklace she was making. She couldn't decide how to form the water and spray as the animal leaped from the water. The beach always helped her work out the kinks, mull over a motif which wasn't jelling. Once she had that image in her brain, she could transfer the picture to graph paper and then begin the actual weaving.

She put her wallet in her back jeans pocket, picked up her car keys, put on her shoes, and headed out. She parked two streets north of the hotel beside a red Beamer like the one she'd lusted after. The car had a Miami-Dade specialty tag and a beach sticker. Collier County property owners and taxpayers received stickers free, but anyone could buy a sticker: people from the east coast, tourists, renters. She wasn't sure how she felt about non-property owners being able to obtain a sticker since there was limited parking, certainly not enough even for taxpayers. Didn't make sense. Go figure.

This specialty tag spelled out STELER. She sounded it out. Stellar? Something astronomical? Or steeler? A fan maybe? Huh. Is that what it meant?

The only other vehicle in the lot was a handicap van with a wheelchair lift. She could see hand controls and no driver's seat when she peeked inside. She'd never considered how difficult it was for a person who couldn't walk to visit the beach. Bizarre juxtaposition. Hotshot fast car parked beside a handicap machine.

The short walk worked off the restless, but brought her no solution to her design problem and she let it go when she reached the waterfront bar and sat to watch the tourists and trade gossip with Doug the bartender. She had one drink and walked the quarter mile back.

As she neared the parking lot, she saw flashing red and blue lights bouncing off the sand and slowed her steps. She couldn't see the lot, but a young patrolman stood at the foot of the boardwalk path. "My car is parked up there. Can I go get it?"

He came to full alert. "Your car? Ma'am? What kind of car?"

"Tan Ford Edge."

"And your name?"

"Robin Garman."

"Stay right here, ma'am and I'll check."

He was gone a few minutes and returned with a man in khaki pants and a blue shirt with a badge clipped to his belt. The patrolman introduced him as Detective Andrew Scott. Cheerful chubby face, tan hair.

"Can I see some ID please, ma'am," the detective asked.

"Sure." She reached for her wallet. "What happened?"

"We're still investigating."

"Oh." Well, that was sure informative. She handed him her driver's license.

"That your car in the parking area?" he motioned his head in the direction of the lot.

"If it's a tan Ford Edge, probably."

"Is it or isn't it?"

Maybe not so cheerful.

"Detective Scott, I parked my Ford Edge in the lot about an hour ago. If there is one of that description there, then it's probably mine. But I can't see it, so I can't say for sure. I'm not trying to be difficult, just accurate."

He stopped to study her. "Fair enough. Let's go look." He led her back up the path.

"That's my car and that's where I parked it. What happened? I don't see anything wrong."

"Let me ask a few more questions. I don't want to influence your replies. You parked about an hour ago. Did you see anyone here?"

"No."

"Did you see any vehicles parked here?"

"Red Beamer from Miami and a handicap van, green. Had a wheel-chair lift."

He studied her again. "Red Beamer? Are you sure?"

"Yes. I noticed it because I wanted that car." In red. Sexy. But it wasn't the least bit practical, so she'd bought the SUV.

"How do you know it was from Miami?"

"The license tag and frame said Miami-Dade."

"Notice the number?" he asked not waiting for an answer before he asked, "Anyone inside?"

"I didn't notice if there was anyone inside. I wasn't staring. The tag was S-T-E-L-E-R." She spelled it out.

He stopped writing. "You remember the tag?"

She shrugged. "I was trying to figure what the letters stood for, and best I could come up with was something to do with stars. Or football. A mindless puzzle."

He nodded wordlessly. Pulled out his phone and read the number to someone and told them to run it. Then he started another track. "You didn't answer your phone."

"I didn't bring it with me. No reason to take it for a walk on the beach and a drink at the bar. I brought money and my ID." She had left her cell home on purpose. She didn't want to keep checking it.

"Okay. Hold on a minute." He hit the speed dial on his cell. "We don't need a warrant. The lady is here."

Robin heard an angry voice through the phone.

"She says she took a walk on the beach and stopped at the bar for a drink."

She heard more yelling. Scott snorted. "Yeah, yeah. Go check with the bartender and then we'll see you back at the station."

"Can you tell me now what happened?" she asked when he put his cell away.

"Soon. Would you come down to police headquarters and make a statement?"

"Is that a request?" He obviously wasn't going to tell her anything. So, she'd read about it in the morning paper or see it tonight on TV.

"Yes."

"I guess. Where is it?"

"Where is what?"

"Your headquarters?" What was it with these law enforcement types? Did they think everyone knew where their office was?

"Oh, I'll drive you and bring you back to your car when we're done."

"How about I follow you in my own car. Then no one has to worry about me getting home." She wanted to be free to leave when she was ready. Her little walk had become a major undertaking.

They each got in their respective cars and she waited while he spoke on his cell and then followed him out. He drove slowly and she didn't have any trouble keeping up with him and was even able to watch the patrol car following close behind. That must have been who he was talking to on the phone.

Turned out she did know where the station was located. She had forgotten because it was off a small side road hidden behind a wall of trees. She'd never been down there. She parked in a visitor slot and Detective Scott led her inside and down a long hall to a large noisy squad room. Most desks were empty but a few were occupied by what she assumed were detectives who wore badges on their belts and had holsters either under their arms or at their waists. One female. Maybe there were more women out in the field.

Detective Scott motioned for her to sit by a desk and he sat behind it and handed her a paper and a pen. "Why don't you write down what you did tonight and when. Then we'll talk."

She was nervous and hesitated. "Can you at least tell me what happened?"

He considered. "The handicap van was stolen. It's the third one this month. You might have supplied our first lead."

"I heard about those. I can't imagine someone stealing from a handicapped person, stealing from the helpless." She had been disturbed with the meanness of such an act, but then most crooks stole from the helpless. Then she added, "You were scaring me; I was beginning to think I might need a lawyer." She picked up the pen, thought a minute, and began writing.

His phone rang two times while she wrote. His conversation was mostly yeah and okay and he scribbled things in his notebook.

When she finished, she passed it over and he read it through.

"Okay, a couple more questions. Where were you before you went to the beach?"

"Home."

He read off her address.

"Yes, that's where I live."

"Can anyone vouch for you being there?"

"No, I live alone now." Where was this going?

"You decided to go to the beach?"

"Yes, I was restless." Suddenly she remembered. "Oh, I had a phone call on the landline which is why I was restless."

"Can the caller vouch for you?"

She managed to keep her face straight. "Probably. It was the FBI."

"The FBI? Are you in trouble with the FBI?"

"Goodness no. Of course not. It might be a long story." She waited for him to give her the go-ahead and told him about the bogus wines.

"I heard about that. Yeah. What's the Agent's name? I'll give him a call."

That stopped her and she leaned back. "You're going to check if he called me? Do you honestly believe I would make up something like that?"

"I'm just eliminating you as a suspect. Routine."

She listened as he talked to Agent Tucker. He didn't seem to have any problem telling Tucker all about the missing van. Had he forgotten she was there? No. He kept glancing at her as he told Tucker about the case. And told her too. She couldn't not listen, besides, she was curious. Scott disclosed that at first they'd thought she was either a victim or an accomplice, had maybe dropped off the car thief.

"We ran the Beamer's tag and have a name and address. Dade County is going to run a car by for us." He listened some more, writing something down and then finished up. "Either Detective Ramirez or I will call if we need help. Thanks." He put his cell down on the desktop.

"Ramirez? Did you say Ramirez?" It was out before she could stop herself.

**

It hadn't been easy to verify Robin's statement; David fought for every answer he got. The bartender looked at his badge and read his name aloud. Slowly. Looked him up and down. Evaluating him. David recognized the appraisal.

"What do you want to know?"

David displayed Robin's license photo on his cell. "Recognize her?"

The bartender glanced down. "Yeah. Why?"

"She's a witness. Helping us with an investigation. Do you know her?"

The bartender relaxed a fraction.

"Okay. Yeah, I know her."

"Have you seen her recently?"

"Little while ago."

"When? How long was she here?"

"Little while ago. Stayed maybe, an hour."

"Drunk?"

David wasn't sure why he'd asked that, but it got a reaction.

"Robin drunk?" The guy laughed. "Hardly."

David didn't like that. She'd been hanging at a bar. On a first name basis with the bartender. "You know her name? You on a first name basis with all your customers?"

"No. Not all."

"She chat you up? Pick up a customer? You maybe?"

"Look mister..."

"Detective. Detective Ramirez."

"Detective Ramirez. What is it you want to know? You said she was a witness helping you. Your question makes it sound like you think she's soliciting. No one solicits in here. We're not that kind of a bar."

"Answer my question. She pick up customers?" Way to antagonize a witness.

"No." And then he surprisingly volunteered additional information. "She comes in sometimes, has a drink. We chat, as you say."

"She was here tonight for an hour or so, had a drink, and chatted."

"Correct."

"What was she drinking?" He saw the bartender's lips quirk.

"Milk with a shot of cream."

"Milk with a sho…" he stopped. "Alcoholic?"

"Nope. But heavy on the fat." The bartender was laughing at him. "Helps her sleep she says. If she's here in the daytime, she'll get a virgin Cape Codder."

"What's a Cape Codder?"

"Cranberry juice and vodka."

"She comes here and doesn't drink?"

"Sometimes she'll have a glass of wine. We're known for our cellar."

"She leave with anyone tonight? Meet up with anyone?"

"Came in alone, left alone."

"You sure?"

"Yep. We done? I've got a wine order to put in." He walked away when David nodded.

She came to the bar often enough to be known by the bartender and yet didn't drink or pick up customers. She parked two blocks away and walked. He was trying to decide if it made any sense but gave it up and headed back to the station. He would ask her.

He hadn't called her. Of course, he'd had an excuse. They'd had a home invasion and by the time he'd cleared the case, her attraction had faded. He still thought about her. The happy. The sunny. He filed it away.

******

"My partner, Detective Ramirez. I believe you two know each other. He said the bartender confirmed your story."

"Story? That wasn't a story. It was what happened." She closed her mouth on her outrage. She wasn't happy David was checking on her. Or that he'd probably shared her seduction with Scott.

"Calm down. Calm down. We had to confirm the facts. Detective Ramirez did. Agent Tucker did. Now we can move on to other suspects. It's routine police procedure."

She was slightly mollified, but then she had a new problem. David was behind her; his aftershave enveloped her. She barely had time to compose her face before he stood in front of her. She saw a flurry of emotions cross his, but couldn't read any of them.

"Robin," he said by way of a greeting and pulled a chair over from the next desk. "What have you got Scott?"

Scott passed David her statement and gave him a verbal update.

David asked, "Dade County's not running a squad car past the address are they?"

"No. One of the detectives is taking his personal vehicle. And this just came in. The owner has a long list of arrests; drug running, robbery, and, ta da, car theft." Scott handed him two more documents. "And he has a junk yard."

David hadn't taken his eyes off her all the time Scott was speaking. It made her a little nervous. Now he looked down and read her statement and then the information on the car owner.

Robin and Scott waited in silence until David asked her, "You didn't see anyone in the parking lot."

Not really a question, but she answered it anyhow, patiently. "No. I did not see anyone in the parking lot."

"How about on the beach? Did you see anyone on the beach?"

She hadn't thought of that. She looked at the picture in her head. "No," she began slowly, thinking it out. "Two runners coming from the north going south. There was a pod of porpoise working the shoreline; I was watching them as I walked. I didn't notice. The couple running was watching them too, and I followed them down the beach to the bar. I wasn't looking for people."

She had her own question. "Where was the man who owned the van?"

"Woman," Scott said. "She said she was to the north of the lot. She saw you."

"Oh." Then she gave a little hah.

"What?" David asked.

"Nothing."

"Maybe something. Tell me," he insisted.

"No, it's nothing."

"Tell us anyhow."

She couldn't keep the annoyance out of her voice. "I went to the beach to walk off energy and work on a beading design. I watched the porpoise." The two men looked puzzled. She turned to Scott. "I mentioned it to you earlier. Well, not the porpoise. I forgot them."

He lifted his shoulder.

She smiled in spite of her annoyance. "I just figured out how to work the design."

"What design?" David asked. "A wine label?"

"No. Not a wine label. A beaded necklace with a matching bracelet. A leaping porpoise. I just figured which glass beads to use for the water. Do you need to know that?"

"You design jewelry? I thought you were a sommelier?" Scott said.

"How come I never heard about this?" David asked.

Another thing they hadn't discussed. Another thing she hadn't told him. She wondered for a moment how much she didn't know about him. But she was irritated now. "I'm a sommelier, and I design jewelry. I'm a business woman." She said it slowly for them, "A person can do more than one thing."

David cleared his throat. "Let's get back to the beach. You saw two runners. Did you see the woman in the wheelchair?"

"No. I didn't see her. But I didn't look at the dunes. I told you. I didn't notice."

Scott said, "Want to add that to your statement?"

"Sure. And then I'd like to go home." She scribbled that she had seen two runners but did not notice anyone else. She almost asked if she should add a drawing of her design or the porpoises but decided it might be uncalled for.

"I'll have your statement typed and you can sign it," Scott said.

"Do I have to wait?" She didn't want to stay this close to David. "Any reason I can't come in tomorrow and sign it?"

Scott looked to David for an answer and when he didn't object said, "Sure come on in tomorrow."

"I'll take you back to your car," David said.

Not happening, she thought and this time she did smile, thankful she had her own wheels. "I have my car, I don't need a ride." She was still looking at Scott. "I'll be in tomorrow." She turned and started out, but David jumped up and said, "I'll walk you to your car."

She let him follow; she didn't know how to stop him.

He waited until they reached her car and touched her arm, turned her around to face him. "Talk to me."

"I told you everything I know. You read my statement."

"No. I mean what's going on?"

"Nothing is going on, Detective."

"What about us?"

"I didn't know there was an 'us', Detective. We've had this conversation before. You said you would call. You didn't. I assumed that meant you didn't intend for there to be an us."

He appeared embarrassed. And guilty?

"Oh, I see," she said. "You either were busy or decided not to call. And I guess from the guilty look you didn't call on purpose. That's sad. But I'll make life easy for you, Detective. I release you from your promise to call. In fact, don't call me. And don't come by; I don't want to see you." She looked down at his hand and in the same calm voice said, "Now, take your hand off my arm, I want to go home."

He seemed surprised he had her arm and let go.

"Thank you." She turned, unlocked the door, opened it, and stepped inside.

He grabbed the door before she could close it. "But you are going to see me. You are a witness in an ongoing investigation."

"Not you. Have your partner contact me if you need anything." She stared him down until he closed the door. As soon as she drove out of the parking lot, she let a tear leak out, more than one and she wiped them off, so she could see to drive. She hadn't realized how much she had wanted him to call. To be friends, and more.

Too bad, so sad. Been there, done that, got the T-Shirt to prove it. Grow up girl, there are plenty of fish in the pond. She sniggered at herself over all the clichés. The whole episode with David was a cliché. She wasn't going to cry over him. Hadn't she brushed off two different men who tried to pick her up at the bar tonight? She was so used to turning men down she almost hadn't realized she'd done it. Next time she'd let one of them pick her up.

She wasn't even kidding herself. She knew she'd never do that. She'd been alone a long time and was used to it. But suddenly she was lonely. Damn David for waking up her libido. He'd been really good at the seduction. She'd believed he really cared. She was such a fool. She'd thought they'd made love. Passionate love. She snorted. She'd been blind. It had been sex. Plain and simple sex.

When she had woken alone, she'd let herself hope he was in the bathroom, hoped for a note in the kitchen. And she'd cried for what she'd lost, for what she'd never had.

He hadn't spent the night. He hadn't called. And she'd let him do it to her again. The thought made her angry. Better mad then sad. She would pick up a man. She could. Maybe the FBI wine expert would be interested. Or Agent Caruso. He'd given off all the I'm available and I'm wonderful vibes.

By the time she arrived home and unlocked her door, she was feeling better and poured herself a glass of wine which she took to the terrace to coast down before going to bed.

Tuesday

Like many offices in town, the FBI office was inside a bank. She hadn't known there was an office in Naples, but then why would she? She walked into the building exactly at ten and took the elevator up to the second floor to a reception area where Agent Tucker met her. He led her down a long hallway and into a large conference room with counters along two walls. The wine cases from Carlisle's sat on the floor and the bottles from each case were on the counter.

In the middle of the conference table in the center of the room was the fake Chateau Mouton Rothschild "R.C." 1945. A cardboard box with five more bottles sat beside it. She walked over for a closer look.

"Amazing, isn't it?" a voice said.

She didn't want to take her eyes off the bottle but looked to see who had spoken. If this is the FBI's expert Johnson, she thought, he must be eighty years old. "Yes, it is. Even if it is a fake." She gestured toward the table. "Is that the case it came in? The cardboard box?"

"Yes. The six bottles came in their own original cardboard box." He laughed aloud.

"Poor Mr. Carlisle," Robin said. "He didn't even know the case should be wood."

Agent Tucker introduced them. "Mrs. Garman, this is Ebert Johnson, our wine expert. He has examined all the wine we confiscated from Mr. Carlisle and we would like you to corroborate his findings."

Ebert took her hand. "It's a pleasure to meet you Mrs. Garman. You have an excellent knowledge of wines. Would you like to examine the Mouton more closely?"

"May I?"

He walked over, picked it up, and handed it to her.

"Oh, my goodness. I know it's a forgery, but it still is exciting." She couldn't help but caress the bottle.

Ebert said, "I have had the rare pleasure of actually sampling the '45. It is ambrosia. Do you think you can identify the flaws?"

"Oh. A test. Aside from the fact we know there are no cases of the 1945 Mouton. And if there were, they wouldn't be cardboard." She sat and held the bottle to the light, examining the top and the labels. She took her time because she enjoyed the challenge of finding the errors, maybe the same way some did crossword puzzles or Sudoku.

"Let's start with the bottle," she said. "I think the shape is off. The capsule…" She saw Agent Tucker frown and pointed at the wrapping over the top of the bottle. "The capsule is plastic heat shrink and shows no fading. It shouldn't be plastic and it should show some fading from age. The cork doesn't have any discoloration either. The wine fills the bottle right up to the cork; there should be some evaporation." She tilted the bottle again under the light. "And, though I have never seen a bottle of 1945, I believe the color is too pale." She looked up at Johnson and saw an approving smile. Good. She wasn't sure why, but it was important he acknowledge her ability.

He nodded and gestured toward the bottle she held, and she continued. "Now for the labels. This one looks brand new, no aging. There is a bit of glue stuck on the bottom corner. I think the print should have a metallic character and the misspelling is humorous; two Ts in Chateau."

She saw his smile light up which encouraged her. "The shield is slightly off center and crooked. I've never heard that mentioned for the real label." She fingered the label's edge. "I'm not sure about the border. If there should be one, I mean. I am sure the label should not say *contains sulfites*. That was a federal mandate put into law long after the '45 was produced." She put the bottle down and looked up with a grin. "Did I pass?"

"Very good. Better than I did, in fact. Let's walk around the room and you can tell me about these other bottles."

It took a long time because she was thorough. Two times he admitted he had missed a feature, once he pointed out a flaw she had overlooked.

He said, "I needed a magnifying glass to determine some were fake. What you did with the naked eye is pretty amazing."

Tucker agreed and suggested lunch during which he updated her with the investigation.

"Carlisle's supplier, Bobby Fallern, was arrested and is in jail. He's not telling us much beyond that he bought the wines from a guy and he doesn't know his name or have a bill of sale. We can't hold him too much longer and he'll be out on bail by the end of the day. Meanwhile, we have a warehouse full of wine which we need to authenticate. That's the real reason we brought you down here. We need another expert. That would be you. It is unusual for us to hire outside, but we're short-handed right now."

"But I'm not an expert. I guessed at the red, based on the fact the rest of the wines he delivered were fake."

"Ebert tested you and qualified you as one."

"But I'm not a policeman. Police woman," she said.

"That's right. You would be a consultant, same as Ebert. Normally the FBI has our own in-house experts, but right now we've been caught short. We'd like you to help him with the warehouse and then be available if we need you for other cases. We'll pay your travel and expenses, and give you a per diem for as long as we need you. Or for as long as you can be available."

Work for the FBI? As a consultant? "Surely you can find agents much more qualified than I am. What about you?"

He shook his head. "Not me, I have other duties and I'm not an expert. We need someone to fill in until one of our specialists is available. Right now, we need someone credentialed and available for the warehouse. Afterwards, it wouldn't be every day; we might not call you at all."

"What would I be doing?"

"Exactly what you did today. Examine the bottles and cases; fill out a card for each one and transcribe your notes into the database."

Today had been interesting. No pressure, simply using her brain to solve a puzzle. Working with two men who seemed to appreciate her knowledge. It might be fun. A change. Might even be a business opportunity.

"Okay," she said, smiling. "I'll do it. What now?"

"We have a dozen forms for you to fill out, and then we take your fingerprints and give you an ID and a badge."

It took another hour to work through the forms and be sworn in, so she didn't arrive at the police station until mid-afternoon.

David was pacing in the corridor. When he saw her, he charged up to her angrily, grabbed her arm, and barked, "Where have you been? You promised to come in this morning. Why aren't you answering your phone?"

She yelped in surprise, drawing the attention of half a dozen officers in the room. He immediately let go of her with a short, "Sorry. But I was worried."

"You needn't be. I can take care of myself. I said I'd be in. My phone is off because I didn't want to be interrupted." She rubbed her arm where he had grabbed her.

"Where were you?"

She smiled. Couldn't help herself. "With the FBI."

"You were with them all day?"

"Yes. Why don't you call and verify that? And, I thought we decided you weren't to call me. Your partner would call."

"He did; you didn't answer."

"Now you know why. If you give me my statement, I'll sign it."

"Come on back to our desks; we have a few more questions."

The officers were still watching them and she could feel their eyes as she followed him and sat in the same chair as yesterday. Not at his desk. "I don't see your partner."

"He's out." David slapped her statement down in front of her onto the desk. "Read it over, initial both pages, sign and date the back page."

She took her time, correcting one spelling error, then she initialed both pages and signed and dated it. She handed it back to him. "May I have a copy?" she asked when he just sat there.

"Oh, sure." He stood and walked to the copy machine. She watched him. Enjoyed looking at him. It was trite, but he was exciting when he was angry. Too bad he was such a jerk. He returned to his desk and handed her one set of papers.

"You said you had questions?" she said as she folded her copy and put it in her purse, not looking at him.

"You were with the FBI? All Day?" He picked up a pen, fiddling with it.

"Yes, I already told you that."

"What were you doing there, all day?"

She did look at him now, straight into those crystal blue eyes. There wasn't any heat in them now. Just cold anger.

"They told me not to talk about it," she said with a smile. She didn't care if he believed her or not.

"I'm a cop. You can tell me."

"Sorry."

"You really expect me to believe you spent all day with the FBI? You must be in big trouble."

"I really don't care what you believe, Detective Ramirez. How I spend my time is my business. If you have any official reason to know where I was today, call them and ask. They might tell you. I'm not going to."

When he made no move toward his phone, she stood. "May I go now?"

He threw the pen down. "Yeah. For now."

She turned and left with all eyes on her again. She walked out with her head up and her back straight even though her knees felt weak. He churned up too many conflicting emotions. She'd stood up to him. Stared him down.

The ride home didn't calm her and she couldn't settle. Because of him. She paced, picked up a vase and moved it to another table. She brushed imaginary crumbs off the counter, then stood at the window and looked out at nothing. Finally, she decided to go back to the beach and walk off the anger before her meeting.

This time she parked at the hotel and strolled north, breathing in the sensations. At times like this, she wished she ran, but that had never worked for her. Neither did music and ear buds. She didn't understand why people wore them at the beach. Why would you come to the beach and then block out the sea sounds? The breaking waves and screaming seagulls were as much a part of the experience as the sand, water, and the smell of salt in the air.

The surf calmed her. By the time she'd walked a mile, an alternate approach to her porpoise design popped into her head. She stopped short to examine it. Simple. Too simple. The stitch. She'd been thinking in terms of the wrong stitch. She could make it work with the peyote stitch, and she knew exactly the beads which would be perfect. Exhilarated, she turned back. She was hungry. A half order of conch fritters at the hotel bar would hold her until supper. She could sketch the design while she ate.

After ordering she was reaching for a napkin to draw her design when a man sat down beside her. "Buy you a drink?"

"No, thanks, I'm fine. I already have one." She held up her glass of milk for him to see. She didn't want to talk to anyone; she wanted to draw her design.

"Well," the guy drawled, "let me buy you the next one. I'm Donny."

She was about to let him down easy when he glanced up behind her and turned pale.

"Donny?" she asked and turned to see David bearing down on them, glowering.

Donny edged nervously out of his seat. "Sorry. Thought you were alone." He scampered away fast.

"What the hell do you think you're doing?" David growled at her.

For a moment, she was speechless, then puzzled. "Me? What am I doing?"

"You're picking up creeps in a bar."

"What? You mean Donny? You think I was picking up Donny?" She was furious. How dare he? Accuse her. Feel he had the right to accuse her.

"Donny? First name basis already?" he said with a snarl. "What were you going to do? Take him back to your place?"

She took a deep breath and went for it. "No. Donny and me, we were going up to his room here at the hotel."

He sneered. "Thought you didn't do one-night-stands."

"Not until you taught me how. Love 'em and leave 'em before the sun comes up because it's only sex. Isn't that what you said?" She threw the phrase at him and saw it hit the mark.

His mouth worked, but before he could say anything the waitress set her snack down. Mel leaned over Robin and said, "If this man is bothering you, I'll have Doug take him outside."

Robin stared at Mel a second, feeling flushed and angry. She turned back to David. "Yes. This man is bothering me, but I think he's leaving."

He wasn't moving, his mouth was an angry slit.

"You need to leave, David. Don't say anything. Not a word. Unless you want me to call your partner to come and get you. Just leave."

He stood scowling at them. The waitress asked, "What will it be honey?"

"I'm going." He turned and strode out.

Robin watched him go. "Thanks Mel."

"Don't mention it. He looked really mad. Your husband?"

Robin laughed. "No. Hardly. He's not the marrying kind. I don't think I'm hungry anymore. Can I take this home?"

"Sure, let me box it up. You finish your drink and give him time to get off the property. I'll send Doug to check he's gone."

"No. Wait. I changed my mind. He can't do this to me. I'm going to eat here and sketch. That's what I planned."

Mel was smiling now. "You go girl. Show him he can't push you around."

It took concentration to get back her good feeling but once she started to sketch, she calmed down and forgot to eat. It was only when Mel came back to tell her the bouncer had seen David leave that she became aware again and picked up a fritter, but it was cold. Mel saw and took it away to nuke it, brought it back steaming.

Robin ate while she sketched, then watched the sunset. At six she met with the manager of the gift shop and then some more folks joined them for a light supper while listening to a new band.

She was half afraid David would be waiting outside when she left, but he must have come to his senses. And he wasn't in his car in her driveway or waiting on her porch either. She let out a sigh, surprised to find she was almost disappointed and snickered at herself for hoping David would be here. Fickle woman. She flapped her hand in self-disgust as she got out of her car and dropped her keys. When she bent to pick them up she heard something else fall, two thunks; she searched but didn't see anything on the ground.

Tires screeched across the street and a car sped past. Some kid out joyriding.

Inside, she put on her blue bunny pajamas and slippers, poured a glass of wine, and sat at the counter. She used colored pencils to put her porpoise design on the special graph paper for beading and swiftly filled in the numbered columns and rows, creating the blue-green water and silver spray using the two-drop peyote stitch and size eleven beads. The bracelet would be the same design, only smaller.

Wednesday

She worked side-by-side with Ebert in the warehouse, a huge flat-topped metal building with a front door beside a large truck bay and a small side door about a third of the way toward the back. It was about a thousand square feet inside. A small glass-enclosed office with two desks and four file cabinets took up half the front wall. A woman was typing on a computer at one desk; a man was going through a pile of papers at the other. Tucker explained the agents were searching through shipping orders and accounts.

A restroom was beside the office and cases of whiskey and beer were stacked along the remainder of the wall. Someone else would examine those. The wine cases were on pallets in the middle of the room, ten double rows from front to back. Most rows were four to six cases high. There were also cases stacked on both side walls and the back wall. No racks of single bottles, no caskets, no barrels.

She and Ebert each had a mobile rolling table and chair, and a grid map with each case numbered by location. The process began with a technician who dusted a case for prints and labeled it and then passed it to her or Ebert who examined the case and each bottle inside. If they found anything fake, they were to attach a yellow sticker to the case and enter comments on a tablet. Then each bottle would be dusted for prints and the case moved to the evidence locker to ensure a legal chain of custody for the evidence. Simple and methodical. Except there were no fakes.

By late morning, Robin was bored. The task was disappointing, and tedious. No forgeries. She had a moment of hope when the tech brought her a case of the champagne. But these labels had the iridescent design. She checked for other signs of forgery and didn't find any. Maybe Carlisle's supplier had a secret warehouse. She tried to contain her disappointment because that was good, wasn't it? No fakes. FBI sub-contracting wasn't going to be the new sideline for Fine Wines. The specialty niche was too small. Only one customer.

Her mind was wandering; her stomach was growling. Almost lunch. They had completed all the aisles and reached the corridor running along the back to the side door. She hadn't remembered the door being so close to the back of the building. She'd thought it was more toward the center. She really was bored if she was questioning the door's location.

Ebert walked over. "All we have left are these double stacks on the back wall. The labels indicate they're all cheap wines. Chances of them being fake are slim since there's no money selling cheap bottles. What say we have lunch and then come back and finish?"

"Great. I need nourishment and don't think I can face one more case right now. I hope we can finish today, because I have my regular work tomorrow." Her wine class. Teaching, interacting with people. She was looking forward to it even more after this dull day of examining dusty cheap wines.

They spent a pleasant hour in an outdoor restaurant where Ebert entertained her with funny tales, which he told well. She liked him a lot, but not as a new lover. And she'd sent Donny away yesterday. She had forgotten she was going to let a man pick her up at the bar. Maybe she belonged locked in a warehouse with the dull wines.

Back at the warehouse, the tech hefted the first box from the row across the back of the building. "Feels light." He set it down. The case was already open and the bottles inside were empty.

"Well that's weird," Robin said. "Why store a case of empty bottles? A case of washed empty bottles?" And then Robin answered her own question. "Because he's going to use the bottles for phony wine." She pulled one out. "These are the same bottles he used for the bogus red wine." The find was almost anticlimactic.

The technician dusted the case and lifted the next. "This one is light, too." He brought it over and immediately went for another. The next eighteen cases, the whole front row, contained empty bottles. The tech lifted the top case off the back stack and stopped. "This one is empty. This too. I think this whole back row is empty." He quickly moved three more cases.

"Look," Robin exclaimed. "A door frame. The empty cases are hiding a door frame. There's another room back there."

The tech cleared the door and turned the knob. It was locked. He pulled out his cell. "I'll call Agent Tucker."

Ebert said, "We might as well finish labeling these cases; I have a feeling the work will be a whole lot different behind that door." The technicians dusted the bottles. They were all wiped clean.

Tucker arrived shortly after they finished with the empty boxes. "Don't know how we missed this." He shook his head. "There are two keys on the ring we couldn't identify." He tried one on the lock and it clicked. He opened the door.

"Stay back. Let me make sure it's safe." Tucker pulled out his flashlight, entered with the lab tech right behind with his own flashlight. They were gone about two minutes when Tucker came back and snapped on the lights. "All clear," he said, "come on in."

The hidden room ran the length of the building and was about ten feet deep, with an interior door on the side wall. Wine cases were stacked along the back wall. A desk with a computer and printer was on the near wall and a long counter down the middle of the room had a large sink. For washing used bottles and removing the labels, Robin supposed. An assembly line of clean bottles stood on the counter top, alongside funnels and gallon jugs of cheap wine, both red and white to fill the empty bottles.

Robin walked over to look closer at the corking area and a pile of capsules. She wandered to the cartons on the back wall. "Here are more cases of my red." She took a few more steps. "And the champagne. Another red and two white wines. Do you think these are the counterfeit wines?"

"Don't touch," Tucker ordered as she reached out.

"I guess I forgot for a minute there, sorry." She leaned closer. "Yeah, I think these are fake."

"We'll dust the cases and bottles, then you and Ebert can take a closer look." He issued instructions as he headed for the closed interior door.

Robin moved over to the desk. "Here's a pile of blank labels. And stencils, good stencils. Glue. Regular printer paper; I don't see any specialty paper. One very good label here." She pointed and walked around the desk. "More labels, these are bad fakes." She glanced into the trash can. "Reject labels for the ice wines. Hard to believe he actually had some he didn't use; the ones on the bottles were so bad. You know, this lab is like the bogus wines; it has a split personality. Some very good forgeries and some very bad. Do you think there might be more than one forger?" she asked.

Ebert was right behind her examining a label. "Yeah, the guy who did the champagne is an artist. The one who did the ice wines is a slob. I vote for two."

Tucker used a key on the door on the far wall, turned the knob gently, and slowly opened it. Robin and Ebert wandered over. Tucker cursed softly and snapped on the light. She peeked around him and choked out a gasp. Ebert grabbed her arm, pulled her back to the desk, and sat her in the chair. She leaned over and lowered her head between her knees trying to keep her lunch from coming up. "Ohhh." She closed her eyes.

She vaguely heard Tucker talking on his phone and tried to concentrate on what he was saying, not on what she'd seen.

Taking deep breaths, she opened her eyes and stared at the floor because with her eyes closed all she could see was the image burned onto the inside of her eyelids of a man lying on the floor in a pool of blood. She became aware Ebert was patting her shoulder and looked up at him. "I'm okay," she said.

"I'm doing it as much for myself as you," he said with an embarrassed smile and continued to pat her.

Robin caught the end of Tucker's conversation notifying the locals he had found a body. "Yeah, I thought you guys would want to know. I have my team coming out too. We'll wait for you."

"Who, who was that on the floor?" she asked in a shaky whisper. She couldn't say dead man.

Tucker rifled the words. "Carlisle's supplier. Bobby Fallern. Very, very dead." He glanced around. "This is a crime scene now and we better move out of here to the front office. Can you walk? Are you okay?"

"I'm okay. I can walk." She stood and proved it. "I'm sorry. I got fingerprints on the chair." She straightened her shoulders and followed Tucker with Ebert hovering beside her, half supporting her, half hanging on.

They had reached the office when they heard sirens. "That will be the locals," Tucker said and went out to meet them.

Of course, it was David with Detective Scott. David stopped short when he saw her through the glass.

"What is she doing here?"

"Ms. Garman and Ebert Johnson are FBI consultants. They have been cataloging the wines stored here. During their appraisal, they discovered a door on the back wall which had been hidden behind empty wine cases. They called me and I unlocked the door. We found a room that runs across the length of the building where we believe the bogus wines were bottled and labeled. We found Fallern dead in a closet off that room. We immediately backed out and called you. We didn't touch anything in either room, except the door and maybe the chair."

"Show us," David ordered. "Anyone go into the murder scene?"

"Me and a tech. We didn't know it was a murder scene. As soon as we saw Fallern, we came to the front office to wait for you. I'll lead you back." Their voices receded.

"We're going to be here a long time and answer a lot of questions," Ebert said. "We were so close to actually handling the bogus wine. Touching the labels. All that work and we didn't even get to play with the fake stuff." That jerked a chuckle out of her. Ebert was right. They were being cheated. And worse, she would have to deal with David again.

The detectives returned and Scott said, "We'll ask you some questions individually, shortly. Meanwhile, we prefer you don't talk to each other."

Agent Caruso arrived and strutted into the office. He looked around and immediately came over to take her hand. Solicitous. Sympathetic. Flirting? Now? She pulled her hand away and saw David's angry scowl before he went to join his men in the back of the warehouse.

Shortly, Scott had said, but after an hour and a half she realized they were operating on hospital time; no one in a hospital ever quoted an exact time. It was always an indefinite period used to imply the belief that whatever you were waiting for would happen shortly, soon, not too long, in a little while, in a few minutes…She pulled out her sketchbook and outlined a triple orchid pattern.

Caruso sat on the edge of the desk, beside her chair, too close. Was he trying to intimidate her? No, still flirting. He said something stupid about the etchings he had which she should come see. She could handle flirting; it was part of her job description. Some men always tried to be close, thought any woman was fair game. As a successful business-woman, she'd learned early to step aside or move out of reach, to gently remove an inappropriate hand and fill it with a wine glass. She could manage intimidation too, knew how to control situations before they became uncomfortable. But an FBI Agent? A cop? That was different. She chose to ignore him and worked on her drawing.

After another half hour Ramirez, Scott, and two other detectives came in. The detectives separated them and David led her to a corner of the room. She almost balked, but remembered a man was dead.

He gazed at her for a moment. "Tell me how you and Ebert worked."

She explained their process. He nodded and wrote in his notebook.

"When did you discover the room?"

"After lunch, when we moved the empty boxes, we found the room hidden behind them."

"You touch anything?"

"No. Not then."

"When?"

"When Agent Tucker turned on the light and I, um, saw, um…" She hesitated over the word body, feeling her stomach come up. He touched her shoulder and she was comforted for a moment until she remembered who he was and leaned away.

He frowned, changed the subject. "Okay, where were you yesterday?"

"You know where I was. At the FBI office, at the police station, at the hotel bar."

"Lunch, today? Go out by yourself?"

"No, we ate together." Her eyes widened as she realized why he was asking. "You can't possibly be implying I had anything to do with that man's death."

"Where did you go when you finished with us yesterday?"

He wasn't going to answer her question.

"I went home for a bit and then for a walk on the beach. I was stiff from sitting all day." She stopped.

He waited for her to continue. He knew very well where she had gone.

"I stopped at the Beach Bar. You saw me there," she said.

"Your home away from home. Hang out there and pick up men a lot do you?"

She gave him an angry glare. It was her fault. She never should have wised-off. Instead, she should have told him the truth. She often walked on the beach and stopped at the Beach Bar to visit with friends. Couldn't believe they hadn't walked on the beach together when they were dating or that she hadn't introduced him to her friends. She wondered if he had been as remiss about his free time. Well duh. One-night-stand? Of course he hadn't shared. On purpose. You don't share with the flavor of the day.

"Sometimes. Sometimes I go there."

"How long were you there?"

"A couple hours, a few hours. I don't know."

"So you were in the bar from about five-thirty to seven-thirty?"

"More like five-thirty to ten," she admitted.

"Can someone verify that?"

"Any number of people."

"Then where did you go?"

"Home."

"Alone?"

"You need to know, why?"

"Alibi."

"When did that man die?"

"We don't know yet for sure."

"I heard the detective tell you it was sometime yesterday or early last night." The tech had said between ten AM and seven PM, sometime after he got out of jail Tuesday.

"I want to know what you did when you left the hotel bar."

"I don't think I need to tell you. Assume I don't have an alibi after I left the hotel. Can I go now?" she waited while he considered her response.

"Yeah."

She stood. "Detective Ramirez. Don't call me. If you have official business, have Detective Scott contact me. I won't answer your calls."

"No problem," he said with a growl. "Don't leave town."

She almost let the anger take over, but she kept her face blank and walked out. *Don't leave town?*

Tucker stopped her at the door and apologized for the circumstances.

"Unless you killed that man, it's not your fault," she told him.

"Well, still. Sorry."

"How was he killed?" She didn't really want to know, but knowing would be better than wondering. There had been so much blood.

"Shot. We'll know more after the autopsy, but it looks like two times in the face, once in the gut. Once in the groin."

She winced.

"Pretty ugly. Someone was very angry at him. Sorry you had to see that." He walked her to her car. "I want to thank you for your help here today. I'll call later if we need you to come back."

She drove home trying not to think of bullets thudding into a body. Of blood. She collapsed on her couch and sat there a long time running the facts around in her head. Finally, even though it was too early, she poured a glass of wine and took it to the garden.

**

Ramirez headed back to the beach bar. He didn't know what it was about Garman that struck a nerve. She always made him act like some simple-minded idiot. He'd used the excuse of a murder investigation to delve into her private life. He didn't feel guilty. Don't leave town? That was stupid. He had seen the anger in her eyes and had expected her to tell him off, but she'd left the room silently.

The chemistry between them was unbelievable. After she'd dragged him into her bed, she'd surprised him with her lovemaking. Passionate. Giving pleasure, satisfying him. She wasn't the prim and proper innocent she'd claimed. And he should have called her the next day. But he never called the woman.

He was confused by his reactions to her. Sunday he'd gone to her home to clear things up. For some reason he'd felt it was important for her to know he was doing his job, not going home with those women. That wasn't his style. He only did one-night-stands, but he'd have a meal or a drink with the woman first. With Robin, dinner hadn't been enough. The more time he spent with her, the more he wanted to be with her. He actually looked forward to their dates. That he thought of their time together as dates baffled him. He never dated.

And then he was asking if he could please call, begging. She'd said yes. But he'd come to his senses. Sure, he thought about her all the time. Got hard. Reached for the phone. But reason always came to his rescue. He knew he couldn't get mixed up with her. She was different. Trouble. He wasn't going back for seconds with this one. That would be a mistake.

Yesterday, when he'd found her hanging out at the bar and seen that man picking her up, he'd lost it. Every part of him iced over. Except his mouth. Idiot. Then he'd doubled-down, accusing her of picking up men. Innocent? No way. She was on a first name basis with the bartender and staff. It made his blood boil to think of her picking up strange men. He shook himself. None of his business if she did pick up men. They were over. He was not some jealous lover. They had no exclusivity agreement. They were not even dating. She was a friend, not a mistress. Not even a friend.

That hadn't stop him from provoking her, suggesting a replay would remove the one-night-stand label. Making a fool out of himself.

The bartender wasn't any friendlier this second visit. The first time David had come in to check after the van was stolen, the bartender had been friendly and still David had fought for every answer he got. Today, the bartender was hostile. When David asked if Robin left alone, Doug wanted to know why.

"Because I asked." He could do intimidating.

"You asked last time too and it wasn't relevant. Robin said you were harassing her, so here's the deal. You convince me you need to know, or I call the manager and he can call your boss."

"A man has been murdered," he said in a cold voice.

"You think she murdered someone? No way."

"No. I don't think she murdered anyone. I'm trying to verify her alibi. She said she was here. Can you confirm?"

"When?"

"Last night."

"Yeah. She was here."

"What time was she here?" The man didn't offer up a free piece of information.

"Hmm. She stayed until a little after ten."

David noted it down.

"Alone?"

Doug pursed his lips. "Last night. Mostly. I had to peel a guy off of her."

"What do you mean?"

"Guy thought he could pick her up because she was in the bar alone. Wouldn't back off. I had to show him the door."

"That happen a lot in here? She pick up men?" The idea made him clench his notepad.

"Didn't say that. I said a tourist tried to pick her up and she wasn't interested. He wouldn't take no for an answer. She didn't kill him though, because he came back in today to apologize. Too much to drink made him stupid. He's here now, if you want to talk to him."

"She was here from five-thirty until after ten?" He was going to break his pen his fingers grasped it so tightly. God, almost five hours in a bar? Alone?

"That's what I said."

"How much after?"

"Maybe ten-fifteen, ten-twenty."

"She sit and drink all that time?"

Doug was making him work for every single bit of information. He was enjoying it too. Almost like a straight-man.

"She had a meeting."

"A meeting about?" David asked.

"Couldn't say."

Couldn't or wouldn't. He'd come back to it.

"With?"

The bartender thought about it. "My manager."

"She met with your manager from five-thirty to ten."

"No. More like seven to eight."

"What happened at eight?"

"More people joined them."

Doug wasn't volunteering anything. Two facts David had to dig for.

"They eat here?"

"Yeah, they did. We get food from the restaurant. Lot of managers and employees eat here."

"You know who these people were?"

"Employees, manager for the shops on premises."

"Your manager here now?"

"Nope."

"Give me his contact information. And the shops guy too while you're at it."

The bartender went to his Rolodex and read off the information.

"What happened after dinner?"

"They stayed and watched the show. We had a local band auditioning."

"They just sit there?"

"No. Danced, clapped, sang along. The show ran until two AM." Doug folded his arms across his chest. "Are we done?"

"For now. I might be back." He called the bar manager and made an appointment in an hour. Since he had time, he took a walk through the promenade of shops. Stopped at a window showcasing local artists. Black and white photographs of the Everglades, artistic, usable pottery, blown glass figurines, and beaded jewelry. He looked closer. A local newspaper review was prominently displayed in the window with a picture of Robin and Robin's jewelry. Huh?

A card described the necklace as *a woven band of fiery Swarovski crystals below which floats a delicate red and orange dragonfly with wings outlined in lustrous natural pearls, diamond crystals for eyes. The matching bracelet has the dragonfly locked in the band. Earrings to match.* High three figures for the set. Beside it was something called a bib-style necklace, described as delicate flower shapes attached by thin strands of seed beads. Again, the Swarovski crystals. This necklace was airy and light. The stones clear with a touch of purple in the blossoms, green in the leaves. He was surprised. When she'd said she designed jewelry, he'd thought leather bracelets. He walked inside.

A saleswoman came over. "I saw you looking at Ms. Garman's designs. They are lovely, aren't they? Can I take one out for you, sir? We are terribly excited to be carrying her jewelry. Very unique. Handmade, you know, one of a kind. She accepts custom orders, if one of these is not quite right."

"No. No, thank you. Not right now. But they are nice."

"If you're looking for bead work you be sure to stop in at the main jewelry shop. They carry nationally known designers. Soon Ms. Garman will be selling her pieces in that shop."

"I'll do that," he said and did look in the window of the jewelry store; more beaded necklaces, also Swarovski crystals. But he didn't think these pieces were as nice as Robin's. Cost was in the high four figures. Must be the difference between a local artist and a famous designer.

How had he not known? He was a detective for God's sake. How had he not known she had such talent? The answer was simple. He'd never asked. He'd never let the conversation drift toward work or spare time. His excuse? He was undercover and it was safer. If he had asked about her job, she would want to know about his. How could he have been so blind? Disinterested? Uncaring? He knew why. Any interest would have implied commitment. He should have realized she wasn't simply a wine steward. That she ran the business. Built it herself, according to Sally. And she made magnificent jewelry. What else didn't he know? The thought stopped him. He didn't know how many men she picked up at the bar.

He headed back to the bar and his meeting.

The bar manager, James Seldon, welcomed him with some reservation. He was a friendly older man, a little soft around the gut. He motioned David to a chair and sat behind his desk. "I'm only talking to you Detective to try to help Robin. I checked into you and hear you're good at your job, but that doesn't alter the fact Robin seems to be having a problem with you." He held up his hand to stop David before he could object. "Let me finish. Robin didn't say you were harassing her, merely that you had some personal history which had become messy. That maybe you were asking inappropriate questions. Sit and ask. If I think you're out of line, I'll let you know."

David kept to the basics and Seldon confirmed everything Doug had said, adding, "A year or so back we decided to keep a wine cellar. Many of our guests are connoisseurs and we wanted to accommodate them, not have them go elsewhere. I asked Robin for input, and she put a list together of both popular and rare or exotic wines. We have since developed a reputation as the place to find vintage wines. Locals are coming in as well as guests. If we don't have what they want, we order it. She also helped with a list for room service and the restaurant. So, yes, she has been spending more time than usual in our bar. It takes time to refine a list like that. She is also a friend."

"Does she drink?"

"Not much. A glass of fine wine sometimes, but I think Doug already told you. He is a little protective of her. We all are." He smiled.

"Do you always hold your meetings in the bar?"

"Most times. I dislike boardrooms and conference rooms. Those meetings seem to go on forever. The back booth is relaxing. We accomplish a lot in less time over good meals. Employees and managers actually look forward to meetings and it helps make the bar appear to be occupied during the day. When customers peek in the room and see us, they feel more comfortable coming in."

"Your meeting last night was about wine lists?"

"My meeting was, yes."

"But the shop manager, that meeting was about jewelry?"

"Oh, you know about that do you? Doug didn't mention he'd told you."

"You said yourself, I'm a good detective. I detected it." And he'd talked to the manager.

"He had contracts for her to sign."

"She helps you with wine and you get her a contract with the shop. Quid pro quo."

"No. She helped with the wine, pro bono. She earned the space in the shop. She makes stunning jewelry. When she saw the necklaces in the jewelry store she went home for some pieces of her own and went right over and talked to Kenneth. Didn't take much to convince him to display them. Those first pieces sold quickly. Many of our guests want to take home local art. Her jewelry is affordable and beautiful and she offered to do some meet-and-greets and put on a demonstration. She sold herself. Management is ecstatic. They signed contracts last night after working out the final details. She also sells her designs at a consignment boutique at Cougars Cove which has been displaying her jewelry for years."

One of their dates had been a boat ride out of Cougars Cove. She'd never mentioned her jewelry.

"Last night we had dinner, a gourmet dinner from our restaurant. My wife joined us. Other employees came by and we made a night of it."

"You know her well?"

"I would think so. About fifteen years."

"She stayed at the table all night? Didn't leave at all?"

Seldon gave it some thought. "Well, she danced some. We all did. She went to the ladies once. My wife went with her. They never go alone you know." Again he smiled.

"She leave alone?"

"Doug said you would ask that. And he told me how he replied. I think my answer is the same."

David jumped on that. "So she did leave with someone."

"No. I didn't say that. My impression is she, um, feels that would be a personal question, not an official one. Until you can show the question is official, I choose not to talk about her personal life."

Did she or didn't she? He didn't need to know officially. And, he shouldn't care personally. But he did.

Thursday

Her early afternoon wine appreciation class was a brilliant success and Robin left the wine tasting room exuberant. The students were as eager and enthusiastic to learn as she was to teach and it was rewarding to have the time to go into detail about the wines and wineries, and offer tastings of the vintages discussed. Robin had expected a good response but hadn't expected this level of participation.

She stopped in to celebrate a moment with Rome and Sally. "The practice sessions with our employees as students paid off and the class went off without a hitch. If the interest continues, we can open additional classes."

They discussed details and then Rome asked, "Have you heard anything more about the fake wine? Or what happened to Fallern? Who killed him?"

Robin snorted. "Humph. No. Like you, just what I read in the newspaper. No one has said anything to me."

"You think Carlisle might have killed that guy?"

She shook her head. "I'd guess, no. Carlisle is a bully. Aren't bullies cowards? I might be able to imagine Carlisle shooting someone in the back, but not face to face. Not that I know anything about murderers. And why would he kill Fallern?"

"Angry at being cheated?"

"I just don't know. But I think there were two forgers. Fallern made the sloppy labels. Someone else, better crafted in forgery, made the others. Maybe that guy did it."

"Well, we'll know when the cops catch up with him. You sure have gotten mixed up in a bunch of strange situations lately, Robin. Nothing happen today, yet?" Rome joked.

Robin hesitated.

"What?" Rome leaned forward in his chair. "Don't tell me something happened today."

"I don't know. I'm not sure." She bit her bottom lip. "A car almost ran me down in front of the coffee shop. But I heard him coming, I heard the engine revving, and jumped back. But for a second, I thought he was aiming for me."

Rome stood and came around the desk. "What? Why didn't you say something earlier?"

She held up her hand in a stop motion. "Calm down, Rome. It really wasn't anywhere near that close." Though it had seemed so at the time. "When you asked what had happened today, it came to mind. The driver wasn't paying attention. I don't think he even noticed the traffic light."

"A man driving?"

"Don't know. All I saw was a big black car."

"Did you report it?"

"What's to report? There was a man in the crosswalk with me; neither of us thought to get the license number. Probably somebody late for an appointment. Look, I didn't even spill my coffee." But it was a near miss. If she hadn't heard him and looked up, she'd have stepped directly in front of him.

Rome frowned. She wasn't sure she'd convinced him, but he let it go. "Well, be careful. Okay?"

"Yes, Dad." She smiled at him and picked up her purse. "Now I'm going home to clean up and head to the hotel for my meeting with the shop manager."

She should have been excited about the classes, but her sneaky mind went back to David. She didn't hate him, wasn't going to give him that much power over her. But it saddened her. They could have been good together. That's what she'd think in a weak moment and then she'd remind herself it had all been fake. The David she loved didn't exist. Still, she thought of him. Not all of the time, but most of the time. She couldn't not think of him. She'd be looking in her closet and think, *I should wear the blue blouse. David said he liked it.* She'd walk by a spot where they had eaten and remember how he stole her French fries. Even this morning, she'd been soaping in the shower and remembered his hands doing the same. Touching those places, making her body thrum. Making her feel beautiful, alive, loved.

She wanted to forget him. But her mind played tricks. She'd dreamt about him, twice. One dream left her panting and begging for more. Begging for release. She promised herself, next time she would sleep a little longer, keep the dream going until she climaxed so she wouldn't wake up sexually frustrated.

In the second dream, he'd been screaming at her, calling her filthy names. He'd been ugly. With horns. Groping himself. Ugh. She'd woken with tears in her eyes. He didn't get to do that to her; she wouldn't let him. She'd poured a shot of brandy and gone back to bed.

He'd been so convincing. So sincere. So loving. Completely fooled her. He had done what men through the ages have done. She'd given him a challenge, the lonely widow who didn't know how to play the game. She laughed at herself. She couldn't have been much of a challenge.

It was just sad. She hated him for stirring up those feeling and emotions she had buried for so long. Maybe it's time to get on with that part of her life.

She shoved him out of her mind.

An hour later, she drove to the hotel where she dropped off a necklace from her stock to replace the window set which had sold and she picked up two special orders. Then, she headed for the bar.

Doug gave her a funny look when she walked in, nodding toward the corner. She gazed around, wondering. Her heart stopped a moment. David. Their eyes met. She grimaced. Today had been going so well. She turned away and sat down quickly because she couldn't trust her legs. Apparently they went weak from the sight of him. She put her briefcase and folders down on the seat beside her and Doug leaned forward over the bar. "He came in early. Been nursing one drink. Funny he would come here where he knows he's not particularly welcome."

She shrugged, decided not to think about him. "Hit me with a Cape Coder, I'm celebrating. But virgin, I dropped off a new piece. Part of me hated to sell it."

"Take a picture?"

"Yeah." She showed him.

"Pretty."

She smiled, pleased. "I also picked up two special orders."

She was aware of David, could feel him approach and prepared herself with a blank expression. He sat beside her, his thigh pressing against hers. The room was suddenly warm. Her brain flashed on the hours they'd spent together.

She crossed that leg over the other and saw him smirk.

"If you touch me again, Doug will throw you out." She said it quietly. The same way she might say the sun is shining.

Doug put her drink down on a napkin and scowled at David. "What she said."

"Sorry. Really. I simply want to talk."

"I'm listening." Doug moved away down the bar and she fiddled with her glass. Her stomach didn't want anything; the air was filled with his scent.

"Not here."

"Here is where I am, Detective. I have an appointment in…" She looked at the watch on her wrist. The beaded band sparkled, gave her a moment of pleasure. "In ten minutes." She didn't, but he didn't have to know that. "I'm busy Detective. I don't really want to talk to you. I thought I told you that. Since you don't seem to understand, let me tell you one more time. I do not want to talk to you. We had a fling. It's over. I'm not interested. I don't even like you."

"You liked me well enough before."

"Not you, Detective. A man called David, who said he loved me."

There was a long silence.

"I miss you," he said.

"Yeah? I miss the man I thought you were."

"I want a second chance."

"You had a second chance. And a third chance. You chose not to pursue them, not to call. You won already, Detective. Remember. You had me. You got what you wanted." Maybe she hadn't satisfied him. That was a part of her misery. She hadn't measured up in the bedroom.

"I made a mistake."

"Yeah, you did. We both did. But it's time to move on. You don't want more than one night. You don't even want a whole night. There are a lot of women out there who want to play, Detective; go find one of them. You broke my heart once. That should be enough for any man. Now leave me alone. Please."

Doug wandered over, asked David if he wanted a drink. David shook his head and went back to his table.

Seldon came to sit by her. "How are you doing? Heard about the wine forger."

She gave him a weak smile. "Okay. I'm trying to convince myself it was a very vivid movie." She put her hand to her mouth. "Oh, I shouldn't have said that. You didn't need to hear that."

He patted her shoulder. "Seen more than my share of dead bodies. Really, you doing okay?"

For a moment she was startled. "Oh, the war. I'm sorry. And yes, I'm doing okay. I started the new wine class today." She was thankful for the change of subject and told him, perhaps with more detail than he wanted. But he listened politely. When she wound down he took out the wine list and they reviewed it together. She suggested a couple of new reds and a moscato. "Sweet. White. Crisp. Some older ladies like it. A dessert wine, but a nice end to an evening."

He folded the amended list and put it back in his pocket. Leaned over and kissed her forehead. "Thanks."

She pushed her drink away; she hadn't touched it. "Okay, I'm off home for a quiet evening of beading. I have two new special orders." She picked up her briefcase and purse.

"You going the beach route?" he asked.

"No. I'm in the parking lot."

She was aware David followed her but thought she could easily reach her car before he caught up. She hurried out the door and down the sidewalk.

Someone grabbed her from behind. Grabbed her arms tightly, pinning them to her sides. Not David. A stranger.

She screamed.

The man was dragging her toward a car.

She threw her head back hard against his face. Heard a curse. Someone yelled, "Stop! Police!"

The man threw her down. Turned, and fled.

David raced to her, bent down. "Honey? Are you all right, honey?"

"I'm okay. Just knocked breathless."

He looked up, but didn't leave her as Doug raced past after the mugger.

"Let me see." David was feeling her all over, checking for broken bones. His hands were shaking when he touched her. "It's okay honey. It's okay."

She saw the mugger reach a car which was waiting with the passenger door open. The man jumped in and the vehicle took off. Robin pulled herself up to a sitting position still catching her breath and David drew her tight to him, almost too tight. Stroking her head and her back, talking to her in a soothing tone. "Everything is okay; I have you now."

Doug walked back. "He got away. Dived into a car. Dark color sedan, no tag. She okay? You okay, Robin?" Doug leaned down, looking at her, concern etched on his face.

"Yes. I just got the breath knocked out of me." She put a hand down.

"Ouch."

"What?" both men said.

"My hand, I scraped my hand." She held it out for them to see and looked at her other hand. "Both hands. Let me up."

Each took an arm and gently lifted her to her feet. She swayed for a second and then shook them off.

"Can you stand?" Doug asked.

"Yes, I'm okay." She walked over to where she'd dropped her purse and briefcase, but when she reached down to for them she staggered and had to grab onto David to keep her balance. Both men grabbed her again.

"Give it a minute, sweetheart." David held her, supported her.

"I'm okay, just a little dizzy from the excitement."

"Come back inside and sit down," Doug said. "Detective Ramirez will bring your stuff." Doug led her slowly inside. When she started for the ladies' room he stopped her. "No, we'll go to the office." He led her through the bar where Mel ran over. "What happened? Is she all right?"

"She's okay. Got jumped in the parking lot. Notify security." Mel patted her gently on the shoulder and reached for the phone as Doug led her to the office and sat her in a chair, pulled open a drawer, and took out a first aid kit.

David stomped in behind them. "Tell me what happened."

"You saw about as much as I know. Some guy jumped out from between two cars and grabbed me. I screamed and threw my head back. You cursed and hollered 'stop, police'. He threw me down."

"Did you get a look at his face?"

"No, all I saw was a black shadow. He grabbed me from behind and pinned my arms."

"Did he hurt you? You screamed."

"No, he scared me. I screamed. You cursed. No wait. You didn't curse. That was him. I whipped my head back and hit his nose. I think. You hollered 'stop police'. He threw me down and took off." She looked at her hands. "That's how I scraped my hands. And then you were there asking me if I was all right." And calling me honey.

Ramirez grabbed the first aid kit away from Doug and began to clean her hands with a wet wipe. She let him. He lathered ointment on the scrapes and covered them with a sterile strip, and wrapping that with stretchy tape to hold it in place. Did the same with her other hand.

"You hurt anywhere else?" he asked when he finished.

"No. Guess I landed on my hands. Maybe the back of my head where I hit his nose or jaw." She raised her hand to feel, but he pushed it away and gently probed the back of her head.

"Small lump. No cuts. The skin isn't broken."

She moved her head back; his face, lips, were close and she was still feeling a little vulnerable.

"Where did you learn a move like that?" he asked.

"Nowhere. It was panic. I was trying to get away." She had taken self-defense lessons, but none of them had kicked in. It all happened too fast. She stood. "I'm going home."

Both men moved to stop her, exchanged some sort of silent communication and shook their heads.

"Not yet. When you do, Detective Ramirez will follow you to make sure you get there safely," Doug said.

"It's broad daylight outside. No one is going to bother me."

"But someone did. In our parking lot. That shouldn't have happened. We're supposed to have good security."

"You and Detective Ramirez work on it. I'm going home. Alone." She reached for her purse.

David said, "I'll follow you. And check your house before you go inside."

That stopped her. "Why wouldn't my house be safe? I was mugged in the parking lot. What's wrong with the two of you? No one needs to follow me home."

The two men did the silent communication thing again. They were scaring her.

It was Doug who spoke. "A mugger would have grabbed your purse. Or your briefcase. This guy grabbed you and had a car waiting with the door open."

She looked at him. Then at David who nodded agreement. She sat down. "You're wrong. There's no reason for anyone to grab me. No one is going to pay ransom for me."

"Well that's the question, isn't it?" said Doug. "Why would someone grab you? And there are people who would pay a ransom for you? Your partners?"

"Of course they would, but they don't have a lot of money." She reasoned it out. "Not enough to justify someone grabbing me. It must be a mistake. They confused me with one of the paying guests." She hung onto that thought. "They got me mixed up with someone else."

David rolled his eyes. "I'm calling in a team to go over the parking lot. I'll escort you home as soon as they arrive."

Seldon came in with a security tech and a copy of the hotel video tapes. "Security queued them up for the time of the attack."

The angle was different, more from the front of the building. A shadowy shape lunged out from between two cars, grabbed Robin, and started to drag her away. Robin snapped her head back and connected. Something distracted the mugger and he turned to look toward the door. Then threw her down and ran. The tape was fuzzy, but even if it had been clear, the guy wore a stocking mask.

Next, Ramirez came running and stood over Robin then bent down and grabbed her close waving Doug after the mugger who jumped into the waiting car through the open door. The car, an SUV, tore out of the lot.

She tried to watch the video objectively, but it was unnerving, and she had to look down for a minute and take deep breaths to calm herself. Seldon was studying her when she raised her head.

David was standing over the security tech. "Can you go back to when Robin arrived?"

The man tapped keys and watched Robin pull into the lot and park and slide out of her car. Another vehicle pulled in and stopped. After she walked inside, the SUV backed and turned, parked. The tape showed other vehicles come and go; one blurry man exited the vehicle and went inside, came back a few minutes later. There was no further movement from the car until Robin walked out the door and the mugger exited the car and attacked her.

"That's it then. That's them. They followed you here and waited. This was not a case of mistaken identity," David declared in a flat tone and Robin sagged inside.

Directing her comment to Seldon, Robin said, "I think someone may have tried to run me down yesterday."

"What the hell?" David stalked over to stand in front of her.

Seldon backed David away. "Stand down, Detective." He turned to her and said, "Go ahead, honey, tell us."

She described the near miss in front of the coffee shop. "But, really, it was an accident. The man wasn't looking; he was in a hurry,"

"I'll see if there are any cameras around the crosswalk." David pulled out his cell again and issued orders, tight lipped. He disconnected when Scott arrived with his forensics team and briefed them. Scott had her repeat her story and watched the tape.

"Will you come out with us, ma'am, and show us where it happened?" Scott asked.

She walked them through it again with Ramirez and Doug adding their parts. Scott's crew went to work and they went back to the office. Seldon watched her, worried.

"I'm okay," she insisted. "I almost got mugged."

"You sure? How are your hands? Do they hurt?" He reached for her bandaged hands.

She held them up and waved them. "Not really. I'm more concerned about my slacks. I tore them when I fell."

Seldon turned to Doug. "How come you were out there?"

Doug nodded to David. "Her cop was hanging in the bar nursing a beer waiting for her. She asked him to leave her alone. Later I saw him follow her out and went to make sure she got to her car okay. Left Mel running the bar. Got there in time to chase the guy and see him get away."

"I don't want you going home alone," Seldon told her.

"Don't be ridiculous. It was just a mugging."

"No. It wasn't."

"Well then, it was a mistake. No one is after me. It was a coincidence. A car pulled in and parked behind me in an empty space."

Seldon frowned. "You could be right, but I'll feel better if you don't go out alone. I know a guy I can call." He picked up his cell and hit the speed dial. "What about your house? Do you have any security?"

"No. And I don't need any." But a part of her thought maybe she should get a system.

Seldon said, "I'll have someone there in the morning."

She was about to argue when Ramirez came back in. "I'm done here. I can follow you home and check your house."

She threw up her hands. "Fine," she said and marched out.

At her house, he made her wait at the door while he checked the interior. She could hear him walking from room to room. He finally came back. "It's safe."

"Of course it is. I'm sure this was all a mistake."

"We need to talk."

She ignored the comment. "I appreciate you checking my house. I will feel safe now and I'll bolt the door as soon as you leave." But he didn't move.

"We need to talk," he said again.

Talk? Personal or business, she almost asked, as if that would make a difference. "Not in the doorway and I need a glass of wine." She led him into the kitchen, pulled a bottle of wine from the fridge, took two glasses from the rack, and poured. She handed him one. With her eyes closed, she inhaled the bouquet and sipped, imagining calm seas with seagulls wheeling. Beaded seagulls. She sat on a stool at the counter and waited.

He didn't say anything; didn't drink any wine.

"You wanted to talk?" She didn't look at him, kept her gaze on her wine.

"Nice place you have here."

So, he wasn't going to get right to it. "You've been here before."

"Yeah, but you dragged me directly into the bedroom. I didn't have a chance to look around."

She felt herself turn red, which made her cross. She looked directly at him. "Right, and you were long gone before the sun rose."

He fingered his wine glass then wiped his hand over his face. "I tried to explain. I told you, I'm sorry."

He pushed the glass around on the counter. "I think I should stay here tonight."

"Not happening. I'll lock the door when you leave."

"I'll stay on the couch."

Right, like she would be able to sleep knowing he was right out here. She chose to misunderstand him. "Why bother, you don't spend the night anyway, remember?" He winced. "Sorry. You probably didn't deserve that, and you might actually be trying to help me."

"Right and right."

She spoke softly. "David, no one is after me. I'm not rich. I'm not famous. I don't have a vault of diamonds or government secrets. I'll be okay. It's time for you to go." She led him to the front room. "I'll lock the door when you leave. I promise."

"Look, security is not what I wanted to talk about."

She waited, head tilted, looking over his shoulder. He was so close she could feel the heat. She crossed her arms over her chest, a barrier between them.

"Forget it," he said. "I'll put a man out front. Come down to the station tomorrow to sign your statement."

He stalked out, pulling the door shut behind him. She leaned against it, feeling the coolness on her forehead.

He yelled through the door. "Lock the door."

She locked it, looked out the peephole and watched him walk to his car and get in. She heard the engine start, but he didn't leave. She leaned her head against the door again.

Now what? Does he think I'm going to call him back? She had to admit she was tempted. And he wouldn't be spending the night on the couch if she did.

Part of the night, she corrected herself. Not doing that. Not yet anyway. Not quite ready for another one-night fling.

She pulled her head away from the door. Was he gone? She looked back out the peephole and saw him drive away.

So many emotions warred inside her. Joy. She'd sold jewelry at the hotel. Terror. She'd been mugged. Confusion. David had been waiting for her. The last was the one she decided to tackle, but not without her wine. She sat for a while thinking about him hanging out in the bar. Waiting for her. Wanting to get back together.

She laughed at herself derisively. Sure. He couldn't live without her.

Took a sip of wine and saw the seagulls wheeling. Nodded her head and grabbed her graph paper to draw them. She had finally succeeded in distracting herself. She worked for another hour, put her glass in the sink, emptied David's, and went to bed.

**

Nursing his beer, David shook his head in frustration. He'd screwed up. Blown it. Being near her made him forget all his moves. He became tongue-tied. Acted like a caveman. He'd courted her once successfully;

he should be able to do it again. Yet he kept tripping because, somehow, it seemed there was more at stake now.

He wasn't sure what he'd thrown away when he'd left that morning, but he knew she was more than a flirtation. Whatever it was he felt when he was with her, he missed it when she was gone. He should never have left, and he'd known that when he'd walked out. No, snuck out. He should have called her as soon as he got home. Or later that morning at the latest and explained he had panicked. He didn't understand then why he felt panicked, and he'd let it go, believing her memory would fade. It hadn't. Not nearly. And, he'd screwed up his chances yet again.

She'd given him a chance Saturday morning. Why hadn't he taken it? Why was he afraid to call? And tonight? The bartender stood over her like a guardian angel, protecting her from him for god's sake. That had burned. He'd jumped up and gone after her when she left, to get her alone. Talk some sense to her. When that dark shape grabbed her, he'd screamed, "Stop. Police." It was instinctive. Had to have been because he'd gone cold and froze for a second. His gut had knotted and stayed that way until he'd assured himself she was unhurt. Except for her poor hands. He'd wanted to kiss them and make them better, but she'd pulled them away. And then Doug had arrived and there was too much to do.

And tonight at her house, he'd had another chance. He should have talked to her, told her how he felt, but instead he'd turned into some idiot high school kid when she'd crossed her arms and shut him out.

He kicked out at the wall, grunted, and sat in his chair to drink more beer.

Friday

She woke in terror, gasping for breath, her arms pinned to her sides. She struggled. Thrashed. Realized the sheets were twisted around her, holding her tight. She rolled off them and broke free. Dragged in a breath.

Shaking, she sat up. Took in several more, deep breaths.

When the shaking lessened she rubbed her face and felt hot tears. Wiped them away. An unsteady breath was followed by a hiccup. She was afraid to open her eyes but pride forced her. It was dark. Well, duh. Her breathing was returning to normal and her heartbeat slowing. She shivered and realized she was soaked with sweat. Her hair was wet. The sheets, too. She untangled them and forced herself out of bed onto unsteady legs.

So much for taking the mugging in stride. She'd thought she'd handled it well, but her brain had other ideas. Her brain was a wimp. A giggle escaped. Get a grip, girl. So what? Deal with it.

Maybe she should have let David stay.

She wiped her eyes, turned on the light, and checked the time. Three-thirty. She shook her head. A shower, clean clothes, then coffee. She wasn't going back to bed tonight.

**

Five hours later, she opened the front door with a questioning smile to the three men standing there. Two of the men stared at her. The third was shaking his head with a frown of disapproval.

"You don't open the door without checking through your peep hole. You don't open the door to strangers. You ask for ID before opening the door."

Exactly what she needed, a strange man chastising her on her own doorstep. She hesitated, torn between slamming the door and an angry retort. Which gave her time to think. The man was right. But still.

"Who are you? What do you want? May I see some identification please?" Just because he was right didn't mean she couldn't give him a hard time. "Do I have to shut the door and ask you to put it in front of the peephole?"

The man leveled a troubled stare at her. "Mrs. Garman, Seldon sent me to wire your house, but it doesn't matter how good a system I put in if you mindlessly open the door." No apology, no sorry. Only the flat statement.

He pulled his wallet out of his pocket and flipped it open. "I'm Tommy. My ID." His two partners did the same "Seldon," he nodded toward the street where Seldon was parking behind a white panel truck, "can vouch for us."

She hadn't checked his name, had barely glanced at his photo, but she waved to Seldon and asked Tommy, "Why don't you have any lettering on your van?"

"We don't like to advertise we're in the process of installing security. Neighbors see that and wonder why the homeowner needs protection. We'll put up warning signs when we're done because the signs themselves are a deterrent." He lifted a shoulder into a half-shrug. "Burglars are lazy and will go to a place without signs. Some homeowners don't like the notoriety a sign attracts and in that case we don't use them."

Seldon was at the doorstep then with another man. A solid, sturdy self-possessed man with broad shoulders and slim hips. Really good looking.

Tommy shook hands with the stranger. "Colin, your aunt's software is working great."

"Wouldn't expect anything else from my step-auntie." The man's lips twitched as if there was a joke she was missing.

Seldon made introductions. "This is a friend who sometimes does some bodyguard work, Colin Gibbs."

"Ma'am." Gibbs turned a killer smile on her. She wasn't dead. She could look and enjoy. She thought about swooning and took a breath, putting a hand on her heart. Wasn't surprised he had a ring on his finger, some lucky woman had this guy collared.

She gave him a smile and invited them in, opening the door wider. "Come in."

Seldon said, "I thought you would give me trouble."

"Well, of course, I'm going to give you trouble, James. But inside, not on the doorstep. You should have discussed security arrangements with me first."

Tommy nervously looked between the two of them. "Ah, Seldon, we'll get started on the exterior perimeter, then we'll come inside." He and his men split off to walk around the outside of the house.

She motioned James and Colin inside, telling Tommy, "There'll be coffee and fixings in the kitchen when you're done."

Seldon and Colin followed her to the kitchen where she fixed mugs for the three of them. She arranged cream and sugar, and a box of Sally's breakfast muffins on the table. "New recipe," she said and started a new pot. She set out clean cups for the security guys.

"Okay, I should get some home security, but I was thinking of a dog."

Neither man smiled.

"You can get a dog, too, if that's what you want, but you need a secure home system with backup, and Tommy is the best in in the business. Colin will be your personal protection, I don't want you out alone."

"I'll hire Tommy. But no bodyguard. I'm a big girl and can take care of myself." She cringed a little inside when she remembered the nightmare. That scared her more than the mugging. Could Colin protect her from nightmares? She turned to him. "I'm sorry, Mr. Gibbs that you wasted your time coming here. I don't need protection. Muffin?" She held out the box.

Seldon reached out and touched her hand. "Now Robin, just listen. Please?"

She sighed and set the box down. "I don't think you can convince me, but I'll listen."

He grimaced. "Someone tried to grab you yesterday. To run you down a few days ago. They're not going to give up. If they tried once, they'll try again. Let Colin stay around for a few days. What's it going to hurt?"

Gibbs took up the argument. "You have to admit it looks like more than coincidence. Wouldn't hurt to have me around in case there's another incident. Or until the cops determine the muggers are after someone else and that the speeding car was just an accident. But James has good instincts. If he thinks you need protection, he's likely right. You should listen."

"Mr. Gibbs, I don't need a bodyguard; I'd feel silly. It was a mugging." She added cream and sugar to the tad of coffee in her cup; she'd had too much caffeine. "Or the guy mistook me for someone else. He made a mistake."

"What do you say we try a compromise?" Colin suggested.

"Such as?"

"James or I will take you to work. You stay in your office. James or I will bring you home. You stay home. You don't go out. If you need to go out, call one of us. For a few days anyway, until we get this straightened out."

She gave it some thought. It wasn't as if she had any plans to go anywhere. She didn't date or party. And these were men she knew she could trust with her life.

"Please," Seldon almost begged. "It's a reasonable suggestion."

It wouldn't hurt, she guessed, and it would make James happy. She could do it for a few days. For him. "Okay. I can do that." She held up a hand. "For a few days, or until the police agree no one is after me."

Seldon breathed a sigh of relief. "Three days. That should be enough time."

"I have work today and I need to go out tomorrow night. I have an event scheduled."

"Cancel it."

"I can't. It's the annual musical soiree." It was a big annual event in Naples which raised a good deal of money for children.

"Big date?" Colin asked.

"I'll be working."

"You can call in sick."

"No, I'm the wine steward. The charity is paying my company to run the event and they expect me to be there."

Colin thought about it. "I could attend as a waiter maybe?"

"The employees are all vetted ahead of time, so that won't work. Look, there will be a lot of people there. It's by invitation. There's security. I'll be safe."

Seldon shook his head. "Colin will take you."

She rolled her eyes. "People will think he's my boyfriend. Worse. He has got to be ten years younger. People will think I'm a cougar."

James turned red.

Colin's lips twitched. "Works for me."

She laughed out loud and gave in. She liked him and the twitch was adorable. He was cute. It would be fun to take him to the party.

"The event is black tie," she warned.

"Not a problem."

This man? In a tux? She could almost feel her tongue hanging out now when he was in a t-shirt with all his muscles outlined and jeans which fit really nicely. Mentally, she slapped herself. She had the impression he knew what she was thinking but was saved from further embarrassment by Tommy knocking on the back door.

She let them in and they completed the interior inspection before returning to the kitchen for coffee. She peered over Tommy's shoulder as he manipulated the data on his tablet and he explained what he was doing. "We have new software made to my specifications by a software writer up north, Colin's aunt." Something about the aunt tickled him, too. "Very user friendly with all the bells and whistles I need. We enter all the measurements for doors and windows, then the application gives us a sketch, lists appropriate materials and the amount needed, gives a range of options and prices. It eliminates a lot of tedious mathematics. Another screen fills in man hours, payroll for each man, and all the associated tax work. I'll have three bids for you in two minutes."

True to his word, he gave her the estimates, explained the different levels of security and recommended the highest one. After consideration, she accepted.

"I'll print out a contract and we could start immediately. One of my clients had a last minute change of plans so we're free and I have everything we need in the truck." He paused. "I want to remind you the system won't work if you don't use it."

"I'll use it. You're installing it; I'll use it."

"Good."

Colin handed her a card. "Whenever you need me. Whenever you want to go out."

She gave it a quick glance and then looked again. "The Inn on Main Street? You live at the Inn?"

"Behind actually. My wife owns the Inn; it's been in her family for generations." She heard the pride in his voice.

"I love that place. I always time my visits to Cougars Cove at teatime." She laughed. "I wasn't too far off with the cougar joke."

He grinned. "The inn is my day job. Sometimes I help out Tommy or James, a couple of others."

"Well, you lucked out with me. The musical soiree is the event of the season. Some people would kill for a ticket. You get to go for free."

As they walked out the door, Seldon said, "I'll come back later and take you to work."

**

Robin introduced the Cuisines for Wines cooking class for Sally with a bold red Italian she uncorked and decanted. She described the vintage and bouquet as she poured a glass for each of the student chefs. Then Sally took over. She demonstrated step by step how to plan, shop, prepare, cook, and serve a complete Italian feast. The students partook of samples of each course prepared ahead by staff: appetizer, main course, dessert. At the end of the class, each student received a silver sack with the Fine Wines logo containing menus, detailed preparation advice, and cooking instructions. The sack also held two full dinner portions and a bottle of wine. It was an expensive gift, but the fee for the class covered it and the goodwill and return on investment would be huge.

After class Robin, Sally, and Rome dissected the demonstration, revamping the areas where the class had not run as smoothly as expected. They reviewed the schedule for next week and selected the staff trainees to assist. The next three class sessions would cover French, German, and American wine and foods.

Sally danced around. "It was really terrific. The students were surprised and pleased about the bottle of wine. And the dinner for two. One woman told me the silver sack was the icing. She was thrilled. She said she'd already received her money's worth with the first class. She couldn't wait to get home and share the meal and the free wine with her husband."

"Giving them each a bottle lowers our profit," Rome said. "But you're right, we more than make up for it with goodwill and great public relations. Most of the students tonight took extra copies of our class schedules to share with friends."

They gloated for a while and then Sally changed the subject. "How is your jewelry selling at the hotel?"

"Great. I have special orders already. Two sets: necklace, earrings, and bracelet. They'll keep me busy. I'm doing better at the hotel than down at Cougars Cove. I wasn't sure I was ready for the high end market, but it seems to be working. The staff is great and it's fun. I'll give a demonstration a week from Sunday."

Her enthusiasm faded when she remembered how the prior afternoon had ended. She told them about David and the mugging, Seldon's insistence on a security system, and the bodyguard.

Rome's face creased in concern. "Are you okay? You weren't hurt?"

Robin held up her palms, no bandages. "See, hardly any sign. I'm fine. I'm sure it was a case of mistaken identity, but I'm letting James have his way for a few days. I think it may be overreaction, but it was a little scary and all the security makes me feel more comfortable. And my new bodyguard, Colin Gibbs, will be my date. You'll get to meet him when he picks me up." She grinned. "I'll have this yummy guy following me around for a few days."

Rome still looked concerned. "Wiring your house and a bodyguard are good ideas. Too much is happening to you lately. The counterfeit wine, the stolen car, the dead guy. Now this mugging. You should wear a panic button."

"Panic button?" Robin shook her head. "The name scares me."

"Well, call it something else then, dog whistle. Whatever. You should get one."

"When did you become so bossy?" She teased him, jollying him out of his unease. She wasn't used to having people worry about her, though it was rather nice. For a moment she was jealous of Sally. "If I do get one, it can't be ugly. Will it match my wardrobe?"

"I'm sure they have something which pairs well with sweats and shorts." Rome snorted, trying not to laugh, which was what she'd intended.

"Back to the event tomorrow," he said. "We're all set. All you have to do is show up. No planning, no prep, no clean-up. Simply do your sommelier thing."

"That will be different, no worries, almost like attending the party. Walk around and talk to people about wine. Tough job. I think I can manage."

When Colin arrived to take her home, she introduced him to her friends. Sally gave her a thumbs up while Colin shook hands with Rome. "This is quite a place," he said looking around.

"Robin built it from the ground up. Took on Sally who manages the food service side; me, later, to run the wine end."

"Come on. I'll give you a tour," Robin offered and took him around the building explaining the operation. His interest wasn't an act; he didn't seem to miss anything and was clearly impressed. She added intelligent to her first impression of strength and ability.

"Sally and Rome are taking over the day-to-day operation while I concentrate on our education section. I'm pretty much retired from planning and working parties and events."

He stood by the stove in the classroom. "My wife has wanted to add wines to our menu for some time, something beyond the basic red or white, but hasn't known where to start. Your wine class sounds perfect for her. Maybe the cuisine class for the cook. We call her cook, not chef." He flashed that smile. "You might consider classes for professionals like her. Small inns, restaurants."

"Hadn't thought about that. Maybe we'll practice with your wife. Have her call me. I think we can work something out which would be beneficial to both of us."

On the ride home she asked, "You know all about me. How about you?"

"Grew up in the north, Maryland. Joined the army. Met my wife when I was stationed in Homestead. We fell in love at first sight and now we have a six-year-old daughter." His eyes lit up. "My wife inherited the Inn and loves running it. The people who work for her, well their parents worked for her parents. It's like a big family. I help some, still learning the ropes. I do some protection work on the side."

There was more she wanted to know about him, like where he'd learned that quiet confidence. Time enough to discover answers.

Tommy had the system installed by the time she arrived home and he made her turn it on and then off a dozen times. Arm to stay, clear; arm for away, clear. She wrote the instructions down, step by step. He gave her a special code to use in case she was trapped inside by someone forcing her to clear it. If she typed in the special code, it turned the alarm off and notified the monitor she was in trouble.

Both men watched her arm and dis-arm the security pad a final time and then Tommy took his leave. Colin said, "I'll come by tomorrow to take you to work." Then he waited outside the door to hear her re-arm the system.

Her answering machine held no updates on her mugger, she gathered her beading supplies, settled at the kitchen counter, and started on the special orders. She began with the earrings, simple, dangling columnar beads. For this project she used glass tube beads, both straight and spiral, different lengths and colors. She liked the radiance, the way they reflected light and color. By bedtime, she had them completed. Tomorrow she'd start the matching necklaces and bracelets.

Saturday

The same nightmare woke her, shaking, with tears in her eyes. Tonight's dream was not as bad as last night, maybe her sub-conscious was dealing with the problem. Same time as last night, though, so maybe she should set her alarm for three-thirty and skip the nightmare. She got up and made hot chamomile tea to help calm herself and then curled up on the couch where she read until daylight.

When she felt it was late enough, she called the police station for an update, but neither detective was available. Why should she be surprised? No one had contacted her after the counterfeit wine, or the stolen van, or the murder. Why would she expect a call because of a mugging? Especially since she had told him, pretty emphatically, not to call. That didn't explain Scott, though. She left a message for one of them to call back.

She wished David would call. She hoped he wouldn't. She picked up her beading and headed for the deck. She would concentrate on bead counts in the spiral choker and add a star-shaped drop at the center of the necklace.

It was a beautiful day, blue sky with puffy white clouds. She noticed swallowtail butterflies in the peach bougainvillea, their yellow and black stripes vibrant against the colored blossoms and the dark green leaves. It would make a nice embroidered necklace. She stopped beading to sketch it quickly. She wrote a quick description with the date and used arrows to point out the colors. She would have to check her book and find out which type of swallowtail these were. She didn't know much about butterflies and she wanted the detail to be correct.

Tommy had given her a few remote security hand-held buttons, suggesting she keep one in the shower, another by the bed. She had one of them close to hand and was surprised how comfortable it made her feel. While she beaded, she considered the database problems at Fine Wines, one program for the wine inventory, another for food and supplies. A third for income and expenses. A fourth for payroll and taxes. And still another to track events and personnel. It was frustrating. The systems should connect. Talk to each other. Personnel at events should link up to payroll. Items taken from inventory should move directly to purchasing. She shouldn't have to open and close applications and reenter data. But there weren't any boxed applications specifically targeting her type of business and she had no one on board who could tweak the software. Ian, one of the cooks' sons, knew computers, but he said what she wanted was beyond his expertise.

They might have to hire a techie. Or… She would talk to Colin about his aunt. And learn why he grinned when he spoke of her.

**

The detectives didn't call, but Agent Tucker did. Déjà vu, almost. He had a new assignment for her. The FBI had arrested a mob boss in New Jersey and confiscated all his possessions under the RICO Act. He'd had to explain the abbreviation to her, the Racketeer Influenced and Corrupt Organization Act, buying, transporting and selling drugs across state lines.

"He has a winter home in Naples which includes a large wine cellar with an extensive collection. We need to make an inventory, and, since Ebert is cataloging the cellar up north, we'd like you to certify the one here."

"What does it involve?"

"The wines are in a digital inventory and we want you assure the physical collection matches the electronic. As an official consultant for the FBI, you decide your own hours and use your own people if you need assistance. Come and look before you decide. See where you'll be working. I guarantee you'll be tempted."

"The place will make a difference?" Probably any place would be better than the warehouse.

"I think so. The cellar is remarkable, and the wines? You'll like them. I'll pick you up at eleven and have you back by noon."

She disconnected with a little smile wondering what Tucker had that made him sure she'd bite. Being an FBI consultant was looking up.

She had barely finished the thought when her cell rang again.

"Ms. Garman," an officious voice began, "I'm Brad Carlisle's attorney, Kent Lynch."

Was Carlisle suing her? "Yes, Mr. Lynch."

"Ms. Garman, since you found the fake wines in Mr. Carlisle's wine cellar, his insurance company is concerned."

They should be. No telling what else he bought could be fake. "I'm not to blame for that, Mr. Lynch. I found the wines; I didn't put them there."

"Well, be that as it may, the problem began with you."

"No, Mr. Lynch, the problem began when Mr. Carlisle bought fake wines."

Lynch's tone changed from arrogant to conciliatory. "I'm not accusing you of anything," he said, though he clearly had been. "I want to hire you as an expert to ascertain the authenticity of the remaining wines in his collection."

"I'm afraid I can't do that Mr. Lynch."

"My client will be happy to pay you for the work." He named a figure well above her normal rate. It was tempting, and she did have the free time, but she also had concerns.

"If I take the job, it will be to determine if there are fake wines. If I do find fakes, I will be obligated to report my findings to the authorities."

"You will report to us; we would inform the authorities."

"Of course, I will inform you first, but I will also notify the authorities."

There was a long pause. "That will be fine. We can go along with that."

"I repeat; you will not be paying me to ignore counterfeit wines." She knew she would find them. The only questions were how many and did Carlisle know about them?

"Not trying to do that, Ms. Garman. I'm paying to get the job done quickly. The insurance company is threatening to drop all his coverage."

"Why me? I was under the impression Mr. Carlisle didn't like me very much."

"He doesn't. But the insurance agent recommended you and your findings will be accepted by everyone. Mr. Carlisle requests you complete the work while he is out of town this week. He's leaving tonight. Can you do it?"

"I need to look at my schedule."

"I must have an answer now," he said. The arrogance was back.

"In that case, the answer is no. I can't do it."

"I'll remind you we are paying well above the going rate."

"I still need to check my schedule. I have other commitments."

"Cancel them."

"No."

"Work around them then."

"Mr. Lynch, stop bullying me. You cannot intimidate me. I am not interested in a job where I will be constantly harassed."

He talked over her. "Ms. Garman, let me—"

"No, let me. That's exactly what I mean. You need to back off. If you want me for this job, it will be under my terms. I will be in complete control of my time. I will have free access whenever I want and have complete autonomy. Once I sign a contract, and up until I say the job is completed, I will not hear from you or see you at any time unless we make an appointment in your office. I will not be hurried or harassed on a daily basis."

"We don't need a contract."

"You might not. I do. If I find any fake wines, I will notify the proper authorities, whomever and whenever I deem fit. And, I am to be paid up front when I sign the contract."

There was a long silence. She thought he might have hung up.

"I don't think we could agree to those terms."

"Fine. Goodbye, Mr. Lynch."

"Wait, wait. Half now, half when you are done."

"No. All up front. I had a little trouble with my bill the last time I dealt with Mr. Carlisle. He tried to stop payment." Hadn't done him any good, but it irritated. "You say you have researched me; you know my word is good. In any event, you'll have a contract."

"For this sort of money, I would expect you to do a complete inventory too."

"Mr. Carlisle should already have an inventory, especially if his cellar is insured. An inventory for insurance purposes would take considerable time; I have seen his cellar, so I have some idea of the work involved." She remembered the racks were only about a third full with cases still on the floor. She hadn't looked at those. "I would have to hire one or two assistants to help. Let's just say an inventory for insurance purposes would be double the amount you mentioned. Separate contract, same terms."

"That's unreasonable."

It was, but she really didn't want the job. She waited.

Finally he said, "I'll have the contracts drawn up and hand-delivered to your office today."

"Fine. Don't play games with me Mr. Lynch. I don't need this job." She hung up. She hated being a hard-nose but had learned it was the only way to protect herself. Some men thought they could overpower a woman with their authority and arrogance. She supposed they did the same thing with men, too. It wasn't just male over female dominance; it only felt that way.

Overall, a pretty successful morning, she reflected. Some beading completed and two jobs accepted. Might be a future in wine inventory; she'd have to research the need. How many wine cellars were in Naples? How many inventory systems? Fine Wines used an Apple database to track everything. She wondered what Tucker's mob boss used. She expected, top of the line digital.

Carlisle probably had a paper inventory, many pieces of paper, scattered. She'd use Cellartracker online to set up his inventory because he'd need something simple to update the cellar each time he added or removed a bottle. The software pulled descriptions and prices from the cloud. She'd hire Ian, a fast and enthusiastic learner, to help. It would be good work experience for him. He wasn't allowed around any open bottles, too young, but he knew about wines: their histories and descriptions, growing and harvesting, fermenting, aging, and bottling. And he knew about the bogus wines she'd already found at Carlisle's and some of what they had discovered in the warehouse.

She called Rome and gave him a heads up; then she hurried to dress for Agent Tucker.

Tucker rang her bell as she was stepping into her shoes. She could see him on the small screen Tommy had installed in the kitchen which was connected to the camera over the front door, so she didn't have to use the peephole.

Tucker opened the front passenger door for her and Agent Caruso, in the back seat, leaned forward to rest his hand on her shoulder in greeting. Agent Tucker said, "The house we seized is under the Department of Justice Asset Forfeiture Program. It's being managed by a subcontractor under the U. S. Marshall's Office, and it's our job to ascertain the value and authenticity of the wine cellar. We were going to have the sub-contractor do it, but my boss wants a wine expert. As I said on the phone, there is a very sophisticated digital system and you can bring in help if you need. Stan will handle any questions or problems."

They drove down Gordon Drive, pulled into a driveway, and parked in front of a three-car garage. The house was huge, one house away from the water, on elevated land. She wondered about that. A hill? In Naples? On the beach? They must have trucked in the fill. A lot of fill. She asked Agent Tucker.

"Yes. The owner, Dutch, built the hill. He had the fill trucked in. He wanted a basement wine cellar and a garage for his cars. He has three cars for everyday use, a Mercedes, a 'Vette, and a Porsche."

"He has three cars? To drive around Naples?"

"He has seven cars. He collects them. The other four are in the cellar—an air-conditioned cellar. A 1967 Ford Shelby GT500, a 1969 Ford Mustang Boss 429, a 1964 Jaguar E-Type Factory 'Semi-Lightweight' Sports Racer, and a 1970 Plymouth Road Runner Hemi

Superbird. Each worth between $150,000 and $300,000. They occupy half the cellar. The custom-built wine cellar occupies the other half. The room is thermostatically controlled with its own air conditioning unit and a generator for power outages. It contains about six thousand bottles."

He stepped out of the car. "You can work anytime you want; someone will always be on site during the day. Stan can arrange evening hours." He led her inside through a side door. The entryway opened to a huge living room, a piano off to one side. She could see a dining room on the left and a pool through what appeared to be a glass wall at the back of the house. A pool bar and a waterfall. How had he managed that?

Ahead she saw a tall woman, the type David liked with blond hair flowing over her shoulders. She was standing in front of a desk talking to two men almost hidden by monitors. Tucker introduced the men as agents and the woman, a Ms. Leach, was the sub-contractor cataloging everything inside the building except the wine cellar. The agents nodded over their monitors. Ms. Leach barely spared her a glance, an angry glance, and handed Agent Tucker a flyer.

"This is the proposed format for the announcement for the house auction."

Stan moved very close to Leach, almost touching, placing his hand on her shoulder as he viewed the copy Ms. Leach held. Apparently the type appealed to him as well as David. Leach smiled as she gave Caruso his own copy of the brochure. Ignoring Robin, she said, 'I'll be upstairs," and she left the room clutching her huge purse close under her arm.

Robin shook her head. Wonder what I did to tick her off? The woman was angry and almost appeared frightened. Of what? Not Stan? He came back to stand near her. He was like a butterfly, no, a thirsty bee buzzing the pretty flowers. She plucked the brochure out of his hand and read it.

The house sat on a one-acre lot, on a manmade hill. Fill raised the whole lot five feet above street level. The brochure went into more detail than Agent Tucker had. The hill's purpose was two-fold: to provide protection against hurricane storm surges and allow space for the built-in underground wine cellar and garage; the natural insulation also provided a cool dry environment and cut down on air-conditioning.

According to the brochure, four muscle cars and the wines were to be auctioned individually.

She counted on her fingers as she read: two master suites, six more bedrooms, ten baths; three dining rooms, two inside, one casual, one formal, with the third outside by the heated infinity pool; lap pool, Jacuzzi, and, the waterfall from the second story into the pool. Two indoor/outdoor social areas including radial bars. Two full kitchens with granite countertops and stainless-steel appliances. A billiards room, a fitness center, and a theater. Five gas fireplaces, marble and hardwood floors, and tray ceilings with something called crown moldings.

And the man didn't even live here.

Tucker pointed out the elevator, but led her down ornate stairs to the basement where he unlocked a solid wooden door.

"The cars are parked over to the right."

He turned to the left and a light switched on automatically as they approached a double glass door etched with herons in flight. It opened to a room which was all glass and wood and mirrors with a crystal chandelier. An island bar, how many did that make? Three? Four? This would be a wine bar, though, unlike the ones in the social areas upstairs. There were eight stools with backs and comfortable leather cushions arranged in front of it.

Three walls held ceiling-high wine racks constructed from a warm dark wood. The standard racks contained slatted bins, diamond cubed storage cases, and base cabinets with etched glass doors or drawers. The corner racks were curved. Each rack, row, cabinet, and drawer was labeled with a number and a bronze heron.

The floor was a breathtaking Everglades mural of painted porcelain tile. Overhead, another mural of blue sky with puffy white clouds and flocks of birds in flight.

Robin walked around the room, stopped in front of a glass and metal gate set in one wall. The gate had the recurring etched bird. She peeked inside. It was dark but she could make out counters with wine bottles, and more racks, waist high. No dead bodies.

"Rare bottles," Tucker said. "Locked for now. You will be given access later."

She walked back to the bar and turned on the digital inventory unit; saw it gave each bottle an ID number and listed its location, date of purchase, supplier, previous owners, cost, and a summary of age, aroma, tastes, overtones. Everything. "Looks like everything is here in the inventory, even current value, though that may be different when they go to auction. Do you want me to do spot checks? Or touch every bottle?"

"Spot check first. Stan has a list of random numbers for you; fifty bottles. If everything checks out, we'll leave it at that. If not, we either repeat with the next fifty or, if necessary, touch every bottle. If you use some of your own people to help, give Agent Caruso their names. We'll complete a more in-depth examination of the expensive rare wines in the locked cage."

"Probably a few million dollars' worth of wine here," she said.

"Are you serious?" Caruso asked, gawking around and standing a little too close.

She stepped away. "Not unusual for wealthy connoisseurs. And there have been some write-ups about the wines he owns. This whole place is way over the top. He probably pays more for his electricity to keep his cars and wine cool than I do for my house mortgage."

Back in the car she told Tucker about her other job offer. He laughed. "The insurance company called me. Carlisle put in a claim for the counterfeit wine. I don't think they're going to pay him and I'm not surprised they're demanding an appraisal. I mentioned your name, but they were already thinking about you. Fine Wines has a good reputation."

**

Colin elected to use his own car again to drive her to work for the Saturday cuisine class. He quietly chewed her out, gently but thoroughly, when she told him about her trip with Tucker.

"But he's FBI," she grumbled. The FBI? Really? What was wrong with going with the FBI?

"Doesn't matter if he is the president. While I'm responsible for your safety, you go nowhere without me."

She didn't understand. "I'm new to this. I'm still learning. Why aren't I safe with the FBI? You don't think they'd hurt me do you?"

"No. But they aren't watching out for your safety, guarding you. They're not expecting to need to protect you. That is a special type of work. That's why presidents have the Secret Service. Look, Robin, it's only a few days. Let me do my job."

She could do as he wanted for a few days. "I won't do it again," she promised and said, "Tommy showed me the software your aunt wrote for him. Fine Wines desperately needs something like that; we're using multiple programs and it's a pain. We need one software which will do everything, especially since we expanded into education. Do you suppose your aunt would be able to help us?"

"Yeah. My, um, aunt." His lips quirked. "It's what she does. She writes code for a living, creates multi-faceted databases which interface with all areas of a business.

"How do I hire her? Your aunt?"

"I'll have her call you."

"Why do you smile when you say aunt?"

He snorted. "She's kind of a hacker. Her whole family, my, um, stepmother's, are computer geeks. My dad's a cop. He married into a family of over-achieving techies. They keep him on his toes."

"You mean they break the law?"

"Nah. But I think they push it around some."

Colin watched from the back of the room and drove her home afterward where he walked her to the door and waited while she cleared the system and reset it. Tommy would be proud of her.

He was back three hours later for the event and was every bit as yummy in his tux as she had imagined. "We need to take my car tonight; it has supplies," she told him as he started toward his own vehicle. He looked it over and walked her to the passenger door, opened it for her and went around to the driver side. He stopped. Lost the smile. Called her over.

When she got to that side of the car, he pointed to two small holes in the door frame. "These are fresh. How did this happen?"

She shrugged her shoulders. Two holes. She reached to touch one spot and Colin caught her hand.

"I don't know. I haven't noticed it." Why had he turned so serious? "Can't be termites, it's not wood. Doesn't look like dirt dobbers." They were a kind of wasp which built mud nests.

"Not bugs," he said. "Bullets."

She went still. Searched his face. He was serious. She shook her head. "No. Can't be."

"They are. Bullet holes. They would have made a noise. You would have heard them smack into the car."

She was still shaking her head. Couldn't seem to stop. Bullet holes?

"Think, Ms. Garman. Anything strange, anything unusual happen the last few days?"

She thought. Considered. "No." She put a hand up. "Unless maybe…"

"Maybe what?" Colin demanded.

"Well. The other night I dropped my keys and I thought I heard two more things fall, but I hadn't dropped anything else. I guess that could be it. Then a car peeled off. Is that what you mean?"

"What night? When?"

"Um. Let me think. I was coming home from the hotel. From a meeting. Tuesday night."

"The guy who sold the fake wine. He was shot Wednesday?" Seldon had filled him in.

Robin corrected him without thinking. "No. He was shot Tuesday. Late they thought, the last I talked to them. We found Mr. Fallern Wednesday." Colin didn't like that.

"We need to call the cops. Who is handling that shooting?"

She told him and gave him the phone number. "He never answers, though," she warned him and almost smiled when Colin was forced to leave a message for the detective to call him back.

She was scared now. Could feel tremors start. Colin held her gently by the shoulders. "It's all right. You're going to be okay. This happened days ago. We're going to go to that event and do our jobs. You will discuss wines. I will protect you." He waited for her to look up at him. "You can do it," he said. Not asking, telling.

She bit her lips, steadied herself. "I can."

She got back into her car, her shot up car, and directed him to the convention center's back door where she gave him the nickel tour of the food truck, pointing out equipment and storage. Everything seemed normal. "We can hold an event almost anywhere with this; plus, we don't have to depend on the client's kitchen."

He lingered by the grill. "How about the dock at Cougars Cove? Could you run a food and wine event there?"

"Sure. We could park in any of the lots or even right in front of the marina. Serve from the truck itself or set up tables and chairs. We rent them, and sometimes we rent a tent. Why? Are you going to hire us for a wine tasting?"

"I'm on the Dock Committee. We have the Fourth of July covered, but we need something for the fifth and sixth. A wine tasting might be it. I'll ask and get back to you."

She liked this man and his ability to find her customers. She checked her schedule on her cell. "You're in luck. We're going to be at the fireworks on the Fourth, but we have the next two days open. I'll pencil the Dock in."

"Good. Now. Ground rules for the benefit. We go in together. I stay close. You keep an eye on me, if I motion for you to move, you move. You see anything or anyone that makes you nervous, you signal me. I'll always be within a few steps."

She nodded and walked inside on his arm. She soon forgot the bullet holes as she circulated from individual to couples, to groups, to individuals. She loved this part of the job. Meeting new people, sharing her knowledge, an interesting tidbit, or a fascinating fact about the wines of the evening. At one point she told a tale about the winemaker. Entertaining, knowing what her audience would enjoy was one of her talents. She caught a few curious looks when Colin came by to bring her a champagne flute.

"I can't drink."

"It's water. Everything going okay?"

"Yes. It's a great group of people. Thank you." She turned back to another group and looked straight into David's eyes across the room. She stiffened, gave him a brief nod and turned away. Colin touched her arm.

"What?" he whispered.

"Oh. Nothing. Just a mistake I made."

"That guy?" he asked.

"Yeah. Made a mistake with him."

"He looks familiar."

"David Ramirez. He's a cop."

"Yeah. That's him. Heard good things about him."

"Well don't let your daughter near him."

"She's six."

"When she's older. He's a player."

"Hadn't heard that."

She looked at him with a question.

"What? People talk. Cops talk. Especially cops. Good cop, bad cop. Skirt chaser. That's not what they say about him. He's got a date tonight," he said watching over her shoulder.

Robin turned for a quick look. "Pretty." Not buxom or blond. Perfect figure in designer clothes.

"If you like the type. You okay?"

She nodded and continued to mingle and socialize, checking every few minutes with Colin. She turned away from a patron and found David right in front of her. Hadn't been forewarned by his aftershave.

"Oh." She drew back, startled and angry with herself because her heart was fluttering and she couldn't think of anything to say.

"Robin."

"Detective Ramirez." She forced herself to smile, slightly to the left of his head. "How nice to see you. Is your company providing the security?" She hadn't thought to check. Not because she wasn't thinking about him, she had been, just not on a business level.

"No. But I have some cops working the floor. Didn't expect to see you here tonight."

"We have the wine contract and are sharing the food catering."

"Thought you weren't doing events anymore."

"You don't listen very well. I still do events." Before he could reply she went on the offensive. "And you don't return phone calls, either. You never called me back."

He looked puzzled.

"Neither you nor Scott returned my calls."

"Why would we?"

"Because you said I was targeted for abduction." She almost stamped her foot. Was annoyed and frustrated she had to remind him.

"As I recall, you said it was a random mugging."

"Yes. That's what I said. You insisted it was a premeditated kidnapping." She couldn't keep the irritation out of her voice.

"I was wrong."

"You couldn't pick up a phone and tell me?"

"Sorry. Didn't seem necessary." He didn't sound sorry.

"As a cop, you make it a practice not to return calls to victims of a crime?"

"Scott should have. I was busy. Didn't realize you thought you were a victim."

He was busy. Didn't realize there was a problem. This was the man she fell in love with? Couldn't even take a few minutes to return her calls; to check on her?

This wasn't the caring man she'd fallen for. That man had made her feel cherished, treasured. She'd loved the way his face lit up when he saw her. The smile he kept just for her. The soft words. The touch of his hand. He'd been so real. So smooth. She'd fallen hard and then he'd bound her to him with a night of passion.

Hah. She slapped herself mentally. Part of a night. Her fairytale prince had turned into a snake before the sun came up. What had she been to him she wondered, not for the first time. A notch on his bedpost? A number in his black book? A point on a graph? How did she rate? Was three weeks the average amount of time he spent on a seduction? Did sex with an almost virgin even fit on his chart? Almost virgin because she'd been celibate for thirteen years. Was that why he hadn't stayed the night? She pulled herself back to the conversation.

"I see you have a date." She nodded toward the woman.

"That's business. Who's the new boyfriend?"

"Boyfriend?"

"The kid over there, the one you can't keep your eyes off."

She glanced over to see Colin watching, ready to come over. She shook her head at him. She wasn't surprised David had assumed Colin was her boyfriend. Colin certainly acted like her date to any observer. Her checking with him every few minutes would seem to be two lovers separated by work. She wasn't sure what to say. She didn't have to explain herself to him. He was the one who left. And didn't call.

"His name is Colin. He returns my calls."

"The guy's a little young for you isn't he? Your new boy toy? You trolling the grade schools now? Kind of makes you a cougar."

She'd told Colin exactly that; hadn't expected this man she'd thought had loved her to be the one name calling. What difference should it make if she dated a younger man? David was with a younger woman. She wasn't going to let him know he'd struck a nerve.

"Hmm. No. Not too young. Just about right I think. He found me. Do you want to meet him?"

"Don't have time. He's married."

"How do you know?"

"Wedding band. Younger married men keep you satisfied in the sack I imagine."

She wasn't sure what to say. He had her off balance. Why did he care? Before she could formulate a response, he continued, "Guess I loosened some hidden sexuality. You had it locked down pretty tight."

He had. Damn him. She hated him for that. For bringing back those physical needs she had carefully packed away. The jab hurt and made her angry.

"Can't imagine why you should be concerned. The lonely widow finds a young sexy man. You have your own younger date tonight. But wait. It's business, you said. Like the last time? Except this one isn't blond or buxom."

"That's right. She's not a date. She's work."

"Convenient for you. Security work? Police work? Never mind. Who you date is none of my business." Would tonight be his lucky night?

"Robin. She's not a date."

"So you said. It's okay. You can date. None of my business." She didn't want to know. She didn't want to care. But she did. Even now, she wanted him. Hated him. If he got lucky, would he leave early? She had to get away.

"Thank you for the update on the status of my case. Excuse me, I need to go powder my nose. You better find your, um, work. I don't see her anymore. Maybe she got lonely."

Turning so he couldn't see her tears, she left and wove through the crowd headed to the ladies' room. She needed time.

Colin caught up to her. "You okay?"

She nodded and, keeping her head turned away, said, "The detective says it was a random mugging, no one tried to grab me. I guess you can go home now."

"He said more than that."

"He asked about my new boy toy." She tried a smile, but knew it didn't work; she held the tears in check. She was not going to cry. At least not out here. Maybe in the ladies'.

He noticed. "Guess he didn't like the idea of you getting it on with me. Take a few minutes to pull yourself together." Put his left hand on her back and guided her down a short hallway to the restroom. A 'closed' sign hung on the door. He took her empty glass and handed her his goblet of water.

"Wait here, I'll take a look inside."

She peeked over his shoulder before she remembered the last time she'd done that and seen a dead body, but all she saw now was a plush seating area with two small white love seats, three chairs, two vanities. Neatly folded towels sat stacked on the counter. Mirrors hung all around the room. The ones on the wall to the right reflected the area of stalls and wash basins around a corner. David's date was sitting at one of the mirrors fixing her lipstick. Her eyes went wide when Colin stepped in. He put his finger across his lips and strode the three steps past the dividing wall to look down the aisle toward another exit on the far side of the stalls and examine the stalls. The doors were white louvered wood and all of them were open. The stalls empty. He backed out and reached for Robin. Held her close as she stepped in and whispered in her ear.

"Take a few minutes. Catch your breath. I'll be right outside." The embrace while he delivered his message was meant to appear intimate. She'd told Colin he wasn't needed and, instead of leaving, he had escorted her here, made sure she was safe. A nice guy. He gave her an encouraging stroke down her arm, an action not hidden from David's date.

"Wow," the woman said as he disappeared out the door.

Robin turned to David's *not a date*. Just my luck, she thought. First David, now his date repairing her face. No tears in here now.

"Yeah."

"That's some man."

"Yeah." Robin couldn't find words for David's date.

"Sorry I spoiled your plans." She gave Robin a knowing look. "I can leave if you want to call him back."

"What? What?" She put her hand to her throat. "You think we were going to …" she couldn't finish the thought. "No. We weren't… It wasn't…." She stopped. She knew what it looked like. The woman had misinterpreted the hug exactly as Colin had intended, because he'd needed the excuse to be in the ladies' room. Robin walked past her through the lounge to a sink, put the goblet down on the counter, and splashed cold water on her face. She sighed as the cold calmed her nerves. Grabbing one of the soft towels, she patted her face dry. She really wanted a few minutes alone.

"You're the sommelier," the woman said.

"Yes." Resigned, Robin drew on some calmness. "Are you enjoying our wines?"

"Very much. This is a marvelous benefit and I understand your firm is donating some bottles for the auction?"

"Yes, we are. Three cases of very fine ice wines. Our donation for the children."

"It is a very good cause. I'll be sure to enter a bid." She stood. "I need to be back on the floor." She turned to leave but the emergency exit door crashed open and four waiters pushed inside. Black ski masks covered their faces. The one in front pointed a gun at them.

Robin stopped breathing.

"Don't move ladies and no one will be hurt," the lead man said. He motioned to his friends to go around. "Get her."

Me? Are they coming after me?

"What about the other one?"

The first man, the leader, looked again. She knew what he saw. Two women, almost the same height, similar features, same color mouse-brown hair, one in a red cocktail dress, the other in green. Two women when he'd expected one? "Take both of them. We don't want anyone raising the alarm."

Breathe, Robin told herself. Breathe. They aren't going to kill us. Not right away. They're going to take both of us. Somewhere. She closed her eyes a second. Reached to her necklace. No, not a panic button. She had never seriously considered a panic button. If she had, she could push it now.

She dropped her hand. Felt the goblet. Slid it off the counter. It fell to the tile floor and shattered with a loud crash.

"What the hell?" The leader made a move toward her.

"Sorry. Sorry. It slipped. You scared me." She raised her hands, palm out, her voice rising with each word as she backed up. She bumped into David's not-a-date, forcing her backwards toward the door. Surely Colin heard the crash.

"Shut up. Shut up. Stand still." The leader made a threatening move with the gun and the three men moved toward her. Robin whimpered, "Don't hurt me." She backed up another step, two, forcing the other woman closer to the door.

She saw it open out of the corner of her eye. Colin slipped through, gun in hand, watching the men in the mirrors.

**

The waiters were focused on the women. The first one reached out to grab her; blocking the leader's view.

Colin grabbed David's not-a-date and flung her toward the door. "Out. Scream." he ordered in a loud whisper. "Scream." She screamed.

He took one step and hit the first guy with a straight punch to the throat. The man collapsed. The second guy couldn't stop his forward momentum. He tripped over his buddy. Went down.

Colin shoved Robin toward the door. "Out. Out. Scream."

She let out the scream which was deafening in the small room and spilled out into the hallway. Colin ducked down behind the wall, and as the third thug moved forward, Colin kicked him in the thigh. When the second guy tried to stand, Colin moved into him and hit him fast in the gut, following it with a hard right to his jaw. The man went back down again with a groan and stayed there.

Colin risked a peek around the corner.

The leader fired a shot in his direction. Colin ducked back into cover. A second shot resounded. When he saw Robin still in the door, he angrily motioned her out.

"Put your gun down," he yelled at the leader, showing his own weapon for a fraction of an instant. "I have you covered and there'll be a dozen people here in two seconds."

He threw a glance at Robin, still in the open doorway. "Robin. Get out. Tell security I'm armed. Tell them to go to the other door. Block these guys in."

But it was too late; the leader fired three more times and then the far door slammed shut.

**

David raced in the direction of the screams, mentally kicking himself for being an idiot, letting himself be distracted. He drew his weapon when he heard the shots.

Shit.

Rebuking himself for losing sight of his responsibility, protecting Patsy, who was now missing. He couldn't believe she had wandered off. She knew better than that. No. He couldn't blame her. He had no one to blame but himself. He'd left her alone. He was supposed to stay with her. He kicked himself again for leaving her alone to chastise Robin. His brain had turned to mush when she had walked in with the kid; some circuit had fried. He'd lost it and berated her. As if he had a right. In the short amount of time he'd verbally abused Robin, Patsy had wandered off.

He'd searched the room, she shouldn't have been hard to miss in her bright red dress, but he hadn't found her. He prayed he wasn't too late. Two of his men were behind him and when he reached the hallway to the restrooms, he saw a flash of red. Patsy. Unhurt. Thank God. He heard more shots.

"Shit."

Patsy flung herself at him, grabbing and holding on. "Some men," she gasped, "tried to grab us."

Us? Who? Before he could ask, Robin burst out the door. "There are four men dressed as waiters. They tried to take us. Colin has a gun. My date. Colin. Don't shoot him, David. He saved us."

She'd told him everything he needed to know in a few succinct sentences. Part of him gave her credit for calmness and strength under fire. The other part was cursing. She shouldn't be here. In danger.

More of his men rushed down the corridor toward him. He shoved both women off to them. "Stay with them. Guard them. No one in this corridor. Call the station, get some cars here. No sirens. And Scott. Get Scott here. Tell them to come in the back door." He sent officers around to the exit.

He peered inside the restroom. Edged in. Colin, the boyfriend, the boy toy, motioned for him to cover the thugs on the floor.

"Watch them. There's one more. He has a gun."

David nodded as Colin peeked around the edge of the wall. They could both see the stalls were empty. Colin crept around the dividing wall and into the stall area, ready to duck into one if the exit door opened. He worked his way through the room staying near the stalls. He stopped at the emergency door.

David scrambled to back him up as two of his men entered the room. He watched as Colin pulled the door open, took a quick glance through. The outside door stood wide open. He heard a vehicle accelerate. Colin charged outside, David a second behind, in time to see taillights as the vehicle rounded the corner.

"Damn."

"Yeah," David agreed. He'd backed up the boy toy. Armed boy toy. One who had taken down three thugs and rescued two women. He'd followed the boyfriend back to the door.

"He was moving too fast," Colin said. "Must have had a driver waiting. A van, that's all I could tell. Could have guessed that much. You don't bring a convertible to a kidnapping." Disgusted, Colin reached down to put his gun in his ankle holster.

"Hand over your weapon."

The boy toy, turned in surprise. "You just backed me up."

"And now I want your weapon." His own weapon was still drawn, but lowered; not pointing at Colin. His badge was visible, hooked on his belt.

"Sure." Colin put on the safety, flipped the weapon over and placed it in Ramirez's outstretched hand, butt first. "Hasn't been fired."

Ramirez kept his eyes on him all the time; gave it a sniff test. No odor. "You have a license for it?"

"Yeah. And a license to carry concealed. Can I have it back?"

When Ramirez hesitated Colin added, "Keep it. Can we do this inside? I want to check on Robin." He nodded past David to the door.

Coming to a decision, David stuck Colin's weapon in his belt, holstered his own. "Inside." He needed to check on Robin, too. And Patsy. He couldn't believe he'd lost track of her. He was supposed to be protecting her, but he'd had to badger Robin, find out who the boy toy was. He'd neglected his duty and almost lost Patsy. The boy toy had saved both the women. Against four men. Without firing a shot. Done his job.

His men had the goons on the floor handcuffed. One was still out cold, another breathing heavily and groaning.

"You did them?" he asked the boy toy.

"Yeah."

"That one hurt serious?" He pointed to the one out cold.

"No. He should be coming around soon. I needed him out of the way for a few minutes."

David went over to talk to his men. "Frisk them?"

"Couple of knives, switchblades. A billy club. No guns."

"Get pictures. Here, use my cell." He passed it over. "Where's Patsy?"

"Outside. I got guards with her and the lady sommelier," one of his men, Polinski, replied. "We told everyone your date thought she saw a rat and screamed. Not sure they bought it, but we sent the looky-loos away."

David glanced through the door. Robin and Patsy stood in the hallway side-by-side, gathering strength from each other. More security guards stood nearby.

Colin came up behind him and waved to Robin who looked relieved and waved back.

David turned to him. "I'm Detective Ramirez. Give me your license and carry permit."

Colin handed them over. Ramirez studied the ID first, matched the picture to the face. Did the same with the license to carry. Uniformed deputies came in and removed the three men, leading them out the emergency door. The third one was now awake and walking.

"I'll be down to talk to them when I finish up here," David told his men.

Scott passed them as he entered, asked David, "Who's this?" He studied Colin.

Ramirez passed over the IDs. "Name's Colin Gibbs and he's going to tell us what happened here."

"Walked my date to the door, waited outside, heard a glass crash." He pointed to the shards. "Heard voices, looked in, saw the women, my date with her hands up. Saw the men coming toward them in the mirrors." He pointed to the back wall. "I grabbed my weapon. Threw the other woman toward the door and hit the first guy in the throat. He was the one out cold. His accomplice tripped over him and went down. I dragged Robin out of the line of fire and kicked the third guy in the thigh. Hit the second guy again when he tried to get up. The man at the exit door loosed the first shot. I ducked back behind the wall. When I peeked, he fired again, chasing me back to cover. I warned him to put the gun down. He fired three times and the exit door slammed."

He motioned toward Ramirez. "You came in then. By the time I got to the back door the vehicle was squealing around the corner and out of the parking lot. All I could tell was not a sedan or pick-up."

"You took out three men?" Scott asked with a disbelieving snort.

"Yeah." A simple answer in a tone that implied he did it every day.

David grimaced. "Polinski. Go interview the women. Separate them."

Scott turned to Ramirez waiting for his version.

"I heard the women screaming and two shots fired; came running. I heard three rounds as I came through the door. Those three were down when I got here."

David knew Scott had more questions for him; ones he wasn't going to ask in front of Colin.

"Can I have my weapon back now?" Colin asked.

Gibbs was pretty calm for a guy who had recently been in a fire fight. "I'm keeping it. I want you to come down to the station and fill out a report. I'll check you out there."

"Am I under arrest?"

"No. Not if you come voluntarily."

Colin shook his head in disgust. "Then I want my lawyer here."

"Are you guilty of something? You need a lawyer?" David asked.

"No. Just want to make sure I get my equipment back."

The cops exchanged a look and Scott said, "Go ahead. Call him."

Colin pulled out his cell and walked into the corner while the two detectives conferred. "Scott, run his ID and license. And check the cameras. Maybe they caught these guys before they put on their masks. Oh, and the doors. The alarms should have gone off. These are emergency exits."

**

"Dad?" Colin said when his father picked up.

"Hey, Colin."

"Some men made a grab for my client. No one's hurt and I got three of them. But the cops want me to go to the station and file a report. The cop is my client's ex and I figure he's going to give me a hard time."

"I'll meet you there."

"I can handle him. What I need is someone to watch my client while I'm gone. I don't think there will be a follow-up this quick, but I can't take a chance and Nick, my backup, is out of town."

"Where is she?"

"Here, at the hall."

"I can be there in ten minutes."

"Great, I appreciate your help. Maybe Becca could watch Robin? While you represent me."

There was a long silence on the other end. Then his father said, "I'll ask her." Mumbles came through the phone. Then, Becca asked, "What's her name Colin? How do I recognize her?"

He'd been holding his breath. "Thanks Becca. Dad's going to let you do it?"

"Your father and I have an understanding, Colin. We're both cops. We both go into dangerous situations. We're both experienced and capable of making our own decisions. Tell me what I need to know."

He did and then his father was back on the line. "We'll be there in ten minutes. She's getting her weapon."

"Thanks Dad."

"That's what family is for, Son."

"I'll try to get with Robin, tell her you're coming, but I don't think they'll let me talk to her."

"Becca will handle it. See you in a few."

Colin walked back to the detectives who stopped talking as he approached. "He's coming."

"What? You have him on speed dial? Need him a lot in the middle of the night huh?" David jeered. "Says a lot about a man if an attorney comes that quick. None of it good."

"Yeah. I have him on speed dial."

"Let's go over your story again," Scott said.

This time they stopped him and asked questions, made him back up and repeat. He did it patiently. They were starting on a third round when there was a commotion at the door. His dad's quiet voice asking politely to see his client, Colin Gibbs.

Polinski stuck his head in the door.

David snapped, "Yeah, let him in."

Colin's father stepped inside. "You okay?" he asked.

Colin nodded. "I was about to start the story for the third time for the detectives."

"Go ahead, I'd like to hear what happened."

Colin faced them, not his father, went through the whole thing again. This time the detectives didn't interrupt.

"This appears to be a clear case of my client protecting his, ah, date," the elder Gibbs declared. "What seems to be the problem?"

"We want to be sure of what happened here," Ramirez said.

"Seems to me the women should have backed him up." He looked from one cop to the other. "Or not?"

"We're talking to them now."

Scott asked Colin, "You walked your girlfriend to the john. How come?"

"She was upset. She needed time to compose herself."

"What did you do to make her upset?" Scott asked.

Colin looked to his dad, gave him a look which said he didn't want to answer.

"Why is that relevant to the situation, Detective?" his father asked at the same time Ramirez said, "Scott, leave it alone."

But the detective didn't. "I can see a scenario where your client sets his date up and then rescues her, so he can be a hero."

Colin's father laughed out loud.

"Leave it, Scott," Ramirez repeated.

"No. I want to know. What did you say to upset her?"

"My client doesn't have to answer. Why don't you ask the girl? Why haven't you talked to her yet?"

"We are talking to her. We'll have answers soon," David growled. "And who are you anyhow? I don't believe you told us."

"I'm Colin's attorney. Ryan Gibbs," he said.

Ramirez snorted, sneered at Colin. "Daddy is bailing you out?"

"Yeah," Colin said with a wide smile.

The father did resemble the son, older, a bit thicker but with the same quality of strength and self-confidence.

Polinski came back in.

"What?" David growled.

Polinski looked around nervously. "Patsy says he saved them, though Gibbs's date was already pushing Patsy toward the door when he came in. Ms. Corson? She said the men were going to take both of them." He checked his notes. "When the men came in, one of the thugs asked which woman? The leader said to take them both."

Ryan asked, "Which woman were the men after?"

"Patsy. Patsy Corson. We've been charged with her protection," Scott answered

Colin disagreed. "You don't know that. They may have been after Robin."

Scott repeated his question to Colin. "You want to tell us now what you did to upset your date? We can ask her."

Colin looked to Ramirez who finally said, "He didn't. He didn't say anything. I did. It was personal."

Scott stared at Ramirez, seemed to realize he'd missed a question and said, "Wait. Wait. My mistake. Who are the women who are involved?"

"Patsy Corson and Robin Garman."

"The sommelier? Shit." He shook his head. "Crap, David. Oh, crap. Let me think." A moment later he said, "So which woman were they after?"

"Good question. Do you know?" Colin said.

Everyone looked to Ramirez. "Until just now, I thought they were after Patsy."

Colin broke the long silence. "Robin told me the police don't believe she was the target of an attempted kidnapping Thursday."

Polinski leaned out the door a minute, listened. "Ah, Boss? Ms. Corson wants to come in."

"Bring her."

No one said anything while they waited. Polinski stuck his head out the door again. "Corson won't come in without Ms. Garman and Garman's friend."

"Ah, hell. Bring 'em all in," Scott ordered.

Colin didn't hide his tiny smile when he saw Becca holding Robin's hand.

David introduced Patsy and Robin, then pointed at Becca. "And who's the friend, Robin?"

"My name is Becca. Becca Travis," the woman replied.

"Becca Travis Gibbs actually," Colin said.

"Your wife? Your wife is friends with your girlfriend?" Ramirez asked, disbelief warring with disgust.

Robin looked from Colin to Becca obviously confused.

"Actually," Ryan Gibbs said in his quiet voice. "That would be my wife." The statement brought a different type of confusion, because Becca appeared to be close to Colin's age.

She flashed Ryan a smile and corrected herself, "Becca Travis Gibbs."

Colin spoke before David could make another angry comment. "I've been asked to protect Ms. Garman by some people who believed her to be the target of a kidnapping. We were keeping my role quiet for her safety. You said tonight she was not the target, Patsy was the target. How do you know? Because it looks like my client was almost abducted tonight—for the second time."

**

Not a lover. David almost grinned. Not a lover. "What are you? Some kind of bodyguard?" he asked Colin.

"Some kind. Yeah. Sometimes I am. The rest of the time I'm an innkeeper. The Inn on Main."

David digested that. "And Ms. Travis, uh Gibbs, is here in some special capacity?" He'd be talking to his officers about how they let an unknown woman approach Patsy.

"She's an ex-cop. A very good ex-cop. I asked her to be here to protect Robin while my attorney and I are tied up with you."

David turned to the woman. "You carrying?"

She raised her long skirt to show the butt of a Smith and Wesson snub nose revolver in her blue boot.

"You licensed?"

"Ah ha." Raising the hem above the boot on her other leg she fished down inside. "Licensed to carry in Florida, before you ask."

He nodded. Florida had strict laws about who could carry firearms and provide security.

"Is your father really an attorney?" David asked the boy toy; he'd have to stop thinking of him as that. The man could handle himself in a fight and facing down cops. Kept his cool.

"Yeah." Colin looked to his father for permission and got it. "He is also FBI, Special Agent in Charge Gibbs."

Another stunned silence.

"I suppose you have ID to prove that claim," David said finally.

"I'm on vacation," the senior Gibbs said with a smile as he handed over his ID. "My wife is an FBI consultant," he added. David collected IDs and badge holders.

"Me too," Robin couldn't help saying. "I'm a consultant. But not like you. I simply identify wines."

Becca smiled. "Great. We have common ground; we can compare notes." They sat together on one of the love seats.

"Patsy? Can you tell us what happened tonight?" David asked as he passed the IDs to Scott to run.

"Exactly what I told your detective. I didn't even realize what was happening at first, but Robin knocked the glass off the counter and started backing me toward the entrance. That man came in," she pointed toward Colin, "grabbed my arm and pitched me out the door. He told me to scream. I saw him hit one of those men and then Robin came out yelling."

Robin nodded in agreement. "Colin hit the next guy and pushed me out the door; the leader fired a shot as I ran out and you showed up."

"They both saved me," Patsy added.

David guessed he was lucky the boy toy was there. He handed Patsy his cell phone. "Do you recognize any of these men?"

"Are these the men who tried to grab us?" Patsy asked fingering through the photos and shaking her head. "No. I don't recognize these men. Were they actually waiters?"

She passed the cell to Robin. Becca peered over her shoulder.

"We're checking. We don't know if they came in the back door or from the event."

"The middle one," Robin said. "I've seen him." She frowned in thought. "Somewhere. I'm not sure where. Grocery store? Maybe a shop? That's it. The shop at the hotel. He was staring through the window."

"When?"

"Um, let me think. Thursday."

David didn't like it. The thug was watching Robin before the mugging? That would mean they were after her, not Patsy. Robin started to pass the phone back to David, but Colin grabbed it. Took a look for himself; passed it to his father who did the same.

David let them look. "You saw him the same day of the incident in the parking lot? Thursday?"

She thought back. "Yes."

"Polinski. Get someone over to the shop at the hotel. See if they have footage." Polinski stepped out to make the call.

"Who were they after? From Ms. Garman's identification, this one was watching her in the shop. I'm curious how you eliminated her as the target," Colin said. "Because there have been two attempts and my client appears to have been the target both times."

"I probably convinced him," Robin said. They all looked at her. "Well, I told him what I told you, Colin. I don't have money. No one would pay money for me. I don't know any state secrets. Or know the formulas for longevity. There is no reason for anyone to want to snatch me. I thought it was a mugging. And tonight Da..., um, the detective told me I wasn't the target." She looked toward Scott. David noticed she never looked at him. Wouldn't even say his name. But she'd used it when she begged him not to shoot her boy toy before he'd entered the restroom. What did that mean?

Scott said, "We determined it was Ms. Corson. Upon further review of the security tapes we saw Ms. Corson come out of the hotel following your same path and go to a similar car, twenty minutes after you. She had two bodyguards with her. And there are reasons for people to abduct her. She's Robert Corson's daughter. Robert Corson of the Corson Restaurants and Wall Street."

"She doesn't have bodyguards?" Colin asked.

Scott nodded. "She does. Both of them are sick. Food poisoning."

"Both guards are sick?"

"Yeah. Hindsight says the illness was a little too convenient."

"Could they have planned to be sick? Are you sure they are sick?

"Oh yeah. One guard is still in the hospital; the other, Floyd Childer was never admitted. He was sent home, back to the hotel, weak as a kitten. Hospital confirmed. We checked."

"You know anything about them? How long they've worked for Corson?" Colin persisted.

"I talked to Corson after we saw the tape and, again, after his men became sick. The one in the hospital, Gus Malkin, has been with Corson for years. Floyd Childer is a new hire, highly recommended. We're looking into their backgrounds and offering protection for Patsy until new guards arrive." He grimaced and continued. "The new men are agents from a reputable firm up north, a highly respected company. They arrive around midnight and will stay a day or two until the regular men are well." Ramirez saw the senior Gibbs exchange a look with his wife.

"You have a comment?"

"Thinking about that gap in protection. The timing is curious."

"More than curious is there have been two attempts and both involve Robin," Colin added. "I'm not ready to consider that coincidence. Was Robin in the wrong place at the wrong time? Twice. What do you know about this attempt? Are you checking the cameras here?"

"Yeah. And the alarms."

"Why?" Patsy asked. "What do you mean alarms."

"Both the back exit door from the ladies' room and the outside door are fire doors; opening them should have set off the alarm. There are cameras covering the hallway and both doors. We might be able to get a look at the leader or whoever disconnected the alarm," David explained. His cell rang and he listened.

When he hung up he said, "Not going to be that easy. The alarms were disconnected and both cameras have been disabled; no one noticed. They don't know how long they haven't been working." He saw Colin getting ready to speak. "As for earlier, they record over the tape every twenty-four hours."

"So someone planned this at least a day ahead," Colin said. "Someone who gained access to the cameras and alarms and knew that her guards would be ill."

"Looks that way."

"And," Colin continued, "someone was here tonight watching. Someone told those men when to hit the ladies' room. Coordinated it."

David looked at him hard. "Yeah. I figured that out."

"Something else you should know," Colin said, "and I don't see how it fits. I think someone tried to shoot Robin, maybe run her down."

If he hadn't seen this man take out three bad guys, David would have laughed at the statement. Instead, he concentrated on breathing. He glanced quickly at Robin, who had her head down, and then back to Gibbs. Barely holding his anger in check, he said through clenched teeth. "Explain." First determine the facts, then get angry.

"Robin told us yesterday someone nearly hit her in the crosswalk." He paused and then added. "On the way here tonight, I found two bullet holes in her car."

David stared at Robin, willing her to look at him. "Someone tried to run you down and you didn't tell me?" he demanded.

She stuttered. "I, I, uh, it seemed like an accident. I'm still not sure. I don't know someone tried to hit me."

"How could you not know?" he bellowed.

She raised her head then and did look at him, angry now. She straightened her shoulders. "I. Didn't. Know. At the time it seemed like a careless driver. Don't you dare yell at me. I'm sure the man with me in the crosswalk didn't report it either. Why don't you go yell at him?" She stood up with her hands clenched and stared vacantly at the wall. Took a deep breath and repeated. "No one is trying to kill me. If they were, why try to kidnap me? They could have killed me tonight. They could have just shot me here." She swallowed, sat down quickly. "None of this makes any sense. The car was just an accident. This, tonight, is a mistake. They had to be after Patsy."

Was she trying to convince herself as much as him?

"What's this about bullet holes?"

Colin explained.

David took a moment to get a grip on his temper. "And you didn't think it was important enough to report it?" he said between clenched teeth.

"He did," Robin said. "Left messages for both of you to call back."

He growled as he pulled out his cell and thumbed through it. Scott doing the same. Disgusted he threw the phone on the counter.

"How do you explain the bullet holes in the car?" he asked quietly.

She waved her arm. "I can't. Maybe they're not bullet holes?"

He snickered. "Sure. Look around, honey. No one is buying that." It didn't make any sense at all. First they try to kill her, then they kidnap her? Why not kill her tonight? He had to find out what was going on. But it didn't matter. She was in danger either way. Didn't she understand?

"Scott, get a team to go over her car." He went back to Robin. "Is it here? We're going to want to see where it was parked, run some trajectories."

"It's parked out back. It was in my driveway when I thought I heard two thunks, but I don't know if it happened then. Or exactly where I had it parked in the driveway." Her cell chimed then and she pulled it out of her purse. "It's Rome, my partner. May I take it?"

Scott nodded.

She listened, spoke to Scott. Done talking to me, David guessed. "The event organizers are looking for me and Patsy. We need to get back out on the floor and apparently Patsy has a speech."

Becca edged closer.

"What time is it?" Patsy glanced at her watch in surprise. She jumped up. "Five minutes. I'm scheduled in five minutes."

"Hold it," David ordered. "Let's finish up here." He didn't want Robin out of his sight.

Before he could think of a reason to continue, Colin said, "I want to talk to Robin and Becca before you take me downtown

"You're not going downtown." David swallowed his anger and worry. Patsy did have to be back on the floor and he was her protection, even if he had messed up royally. With a growl he handed Colin his weapon and ID. "Come down tomorrow and make a statement. I take it you're going to keep watch on Robin?"

Colin nodded. "You don't know who they're after. You might think you do, but you don't. My client is still at risk."

David agreed. He wanted Robin kept safe, but he said, "Patsy is the target. No reason for anyone to grab Robin, but I don't like the coincidence. Your, um, Ms. Gibbs, should stay close to her. You too." The boy-toy had proven himself. Not just tough, but hadn't snitched that it was David who had upset Robin. "I'll stay close to Patsy. It would look funny if her date disappeared, especially after all that screaming. My men will be in the hall and on alert. Scott will interview the prisoners and check the video feeds from the hotel."

Patsy had looked like the target, but he should have kept someone on Robin, too. Shouldn't have taken a chance with her life. If she'd been run down, would he have looked for an ulterior motive? Or just accepted it was an accident? And why would someone try to shoot her and then go to the trouble of kidnapping her? Didn't make any sense. He needed to find the answers.

Becca interrupted his musing. "I need my credentials back, please."

Scott handed them over along with her husband's.

Colin told Robin, "One of us will be with you at all times. I don't expect anyone to try again tonight, but we can't take the chance. Between my dad, me, and, um, Becca, we can work it out. But I'd like two more men," Colin said, looking at his father.

Ryan Gibbs pulled out his cell, "I'll get them here by morning."

**

Patsy's speech motivated the attendees to reach for their checkbooks. Or it might have been her promise that her father's company would match whatever amount was raised. She pointed out the chief financial officer who would write the check at the end of the auction. The patrons placed more bids and drank more wine, which kept Robin busy with the wine service, and circulating, assisting Rome and two new sommeliers, though her mind was only half on the work. Becca, Colin, or his dad, Ryan, one of them, was always close by. The trained agents were inconspicuous, she imagined, to anyone who might be watching.

The guests were generous, having fun while donating to a good cause. Coffee and dessert were served and the winners of the silent auction were announced. Fine Wines' donation had been purchased for three times its face value. There was cheering and clapping when the participants were told the total raised by the event, far more than the planners had expected. The chief financial officer made out his check with a flourish, doubling the amount to more cheers. It was a good evening for Fine Wines.

The party wound down and the sommeliers were finally done. Colin and Becca walked her to the exit with Becca leaning in as if telling a secret. The same as she'd done after the shooting when Becca had simply swept down the hall riding the attorney's wake, dodged over to Robin, and hugged her close. She'd whispered in her ear, "I'm Becca. Colin sent me. I'm to keep you safe. Make believe I'm your best friend." Then she'd demanded Robin tell her exactly what happened. Like Colin and his dad, Becca had a quality of strength and competence. No bluster, just quiet power. A bond was created between the three women while they waited in the hallway.

Their shoulders were touching as Becca said, "We're going to your place for a strategy session. Ryan will make sure no one is tailing us."

"Do you think they might be? Wait, that's a stupid question. Do you really think someone could be after me? Isn't the fact that Patsy's guards are both sick, doesn't that mean she's the target? And she's wealthy," Robin said as they exited the building.

"That could be coincidence, but no one likes coincidences. You were near Patsy both times. Look a little like her. Whether they were after you or not, they tried to snatch you. That puts you at risk. Ramirez is checking to see if anyone besides the guards was sick, eliminate that coincidence."

"Did he find anything on the video at the shop?"

"Don't know."

Robin didn't ask any more questions during the ride and both Colin and Seldon were waiting when they reached her bungalow. She disarmed the system as the senior Gibbs arrived. When they were all inside, she asked if she should reset the alarm, unsure of the protocol.

"Always when you come in, reset the alarm," Colin instructed and then introduced Seldon to his family. Robin smiled when he stumbled over his father's wife, his stepmother. Colin hadn't found the right words yet. The hesitation and awkwardness softened him.

The new stepmother seemed to find his discomfort humorous but suggested, "Colin, you should try my dad and his wife, Becca. Or Becca, my dad's wife." She shook hands with Seldon, putting both men at ease.

"Can I get anyone drinks?" Robin asked and took orders for coffee and one tea and headed to the kitchen. They all followed. It was clear Colin had updated Seldon.

"There's no reason to grab Robin," Seldon said.

"I told them that. There isn't any reason for anyone to abduct me. It has to be a coincidence." They were silent as Robin poured coffee.

"What did you mean when you said you consult for the FBI?" Becca asked.

"Oh. I help out when they need an expert on counterfeit wines. At least I did once and now they have another job, um, case for me."

"You said you went with them this morning. Tell me more about what they want," Colin asked.

"Some guy was arrested up north. He has a second or third home here with a wine cellar. Their other expert is busy with the main house, so they asked me to audit, authenticate, and price the wine inventory here."

"How did they find you? Select you?" Becca asked.

Robin described the circumstances of the Fine Wines event with Carlisle. Which led to Agent Tucker, which led to her helping Ebert. Which led to... "Oh my gosh. How could I forget? A man died in the warehouse."

"Explain."

She did.

"Any one of those could be the cause," Ryan said. "Either the fake wines, the murder, or the new job for the FBI."

"Wait a minute," Seldon injected. He pointed at her. "What about the time that Ramirez guy came looking for you? That wasn't part of any fake wines."

"No. That was a car theft." She told the others, "I was parked in the lot where a handicapped van had been stolen. The detective was checking my alibi." She stopped because they were looking at her as if she had purple hair.

"Wow girl. You have a client with counterfeit wines, whom you turn in. You find a body while authenticating wines. You're suspected of stealing a car." Becca was enumerating these points on her fingers.

"No. They don't think I stole the car. They were tracking me down because my car was in the same lot. The wanted to know if I saw anything. I wasn't involved."

"Did you? See anything?" Becca asked.

"I gave them the tag number of a car which was there. I noticed because it was on a car I liked and the tag was a brainteaser."

"They find the car?"

"They traced the tag to a place in Miami. I overheard Detective Scott tell Agent Tucker."

"And…"

"That's all they've told me. I know it sounds like a lot, but really, I was merely a bystander. An innocent bystander." She was. She shouldn't have to defend herself.

"But the thieves could have found out you fingered them and are looking for payback."

"I don't know. Wouldn't they, the cops, have told me?"

"Maybe. We don't always tell witnesses about threats. But I'm sure the detective would have said something tonight," Becca replied. "Anything else happening we should know about?"

"I'm supposed to do an authentication for Mr. Carlisle. His attorney arranged it because his insurance company demanded it. Tomorrow."

The senior Gibbs stirred his tea. "Grabbing you might delay either of those authentications. Don't ask me why someone would want to do that. Or someone might want payback for you exposing the counterfeit wines. But, rather than extracting it on a public street, they would go after you in a quiet secluded place, I would think."

Robin swallowed. The image he drew scared her. And he'd said it so calmly. "That's a scary thought. But the wines would have been discovered at the event."

"It might not matter. Sometimes perception is more important than reality. You called the cops on Carlisle. He might have taken offense."

"I didn't. I would have, but Dav—um, Detective Ramirez made the call."

"Why?"

"He was there when I discovered the fake wines."

Ryan waited.

"He's a partner in a security firm and his firm was hired for the event. He was there finalizing plans. He forced the issue. He was the one who actually called in the police. Mr. Carlisle should be more annoyed at him than me." She paused a moment. "Although, I guess I'm responsible for discovering the deception and insisting on calling the authorities."

"Ramirez called the FBI?"

"Yes."

"The responding agent was this guy Tucker? The agent who hired you as a consultant to inventory the warehouse belonging to Carlisle's supplier?"

"Yes."

"The supplier is the man you found murdered."

"Yes. Well, I was there when he was discovered."

"Has the FBI solved the murder?"

"Agent Tucker didn't say anything about the case this morning. I didn't feel it was my place to ask. Besides, the local police have the case. Detectives Scott and Ramirez."

Her account was greeted by short silence which Seldon broke. "All the odd things which have happened to you this month, Ramirez has been involved in all of them?"

"What? No." She said that before she thought. "Well, maybe. But, he hasn't caused them. He backed me up with Carlisle and insisted we call the FBI. He interviewed me on the van and at the warehouse. He saved me from the mugger at the hotel." They were all still silent.

"Wait a minute. You can't think… No. No way. David would never hurt me. You can't be thinking that." She looked at their faces. David wouldn't hurt her. She knew he wouldn't. Even though he had hurt her. He hadn't set out to hurt her. Not from his point of view anyhow. He wouldn't hurt her physically.

"No one is accusing him, Robin. But we should consider it." Becca's eyes were full of sympathy. "How involved are you with Detective Ramirez?"

Robin glanced down. Becca couldn't know. Could she? "What do you mean?"

"You can't look at him. Can't even say his name. Except, just now when you were defending him, you spoke his name for the first time. He, on the other hand, can't take his eyes off you."

Really? She hadn't noticed that. But then she hadn't been looking at him. She looked up at Becca. Now what, admit to being a fool?

Ryan offered her some comfort. "I don't think Ramirez would plan anything so elaborate. He wouldn't have to; he'd have easy access if he wanted to grab you or hurt you. He could walk up to your door or stop you in a parking lot."

Robin studied him, a softer, kinder version of Colin, she thought. At least he appeared to be. But Ryan's gentleness made it easier for her to tell the truth even though she was mortified.

She looked Becca in the eye. "A one-night stand. Not even a whole night. He broke it off, not me. He would have no reason to come after me."

"Yet he was waiting for you in the bar," Seldon said.

"Yes, he wanted to get back together. But he's said that before," she argued. "Begged to get back together and then disappeared." She shrugged her shoulders. "He'd promise to call or come over and then, silence. This time was no different. He never even returned my calls about the mugging."

"It's not Ramirez," Colin said. "Let's not get sidetracked here. Someone tried two times to hurt Robin. Two times to grab her. Probably her. We can't take the chance she wasn't the target. We have to determine who and why and why they changed methods. If they changed methods. Why did someone try to kill her? Why did they stop trying? Are they the same ones trying to abduct her? There's a far out possibility we're dealing with two different criminals." He paused.

"Probably not the cars thieves. If they knew her role, she'd be dead, not disappeared. But we should ask Ramirez about the status on that case. We need to know.

"Next, Carlisle and his attorney. Is there any benefit for them to delay Robin's certification of his wines? Or to stop her from doing it altogether? Both the insurance company and the attorney know there are more fake wines; it's simply a matter of determining how many. Almost the same reasoning with the FBI assignment. Doesn't change anything if there are fake wines."

"Might give Carlisle time to replace phony wines with the real stuff," Seldon suggested.

Robin spoke up. "That would imply he knows which wines are fake and I don't think he has a clue. The insurance company wants me to ascertain and document how many forgeries he has. To tell the truth, I'm curious. That's why I took the job."

"Does the attorney know Carlisle has counterfeits?" Ryan asked.

She shook her head. "I don't know anything about him, but he does suspect or he's an idiot. We argued about me reporting any bogus wines to the authorities. I won." She had another thought. "Besides, how can it be either of those jobs? I didn't even get them until this morning. The mugging was Thursday."

"But Carlisle and the FBI knew they would be hiring you. Maybe someone else did too. Do you have keys to either place?"

"No. Carlisle's contract states a representative will meet me at the door and stay with me on the premises. And Agent Tucker said there'll be FBI personnel at the mob boss's house. If I need to get in after-hours, an agent will meet me."

"Does the felon, the wine owner, have a name?" Becca asked as she refilled cups.

"I have it written down, I'll get it."

She was right back and gave Becca the paperwork.

"Dutch Lemay," Becca read looking around.

"Isn't he the guy with the cars?" Seldon asked.

"Yeah. He has a collection of exotic cars. He have any at his house?" Colin was interested.

"That's what Tucker said. I didn't get to see them. He has three in a regular garage on the ground floor for everyday use. Another four in a climate controlled basement. One, I think a Shelly or something and another is a Superbird."

Seldon rubbed his hands together. "Wow. I've heard he has some classics. I sure would like to see them."

"Why?" The cars hadn't meant anything to Robin; but apparently they did to him.

"Great cars. Classics," Ryan agreed.

"You too?" Becca asked him surprised.

"Give a week's pay to sit in a Shelby."

"It's a car." Becca looked clearly puzzled by his attitude. "How come I didn't know this about you?" she asked Ryan. "You drive a pickup."

"It's not a car," Seldon came to his rescue. "Calling it a car is like calling a race horse a pony. I'd like to sit in the Superbird."

"Can we get back on track, please?" Colin waited as they settled down then asked, "Robin, can you go away for a few days?"

"No. I have to be at Carlisle's tomorrow and Dutch's on Monday."

"Can you postpone? Patsy will be leaving Wednesday or Thursday, after that maybe you'll be in the clear," Seldon said.

She shook her head. "No. Both Carlisle and Tucker are anxious for me to finish." Robin was surprised to find herself arguing the other side now. "You don't know the problem will end with Patsy leaving. If these people are after me, wouldn't they just follow me? What about when I come back. I can't put my life on hold."

She'd been on hold for fifteen years. Not that she thought of it that way. She'd done what she had to do to support herself. She'd enjoyed her work, building a business which let her share her love of wine. She was lucky, no, not lucky. She had worked damn hard to be successful, to create a niche, to become successful. But now it was her turn. Her time to do what she'd always wanted. Teach. She might not be doing such a good job with the love life part, but her wine class was a success and she'd discovered a new sideline in wine inventory. Her jewelry was being noticed and selling.

"She's right, Seldon. Running away isn't going to help. We can't take a chance they might follow her. This is the best place to protect her. We've got more help coming in the morning. Right, Dad?"

Ryan nodded.

"I can stay tonight," Becca offered as she looked to Ryan for confirmation.

"We both will."

"Good. My dad has been on protection details before," Colin told her, caught himself and smiled. "My mom. too."

Guess he finally figured out what to call her. Robin saw it pleased Becca whose face lit up. "Who is coming in the morning?" she asked her husband.

"Mary Lee. Jake is sending her, and Jen, maybe. Not Daffy. He went out on assignment late this afternoon. But he'll be free on Wednesday or Thursday."

"Are they FBI agents?" Robin asked.

"Professional bodyguards."

"You vouch for them, Colin?" Seldon asked.

"Mary Lee and Daffy are two of the best in the business. By Jen do you mean Jen Garrett?" he asked his father.

"Yeah."

"Good woman. Professional. She can guard my back."

Robin said, "You called in two bodyguards? Is that necessary? Wait, don't answer. You're the experts. How much does a bodyguard cost?" She was thinking, Sunday, Monday, maybe Tuesday, maybe Wednesday. And if she paid them shouldn't she pay Colin?

"Not your problem. Won't be a charge to you. Mary Lee is almost family. Jen, too," Becca told her.

It was a lot to take in. Robin wasn't sure what to say. She tried a question. "What's a daffy?"

"Nickname," Becca answered. "Daffy and Mary Lee are freelance operatives who work for my brother-in-law who is part owner of a security business. Jen is married to his partner."

"Your family is all cops and bodyguards?"

"Some are, I guess. Most of my family are computer nerds." She turned to Colin and boldly proposed, "Colin is comping them nights at his Inn. Right, Colin?"

Robin laughed and threw up her hands. "Okay, okay. I give up. Sounds like you got a whole village when your dad got married, Colin. Becca and Ryan stay with me tonight. Mary Lee and Jen go with me tomorrow. To Carlisle's?"

"Right."

"You going Monday, Gibbs?" Becca asked. "Get a look at the car?"

"No. Probably not. Let the professionals deal with it. We can fill in where needed."

"I can help too, Colin," Seldon offered. "You can call on me. I'm not a professional, but I can provide support."

"We might need you. Right now we're playing it by ear. There's an awful lot we don't know.

"What about Ramirez?" Ryan asked his son. "Do you think he will share?"

"That was the impression I got. He'll let us know if he learns anything."

"If not, Cilla can get us a look at whatever he has," Becca said. "She could start tonight. If Ramirez shares, we don't have to tell him."

The senior Gibbs looked into his tea cup. "I didn't hear anything about Cilla hacking into official files."

Robin looked back and forth at both of them. "What do you mean?"

"Nothing," Becca replied, then relented. "My sister could take a look at Ramirez's files and give us a heads up."

"What does that mean? How can she look at his files? I don't understand."

"Don't ask," Ryan said. "At least, don't ask with me in the room. Ask her later. Besides, I have a little pull with the local FBI office. I should be able to get anything Ramirez won't share. I'll call them in the morning. Right now, I want to take a look at the security here."

"It's a good system," Seldon said. "A friend did it for me. He does good work. Go look and you'll see. Top of the line."

Colin said, "He owed me too, because I connected him to Cilla for software. Come on, I'll take you through the house." Becca went with them while Robin made more coffee.

Ryan was smiling when they came back. "You got some real mojo. Top of the line security with an excellent install. They put in stuff I've only read about, never seen. Who monitors?"

"Same people. They monitor twenty-four, seven."

"Back to tomorrow, Robin," Colin said. "Are you going alone or taking assistants with you?"

"I'll need at least two people at Carlisle's. His inventory, if he even has one, will be out of date and incomplete. I'll want one person at the mob boss's."

Colin nodded. "Will your help be wine experts, or can the bodyguards do the job?"

"I want at least one of my people tomorrow. I like to give them work when I can, and I'll set up a whole new database for Carlisle. Of course, we'll have to deal with forged wines and that will take time, but it's a small cellar."

"Dutch has a top-of-the-line digital inventory, it should just be a matter of checking barcodes. I guess anyone who can lift a bottle and use a computer can do the job. I'll want Ian at Carlisle's, but I don't want to put him in danger."

"He should be okay, but the fewer civilians involved the better," Colin said. "If you need more help, my dad, Becca, or Seldon can fill in. You're doing Carlisle's tomorrow. Dutch's Monday. Monday can be a repeat of Sunday. What happens Tuesday?"

"Tuesday, I have a wine class in the afternoon at the office."

"When are the guards due in, Dad?"

"Be here at nine in the morning."

"Then we meet back here at nine. I'll give Ramirez a call and have him meet with us." Colin looked around at the group. "Let's call it a day."

They broke up, Seldon saying, "Call me if you need me." He and Colin left together, Robin disarming the security system to let them out and then re-arming it.

She showed Becca and Ryan to the spare room, pointed out the TV remote, said, "There are towels and toiletries in the bathroom. Help yourselves. Clean linens on the beds." Then she asked the question she'd been wondering about. "Why are you guys staying and not Colin?"

"Colin has to go talk to his wife."

"Why not a phone call? I'm not complaining, just curious."

"He was in a shootout tonight. She needs to hear it from him. Needs to be able to see he's okay. Touch him."

"Oh." It sounded as if Becca was talking from experience. Which side had Becca been on? The speaker or the toucher?

Ryan left the two women alone.

"Tell me more about your sister looking at Ramirez's files," said Robin.

"My sister is a hacker. Sometimes she hacks into files."

"She can do that? Police files?" Robin wasn't sure what she'd thought Colin meant when he said his sister-in-law was a hacker. Certainly not that she could look at police files.

"We all can. She's better at it than I am. My brother John is even better."

"It's illegal isn't it?"

"Yeah, which is why Gibbs doesn't want to know about it. Prefers I hold off. So, I'll hold off."

"How does Mr. Gibbs handle it when your sister hacks into official records?"

"Mostly she doesn't, because we can't use anything she finds that way in court. If we want her to hack records, he gets a warrant. This time, we'll wait to see if your boyfriend wants to help."

Robin walked over to the bed. "He's not my boyfriend. I told you."

"Yeah, yeah. But your actions don't fit that scenario."

"No. I told you. One-night stand." Robin never thought she'd be insisting someone believe she acted promiscuously.

"More than that. Remember, you can't look at him. He can't take his eyes off you. Something going on there."

Dejected, Robin sat on the bed. "I fell in love with a smooth talker who convinced me we were a perfect match. I thought I was getting forever, but he only wanted sex and I became the proverbial one-night stand. I'm embarrassed and mortified I fell for his sweet talk. Later, when I should have known better, I gave him another chance. Two chances, actually. But I wasn't even worth the effort of him picking up a phone to call." She wasn't going to cry or whine about it. "That's why I can't look at him; all I see is the face of the man who used me."

"A man doesn't look at a woman the way he looks at you if he isn't emotionally involved."

Robin just stared at Becca for a moment. "Colin said something similar, but you're both wrong. He couldn't have talked to me the way he did tonight if he had any feelings for me." She motioned to the dresser. "Some night clothes in there. Robes in the bathroom."

They worked together turning down the bed and Becca asked, "You meet him at Carlisle's that night? Is that how it started? Because he backed you up?"

"No, it was all over by then. We met at a Fine Wines event; he was one of the guards. We drifted together and talked. Became friends, or so I thought, and then more. I didn't know it at the time, but he was there undercover, after a burglar."

Becca became very still. "You were involved in another crime?"

"Not really. Some woman was heisting, his word, jewelry and cash during events. Ramirez caught her in the act and put her in jail."

Becca sat on the edge of the bed. "Tell me more."

"I don't know much."

Robin filled her in and Becca said, "Something else to ask him."

"Feel free to help yourself to anything in the kitchen. Or watch TV. I'm exhausted." She headed out the door. "See you in the morning."

Even though Robin was drained and dog-tired she tossed and turned, seeing again the men rushing in the door. The gun pointing at them. Finally, she gave up trying to sleep and reached for her book.

Sunday

It began sweetly, softly. She was dancing with David. Slow dancing. Her head tucked warmly by his cheek, his mouth near her ear crooning words of love.

Suddenly the music stopped with a cacophonous clash and he shoved her away. She stumbled backward, staring and bewildered.

His face was angry, an ugly mask.

She reached for him, her arm outstretched, her hand open. "What? Why? What happened?"

He screamed, spewing hateful, horrible words.

She backed up a few steps, put her hand to her trembling lips, felt the tears stream down her face. No. It didn't happen this way.

"Whore! Bitch! Slut!" he bellowed.

She turned and ran. Into a room. A dark room. The door slammed shut behind her.

A shape materialized. Shimmering. Hooded. Hulking. Evil.

She dropped the glass she was holding.

They both watched it fall. Float, slowly down. It took a long time. The glass landed, silently, rolled to a stop.

The shape growled.

She felt it steal closer.

It pointed a shiny gun at her. She could see the dark core of the barrel, pointing between her eyes before it lowered and aimed at her heart.

"Bitch!"

"No! No! No!" she screamed.

He shot her three times.

There was a great pressure in her chest. Under her right breast. All the bullets had hit the same spot.

She came awake on her stomach, breathing in gulps.

A dream. A dream. It's a dream.

Squeezing her eyes shut, she gasped for breath and moaned. Afraid to move. She hurt.

How could she hurt from a dream? She reached toward the pain. Felt beneath her.

Wet. She was wet. Blood? No. It was a dream. Couldn't be blood.

Sweat. It was sweat. She sighed with relief, but she was still shaking from the terror, gasping. She felt further and her hand touched something hard and jammed it further into her breast.

Her book. She'd fallen asleep reading a book and rolled over onto it. She caught her breath and forced her eyes open.

The door swung open slowly. Silently.

A small whimper escaped her lips.

In the dimness, she saw Becca crouched there. A gun in her hand.

Robin tried to speak. Nothing came out. She tried again. "I'm okay. It was a dream."

Becca put a finger to her lips, signaling silence. She swiftly scanned the room and came in low, moving fast to the left. Ryan came in behind, high and to the right. Also armed. Becca checked the bathroom. The shower. Ryan opened the closet. Rifled through it. Looked under the bed. He tried the window as Becca came to stand beside the bed and turned on the light.

"Not a dream," Becca said, a hand on her shoulder. "A nightmare. We heard you call out."

Ryan put his gun away, stuffing it into the waistband of his sweats. He wore no shirt, Robin noticed. Well built. Huh? What was wrong with her? Why was she staring at his chest?

Becca had on an oversize t-shirt. His? Where would she put her gun?

The nightmare had scrambled her brains.

"Not surprising you should have nightmares. I'll go warm some milk." Becca exchanged a silent message with Ryan and left the room.

He smiled at her. "Don't look so alarmed. Becca doesn't cook, but she can warm milk." He sat beside her and took her hand. Held it gently. Patted it. "She can do that. She has watched me do it for her enough times."

"She, um, she has nightmares?" Robin managed to say. Distracted. What he wanted, she expected.

"Not much anymore. But she wakes with the terrors. Sweaty and shaking. The warm milk seems to help."

Robin was feeling calmer. She sat up and he fluffed the pillow behind her. She tried a smile. "I'm okay. I'm embarrassed I woke you."

"That's what we are here for. To protect you. That is what we are doing. Simply because the danger isn't physical, doesn't mean you don't need help and comfort."

"You don't have to sit with me." She looked down.

"You don't think I would leave you alone? You had a tough day. You held up well and still are. Nightmares are nothing to be ashamed of; you can't control how the mind works. It will let you think you're doing fine, and then it will sneak you a sharp jab. Which is what your brain was doing tonight; it was processing the fear left over from the attempted kidnapping. Walking you through it again in a safer environment. Giving you a chance to examine what happened. A chance to ease the terror."

"I don't want it to."

He laughed. "That's the thing. You can't stop it; it hasn't finished yet. You always see more than you think. Hear more. Your brain is reconciling what you remember with what you have forgotten. You may have more nightmares, but you can help your brain. You can direct the dreams."

"What do you mean?"

"Before you fall asleep, you set a trip wire to wake yourself up. It's simple. Tell yourself to wake up when the first discordant note sounds. Or better yet, direct the action. Channel it into the real ending. The safe ending."

"I can do that?"

He nodded. "Try it. You'll see." He patted her hand again.

Becca came back with a steaming mug. She'd put on some pants. Probably had her ankle holster on under them. She and Ryan exchanged another silent message. "I'll leave you two alone." They traded places.

"I imagine he told you he warms milk for me. I drink it because he thinks the milk comforts me. He doesn't realize it's him warming the milk that comforts. That he cares. Try it," she said.

Robin had to hold the mug with both hands. She took a sip, to make Becca happy. Must be what Becca does for Ryan, she thought. Aloud she said, "You two work well together."

"Yeah, we do," she said with a satisfied grin. "But if you mean how we came into the room, we planned that outside the door. Take a few more sips. Do you want to talk about it? Sometimes it helps me to talk about it. Get it out in the open. Makes the horror less real. Was it about the kidnapping?"

Robin nodded. "But it was different. It wasn't what happened. David called me filthy names and I ran. Into an empty room. A creature was there. He called me names. He shot me. Three times. He shot me. Colin wasn't there; he didn't save me." Did that sound whiny?

"Start at the beginning," Becca said and listened to every word, urging her to continue when she stalled. Getting her to drink all the milk.

David screaming at her was the part which upset her. That hurt more than the bullets. Him calling her names which she'd called herself. Slut. She wasn't a slut. Was that what the nightmare was telling her? She wasn't a slut. Or a whore. Or a bitch. She was simply a woman in love. Wasn't going to scold herself for having sex. She could face the truth. She fell in love or lust and fell into bed. That simple.

Robin was shivering by the time she finished the milk.

"You need a hot shower. Go ahead. I'll put on dry sheets for you. Ryan should be back with another mug of milk."

When Ryan returned, he replaced the empty cup with a full one. "We'll wait for you in the kitchen, if you want company. Or you can crawl back into bed. If you don't come out, we'll look in. Leave the door ajar."

The shower was hot and felt good. She took her time, letting the water wash away the rest of the terror. When she got out and dried off, she found Becca had laid out a clean nightgown. She dressed and wrapped a second towel around her hair. Wouldn't bother to blow it dry. She swallowed a mouthful of milk, climbed back into bed, and, exhausted, fell asleep.

**

She woke to the smell of coffee and bacon and realized she was hungry. She checked the time. Late, almost eight thirty. Memory came flooding back, the nightmare, the warm milk, and the comforting suggestions. Could she channel the dream the next time? Tonight at three-thirty? She'd try. Positive thinking might work.

Voices in the kitchen brought her out of her reverie and she jumped out of bed and used the bathroom. Her reflection in the mirror was frightful; the towel had come off during the night and her hair had dried in a tangle. She dampened it and brushed it out, then patted on some make-up to cover the dark circles under her eyes. She pulled on old jeans, and was reaching for an older t-shirt when she remembered she was going to Carlisle's and slipped on a nice shirt instead and headed for the kitchen.

"I smell coffee and bacon, Becca, two of my favorites. Oh." She stopped short. It wasn't Becca cooking; it was Ryan. And furthermore, he was cooking for an army. He had a platter of bacon, her large fry pan full of scrambled eggs, and he was flipping pancakes. Becca was setting the table.

"I can't eat all that," Robin joked, taking the cup of coffee Becca handed her.

"We are expecting company. Your bodyguards and Colin."

"Oh. What can I do?"

Ryan bobbed his head toward the table. "Help Becca."

But Becca had the table set and the coffee made. The teapot was hot and milk and sugar were on the table along with maple syrup and butter. "Looks like she has it all done. I can help with the cooking." Although it looked like he had that under control, too.

"You cook?"

"Some. I can do eggs and pancakes. Toast and cereal."

He laughed. "Becca can do cereal too. She doesn't cook. None of the women in her family cook." Robin recalled he'd told her that last night.

"Proud of it, too," Becca said. "But that's not fair, Gibbs. Cilla can do that potato thing and Penney can do tea and fill a bowl with chips."

"Yeah, there is that." Gibbs chuckled. The doorbell rang and they all turned to the monitor. "It's Colin. Why don't you go let him in?"

Robin disarmed the system and opened the door with a welcoming smile. A black SUV pulled into the drive and they both turned to watch a small woman with short dark, choppy hair step out. Robin caught her breath and gave Colin a nervous glance; the woman was dressed in leather with tats covering both her arms. But he was walking over to the biker chic with a laugh and encircled her in a bear hug.

"What about me?" complained the woman exiting the driver's side. "Am I chopped liver?"

"Nothing wrong with chopped liver." Colin hugged her too. She was one of the most stunning women Robin had ever seen. Beauty queen, movie star, stunning.

The biker chic picked up a duffle bag and slung it over her shoulder. The beauty queen patted Colin on the cheek and lifted a suitcase and a huge makeup kit out of the back seat. Guess they did their own heavy lifting because Colin didn't try to help either one. These must be her bodyguards.

Colin made the introductions. The biker chic was Jen Garrett; the beauty queen was Mary Lee. Robin didn't ask but wondered, if Lee was a last name or one of those southern names like Billie Bob?

The women left their bags by the door and headed for the kitchen. She heard happy greetings while she reset the alarm.

Ryan put platters of eggs and toast from the warming oven on the table. Becca fetched the pancakes and bacon.

"Perfect timing," Jen said sitting. Mary Lee went for the coffee pot and filled cups. While they ate, Colin updated them.

Robin told them about the wine cellar and cars. Gibbs had to correct her when she called one a big bird.

"Not a big bird, Superbird; they're muscle cars."

Jen's eyes grew wide and a grin split her face. "Really? He has a '70 Road Runner? And I'm going to be able to see it? Touch it?" She jumped up and hugged Ryan.

Robin looked around the table, shared a moment of bewilderment with Becca. The others showed various stages of excitement. Jen explained. "The car is a classic. Only 500 were built and not many remain. I'd do this job for nothing for a chance to see that car. I'd pay to do this job." She did a little jig. "Thank you. Thank you. Thank you. I almost had a chance to see one three years ago, but the client sold it right before I came onboard. When do I get to see it?" She seemed to realize the surprise around the table. "What? Because I'm a biker, I can't appreciate a classic car?" Before anyone could respond the doorbell rang.

"You expecting company?" Jen asked standing to look at the kitchen monitor displaying David on the front stoop staring into the lens.

"Yes. It's the Detective working the case; he's invited," Colin said, and Jen followed Robin to the door.

**

Ramirez was surprised to find three vehicles in the driveway, none of them Robin's. Hers would be in the garage, he decided. The last vehicle in the drive was a black SUV with all the earmarks of an armored car. He climbed the steps to the front door and rang the bell. Spotted the surveillance camera above the door. That was new. He glanced to the shrubbery at the corner of the house. Probably another hidden there. Well-hidden. Security system? Taking the threat seriously? Well, obviously. She'd hired a bodyguard. Or had a boyfriend who worked as a bodyguard. The profession didn't negate a relationship. A married man. With a kid.

He'd read the profile on Gibbs which Scott had printed out. The man had joined the Army right out of high school, rose to the rank of captain, Military Police. Earned a degree in law enforcement while in the service. Now in the reserves. Married with a six-year-old girl. He'd applied for and received his carry concealed when he left the military and was properly licensed under Florida law, Class G with recertification. He was identified as Assistant Manager of the Inn on Main.

David had called a cop he knew on Marco Island, a cop with the same first name, David. "Colin Gibbs? Don't know much. Married one of our local gals. She's third generation. Her family owns the Inn. Why?"

"He says he's a bodyguard, protecting a woman here in town. You know anything about him?"

"No. He does leave town every once in a while, on business. Haven't heard anything about protection though. He'd have to be licensed."

"He is. His father is FBI. Heard of him?" Ramirez asked without much hope.

"Yeah. Him, I know personally."

"You know him?" David sat up. Hadn't expected that.

"Yeah. Worked with him a while back. A big drug bust. You hear about it? You were away at training, I think."

David had. "I was. He's that guy? The one who brought the case to you?" Credit for the bust went to various local police forces. "He the same agent solved that art theft case?"

"Yeah. We got some credit for both cases. Good man; good agent. The man's a good cop. I got nothing but respect for him. Had everyone working together: locals, state, FBI. Salvaged two operations which were going down the tubes. Gave the credit for the art bust to the local fibbies."

"How did an FBI agent get mixed up in your drug case?" David asked.

"Not mine. State guys. Gibbs sort of stepped in it while he was filling in for his son at the Inn. One of those times Colin was out of town. Anyhow, Gibbs met the woman who discovered the stolen art. Woman by the name of May Stratton, May London now, she married my new hire, Nick. He was undercover FDLE working the drug sting and he knew Gibbs from before. All roads converged. You want more? 'Cause Nick recently returned from Gibbs's wedding. Says Gibbs married some young thing. Well, young for him. I didn't meet her when they were here before. She has a good rep too, good cop, by what I hear. They're in town for the christening of Nick's first kid. It's a big deal for us." There was a pause. "Ryan mixed up in your thing?"

"Seems like. Wife too."

"Wife's family runs a security firm up north. From what Nick says."

"Any good?"

"One of the best. Does a lot of government work. Nick met them at the wedding. Sounds like you're working with reliable people."

Yeah, cops gossiped and his friend gossiped freely about the drug arrests, the art theft, the wedding, and David had let him talk, because you learned more when you listened.

Now he was smiling for the camera and rang the bell again.

He wasn't here to warn her off Gibbs. He was here to set things right. He still wasn't sure why he'd jumped on her last night. Why he'd accused her of sleeping with the boy toy. Boy toy? He'd been angry when he saw her with another man. The feeling, the anger, didn't make any sense. He'd left her behind a long time ago. Hadn't even called her back when he'd promised. And hadn't called about the mugging either. Which was a good thing as it turned out. Because if he had, it would have been to tell her she wasn't the target of a kidnapping. She would have been unprotected and she'd be gone now. Probably a dead collateral statistic. He'd screwed up. Badly.

He wanted to hold her. Comfort her. Comfort himself. Jeez, he was messed up. She'd messed him up. He'd finally identified the emotion he felt when he saw her with Colin. Jealousy. Jealous of the boy toy. It had made him crazy. Made him forget his job. Abandon Patsy. Insult Robin. Hurt her so she wouldn't even look at him. He had to fix it. He'd pursued her because she was a challenge, worldly but innocent. Then, the more he was with her, the more he was drawn to her and wanted to be near her. He enjoyed her company, looked forward to their dates. She was sweet, yet strong. Funny. He found he wanted to make her smile, laugh. He thought about her all the time. Yeah, he'd really screwed up.

Scott had noticed. Even mentioned it. Laughed at him. But Scott was wrong, he wasn't in love. He was in like. Like mixed with lust.

He realized he had fallen for her long before she took him to her bed where he found, not the shy, embarrassed woman he'd expected, but a fiery, passionate lover. He'd almost stayed that night; been tempted. But he never stayed. Even with a woman who could make him feel satisfied, he'd left. He'd intended to phone, but caught a murder. Had spent the next twenty-four hours tracking the culprit. He could have called later, but by then he'd convinced himself it was lust. Two adults attracted to each other. So he didn't call. Tried to put her out of his head. But she'd done something to him, and at odd moments he'd hear her laughter. Recall how well they fit together.

Still he hadn't called. Guess he expected he'd get over her like he would a bad cold. One day had turned into two, two into three, and he'd convinced himself he was getting better. He still heard her laughter.

He'd intended to use Monica's mug shots to convince her that he was doing his job, not sleeping with a bunch of women. Only her. He hadn't meant to hurt her; had done it anyway.

And then after the car theft he'd another chance. Which he also blew. He'd waited for her in the bar. Two times. Which led to the attempted abduction, which led to Patsy.

He was going to win her back. But first he had to get control of his emotions. Do his job.

He'd known she wouldn't be alone. Unprotected. But three cars? One probably belonged to lover boy; the other maybe his in-laws? Chaperone? Didn't seem to bother the guy that his stepmother was young enough to be his sister. Give the guy credit for that. Or maybe both men were doing her. Snorted. Called himself an ass. Damn it. Robin had him totally screwed up. He shook his head and rang the bell again.

She opened the door. With the chain on.

"Let me in."

It wasn't quite an order. He saw her glance behind her to a woman covered in tattoos who nodded okay. He held his temper. The door closed and he heard the chain slide; then the door opened long enough for him to step through.

"We're in the kitchen. Come on in," Robin said without looking at him as she reset the alarm.

Damn.

He walked in and greeted the elder Gibbs and his young wife. Said hello to Colin, and stopped when he saw the stunning blonde. His gaze stuck on her for too long. He could only nod, his tongue glued to the top of his mouth. Colin had called her Mary Lee. The other woman, with the tats was Jen. Friends of Robin's?

The wife, Becca, offered coffee and poured him a cup. "Breakfast? Sit. We were just starting."

"Here, beside me." Mary Lee, the beauty queen, motioned to the empty chair next to her.

"You have an update for us?" Colin asked. Becca handed her husband a new tea bag and hot water. Platters of food were on the table. Robin set a dish and silverware in front of him.

"Update?" Colin repeated to get his attention.

"What? Oh. Yeah. We found the guy on the hotel surveillance tape. Standing in front of the gift shop, watching through the window." He took out his cell and pushed a few buttons to pull up the photo. Passed it to Robin. "He was there."

That had been his excuse to come by today. To show her the photo. And the invite from Colin. And talk to Robin if he could get her alone. He owed her an apology.

Robin looked at his cell. "That's him. See how he seems to be glaring? Made me nervous." She glanced at David for a moment and then quickly away.

"We're going to review all the video from the hallways, entrances, exits, and common rooms, before and after this," David said.

"Why?" Robin asked handing back the phone.

"Catch him following you. Or maybe meeting with someone else. We're no closer to knowing why they want you. It does appear it is you they're after, based on this photo. I haven't seen the video yet. The crooks we collared last night, the ones your boyfriend took down…" He stopped. He hadn't intended to say that. "Excuse me, that was uncalled for. I apologize. The ones Colin took down. They know nothing, not even the identity of the guy who hired them. They were promised a thousand apiece, five hundred up front, to grab some woman. They missed the first time. They don't get the money until they deliver you."

Becca passed him the last two pancakes and syrup. "Could Carlisle hold a grudge? Because Robin made him report the fake wines?" she asked.

He considered it while he poured syrup on his pancakes. Hadn't considered Carlisle. "He could hold a grudge because she discovered them and insisted they be reported, but I was the one who called the Feds. If he was going to blame anyone, he'd blame me. I don't see him as either a kidnapper or a killer. Not smart enough and he doesn't have the backbone. He's a bully and a snob. Nothing indicates he could do this."

"How about the fake wines? The guy who sold those?"

"The wines belong to the Feds."

"How is their investigation going?"

"Another thing I don't know. They're not sharing."

Colin looked at his dad.

"I have an appointment with them later this morning. I'll ask them."

"And what? They tell you because you're FBI? Way I hear it, you guys don't even talk to each other." David couldn't help his contempt.

"True, sometimes, but they'll tell me because they know me. Let's just say I'm a good guy and folks like me." He reached for more bacon. "While we are talking about sharing, have you told them about the attempted kidnapping?"

"No. Not a federal offense until state lines are crossed."

"Do you have any objection if I give them a heads up?"

"No. We didn't not tell them. It's not their jurisdiction yet."

They hadn't purposely left the FBI out. He added some cream to his coffee.

"Can you tell us where you are with the murder in the warehouse?" Colin asked.

"Not much there either. We've worked through most of his client list under the pretext of warning them they might have fake wines. Asking questions. We've received a few angry call-backs when the clients found we were right. But no one knows anything. No leads." He swirled a bite of pancake in the syrup.

"There's no reason to think someone is after her because of that. The warehouse was full of FBI agents when the body was discovered. You think for one minute I would let her out there alone if I thought someone was after her?"

He was speaking to her now, waiting for her to look at him. "Robin? You don't think I'd do that do you?"

But she wouldn't look at him. He laid his fork down.

"Robin?" God. She couldn't believe that, could she? He didn't care what the others thought. "Robin?" Desperate now. "I could never do that to anyone let alone someone I, ah, um, like." Had he really almost said love?

The silence around the table was complete. She finally raised her head; looked at him. He searched her eyes, afraid of what he'd see.

"No. David. I told them you would never purposely harm me." An emotionless statement. Not the resoundingly compelling exoneration he'd hoped for. And what did purposely mean?

It was Mrs. Gibbs who brought him back to the subject this time. "What about your arrest of the jewel thief. Could that blow back on Robin? Or the stolen van? Robin mentioned those last night."

"Look, Scott and I have been over and over all this, been through all the files; we worked through most of the night. Nothing. There is nothing in them to put a target on Robin. I'm a cop for God's sake, a good cop. If there'd been anything, anything, I'd have put her in protective custody. In a heartbeat."

"Humor us. Tell us about the other cases. We don't know about either of them." Colin said taking a bite of eggs.

"The van? That case is still open. Miami-Dade and the Feds are running it. They have the address under surveillance. The Feds have been after these guys a long time and this is as close as they've ever gotten. The gang steals vehicles all over the country, puts stolen VIN numbers on them, and resells them. Robin's name is in our files but we never gave it to Miami-Dade. Besides, the thieves don't even know we're watching them." He finally ate his soggy pancake.

"The burglar? We tripped to her when one of her victims discovered jewelry missing the next morning. Since the victim had worn the pieces the day before, it was obvious the theft had taken place during the party. We ran everyone on the guest list and talked to all of them. Most of the men remembered a really well-built blonde. No one knew who she was. Not one of them looked at her face, at least not long enough to be able to describe her. All we could get was racked, twenties to thirties. A couple thought maybe low forties. We had cops working dinner parties and events undercover for a month and caught her with old-fashioned police work. Robin never was involved in the investigation. We, um, dated, but she was never involved in the case."

"You arrested the woman at one of the events?"

"Yeah."

"Could she have seen you and Robin together?"

He shook his head. "We weren't."

"I introduced you," Robin said.

"What?" He gave her a confused look, then remembered. "You did. She came up behind us when we were talking. Could she have heard us? What were we saying?" He was thinking out loud, remembering. Even though Robin was looking down he saw her face turn red.

"Oh. Right. I was saying we should get back together. You were telling me to wait. That's what she saw, heard. That can't be it. Kidnap you? It's overkill." He took a quick breath, raised his hand. "Look. That doesn't make any sense. Why would she go after you? She was the one who wanted the introduction; it wasn't your idea."

"Is she still in jail?" Colin asked. "How did she find out about the events? She have an invitation? Come with somebody?"

"This is stupid," David argued and put his fork down. "All right. All right. She was released on bond and promptly disappeared. We think she found the parties in the newspaper and was able to wheedle her way in. But she's gone."

"Let's go back to Carlisle," Ryan requested.

"Why?"

"Because Robin is heading over there to work shortly."

"Why?" He was beginning to sound like a weird owl. Why instead of who.

"She has been hired by the insurance company to inventory his wines and weed out the fakes." Ryan lifted his tea bag out of his cup and laid it in the saucer.

David gave her a stare. "You don't have to do it now. It's not safe."

"Yes. I do." She wasn't looking at him, but at Mary Lee beside him.

He turned to Colin, who tipped his head, raised his coffee cup. "We've already had this discussion. She says she's going."

"You're going with her." He made that a statement.

"No."

David shook his head. "She doesn't go by herself. I'll take the day off."

"Jen and I'll be with her." Mary Lee said and patted his arm. The calming action angered him.

"She needs a bodyguard, not girlfriends.

"We are bodyguards," Mary Lee informed him.

"Sure." He made sure they could hear the derision in his voice. Turned on Colin. "You let these women protect someone you love? Your wife?"

"We're good," Jen said before Colin could answer.

At the same time Mary Lee said, "I am actually very good at my job."

Part of him knew better, but he couldn't stop himself. "At what? The beauty pageant circuit?"

"Do you need a demonstration?" she asked batting her eyelids and patting his arm again.

"Yeah, lady. I need a demonstration. What are you going to do? Seduce me? Go—"

Before he could finish, he blew out a grunt of pain and found himself bent over the table with his head beside his dish looking across the table top, not quite directly into the barrel of a gun held steadily in the hand of the tattooed chic. Safety on, he saw, trigger finger placed over the guard. His arm was bent up his back and he couldn't move. Breathing was hard. He saw Robin's shocked face through a haze. He had enough presence of mind to whisper, "Uncle."

Mary Lee let go.

The weapon disappeared.

He tried lifting his arm and groaned, shut his eyes. Pride alone gave him the strength to sit up straight. His arm, the one the beauty queen had been patting so gently before she'd twisted it, felt dead. She was massaging it for him now, soothing the burning.

He wanted to snatch it away, but it wasn't working right and Mary Lee held it firmly. "Let me," she said, "I know how to fix it."

"What was…" All he could manage was a croak. He tried again. "What was that?"

"Brazilian jiu-jitsu. With a little of this and a little of that. Lets a smaller person take down someone much larger."

Colin smirked. "She used the same demonstration on me a few weeks ago. The pain goes away in a few minutes. Don't worry, you'll still have a whole functioning arm."

"Good to know." He muttered through the pain. Right now it felt amputated. It was all he could do not to whimper like a baby.

"To answer your question," Ryan said, though David had forgotten he'd asked one, "both women have protected my wife. More than once."

Becca added, "They're two of the best in the business. Work for my brother-in-law's firm, Safe Keeping. Jen is married to his partner, worked with him as a bodyguard before she became his wife. That should make you feel better."

"I don't have anything against women," he argued.

Mary Lee was still working on his arm. "You fell for the dumb blond routine; one of my many skills. It sort of makes you a sexist pig," she said pleasantly.

"I am not a sexist pig. You fooled me, batting your baby blues."

"Exactly."

His arm was only numb now. Someone put a cold cloth on his forehead and he jerked around.

"This will make you feel better," Robin said from behind him. He hadn't noticed her getting the compress; he'd been concentrating on being brave. He reached for the cloth and turned to face her, but she was already sitting down. Not interested if he felt better?

"Hey, no one did that for me." Colin's smirk changed to a complaint. Maybe she did care for him.

"Who's paying you?" David tried another track. He saw various emotions, ranging from uncomfortable to embarrassment. Eyes looking away. "What? Is that a tough question? I mean, obviously Safe Keeping is paying you. Who's paying Safe Keeping?"

Finally, Becca spoke almost apologetically. "I'm paying them. Robin's safety is important to Colin. Mary Lee and Jen volunteered to work gratis; Jake and Ron offered to eat the expense. We had a, um, discussion and we reached a compromise. I'm paying Safe Keeping for top of the line protection. Colin works for free because he's repaying a debt." She looked daggers at Colin when she said that. Obviously angry he wouldn't accept money for himself. "The guards stay until Colin says Robin's safe. And, I think we are all in agreement, she's not safe now."

David gawked. "You can afford to pay two top bodyguards for an extended period? You're married to an FBI agent."

"That's my wife. Strong, smart, fair. And rich." Ryan grinned. "And married to me."

Having no response to that, David turned to Robin. "You have to come downtown and make a statement. Then you should come back here and stay put, at least until we get everything straightened out."

She searched his face. Looked as if she would say something, but then picked up her fork to eat. She didn't eat, but looked down at her food. Then she picked up her plate and utensils, strode to the sink and dumped her remaining breakfast and rinsed everything before placing it in the dishwasher.

She looked at those gathered around the table. "I'll be ready in fifteen minutes. First we go to the police station; then I go to Carlisle's." She left the kitchen and the silence around the table.

Jen followed her. Mary Lee stood. "I need two minutes to do my make-up."

David couldn't help himself. "Bodyguards worry about make-up?" He wasn't thinking. It was a case of open mouth, insert foot. She shifted toward him and he hastily moved out of her reach. He raised his hand. "Uncalled for. Sorry. Mouth worked, brain was dead. I meant to say you don't need makeup." She didn't know she was beautiful?

She walked past him without incapacitating him.

"Those two will stand out in any crowd," he complained.

"Don't judge," Becca told him. "Wait and see." She rose and began clearing dishes. Colin loaded the dishwasher. Ryan put away leftovers. David sat and held his coffee. With his good arm.

A few minutes later he heard Mary Lee come back in and glanced over to see how she had improved on perfect. He actually looked behind this plain, drab woman to see if Mary Lee was behind her. He felt his mouth open and heard Becca chuckle behind him.

"Told you."

Mary Lee's luxurious mane of hair hung limp, dull, and lifeless. Her face was chubby with a fat nose, no cheekbones; even her jaw line was rounded, her body plump.

"Okay. You can twist my arm again," he said. That earned him a smile. He cleared his throat. "What's the plan for today?'

"Jen drives. I ride shotgun. Robin's in the back seat. Robin follows orders, immediately. No questions. Jen's laying it all out for her now."

When Robin came back, David thought her eyes were red but was smart enough to leave it alone.

Jen also was a changed woman. She'd put on a long-sleeved shirt with the sleeves rolled down and buttoned at the wrist hiding the tattoos. She'd taken off the nose ring and one ear had only a single stud. She'd pulled all the metal off the other ear. His surprise must have shown.

She showed him the ear piercings. They were one piece. "This is an ear wrap. It wraps around the outer edge of the ear and looks like piercings."

Learn something new every day, he thought.

**

Robin had spent ten of those fifteen minutes in the bathroom; first, not crying and then wiping her tears and later applying cold water to her face to hide the red and puffy. She'd had to leave the table, otherwise she'd have cried in front of everyone. She blamed the tears on her rough night, not on the feelings she still felt for David. Every kind word brought hope which was dashed by angry comments. One moment he was warm concern, the next, professional disinterest. His changing attitude confused her.

She ignored David when she came out and drove off with Mary Lee and Jen. He followed behind them to the station where he told her guards he would escort her inside.

"We go with her," Jen said.

"She'll be safe in the station."

The two women gave each other a strange smile. "She will be, if we're with her."

"Whatever," he said and waved them ahead. Jen and Robin led the way; Mary Lee brought up the rear. Robin felt David's eyes on her all the time and was relieved to finally be finished and away from him.

Ian, a tall and gangly young man was waiting outside Carlisle's gate. He was quick and smart and absorbed information like a sponge and knew more than most adults about the wines he had never sipped. Another month and he'd be old enough to drink. Robin introduced him to her 'friends' and then rang the bell, identified herself, and requested admittance. It took a few minutes, but the gate slid open and the two cars passed through. The man waiting at the front door was slight, ordinary, and angry, if you could judge by the stiff back and raised chin. "You're late. I expected you earlier. Mr. Carlisle said you would be here an hour ago. He didn't say anything about two cars. Or this many people."

Yes, definitely anger, fostered by Carlisle. "I'm sorry if you expected us sooner. My arrangement with Mr. Lynch did not include a schedule or the number of people who would work with me. Maybe he didn't share that information with Mr. Carlisle." She offered her hand, "And you are?"

"I'm George Franks. I work for Mr. Carlisle." The anger was changing to doubt.

"Mr. Carlisle needs this inventory and appraisal as soon as possible and I came out today as a favor to him. I'm sorry any of us have to be here on a Sunday morning and I'm sure you had other things planned, as did we. I brought help with the hope we can complete the task today and won't have to return. We certainly appreciate you giving up your Sunday to help us."

Franks frowned, uncertain, but mollified. "Mr. Carlisle instructed me to stay all day. The maid has the day off."

"This is inconvenient for all of us, but we are helping Mr. Carlisle out of a difficult situation. I'll do everything I can to finish up today." She was very good at soothing people; she'd had to learn diplomacy early alongside the art of how to fight in a man's world. She'd always treated her customers with respect. With employees she gently suggested better ways for them to complete their duties. In this case Robin was using the misery loves company gambit; it put all of them in the same boat and gave Franks a way out with dignity.

She continued. "You're welcome to accompany us, but it's not necessary; there's no reason you can't be doing your own work. If we need you we'll find you, or should we call?"

Giving him choices and control, calmed him further. She waited for him to decide.

He gave a sharp nod. "Good. I have a briefcase of documents to review. I'll be in the library." He gave her his cell number.

"Do you have Mr. Carlisle's wine inventory for me?"

"Yes, right here." He picked up a file folder of loose papers from a table top and handed it to her. "This is all I've been able to find. I'll keep looking. It's pretty sparse."

"I expected it would be." She passed it to Ian. "I know the way to the wine cellar; you don't have to show us." As she turned to walk down the hall, Jen cut her off. "You between me and Mary Lee." Ian overheard and gave her a puzzled look, but she shrugged her shoulders at him and pointed the way.

"It's not in the cellar?" Jen asked. "Why isn't it in the cellar?"

"There are no cellars in this part of Florida. The water table is too high; it's only a few feet below ground level, wine cellars are on the first floor."

Robin set her laptop on the tasting counter and pulled the handheld scanner out of her briefcase and attached it. "We'll work here, start with the wall to the left and work around the room. Finish up with the boxes last. I'll examine the bottles and hand them to you, Ian. You scan the barcode into the database, assign an ID number, and note the location. Each of the racks is already labeled. That will help."

She called up the application. "Each bottle will have today as a purchase date, with a note in comments explaining the circumstances." She held up the folder. "I'll enter the data when I review the paperwork, what little there is."

She pointed to the screen. "I've set up a check box field for counterfeit wines. Check if counterfeit. That will bring up a sub-form where we can describe the discrepancies. If we find any fake bottles, we'll use an empty carton to store them. When we're all done, we can sort the database by the check box and get a list of all the counterfeits which we will print for the attorney and the FBI."

"What's a field?" Jen wanted to know.

"Column. Data type. It's the proper designation for a column in a database."

"Are you expecting to find counterfeit wines?"

"Yes, I am. Carlisle had his own supplier, remember? And we know Fallern was printing his own labels and had a supply of empty bottles. There was evidence he had a production line going. Carlisle probably was not the only client he scammed." More work for Fine Wines maybe?

"We can help," Mary Lee said.

"How much do you know about wine?"

"Sweet and cheap," Jen mocked. "Both of us."

"I can pass bottles to you, you carry them to Ian to scan. That way I can be working on the next bottle. We'll get a fire line going." Be quicker.

They went to work. Robin picked up each bottle, examined front and back labels, capsule, and level of wine, then she passed the bottle to Jen or Mary Lee who carried it to Ian who scanned it in and labeled it. Robin moved through the racks working across and down each rack fairly quickly. She'd reached the middle of the back wall before she found a fake. Curious, Jen and Ian crowded around her. Mary Lee stayed by the door.

"How can you tell?" Jen asked.

"This particular winery always has an embossed bottle." She turned it so they could see. "Smooth glass. No imprint. The label is decent. Ian, scan in the barcode; see what it reads. This cabernet sauvignon should sell for around $180.00." She pulled more bottles from the diamond shaped bin where they were arranged individually and stood them on the countertop.

"Exactly what the label says," Ian told her, "but like you said, the bottle should be embossed."

"Okay Ian, enter a check in the counterfeit field. I'll dictate what you should type in the memo field." When she saw he was ready, she continued, "Though the skew number is valid…" She stopped, waiting as Ian pecked laboriously at the keyboard. It was painful to watch him try to find keys.

Jen pushed him away from the laptop. "Let me do that; I'm a touch typist."

Robin stared at her.

"I type reports all the time. See if you can dictate faster than I can type."

"Though the skew number is valid, and the label appears real, the bottle is not embossed. I count a dozen bottles in this bin." She stopped, motioned to Jen. "Hit the function key; the software will copy the line. Each bottle will have its own ID number." They labelled the bottles and placed them in an empty case with the beginning and ending ID numbers.

Robin moved to the next bin and pulled out a bottle. "Scan this in." She handed it to Ian as she continued checking all the bottles. "Thirty-six of these. All fake. What did you find?"

"Skew number comes back to that wine. You sure this is a fake?"

"Type the name in Google and click images."

Ian started, one letter at a time, but Jen pushed him away again.

"The labels look the same," Jen said.

"Right. Yes. See the date? The real label for this vintage should be in red. It's a limited production and sells for about a hundred dollars more than other dates. If you didn't know about the red, you'd accept this gray date. Twelve more in the next bin, makes forty-eight. At about one hundred bucks a pop, that's a nice and easy forty-eight-hundred-dollar profit for the seller, less the cost of paper. He probably used empty bottles."

"How do you know all this stuff?" Jen asked.

"The same way you know guns or knives, I would expect. Or Jimmy Choo from Sketchers. Experience. I've been in the wine business for fifteen years."

Jen entered the data and Robin moved on to the next rack and finished the back wall without finding more fakes.

**

She was surprised when Franks entered the room to say, "Ms. Garman, another one of your assistants has arrived."

She almost blurted out she wasn't expecting anyone when David walked in. She'd forgotten about his threat to look in on them later. "Thought you said this afternoon," she grumbled.

"Hate to break it to you, but it is afternoon. Way past lunch."

"We missed lunch?" Ian looked at his watch. "Wow. We can go to Pastrami Dan's."

"Any good?" Jen asked him.

"Very, very good. New York Deli good," he replied, then added, "I'm told. Never been to a New York deli."

"I'm in," Jen said.

"Me too," Mary Lee agreed.

"Let's go," Ian said.

"No, we'll order in. Does he deliver?" Jen asked.

"He does," David said, "but I'll go fetch them. Five pastramis on rye with mustard?" They agreed and he pulled out his cell.

"Make it six."

"You going to eat two, Robin?"

"One for Mr. Franks. We can eat together."

"Done." David placed the order.

"I'll come with you." Ian jumped up.

"Fine. You can do the heavy lifting."

**

The drive gave David time to quiz Ian and find out more about Robin and Fine Wines. But Ian beat him to it. "Why is a cop hanging around Ms. Garman?"

"How do you know I'm a cop?"

"Look like one. Smell like one."

"Smell like one? Where did you get that?"

"The streets. TV. You act like a cop. Asking questions. You didn't answer mine. Does she know you're a cop? And those women act strange. Always watching."

"You're a pretty observant kid. What do you do at Fine Wines? You're a little young aren't you to be in the wine business?"

"Yeah. I'm observant. You still didn't answer my question."

"You answer mine and I will."

"I can tell her you're a cop," he threatened.

"She knows I'm a cop. Tell me about your job; why aren't you in school?"

"Sunday, Dude," he said it with a roll of his eyes. "Besides, I graduated last year, four point oh average," he bragged. "Got a pay raise and a bonus. Started grad school."

"Impressive. How long have you been working for her?"

Ian gave it some thought. "She hired me when I was sixteen. Almost five years."

"Started kind of young." David waited.

"Part time. After school. With the stipulation I finish school."

"What do you do? I thought her business was all wine."

"Right. I can't be around any open wines. But I can mop floors, take out the trash, help the pastry chefs set up. My sister is going to be a pastry chef," he bragged. "I work all over the building, lots of different jobs. I see everything, know everyone. We're like a big family. She let me do that for six months and then let me pick the job I wanted to learn, where I wanted to work."

"Pretty nice of her. You a relative?"

"Nah. My mom works for her."

"So she hired you and your sister?"

"I told you, man, it's a family. She hires all the relatives."

He thought about that. Remembered what Sally had said. "What job did you pick?"

"I picked hers. I want to be what she is."

"A sommelier."

"What? No. Well sort of. I want to have my own business. If it's wine, that's okay. She gave me books, spent time with me, taught me business and wines. I learned vineyards, types of wine, where and how they were grown, aged… all of that. How to order. Number of glasses you can serve from one bottle. Learned how to use the databases. Spent time in accounting and payroll. I'm a man for all areas. And I still clean floors."

"How come?"

"I'm good at it."

"How does being around wines work with the Florida minimum drinking age?" he asked, curious.

"No. I'm not answering anymore questions until you answer mine. It's your turn. Why is a cop hanging around Ms. Garman? And you watch her. Your eyes are always on her. And she doesn't like you much."

Kid was sharp. Or he really had it bad, if a kid could see his need. "We have some history."

"No way. Ms. Garman doesn't mess around."

"Guess you don't know everything."

"Huh. You got something for her. But she doesn't like you. Why's she letting you hang around? And what about those two women? If they're friends, they're new friends."

Kid really was sharp. David knew detectives who wouldn't have spotted anything off with the women. They were beautiful and distracting.

"Like I said, you don't know everything. Besides, she doesn't hate me. She thinks she does. I'll bring her around. Now, tell me how you work with liquor."

"I don't. I'm never in a room where the wine is open. Ever. No exceptions. But it's only the tasting room and now the classrooms that I'm not allowed in. We don't quite fit into the exception for education. Yet." He was referring to the Florida state exception which allowed an underage person to taste, but not swallow, alcohol for educational purposes.

"Has to be accredited, right?"

"Yeah. And we're not. Accredited. Ms. Garman is by the book. I work everywhere else, learning the ropes. I could run the Fine Foods section. And Rome and Sally like me."

"Why should that matter? You're all family."

"Well sure, but now with Rome and Sally running the business, it's a little different. Rome says he has a spot for me when I get my business degree." He was bragging again. "And you still haven't told me what's going on. Why are you here? And those women?"

The kid was like a terrier with a rat. He wouldn't let go. David decided to trust him. "It might be better if you know. You can help. We think, we're not sure, but we think someone is trying to abduct her. Those two women are bodyguards."

The kid's eyes became really big. "No way. Those babes are bodyguards?" He took a breath. "Who would want to grab her? Why?"

"That's what we don't know." He explained the situation and events; could see the kid thinking.

David asked, "How about the men in her life? Any of them angry at her?" He didn't even feel guilty, quizzing a kid to find out about her sex life.

"I told you she doesn't mess around."

"She must date."

"No. She doesn't. Though some guy came to work with her yesterday; and picked her up after."

"Colin Gibbs. He's a bodyguard. Must be other men."

"No. Well, maybe about a month ago. We thought there might be a guy."

Month ago would have been him. "What makes you think that?"

"She was different. Dreamy. Hummed. For a few days. Then, nothing. Kind of sad. We talked about it, and that's all we kids could figure. A guy. And I overheard Sally telling Rome that Robin had a man friend. I'm telling you she doesn't date. We'd have known." He was quiet for a while, thinking. Made David a bit nervous.

Then the kid said slowly, "You have history with her. That was you a month ago. What did you do to her to make her unhappy?" The kid was angry now. "You dumped her, didn't you? That's why she doesn't like you around."

David couldn't cover his grimace.

"Yeah," Ian said. "I nailed it in one. You really hurt her. And what? Now you're protecting her? Sure." The kid slunk into the far corner of his seat and looked out the window. His silence screaming.

"Look, kid, it wasn't like that." Wasn't it? It was exactly like that. "It was a mistake. I made a mistake. I'm goin' to fix it." Why was he explaining to a kid? And why did the kid make him feel like scum?

"I'm not telling you anything else."

David pulled into Dan's, parked, and pulled out his wallet. Handed the kid five twenties. "Get some drinks and salad too." Ian grabbed the money and stomped into the shop. He wasn't in any better mood when he came out loaded down, and they made the return trip in an uneasy silence. Everyone was in the kitchen and Ian went directly to Robin and whispered something to her. She patted him gently on the shoulder, murmured a few words. Then she turned to David with a look of sheer disgust. He stared right back. Now he had one more thing he had to fix.

While they ate, the women compared the food to delis back home. Dan's came near the top.

After lunch they returned to the wine cellar. David asked, "You find any counterfeit wines this morning?"

Robin pointed them out.

"All the phony wines are cabernets. Does that mean something?" Ian asked.

Robin pursed her lips. "Well, maybe reds are easier to imitate. Or maybe, Mr. Carlisle buys reds. I don't know. It's a good question. I'll have to think about it."

All the wines on the side wall were genuine and two hours later they were ready for another break when Franks announced snacks waiting in the kitchen: cheese, crackers, apples, grapes, chips, and cookies. Sodas, coffee, and tea.

"Will you finish today?" he asked.

"Probably. We'll come close if we don't. We have a few racks on the last wall and all the boxes. We have to open each one and examine every bottle. That will take time."

Franks groaned. "So you need to come back tomorrow?"

"No. We have another job tomorrow."

He let out a breath of relief and picked out some grapes. "My anniversary is tomorrow. My family has plans, but I can stay late today."

"We'll see," Robin told him.

"Do you want wine with your snack?" Franks asked as he opened the refrigerator door. "I have two whites and two reds chilled." He stopped. "Oh, do you need to add these to the inventory?"

Robin stood up to take a look. "We should." She pulled out one bottle and examined it. "This is a nice white. The reds are fake though."

"What? How can they be? How can you tell? You didn't even touch them."

"I don't need to. The labels are crooked and blurred. I haven't seen any of these in the wine cellar. Is that where you got them?"

"Yes. They were on the counter."

"Well, I wouldn't drink them."

"We'll take them," David said.

Robin gave him a puzzled look, but he said, "We're required to, according to your contract. Confiscate fake wines."

"Did you find other fake wines?" Franks asked.

David answered before Robin had a chance. "That will be in her report after she completes her research on the web tonight."

Robin followed his lead to distract Franks. "Right. I still have to log in the purchase orders and do some web research. Did you find any more receipts or paperwork?"

"I did find some more receipts." He handed her another folder. David looked over her shoulder and watched as she thumbed through it while Franks was casting surreptitious looks at Mary Lee.

"You a sommelier?" Franks finally asked her.

"No. I work in the IT department. We have a little dark hole for an office. How long have you been married?" Yup. The woman could keep a secret. And distract. The conversation stayed on Franks' family for the rest of the break.

Back in the wine cellar Robin said, "The counter next, Ian, then the cases, then we'll finish the walls. I'm curious about the boxes."

David was curious too. The last time he was here, the boxes held fake wines.

The counter wines were real. And Ian moved to the cases. "Look." He was nearly jumping up and down with excitement. "This is the champagne you said you found. The fake one." He had turned three of the top boxes, displaying the labels.

Robin touched the label. "I think this one case is real. Those two, though? Bogus."

"These were not here before. They're new. Right?" David asked shifting into cop mode.

She closed her eyes, tilted her head as she thought. "No, they were not here." She opened her eyes and looked directly at David. "Mr. Carlisle may have shelved those wines or the FBI might have taken the cases. I'll ask. Do you think Carlisle ordered the same wine again? New purchases, would mean someone else is selling forged wine, because it sure isn't Fallern. Maybe he had a partner. There might be something in the purchase orders or shipping forms in the folder. I only glanced through them."

David reached for the file. His case had reached a dead end and gone cold; he'd never found a partner or anyone who might want Fallern dead. "You work on the cartons; I'll check the sales receipts." But he stopped before he took the folder.

Robin asked, "What's wrong?"

"I don't have legal cause to look. I need a warrant."

She pushed the folder at him. "My contract gives me the right to notify law enforcement if I find any counterfeits. Whoever and whenever I want. That should include me letting you look through this folder. I am notifying you now that I have found fake wines."

He smiled at her and grabbed the folder. "You're a doll. What's that champagne again? How do you spell it?"

Ian looked at Robin, got a nod and took the file away from Ramirez. He thumbed through the pages. "Here. Here. This. Last week. Thursday." He handed it over pointing to a line on the shipping form. "Here's the fake champagne. Delivered along with four cases of a sweet white muscato." He went to turn all the boxes front side forward; David helped. The muscato and the champagne, four cases each.

"You think they're fake, Ms. Garman?"

"You tell me, see how much you remember. I'll examine the sweet whites." She stepped over to the first carton, pulled out her knife, and sliced it open. She checked the name and description on line. Nodded once and inspected the label and bottle closely. "This is fine. Well, a really sweet wine, but authentic." She moved on to the next case and worked quickly through the box.

Ian was slower; he was still working on the first carton.

Robin finished. "These are all genuine. There would be little reason to fake a cheap bottle of wine." She and the women numbered the boxes and entered the bottles and their location into the computer.

Ian was ready for her then and eager to begin with his first bottle of the champagne. "This label is a perfect match for what you told me. To begin, the labels on the boxes are crooked. I gave them all a quick look; they're all the same. The scan of the back label of the bottle returns as a cheap bubbly."

She smiled at him with approval. "Scan them all in; slap numbers on the cartons."

They worked rapidly in silence. The data entry was simple work once the determination of authenticity was made.

David pulled the purchase order from the file. "I need to take this with me," he told her.

"I can't let you take that; can't you write down the information?"

"I need the original in case we ever go to trial. I'll write you a receipt and get you a copy tomorrow."

"No, it's not going to work that way. I have a job to do and a contract. I'll make you a copy."

He didn't like it, but he could always subpoena the original, or the D.A. could. "Okay."

She frowned, started to say something. Stopped.

"What?"

"Well, at the risk that you will want the whole file, it occurs to me it would be helpful to see if the same dealer sold Carlisle any of the other fake wines."

"Thought of that; figured I'd wait until after supper to ask you."

She was surprised at his comment. "After supper?"

"You are inviting me back for supper, aren't you? And I need you to look at the gift shop video, too." That's the excuse he'd used with his boss. He held his breath.

She countered with. "How about this? You may come to dinner, and afterwards I'll review the file; I intended to work on it tonight anyway. I'll make you copies. Sort the database for the fakes and print that list for you."

"Great." He smiled to himself. He'd conned her into it. "I'll pick up dinner on the way.

They packed up and Robin informed Franks they had completed most of the physical inventory, and would return later in the week to finish. "We found a number of counterfeit wines, and I'll have a full report when we're done. I'll notify the FBI tomorrow and the local cops who are investigating a murder related to the fakes. I'll call Mr. Lynch tomorrow and let him know our progress."

David marveled. Robin had told Franks the truth and yet managed not to mention the local cops already knew.

Ian had a date and left first. He wouldn't be with them tomorrow; he had classes. Robin, walking between Jen and Mary Lee, was next. David left last and followed them back to the house, ordering supper on the way.

Ryan Gibbs and his wife were waiting. Colin arrived the same time as the pizzas, wings, and salads. David pulled up the video on his phone of the suspect who had been staring at Robin through the shop window. He passed it around.

"How successful was your visit to FBI headquarters," he asked the senior Gibbs.

"Pretty good. First, they have no leads on the counterfeit wines. Everything they have stops in that room at the back of the warehouse. There is nothing in the warehouse to indicate who the forger is, and they haven't been able to identify him or find a trail. They are pretty sure Bobby Fallern was middleman. He collected empty bottles at locations where he delivered wines. The local agents have verified that. They assume Fallern saw the money the forger was making and decided to go into business for himself. That would explain the two levels of quality.

"The hypothesis is, the forger murdered Fallern when he caught him counterfeiting wines. Did you find anything today that might help?"

"We did. Well, Robin did," David told him. "She found more bogus wines and has some purchase orders to look through."

Gibbs nodded. "Share that with the local office when you contact them. They have quite a bit on Carlisle and will have a package together for you. No convictions or arrests, but an iffy background, slightly across the line. Nothing like forgery, abduction, or murder." He handed David a card. "Here. Contact Agent Tucker in the morning."

Gibbs looked at his notes before continuing. "Second, they wish you had informed them of the attempted kidnapping." He raised his hand. "I smoothed that over for you, but you should give them the details when you speak with them. They'll check informants and look for similar crimes. They did a quick look while I was there and came up empty. Also, if you share, they might have a couple of agents who can work with you. They're not happy one of their own has been targeted." He gave Robin a smile. "Even if she is only a consultant."

Gibbs had accomplished quite a lot. "For a couple of extra men, I'll be on my best behavior."

They finished all the food; there were no left-overs, not even a leaf of lettuce, and clean-up was easy. Everything went into the trash. Robin started coffee and served Sally's cookies, straight from the freezer, in a pretty dish. Soft cookies which could be eaten frozen.

Colin stood. "Robin. Tomorrow, we'll repeat today. Do whatever Mary Lee and Jen say. You don't need me, and as much as I want to see those cars, I don't have time." He headed home.

Robin finally turned toward David, but she looked over his shoulder. "I'll work on the purchase orders and email any dealer names I find, Detective, if you want to wait."

"I can wait."

"I'll be in my office."

"I'll come with you."

She stopped and then shrugged reluctantly. "Whatever," and walked away leaving him to follow.

Not quite the response he'd hoped for.

He started to close the door behind him, when Jen called, "Leave it open, please." He pushed it shut; he wanted to talk to Robin. Alone. But Jen called to him, "Leave it open, please, or I have to be in the room with you."

He was stuck. He left it open a few inches and pulled up a chair beside Robin at the desk.

"I'd rather you sit over there." She pointed to the other side of the desk.

"I'm fine here." He wanted to be near her.

She still wasn't looking at him, instead she glanced through the file. "Fine. Do what you want. You will anyway." She went to work, ignoring him and slapped two forms to the side, grabbed the next receipt and studied it a long time.

Anger was steaming off her. He was doing it again. Every time he got near her, he screwed up. He'd come into the room intending to talk to her, try to explain and apologize for last night. Instead, he was bullying her. Being a jerk. Again. She sat stiffly at her desk; her body language clearly said she didn't want him near. He should move to the other side of the desk as she asked, but somehow that felt like an admission of defeat.

He shook his head. Defeat? What kind of sense did that make? He moved to the other side of the desk and the tension left her body.

She worked through the folder, turning the papers over one by one and when she reached the end of the file, she picked up four sheets she had set aside. "These are for the champagne and two other fake wines we found. I'll make copies for you now and later enter them into the database. I don't have receipts for everything. I didn't expect Carlisle to have good records, but Franks may find some more. I'll let you know."

"I need originals." Didn't hurt to try.

"Right. That's what you said. Get them from the FBI. I'm not turning them over. You can work from the copies." She made him copies.

He didn't push it. He took the papers and followed her back to the kitchen where Ryan was pouring more coffee.

Robin told Jen, "I'll be with the FBI tomorrow; they have agents at the site. You really don't have to come with me."

"We'll be with you. Besides I want to see that car," Jen said.

David declared, "I'm coming too. They were after you, Robin."

"No. Not necessary. Nothing is going to happen." She spoke to Jen, not him.

"Car. Remember? Gotta see the car. And Mary Lee goes where we go."

David tried again. He had to convince her of the danger. Who cared about the car?

"They put a closed sign on the restroom door, Robin. They didn't wait for Patsy to leave when they went in for you."

"No, you're wrong," she said looking in his general direction.

"The sign was on the door; Patsy was still in there when the crooks busted in." Why couldn't she understand? She was in danger. Needed him.

She looked at him now, surprised. "No. You're wrong about the sign. The sign was up when I went in."

"You went into a closed bathroom?"

"Women do it all the time," Jen said. "Nothing unusual in that. The cleaners don't mind. They're generally female and understand."

"I wasn't going to use the facilities. I needed some time alone to, um, to freshen up," she finished, still not looking directly at him.

"If the sign was up before you went in, then—"

He didn't get a chance to finish because Ryan said, "They were after Patsy."

"The video." Mary Lee said. She was watching it on David's phone. "Look. The woman in the back of the shop. Behind Robin. Is that guy looking at her? Not Robin?"

"Patsy. That's Patsy," Becca said. "She's still under protection, isn't she?"

David stood, snatching his phone. Shit. They weren't after Robin. Patsy was the target after all. Had her guards arrived? He speed-dialed Scott. Paced while it rang.

"They're after Patsy," he said as soon as Scott answered. "The hotel video we just got? Shows the creep watching Patsy. We never had the whole tape, only the still photo. And the closed sign was on the restroom door before Robin went in."

"Shit." Scott echoed David's comment of a moment before. "Okay, I'm heading over."

"Take a couple of men. Go to her room. I'll call her." David disconnected and dialed Patsy, looking around the table. He let it ring six times. "No answer." He disconnected, dialed Scott again. "I can't get her."

"I'm on my way. Almost there," Scott said.

David disconnected and waited through long moments of silence; then his cell rang. He put it on speaker.

"The maid says they went for a walk on the beach," Scott said. "Patsy should be okay. She's got those two new guards with her."

"Call them."

"Tried. They're not answering either."

"What kind of bodyguard turns off his cell?" David demanded. "Did we check out Dieffenbachia?"

Ryan asked, "Dieffenbachia? Daffy? Daffy's the guard?"

David looked at him hopefully. "You know him? Can you get him?"

Becca pulled out her cell. Hit a button. "I have his emergency code." Becca hit the button again, paused, and hit it a third time.

They waited.

Her cell buzzed softly. She spoke into it, "They're after Patsy. She's their target." Her eyes widened as she listened. "Wait. Let me put you on speaker. We got the cops here. Go ahead."

A calm voice came through, speaking softly. "We need an ambulance, three down, two bad guys and my partner. We're on the beach, um, a bit south of the hotel. Patsy is fine. Two other men took off running to the north. Just happened."

"Go. Go," David said to Scott, and then hit two keys on his cell and ordered the ambulance and back-up. Told Becca's speaker phone. "This is Detective Ramirez. Ambulance and cops are on the way. Patrol unit will check the parking areas and jot down license tags. Detective Scott and three men are heading for the beach. Descriptions of the two men?"

"Dark pants, white shirts, long sleeves. Both about five feet ten, brown hair. Should stand out on the beach."

"How bad are the injuries?"

"The bad guys are serious. My partner has a flesh wound. I hear sirens. Your men know we got guns right?"

"Yeah."

"Thanks."

David needed to get to the beach, but first he asked Becca, "How do you happen to have a code number for a bodyguard?"

"Daffy, Dieffenbachia, works for my brother-in-law," she said. "Safe Keeping has a code for emergencies when cells are silenced. We all have the number. Also, Daffy is married to another of my sisters."

He snorted. Ex-cop marries FBI agent with an innkeeper son who bodyguards as a hobby. Same ex-cop has a brother-in-law who owns a protection business which employs a second brother-in-law as a bodyguard. An agency which also employs beautiful women who apparently are good at their jobs. "Anyone else I should know about?"

Becca rested her chin on her hands, her elbows on the table. Obviously enjoying herself. "Where do you want me to start?" She smiled brightly.

Gibbs senior chuckled. "Her family is made up of over-achievers, but that's about it for armed men."

"Who's working with Daffy?" Mary Lee asked David.

"Why? Are there more boyfriends? Never mind," David added quickly when he saw the frown. "Sorry." He pulled out his notebook and thumbed through two pages, back to where Patsy had told them the guards' names. "Reydar. Joel Reydar," he read. "Spelled r-e-y-d-a- r.'

"Reydar works for Safekeeping?" Ryan asked surprised.

"You know him?" Mary Lee and David asked at the same time.

"Never met him, but I've heard good things about him. He rates a close second behind Daffy. Good man. We need to find out how badly he's hurt. Daffy may need some backup. Guess I'll head on over. You coming with me," he asked his wife, "or staying with Robin?"

"Hold on a minute," David ordered. He didn't need more civilians at a crime scene. Already too many of them there. "I'm not letting civilians on my crime scene."

"Not quite civilians," Ryan reminded him.

"Jesus. What's wrong with you people? Let us do our job."

"Didn't do it too well at the event. Or this evening." Ryan held up his hand. "Not faulting you. Had the same sort of thing happen to me. Can never have too many good men. Or women. And it looks like Patsy needs more help."

David knew Gibbs was right; he could use experienced people. "What about Robin?"

"Her guards stay with her," Ryan said.

"Why?" Robin asked. "They're after Patsy. You all just said so. And they actually tried for her."

"Nobody here can say you're not at risk. They've tried to take you two times now. Doesn't matter if it's a mistake or not if they get you. The guards stay." Ryan glanced around at everyone. "Do whatever they tell you. Okay?"

David was about to chime in when he realized his opinion might push her in the other direction.

"Ryan's right," Mary Lee said. "We can't take a chance. Always smart to be prepared. Besides, Jen wants to see that car."

Ryan stood, ending the conversation. "Let's go, wifey. Jen, we'll let you know Reydar's status."

Jen nodded and pulled out her phone. "I'll give Ron a heads-up."

Monday

The smell of coffee woke her, still tired. Last night she'd shown Jen and Mary Lee to their room and gone to bed where she'd tossed and turned. Finally, she rose and worked on Carlisle's database until her eyes blurred. She went back to bed and tossed and turned more. Only good thing about it was, she didn't have a nightmare. She lay in bed a few moments longer and then groaned and jumped up and dressed.

Jen handed her coffee. "Mary Lee went to lie down. What are your plans today?"

"We head over to Dutch's. Are you both coming?"

"For sure. Besides, you couldn't keep me away; I need to see that car." Jen sat and sipped her own coffee. "You really got that guy unnerved, you know."

"What do you mean? Who?"

"Your detective. He was ready to hit something when you both came out of your office last night. What happened in there?"

My detective? She didn't think so. "Nothing happened." And she didn't know how she felt about that. He'd gone out of his way to antagonize her, sitting close. Then abruptly he'd backed-off, moved around the desk. Adding physical distance to emotional. Then he'd demanded the original documents. Had she refused because she was angry? She didn't want to think about it. "How is your friend, Reydar?" She sat at the table.

"He's okay. A crease on his shoulder. Enough for a small bandage and bragging rights."

"I'm happy to hear that. What happened on the beach?"

Jen gave her a succinct response. "Patsy was restless, so they took a walk on the beach. Four men dressed like waiters approached them. Reydar waved them off and stepped in front of Patsy. Daffy moved forward. Two of the hoods pulled guns. Reydar pushed Patsy down and was shot as he dropped to cover her. Daffy rammed one of the armed men knocking him right into his accomplice and right into his line of fire. He was shot by his own partner. He's critical. That gave Daffy time to draw his weapon and restrain the shooter. The other two ran away. The cops caught both of them. They're talking, but they don't know anything. Both claim they were hired by the guy in the hospital, and he's not talking; he's in a coma. Your detective is checking their backgrounds, who they hang with, who might have hired them."

"Wow. I can't even imagine." She shook her head. "You guys enjoy that? Getting shot at?"

"Not enjoy and besides we don't get shot at a lot."

"One time would be enough for me."

"You're looking at this the wrong way. It's a job which needs to be done and one we're good at. We save people. We protect their families."

Robin nodded. "Okay. I can see that. Especially since it's me, or Patsy, who is being saved. What kind of name is Reydar? I think I understand Daffy, short for Dieffenbachia?"

"Yeah. It's a sissy name, but it fits him. Not that he's daffy. Sharp, smart, quick. But a nice guy. Reydar is a family name. Some think they call him Radar like the guy in the TV show." She took a quick sip of coffee. "Both men are kind of short with glasses and Reydar comes across as innocent and naïve. But don't fall for that. By the way, Gibbs and Becca went back to the Inn; Daffy and Reydar don't need them."

Robin poured more coffee. "I've got work in my office."

Jen followed her and asked, "Want some help?"

She shook her head. "I need to run a computer sort for names of suppliers for Detective Ramirez. Won't take long; you can sit and watch if you like." She ran the sort from the data she'd entered last night, then emailed it to David.

At least she'd be free of him today. She hated having him so close. She wanted to touch him, share a smile, check his reaction to a joke. It irritated her that she still wanted him. Loved him. That she couldn't make those feelings go away. She didn't sigh.

**

Jen parked on the side street, not in Dutch's driveway, and Robin, with Mary Lee beside her, led them inside to the desk where two agents sat in front of a board of monitors. Agent Caruso stood beside them very close to Ms. Leach, whispering in her ear in a manner which appeared almost intimate. Deja vu. He stepped away quickly when he saw them and grabbed badges; Robin had called the night before with their names. She'd been worried he'd question their credentials, but he didn't even ask to see them. As he handed out the IDs he said, "Agent Tucker said he would call you about some message you left. Did you talk to him?"

She shook her head and reached for her cell.

"Nah, not on your cell. No towers here, no bars."

She checked and sure enough, no bars. Her bodyguards did the same. It gave her a chuckle. "No reception? Here? One of the wealthiest neighborhoods in the country?"

"Right. No towers allowed. But the landline works. If he needs to get in touch, he'll call on the landline and the guys will put him through."

"What?" Jen said with disbelief, "Dutch never heard of cell signal boosters or repeaters? Or network extenders to create a signal for cells through the house broadband network, Voice Over Internet Protocols?"

"Who knows? The guy was a crook," Caruso said. As if that were explanation enough.

Robin asked, "When we break for lunch would it be possible for my team to tour the house... mansion... what do you call it?"

"Mansion. Sure. Feel free. No reason you can't. I'll take you down to the cellar now and then I'm needed back at the office."

Leach frowned and her lips thinned in disapproval. Because they were going to tour the house or because he was leaving, Robin didn't know. Maybe the woman had indigestion or maybe cranky was her normal.

"I know the way. Been here before, remember? You don't need to trouble yourself." Robin wasn't surprised when he immediately accepted her offer.

"Great. That way I can get back to my work." Very important work, his tone implied. "Here's the list of bottles you need to check." He handed it to her and tossed her the whole ring of keys. "Leave these at the desk when you're done." He gave Leach a hungry glance and left.

Robin led her guards downstairs and directly to the cars. Might as well get it over with.

Jen couldn't speak. Her mouth formed a wide O; her eyes were smaller versions. She kept reaching out a hand to touch, but kept pulling it back. Her soft *Wow* sounded like a prayer.

All Robin saw were cars. She could appreciate a classic she guessed, but really. She exchanged a shrug with Mary Lee. She gave Jen a few minutes to look at the cars and then broke her out of her adoration, worship, reverence? She led them inside the wine cellar where amazement replaced the admiration.

Robin made a circuit of the room, stopped at the locked cage. "The rare wines are locked in here. We may get to them on our next visit. During break you can tour or, if you prefer, go back to the cars. Let's get started."

She put the laptop down by the cellar computer and Jen whispered in her ear, "Security cameras. Don't look."

She closed her eyes a moment, mentally shrugged her shoulders, probably wouldn't see them anyway. Didn't really make a difference; she'd do the same job whether there were cameras or not. Dutch's database was top of the line. It updated prices automatically. All she had to do was authenticate the bottles on the list and check the information in the database using other online resources, which was why she'd brought her own laptop. To search for details and images and confirm the values.

"I set up a new database for the wines I'm to examine. Today will go quicker than yesterday because everything is already in an electronic inventory. All I have to do is authenticate the wines and check the prices."

The computer did all the work and she was soon bored with the job; it was all repetitive. The wines were ordinary and unexceptional. Not cheap, just not very good. That was a surprise. The room itself screamed money and affluence. Maybe the guy was wine ignorant. Not a fine wine in the mix. Checking inventory would not be one of her new career choices. Creating an inventory, as she did yesterday, was sort of a challenge. Authenticating an inventory was boring, but some of Fine Wines' trainees might be interested. She'd talk to Rome and Sally.

Jen's eyes kept turning toward the door and the cars and an hour later she snuck out after getting a nod from Mary Lee. Robin stopped to watch. She found the woman's awe entertaining; a nice break from the tedium of logging in uninspiring wines. Tomorrow, the search of the rare and limited production vintages in the locked room would offer some excitement. Great wines she'd never have an opportunity to touch otherwise.

They ordered-in lunch which they ate in front of the cars, foregoing the house tour because she and Mary Lee didn't care and Jen was enthralled with the old cars. Back at work, Robin was on random choice number forty-two when she discovered a forgery right beside it. She noticed it because the label was one she'd seen in the lab the day they'd found the body.

She held the bottle up. "This is a good forgery. A good fake, not the same sloppy work we saw at Carlisle's." Mary Lee and Jen both came over for a close look, and she pointed out the errors. "Both the vineyards and the winery should be on the label, but the winery is missing. The leaves on the vines around the edge are oak leaves, not grape leaves." She set it aside wondering how the FBI would handle fakes in their confiscated wine cellar. Should she call Agent Tucker? Maybe she should call David with the supplier's name; it was in the database and it could tie in to the murder case since the label probably came from Fallern's lab. She decided to wait. She might find more. At least the fake added some excitement to the monotony, and it distracted Jen from the cars for a few minutes, but her guards had seen fakes yesterday and were veterans now.

A long time later, she checked the clock and saw it was nearly quitting time. Quit early and gaze rapturously at cars? Or check out the limited-edition wines? No contest for her, but Jen was looking wistfully through the door.

"We'll call it a day. I expect we'll work on the caged wines in the morning. You can look at the cars for a bit before we go, Jen, and I'll let Agent Caruso know what we found."

Right choice she could see as Jen hurried out. Mary Lee stayed.

Robin pulled out her cell and was puzzled for a moment when it didn't work; then she remembered and looked for the house phone. Found it on the wall in the shape of a wine bottle. She dialed nine for an outside line and left a message on Caruso's voicemail about the fake and asked him to contact Detective Ramirez. She was unsure if she should contact him herself, but then decided it was her frustration that was holding her back. David deserved to know. She tried him, but he didn't answer either. Was she surprised? He had yet to respond to any of her calls. She left him a message and told him to contact Agent Caruso. She tried Scott with the same results. Cops. Didn't they ever answer their phones? She gave up. It was one bottle and a cheap bottle at that.

Maybe she'd go look at the cars and let Jen explain why they were so fascinating; she really didn't know much about cars, beyond what she'd learned when she picked out her own, and she didn't much care. A car was something which transported you with your equipment and supplies to your destination and then got you back home again. She understood there were fast cars, exotic cars, and antique cars, but she couldn't get excited about any of them. Oh, she knew what a Mustang was, and she knew a Shelby was a special kind of Mustang, but if she was going to look at something extraordinary, it was going to be a bottle of wine. She decided to sneak a look inside the cage. She tried her keys, found one which worked and opened the door.

Six clear glass single bottle display cases were lined up on the counter. Glass, not Plexiglas. Each looked to be six by sixteen inches, large enough for a magnum. She held her breath and moved closer. Oh, God, a 1907 Heidsieck Champagne. Her mouth watered and she managed a soft inhale. Okay. Maybe this was what Jen felt about the cars. These were wines she'd read about. Never expected to see. And here they were, collected, hoarded.

"What? What is it? Looks old," Mary Lee asked beside her.

Robin shook her head. Finally found her voice, weak though it was. "It is. The story is, it's from a shipwreck, a freighter sunk by a German U-boat in 1916. Recovered in 1998. A 1907 champagne."

"It was underwater all that time?"

Robin simply nodded.

"Doesn't it go bad when it gets old?

"Ages. We call it, aging." She shrugged her shoulders. "There is some debate about that. It's almost too rare to drink."

"What do people like Dutch do with the wine? Just keep it in this room? I guess if he drank it, it would be gone."

"That's about it. Save it or open it. Have a private tasting inviting only the very rich and powerful."

"Doesn't make a lot of sense to buy something you can't use. At least you can drive the muscle cars and still have a car. They don't go poof or glug as the case may be."

Robin stared at the first bottle, her attention riveted totally on it and reached out to touch it while looking beyond it at the remaining five clear containers. And stopped. "Six of them," she breathed.

Mary Lee moved down the counter. "Why is this one different?" She pointed to the last one on the far right. "Are they different years?"

Robin's eyes had been caught and held by the first bottle. Now she pulled her attention off the bottle and studied the last one. Shook her head. "No. Not different years. This can't be right. It shouldn't be different. Can't be. The provenance, there must be provenance in the file." She opened a file drawer and searched for the forms. Pulled out a file.

Robin sorted through the papers then laid them out beside each bottle. "Hmm. These five sheets are copies. Not the original paperwork. And the ID is altered. But the last one looks genuine. The bottle, too, has a different feel. Looks older."

She studied the paperwork. "The bottles were purchased together about six months ago. All from the same dealer, a dealer with a sterling reputation. Strange no one noticed the alterations in the paperwork or the differences in the bottles at the time."

They were silent for a while, thinking about it.

"They should have, don't you think? Especially since I can see it," Mary Lee said. "What about those bottles on the other counter?"

Robin was still concentrating on the Heidsieck, something about the bottle itself was familiar, niggling her brain, which was funny because she'd never seen a bottle before—except in pictures. She took time now to glance around the room. She walked to the other counter with more glass containers and shook her head. Six more clear glass display cases, each with a bottle of the 1787 Chateau d'Yquem.

"Those can't be forgeries," she said before Mary Lee could ask. "It's one of the most expensive wines in the world and one of the most counterfeited, but Dutch wouldn't buy forgeries."

She found the provenances for these wines and placed them on the counter.

Mary Lee turned the pages over, held them up to the light, felt the signatures. "This is a copy. Not an original. No one signed this page." She did the same with the rest. "All copies."

Robin felt the signature line also. "What does that mean? Dutch bought fakes? You have to be pretty brazen to rip off a crime boss." She bent to check the top rack underneath. "Oh, Domaine de la Romanee-Conti Romanee-Conti Grand Cru." She counted. "A dozen of them. Called the best wine in the world. One for which the price keeps rising because there is greater demand and fewer bottles left unopened. The glitterati call it DRC. The Conti had some excellent growing seasons, very good for the vines. Produced limited editions." She was prattling.

Jen came back in and asked, "What are we looking at?"

"Counterfeit wines. And not ordinary wines but very expensive, limited-edition wines. Wines with forged documentation. If forged is the right word. Maybe just fake."

Jen leaned over to look. "The mob boss bought fake wines? Whoever sold them to him will be swimming with the fishes."

Robin was looking at more files. "He didn't buy fake wines. Look at these photos." She spread them out on top of the documents and the women crowded around. Eight by ten snapshots of the six Heidsieck bottles, lined up on the counter in this room. "The bottles are all the same."

After a long silence Robin continued. "That means the switch took place after he bought them. Took place here. Do you think he did it? Why would he?"

"Or someone did it after he went to jail," Mary Lee suggested.

Another long silence.

"Oh," Robin put her hand to her mouth. "The bottle. I thought it looked familiar and I couldn't figure out why. I saw it. I saw a piece of that black glass on the floor of the warehouse where that man was killed. I was sitting in a chair with my head down, trying not to faint. There was broken glass under the desk. That glass. Can't mistake the weathered pitted look. I better call Agent Tucker." She started to reach for her cell again, remembered in time there was no reception and picked up the house phone and put it to her ear. She pushed the button a couple of times.

She looked at Jen. "The phone's dead."

She pushed the button again. Nothing happened. Except the lights went out. The air conditioner stopped. She looked stupidly at the phone for a second. Did I do that? Pushing the button?

Then she felt Mary Lee and Jen bracket her, blocking her from the doorway. Heard rustling and just knew they were drawing guns.

The lights and air conditioner snapped back on.

"Back-up generator," Mary Lee said. But neither woman relaxed; both had their weapons drawn.

It went dark and the AC died again. Without me pushing the phone button, Robin thought.

Jen said, "Generator shut down."

"Shit. What are the chances." Not a question. "Jen, you have a light?" Mary Lee asked.

A cell phone lit up, pointed at the floor. Turned off immediately. "Don't want to spotlight our position," Jen said.

"I'll check the door. You have Robin." Mary Lee left following her own pencil-thin beam of light out of the room. The beam wound through the main room and around the corner, a dark shadow following off to the side.

Jen's hand pushed Robin down. "Down on the floor. Stay quiet."

They heard a scratching sound and a minute later the beam came back. "Door to the stairs is locked. I could probably pick it, but…"

"Right, we don't know what's on the other side," Jen finished for her.

"I'll run the perimeter, check the garage overhead door." Mary Lee and her pencil beam moved to the main garage and winked out.

Another beam appeared on the far side of Robin. Jen had done something to her cell window. "I'm going to disable the cameras, just in case they're on a separate circuit. Stay where you are." The camera was highlighted. A hand appeared and pulled wires loose.

"Someone was watching us?" Robin whispered. "Someone here? In the house?"

"Most likely. Had to be here to cut the phone line, pull the main power supply. And the generator. Stay here, I'm going to fix the other camera."

Robin saw the wires pulled from the second camera. The beam came back and shut off. "Dutch should have used wireless. No new technology here."

Mary Lee slipped back in. Her voice startled Robin. But not Jen. "We're clear. No one here. I booby-trapped the door; we'll hear if anyone comes through. No other entrance, only the overhead. I checked when we got here; it has a manual override. We can get out that way."

"I pulled the wires on the cameras; we can use the light."

"We're going out," Mary Lee said. "Jen first, you next Robin, me last. Anything happens, do what we tell you. If we say down, you get down, flat, hands over your head. Immediately. We run, you run. Got it?" Mary Lee waited for Robin to acknowledge.

This was the stuff of nightmares. But it wasn't a nightmare. She hoped she'd live to have nightmares. She didn't question they were in trouble. Electric and generator going out at the same time as the phone? Not a coincidence. Phone first. Other way around, if it had been a digital phone, maybe. But this one was a hardwired old-fashioned landline, not dependent on electricity. Everyone had at least one for hurricanes.

Robin nodded, whispered, "Yes."

"Let's go."

Jen turned on her thin flash, held it to the side, leading the way. When they reached the overhead, Jen backed them against the wall, double checked with Mary Lee, then grabbed a cord hanging from the motor on the ceiling in front of the door. She pulled it and the door rose about two feet. She stepped quickly to the door, checked again with Mary Lee, then dropped and rolled under the door and was gone. Robin listened to silence for a moment, then heard a whispered, "Come."

Mary Lee pushed her down and under the door, rolled out after her. Jen took off at a run toward the SUV; she unlocked it as she ran and turned on the engine with her remote. She opened the back door and helped toss Robin in. "Down on the floor. Stay there," she ordered as she closed the door quietly. She got in the front. Mary Lee was already around the other side jumping in. Jen gave one quick look around, gunned the engine, and shot out of the parking spot. She took off to the end of the road, making a scary left heading north on the boulevard.

They hadn't gone far when Mary Lee pulled her cell out. Called Colin. She gave him the bare facts. No cell coverage, fake wines, landlines out, electric off, backup electric off, locked door. Exit through garage.

Not escape, Robin noticed. Exit. It had felt like escape.

Mary Lee asked, "Where do we go? Not the police station. The only people at the house were cops."

Jen slowed the vehicle to blend into the heavy traffic as they waited for a reply. "We weren't followed," she said glancing in the rear view.

Robin dared to speak. "The hotel is up this road. The bar. Bar manager and bartender are friends. One is ex-special forces, worked with Colin."

"You hear?" Mary Lee asked Colin. "Putting you on speaker."

"The hotel could work," Jen said. "It's straight ahead. Who is this bar guy?"

Colin answered, "Seldon. He's okay. Go. I'll call and tell him you're coming. You should be there in three minutes doing the speed limit. He'll meet you out front. Do what he says. I'll get there as soon as I can."

They reached the hotel in less than three minutes and Seldon was waiting on the east side of the street across from the hotel.

"That's him. That's my friend."

He motioned them into the lot. Jen turned in and waited for him to point out a spot hidden behind a wall. She backed the vehicle in.

Meanwhile Mary Lee had her makeup kit open. She pulled out a hairy ball and shook it. Passed it to Robin. "Put this on." She was taking off her shirt, not the least bit embarrassed to be stripping. The hairy ball was a short-cropped mousy brown wig. Robin tugged it onto her head. Mary Lee tossed a shirt at Jen. She pulled another item from her case, unrolled a sun hat, and handed it over to Robin. Then she slipped a tan blouse over her own head. All before Seldon could walk to the car door. No one would recognize them as the three women who had run from Dutch's.

Jen stepped out of the car, told Seldon, "You lead. I'll walk beside you. Robin behind us with Mary Lee. No hurry. Merely a group of tourists out for a walk. Where are we going?"

"Across, through the side entrance, into the bar office. It's private. Colin's on his way." He led the way across the street and down a narrow paved pathway and turned to the right, to a door marked private. Jen walked close beside, head swiveling as if looking at the paintings and photographs on the walls, but she was more likely keeping an eye out for anyone following. Mary Lee sauntered behind her with Robin, keeping a comforting and controlling hand on Robin's arm.

Jen kept her hand on her weapon as Seldon opened the door to the office. She motioned for them to wait and stepped cautiously into the room and disappeared for a moment. Mary Lee kept a restraining hand on Robin's arm. Jen reappeared with an okay gesture motioning to them to enter. Then she closed and secured the door behind them.

Seldon nodded in approval.

Robin's phone had been pinging since they reached the hotel. Now she pulled it out. Calls, text messages. Mary Lee took it away before she could respond. She turned it off, opened it, and took out the battery. "We can't have anyone track it; I'm sorry."

"Doug's bringing in food and drinks. Coffee is on the credenza," Seldon said.

"Who is Doug?" Jen asked.

"He's the bartender," Robin explained before Seldon could answer. "He served with Colin. Seldon and Doug are the ones who called Colin to protect me."

The women relaxed a little. "We'll wait until he comes. Robin, stay away from the door. Out of sight."

Seldon didn't look annoyed at her instructions, but almost proud.

Two minutes later, Doug knocked. "Food's here."

Mary Lee went to the door, stood to the side. She opened it, cautiously looked out to find Doug standing against the far wall holding a tray with sodas and snacks. Seldon reached out for the tray; Doug handed it over. "Colin called," Doug said. "He'll be here in ten." Then he turned and left.

Relaxing a little, Jen said, "I'll take a cup of that coffee." She walked over to the pot.

The phone rang and Seldon put it on speaker. Becca said, "Colin's driving. Robin there?" Becca's phone was on speaker; they could hear the whine of the engine in the background.

"Yes," Jen said. "And two men here who are strangers?" She made that a question.

Colin's voice came from a distance. "Doug and Seldon. Both are good men. I just talked to Doug. He'll keep watch from the bar. You can trust him. Who was in the house with you?" Colin asked.

"We don't know; we've been in the cellar all day. When we got there, two agents on guard duty, plus Agent Caruso, and a Ms. Leach who was completing an inventory. But that was hours ago."

Road noises came through the cell again along with Ryan's voice. "We have to call the FBI. It's their property, their agents."

"My dad's right. What about the local cops? Yes, we want the local cops there too." Colin was thinking out loud, answering his own question. "I'll do it. I'll call Ramirez. Well, Becca will. We'll be there soon." The cell cut off.

Robin pulled her cap off and then stopped. "I can take it off? Right? It's okay now?"

"While we're inside. But keep the wig on," Jen said. "We might as well get comfortable."

Robin wandered over to the drinks. "No wine?" she tried to joke. "Scotch? This is a bar isn't it?" She reached for a Coke and noticed her hand shake. "Can someone tell me what happened? I know why we're hiding and why we rolled under the garage door." She collapsed into a chair because her legs suddenly felt weak. "But why did the power and phones go out to begin with?"

Jen answered. "Probably because you found the fake wines. They were watching on the security cameras. The power going out and the landline failing at the same time were not coincidence. Someone did that. And locked us in the cellar.

"What cameras?" Seldon asked.

"Security cameras spaced around the cellar. Someone was watching. Someone inside the house who could pull the breaker and cut the phone lines."

"That's why you wouldn't go to the police station?"

"Right. We don't know who was in the house at the time. We do know three FBI agents were there earlier. Law enforcement. We don't know their status. Colin will get Ramirez to go check. Ryan will do the same with the FBI."

Mary Lee continued, "Colin hired us to protect you. That's what we did. We got you out because there was no way to know what would happen next. Were we only locked in the cellar? Or were they going to follow up with deadly force?"

Robin concentrated on her breathing. They both sounded so matter of fact, so calm. But this was what they did, Robin reminded herself. Protect people. She stood. "But those guys were after Patsy. Not me. I thought we knew that."

"We thought we did. Now?" Mary Lee shrugged her shoulders. "This looks like it happened because you discovered the fake wines. It doesn't feel like a snatch. But we don't know, and either scenario could be dangerous."

Jen's cell rang; she checked it, nodded as it was followed by a knock at the door. "That's Colin."

Colin, Becca, and Ryan entered. Doug behind them, crowding the room.

Mary Lee said, "This wasn't a snatch and it's not related to Patsy. That wouldn't make any sense. This feels different. The timing's too perfect; immediately after Robin found the wines. Had to be someone on scene to see us and act. Someone who knew where the breaker was, knew about the landline, the cell phones. Someone in the FBI maybe? Or the civilian? What's her name? Leach?"

"Inclined to agree," Colin said. "Doesn't make this any easier. Two different crimes? Kidnapping and fake wines? Is this overkill for fake wines?"

"I think," Robin said slowly, "it's the fake wine bottles. I think the glass is the same as the broken bottle I saw in the warehouse where that man was killed. I think I saw one of those fake bottles."

Colin said, "They think, or know, Robin can match the rare wines at Dutch's to a murder?" He exchanged a look with his dad who took it up.

"Does sound like it's tied to the bogus wines. You said you had a list of wines to check?"

Robin pulled it from her pocket. "Agent Caruso said the bottles were chosen at random; this is the list of ID numbers."

"The bogus wines were on the list?"

"Um. No. Not so far. I found one fake bottle. It was beside one on the list. I wasn't supposed to go into the locked cage today. But I was curious. I knew Dutch had some very rare and exotic wines. None of them were on the random list. I wanted to see if they were in the cage."

"What cage?"

"A locked room in the wine cellar. I assumed those wines would be in there. I wanted to see them. And I had a key. Agent Caruso gave me the whole key ring."

Ryan laid it out. "Maybe opening the door triggered the reaction. Whoever it was, they're smart. Can think on their feet. Spur of the moment. They lock you down and take out a guard or two? Who made the list of wines you were to check? Caruso?"

She nodded. "He gave it to me."

"You call him?"

Robin nodded. "He's not answering his cell."

"Of course he couldn't," said Jen, "if he's at the house. No cell reception. And the landline is cut. So it's either him or he's down. Or locked up the way we were."

"Ramirez should be there by now. He wasn't too interested until I told him you were involved, Robin," Colin said. "Then he demanded to know your location. Got pretty angry when I wouldn't tell him. I don't think it's a good idea to tell him. Not yet." He was asking for her understanding. She nodded again.

"What about Agent Tucker?"

"My dad called him when he couldn't raise Caruso. Agent Tucker is on his way too."

"Aren't you afraid someone will track your cells?" Robin asked. Still smarting at her own being disabled.

"No. No one tracks our cells," Colin replied. "Now we have to decide where to stash you."

"She can stay here in the hotel. Maybe on the same floor as Patsy," Seldon suggested.

"But I have a perfectly good home, Seldon. With new security," Robin argued.

"Think of it as a vacation. Employee discount. Two rooms. Off season, shouldn't be a problem."

Two rooms? Was he kidding? Why two rooms? But Colin was still talking.

"We could work with Patsy's guards. Would be our people plus Patsy's. Double the security for both women."

"Their first job will be to protect Patsy, not Robin," Jen said. "Ours is to protect Robin. But it would double our perimeter defenses. Especially if we had connecting rooms. They are our people, Patsy's guards. Shouldn't be a problem working together."

Before Robin could comment, Colin asked her, "Do you have to call in to work? Will anybody be waiting for you?"

"No. No one is expecting me until my class tomorrow." But then she asked, "Have I put everyone in danger? With this simple inventory?"

Seldon glared. "You didn't do anything. None of this is your fault."

"He's right," Becca said. "The person to blame is the one who cut the power. Seldon, can you get the rooms? Will it raise questions?"

"No. Sometimes the staff will rent a room."

"Next to Patsy. Daffy will have a second room rented. Probably at the end of the corridor. Get the next two connecting."

Seldon returned in fifteen minutes. "I made them in my name. Patsy is by the emergency exit, next is Daffy, we're the next two."

They moved out, with Colin first, Ryan and Becca bringing up the rear. Robin with her cap back on in the middle with Mary lee and Jen on either side of her. They took the service elevator using Seldon's keycard to reach the top floor where the elevator doors opened into a plush hallway. Robin saw Becca nudge Colin, pointing her chin to the cameras. Seldon walked to number 527 and unlocked it.

"Jen and I'll clear the rooms. You folks wait here," Mary Lee said. Again, Robin noted the teamwork. Everyone waited, even Colin. No argument. So there must be rules, protocols. It was the same way the two women had worked together in the wine cellar. Without communication they checked the suite and then unlocked the connecting doors and did the same in the next suite.

Robin was ushered inside to a small dining area with a table and four chairs. To the right she could see a kitchen with a coffee maker and microwave on top of a counter. A small refrigerator with drawers underneath, cupboards overhead. A large living area was straight ahead furnished with a blue couch and two paisley chairs, coffee and end tables. There was a large flat-screen TV on the wall. She could see a slider and balcony and a view of the gulf on the other wall. The bathroom had a Jacuzzi tub and a walk-in shower with a dozen nozzles. To the left was the bedroom with a king-size bed, a small desk and chair and another flat-screen TV. The connecting door led to the second suite which was a mirror image of the one they were in. Plush. She imagined Patsy's rooms were the same.

Mary Lee's cell chimed and she gave it a quick look. "Daffy. Wants to know what's happening. He must be hooked into the hotel security system." She put the phone away and left to confer with the Daffy person.

**

"What the hell do you mean?" David said in a hoarse whisper which was all he could manage when Colin reported the power outage and the escape from Dutch's. "That doesn't make any sense. No one is after Robin. They're after Patsy." Scott glanced over from his desk. David raised a finger for him to wait, found his voice. "No one's after Robin."

"Power and phones went down; my people didn't want to take any chances. They removed Robin from the premises."

Shit. "Is she all right? Where is she?"

"She's okay. She's at a safe place."

Scott stood, concern on his face.

David snarled at him. "It's Gibbs. Someone went after Robin."

"But they're after Patsy," Scott objected and pulled on his shoulder holster.

"I know. That's what we thought anyhow." David shook his head, ran his fingers through his hair.

"Where is she?" he growled into the phone.

"Safe place. That's all you need to know."

"The hell it's all I need to know. Where the hell is she?" He was roaring now.

"No one needs to know where she is."

David knocked his chair back. "Tell me where she is or I'm going to come over there and tear your head off."

In one part of his mind, David could give Gibbs credit; he didn't laugh at the empty threat. The other part wasn't sure it was an empty threat.

"She's safer if no one knows where she is," Colin replied in a reasonable tone.

"I'm. Not. Anyone," he growled.

Scott walked over.

"I'm not anyone," David repeated. He wasn't. He was her…what? Lover? Not anymore. Friend? She'd said not yet; it was too soon. Shit. He took a breath and forced himself to calm down. "I'm not anyone. I'm a cop." That's all he was. A cop who cared about her. "If she's hurt—".

"She's not hurt. My people evacuated her without incident and took her to a safe place. Being a cop doesn't get you her location. Cops were the only ones who knew where she was. I'm on my way to her now," Colin said.

"Tell us what happened; I have you on speaker."

Gibbs outlined the incident. David retrieved his own weapon from a drawer and attached it to his belt. "We're on our way. Stay available," David said and they headed for the exit.

Scott drove. David called Robin. Tried to call; the calls didn't go through. Neither did a call to the mansion.

Scott didn't use the siren—wouldn't do to announce their arrival—and he drove slowly past the house once, before coming back. No cars in the driveway. The place looked quiet. Scott backed in. They stepped out, looking round. Still quiet. They walked to the door, cautiously. Tried it. Locked. Scott knocked. They waited. Nothing.

Scott knocked again. Still nothing.

David went back to the car for flashlights for both of them. "I'll check the outside." He headed around the building, down the drive to the lower garage, checking windows and doors on the way. He could see the garage door raised about two feet. He knew he'd make a good target backlit, but he stooped down and quickly scooted inside, rolling to the left. No noise, no movement. The place felt empty. He made a quick visual of the room; enough light spilled in from outside. It was empty. He held the flashlight out to the side, away from his body, then turned it on and checked the dark corners, under and behind the cars. No one.

He headed to the door at the far end, opened it, and shone the flash around. Wine cellar. Did a walk through, checking behind the counter. Stepped into the cage. Then he went back out and tried the door to the stairs and the elevator. Stairs door locked; not from this side. The elevator door stayed shut. No power. He'd found exactly what Gibbs had said he would. The cellar was clear. He pulled out his cell to tell Scott; no bars. He finished his circuit of the building and returned to his partner.

"All clear. I didn't see any signs of trouble," he told Scott who was holding the mic in the unmarked vehicle.

"I had HQ contact the fibbies. Two agents man the house here all day. It's quitting time, they think the agents might have gone home.

They're trying to contact them. No luck so far. They're sending someone with keys. Ryan Gibbs had already given them a heads up. We're to wait."

A dark blue unmarked sedan pulled in about ten minutes later. It parked next to their car. One man exited, Agent Tucker.

"What do you know, Ramirez?" he asked.

"The place is locked up tight, except for the garage door and the wine cellar. The inner cellar door is locked."

"SWAT team?" Tucker asked.

"Nothing we've heard so far says SWAT. I didn't see any signs of damage inside. You have a key?"

Tucker pulled it out.

Another car approached, Dodge Charger, black. It parked on the street. Ryan Gibbs stepped out of the passenger door and spoke to the driver. Then he walked up the drive. The windows were tinted and David couldn't see the driver.

Gibbs said, "I'm observing. Do we know anything more?"

When David filled him in, Gibbs summed it up. "No one tried to hurt Robin or her crew. They merely cut them off. Locked them up. We can take a quick walk through. Turn the power back on. If we see anything sketchy we can always call in SWAT. Might need a search team if HQ can't locate the two agents. Tucker, you have a floor plan?"

David smirked. Observing. Sure.

Tucker called it up on his tablet and pointed out the rooms. "We go in the front. I'll go to the left and clear the sitting room, Gibbs goes ahead and checks the dining room. Ramirez, and Scott to the right, library and TV room. Den is straight down the hall. That's where my guys were set up."

They drew their weapons. Tucker unlocked the door and they edged in, flashlights held away from their bodies. They checked and cleared each room and met at the desk. Tucker looked at the blank monitors.

"Everything looks normal. Like they shut down and went off duty. This whole thing happened about quitting time. Someone might have come in after my guys left."

"Wouldn't that set off the alarm?" David asked.

"Should."

"Would it work if the power was off?"

Tucker shrugged his shoulders.

"Where's the fuse box?" David asked. That would tell them something.

"Laundry room off the kitchen." Tucker led the way, weapon drawn again. He opened the box on the wall in the corner and, after a quick look around for agreement, reset the breaker. Lights flooded on and they heard the A/C kick in. "Yep, inside job, but before or after the agents left?" Tucker muttered.

Gibbs clicked his tongue. They turned to him. He pointed to the butler's pantry. Double doors, everything in the house was double doors, wedged shut with a broom handle. A rolling serving cart braced in front.

Now they were back on alert, guns pointed toward the doors. Tucker crept beside the doors and shouted, "FBI!"

They heard pounding on the door and two voices yelling over each other. Tucker stayed to one side. David moved to the other. He leaned forward and unlocked the wheel to the cart. Making sure the others were out of the line of fire, he shoved it away then pulled the broom out of the door handles.

The two agents tumbled out. They stopped short when they saw Tucker.

"Sir," one of them said.

"What happened? How did you wind up locked in there?"

They both answered at the same time. Tucker held up a hand. "You first, Edwards."

"Yes, Sir. Ms. Leach, she, um, she said we had to see something she found in the butler's pantry. We went in, and she slammed the door shut and locked it. A few minutes later the lights went out. Came right back on, and then quit again and stayed off. We hollered for her to come back and let us out." He looked at his fellow agent for confirmation; he nodded.

"You have anything to add to that Walters?" Tucker asked.

"No, Sir. She locked us in and left, I guess. Cell phones don't work here. We thought she was playing a joke and would be back." He seemed to realize there were people he didn't know. "What's happening Sir?"

"We were hoping you could tell us." They holstered their weapons and Tucker led them back to the operations desk.

"Why are the monitors dark?" Tucker asked motioning to the panel of twelve monitors.

"Ah, Sir, um, they're always dark." Walters looked to his partner again, who jumped in with an explanation.

"Right, Sir. Always dark. Sometimes when we come on duty they're on. They don't show anything but empty rooms. The pictures are static, except for the desk of course. But they generally go dark. Asleep, I think they call it."

"Asleep." Tucker said quietly. "Asleep? The security monitors go to sleep? You don't question why? Were you asleep too?"

"Oh, no, Sir. We were awake. Working on our laptops. We never went to sleep, Sir."

Tucker wiped his hand over his face. Gibbs looked down. Scott rolled his eyes. David shook his head. It would have been comical if Robin wasn't involved. On so many different levels. FBI agents not monitoring the monitors? How stupid were these two guys? Everything they said made it worse.

"You are stationed here to ensure the house is covered and you don't turn on the monitors for the security cameras?"

"Oh, there's no reason to do that, Sir. No one here but us. They'd turn on if anything happened; the cameras are on motion sensors and the movement would turn on the monitors. They're just asleep."

"What about Ms. Leach? Didn't the monitors follow her? Wasn't she working here?"

They looked at each other again. "Oh, right. I guess she didn't go into any room where the cameras are located?"

"The cameras are in every room, Edwards. Didn't it ever occur to you that something was wrong?" Tucker let his irritation show.

"Um, no, Sir." For the first time Edwards seemed to realize there was a problem.

Tucker walked to the wall and pushed a switch. The monitors jumped to life. All static views of empty rooms. After a few seconds, a different set of rooms. One monitor showing motion, the operation desk.

Walters jumped in to help Edwards. "See, Sir. All static images. No motion. Agent Caruso never said anything. Even today he didn't say anything." The man apparently saw an escape. "Yes sir. He was here this morning for a while. The monitors didn't come on then. And they didn't come on when he came back this afternoon."

Gibbs seized on that. "Caruso was here? What time?"

"I didn't see him," Edwards complained.

"You were in the john when he came in, around three-thirty," Walters replied.

Tucker leaned over and looked at the log. "I don't see where he signed in this afternoon."

"Um, no, Sir. He generally doesn't."

It was Tucker's turn to roll his eyes. "There are sign-in protocols for a reason, Walters."

Walters looked chagrined.

"Was Caruso still here when Ms. Leach took you into the pantry? He hasn't signed out." David figured that didn't mean anything. He was looking over Tucker's shoulder. If Caruso hadn't signed in why would he sign out?

Walters looked at Edwards again who said, "Don't look at me; I never knew he was here. I didn't see him at all, Sir."

Tucker gave him a glare that backed him up a step. Tucker turned the glare on Walters.

"Was he here when Leach walked you into the pantry?" he repeated, barely holding onto his temper.

"I guess so." Walters was nervous now.

"You guess so? Was he or wasn't he?" Tucker bellowed in his face.

"Yes, Sir. He was still here." Walters was looking everywhere but at the Agent. He seemed to realize Caruso wasn't present. "Where is he? Where's Leach?"

"That's what we'd like to know," Tucker growled. "Go sit down. Both of you." Swearing to himself, he turned to the controls.

"Monitors were turned off, but the cameras record to the Cloud. I'll run them back. How far back? What time did you say the door was locked? Maybe, just maybe, we'll see how that happened." He gave an angry glance at his two agents. "Have to let HQ know we found these two idiots, but let's watch the footage first."

"Try three-thirty, when Caruso arrived. It was around four-thirty when Robin accessed the locked room. We think everything was fine until she discovered the fake wines. Colin got the call around four forty-five. Three-thirty to five-thirty, that's the window."

Tucker pushed buttons. Three monitors became active. One displaying the two clerks at the op desk. A second recording showed Leach in a bedroom making notes on a tablet. The third, Robin and her team in the wine cellar. Tucker fast forwarded and they watched everyone speed up.

Leach walked through the room, touching objects, making notes. Sticking what was probably ID numbers on items, making more notes. Taking pictures with her tablet. Taking more pictures, making more notes, sticking on ID numbers. Even fast forwarded, it was boring.

"Wait," Gibbs said. "Go back."

"You see something?"

"I think, maybe." They all watched as the agent re-ran it. Leach moved her carry-all ahead of her on the floor. Bent over a figurine on the dresser, looked it all over. Turned her back to the camera and bent over again. Moved to one of the lamps and made more notes. Took a picture of it. "There. Stop. Go back a little. Slow it down. Watch the figurine. She doesn't photograph it or catalog it."

In slow motion it was obvious.

"She put it in her tote. That's why she was carrying that huge purse," Tucker exclaimed. "She's been stealing items. Not recording them. Think she did the wines too?"

Gibbs shook his head. "Maybe. Fast forward again.

The monitor at the op desk, showed Caruso's arrival. Lucky for Edwards the video would back him up. He wasn't there. A fourth monitor now tracked Caruso walking through the house. He reached the bedroom, snuck in, and grabbed Leach into a clutch. The embrace lasted a long time, even for fast forward. Soon they were stripping each other.

"Jesus," Tucker said.

David didn't want to watch, but couldn't take his eyes off the screen, as the two rolled onto the bed. Gibbs looked away. The rest of the men watched as the heavy breathing turned into quick penetration and moaning. Finally, it was over. The two were lying on the bed, naked, breathing heavily, when the tablet whistled. Leach sat straight up, looking at it.

"The wine cellar," David pointed to the other monitor. "Robin just opened the door on the cage. Must have tripped the alarm on her tablet."

They watched Robin enter the inner wine room.

Back in the bedroom, Caruso made a grab for Leach, but she eluded him, stood and walked to the tablet fully naked. She gave it a quick glance, smiled at Caruso. Tapped some buttons on the phone.

"She put the line on hold," Tucker said.

"Come join me in the shower." She beckoned Caruso and he smiled and jumped after her. They heard her giggle. Through the door the camera caught them in a huge white and black room, bigger than David's whole apartment. A giant white oval tub stood alone in the center of the room. The shower was out of sight.

Leach pushed Caruso backward into the tub and jogged out of the room. She slammed the door shut and pushed the dresser against it.

"Well, guess we know where Caruso is," Tucker said. "That woman thinks fast on her feet. Tempts Caruso into the bathroom and blocks the door. Strong, too. Wonder what she would have done if the door opened in." They watched as she dressed quickly. Threw Caruso's clothes under the bed. Put his weapon in her purse.

"She's armed."

The monitors tracked her back to the op desk where she put her carry-all down and told the two agents they needed to see what she found in the pantry.

"And, of course, my two idiot agents follow her and end up locked in; exactly like Caruso." He shook his head in disgust.

Leach ran down the stairs. Another view showed her locking the door. She came back and pushed more buttons on the phone, then went back into the kitchen and pulled the breaker. Everything went dark. Light came back on again. Leach moved over to a smaller box and pulled that breaker. "The generator," Tucker said. Wiped his hands over his face. "At least she didn't cut the phone line. Simply put the main line on hold." He looked down and released the hold button.

David reached for the phone. "I'll put out an all-points bulletin on her vehicle. Locate her home address; send a unit over."

"She's armed," Tucker reminded him.

"I'll warn my men. If she's connected to the fake wines, she's connected to a murder."

"We might want to watch her. Follow her," Gibbs suggested. "What she did here? She didn't hurt anyone. She's playing for time. Time to go back to her apartment, load up whatever she has. Maybe wire money to different accounts. Disappear."

"Maybe meet a partner. The person who did the wines," David added.

"If so, your men will be dealing with a killer," Gibbs said.

David asked for warrants to search her home, car, phone, and computer records. Plenty of probable cause. He ordered an arrest warrant based on the thefts from Dutch's and Caruso's weapon.

"Someone should look at the tapes; see if she swapped the wines," Gibbs said.

"I'll assign a team to the tapes." Tucker turned to his agents. "You two. Make yourselves useful. Go get Caruso and for God's sake, get him dressed before you come back here. I've seen a whole lot more of him than I ever wanted." He paused until they were at the door. "And, gentlemen. Remember, he may be Leach's partner in more than the horizontal mamba."

When they were gone he said, "How did they ever get so young and so green?" He scowled and used the landline to call in. Then he pushed some buttons and rewound to the morning video.

"I'll run the whole day. Let's see if Caruso is part of this." They watched as the two young agents arrived together. Caruso and Leach came in a few minutes later. After greetings, Caruso surreptitiously pushed the switch that turned off the monitors. Tucker shook his head.

A few minutes later, Leach headed out to work on her inventory in a second floor bedroom. The cameras tracked Caruso to the same room.

"I can't watch this again. Someone tell me when it's over." Tucker groaned. And then watched. It was a repeat of the earlier video. Well, the later video. Except this time the pair never made it to the bed. This time they were standing up against the door. When it was over, Caruso gave her a quick kiss, muttered, *later,* and left. Leach began her inventory. This part of the tape was boring, but better than the steamy X-rated scenes and now that they knew what to look for, they observed her pilfer four more items.

Tucker time-tagged the spots. "I'll have my people go through all of the tapes. Should be able to see who switched out the wines. Find out if Caruso helped or if he was simply here for the nooky. It will take time." He picked up the phone again to get the process started.

Gibbs sat at a desk and turned on his tablet.

"You sending an email?" David asked looking over his shoulder. "You think someone is checking their emails?"

"Text, wife, an update for Colin," he said as he typed.

"No cell service," Tucker reminded him.

"But we do have WI-FI and I can text to her phone number @ vtext.com from the laptop. It will be delivered to her cell. Watch and learn."

"You watch," David told Tucker. "I'll check the cellar door. You have a key?"

Tucker handed it over from the spare set he carried.

Scott went with him. David unlocked the door and walked into the garage; it looked different with the lights on. They cleared the garage again, lowered the door. Went back to the wine cellar and Scott almost grabbed his weapon when the light came on automatically. David checked the door to the cage and found the trip wire; a button, a silent alarm, stuck in the door jamb. "Might be able to find the source for that. It's pretty sophisticated." He couldn't stop the curse. Leach could just as easily have walked into the wine cellar and shot them. Bodyguards notwithstanding.

"Have to get with Tucker and convince him to let our forensics team work with the FBI. Find out who vetted Leach." For now, he took pictures, and they went back upstairs to work out the details.

Caruso came in raging. "These two jerks won't hand over my weapon. They won't even talk to me, except to say, 'Boss wants you'." He confronted Tucker, standing aggressively inside the comfort zone, his upper body leaning forward. His face was scrunched up. He was almost spitting.

The two agents had done something right, David thought, and watched as Tucker turned to his agent after pushing some buttons on the control panel.

"What makes you think they have your weapon? Have you lost it?" he asked in a dangerously quiet tone.

"No, I didn't lose it," he growled.

"You have your gun."

"No. I took it off to, um, shower. One of these jerks must have grabbed it. If one of them doesn't have it; you must, and I want it back. No one touches my gun, no…" His voice trailed off as his eye caught the tape. Tucker had keyed it for the final moments of Caruso's naked butt rolling off Leach. They watched the action unfold again; Caruso locked in the bathroom. Leach taking his weapon.

"No. I don't have your weapon Agent. As you can see. Your playmate took it."

"Shit. She took my gun?"

"Yeah. That's not all she took. Hand over your shield."

"What?"

"Your shield, Caruso. As of right now, you're suspended."

"Because the bitch stole my gun?" He was livid, his face red.

"That would be enough reason. Now shut up and give me your shield."

"You can't do this." He stepped even closer to Tucker, threatening and defiant.

"I can. And you should consider yourself lucky if that is all I do. Now, back off."

Caruso frowned, his hands were tight fists. "She stole my weapon. Someone needs to arrest her. I'm not the one at fault here."

David couldn't believe the guy was arguing. They had all seen the video.

"She stole your weapon after you had intimate relations, on the job, in a government-seized building."

"So, I took a few minutes out to grab some pussy. What's the big deal?"

"You mean besides burning up the sheets instead of doing your job?"

"What job? All I had to do was be on the property. I'm on the fucking property. I took a few minutes to myself." He smirked. "Call it a coffee break."

Not smart, David thought. First arguing and lying and now trying to defend a bad position. The man turned his stomach. He remembered the way Caruso had held onto Robin's hand back at the warehouse.

Tucker was as disgusted as David. "Not a few minutes. But I'm not going to argue the point. Ms. Leach has been recorded stealing valuables from this house. You are responsible for the security of this house and its contents. It remains to be determined if you were in collusion with her or not. Until we have ascertained that fact, you are suspended."

"What? What? I don't believe it. Stealing? You don't know what you're talking about." Disbelief added to the rage.

"That's the problem. You don't know. I could show you the video, but I'm not going to waste my time. We observed you turn off the monitors. That was recorded to the web."

"So what? This whole thing is crazy. I'm not stealing. No one's stealing. I turned off the monitors because the bitch didn't want to fuck with them on. No one stole anything. You're making a big deal out of this because you never wanted me in charge here."

Tucker drove his point home. "You didn't do your job. You were negligent at the very least."

"Alice? Stealing? She's a dumb blonde." He looked to the other two agents as anger began to change to doubt and confusion.

"Dumb blonde with your weapon. It might turn out that, of the two of you, she isn't the dumb blonde. Hand over your shield. Now. Don't make me ask again."

"This is crap." Caruso snarled, but handed over his wallet. "My uncle will be talking to your supervisor."

"Your uncle can't help you out of this. If you were working with her, I promise you, you'll go to jail. I promise you. Now, sit down, and be quiet." He included the other two in the order. They sat.

Caruso opened his mouth. His jaw worked a moment

Tucker pointed. "I said sit. Be quiet. When I want to hear from you, I'll let you know. You're lucky not to be walking out in handcuffs. And that might still happen. Sit. " Caruso sat as if he'd been knee-capped. With his mouth open.

Gibbs spoke. "That last figurine, I think I can identify it." He tapped keys on his laptop. "Can you go back to it and enlarge the base? She tips it over to check the signature."

Tucker did, and Gibbs read the identifying mark. "Lladro."

"Even I recognize Lladro. Can't you buy those for few hundred dollars?" Tucker asked.

"Some, yes. But this isn't one of them. Here." He turned his laptop around. "Lladro. Oriental Horse. Glazed. Eighteen thousand dollars."

They stared over his shoulder at the laptop.

"She took four items today. Say fifteen to twenty thousand each. Sixty to eighty thousand dollars is a nice take for one day's work."

And how many days had she been doing it? David wondered. He picked up the clipboard. Thumbed through it. Tipped his head to the two agents. "Your guys had her sign in. Or maybe she had to for inventory purposes." He continued thumbing through the sheets. "Ten, eleven, twelve. Looks like fifteen days in the last three weeks. A million bucks. Not counting the wines."

"May I ask Agent Caruso a few questions?" Gibbs asked Tucker politely.

Caruso jumped up. "Who the hell are you? And what the hell are you doing on government property? And these two?" Caruso growled, pointing to Scott and David.

"The one person who might be able to save your ass. Special Agent in Charge, Ryan Gibbs," Tucker said. "Now sit down."

Caruso glanced at his boss, ready to argue, but changed his mind and sat.

David leaned back against the wall, arms across his chest, enjoying the scene. He had his own questions. Be interesting to see if Gibbs had the same ones.

Ryan sat on the corner of the desk, non-threatening, amiable, and explained his involvement in a friendly, confidential manner. "I'm out of D.C. Visiting actually. Got dragged into this by a friend. We are all on the same side here and I think if we sit down and talk we may come up with some solutions which will make us happy. You don't have to answer any of my questions if they make you uncomfortable, but I don't think you will find them out of line."

Caruso looked around the room at the angry faces; his eyes caught his naked self on the monitor. Tucker had rewound the tape and paused it. Caruso wisely chose to talk to the man who offered hope.

"I don't answer any questions I don't like." A statement.

"Correct. That's fair. Anything you say or elect not to say, stays right here. This is a friendly discussion. We are simply interested in what you know about Ms. Leach. Hopefully your answers will give us a clearer picture.

"Okay."

"When did you meet her?"

He thought about it. "When Agent Tucker and I went to her office."

Tucker nodded agreement. "Three weeks ago. She's the assigned cataloger and we reviewed her duties."

"When did you see her next?"

Caruso pursed his lips, looked round the room again, nervously. At last he said, "That night. She came on real strong during our meeting and we hooked up later."

"Go to her place?" Gibbs asked.

"Why? How can it matter where we went?"

"Don't know until you tell us."

"Uh. She didn't want to go to her place. Said she had kids. Didn't know me well enough to go to mine. We went to a motel."

He must have heard how silly that sounded. *Not know him well enough to go to his place, but well enough to go to a motel for sex?* He shrugged his shoulders. "Made sense at the time."

"See her since then?"

"Few more times at the motel, and then she started her work here. All the beds and everything…"

"You suggest it?"

"Yeah. She said the motel was cold."

"She suggested it, not you?"

"I guess. Yeah. She was complaining about the motel and still wouldn't come to my place."

"She ever ask you about your work here?"

"Nah. Well, stuff like what times I'd be here. How many people on duty, normal stuff she needed to know for her job. Or, um, stuff."

"How about the monitors? You said she was concerned about them."

"Yeah. She freaked out. She didn't want to do anything if there were cameras recording. She wanted to know if they were in all the rooms." He stopped. Looked around again. Stared at the image of himself frozen on the screen. "When I told her they were, she cried and I said I'd turn them off."

"The cameras?"

"No. The monitors. I showed her how to do it, too, when she was still anxious."

"Didn't she worry that the cameras were still running?"

"Yes, but I told her they were live. I didn't tell her they recorded to the Cloud. That would have put her totally off any, um, doing anything. She bought it." He smirked.

Tucker broke in with a question David wanted to ask. "You weren't *freaked out* about your, um, escapades being stored on the web?"

He raised a shoulder. "I didn't think anyone was ever going to look at them. Besides, I thought I could always wipe them." He heard himself and hurriedly added. "I didn't do it. I didn't wipe them. Besides you promised nothing I said would be used against me."

"It won't. How come you didn't delete any files?" Gibbs asked.

Caruso did the eyes around the room again. Mumbled, "Didn't have the password."

Gibbs nodded. Didn't seem to care the agent had admitted he intended to destroy government files.

"You ever look in her purse?"

"No. Why would I?"

"I want you to think about this next question before you answer. Would you have checked her valise if you weren't shagging her?"

Caruso answered immediately. "No. She was vetted." David could see when it hit him. "Maybe." He looked down, rubbed his hand across his face. "She was playin' me? That's the way she was getting the stuff out? In her purse?"

Gibbs nodded sympathetically. "Yeah." He let that sink in and then said, "You never went to her place?"

"No."

"Or yours?"

Caruso closed his eyes. "One time. Sort of. She changed her mind almost as soon as we got there."

"When was that?"

"Saturday."

"Some reason she wanted to go there?"

"She said she knew me better. But then she changed her mind and asked me to take her back to the motel."

"You do that?"

"Yeah. It's what she wanted. No skin off my nose where we fucked."

David hid his cringe. The guy was a worm.

"When did she find out Ms. Garman would be doing the wine inventory?"

Hunh? David saw the answer before Caruso said it.

"Saturday. I told her when we met. She didn't like it. That's when she suggested my place. She asked me all kinds of questions. Wanted to know why she couldn't do the wines herself and I told her it was Tucker's decision. Period. I told her the sommelier would start with the regular stuff Monday. Sometime later for the more classy wines. She asked if the guy was doing a complete inventory and I told her a spot check from a list of random ID numbers which I would make."

"How did you set up the list?" Gibbs appeared to be simply curious.

"Didn't. Let her do it. After she did me." He smirked again. "She called it a makeup gift for letting me down at my place. Promised me today." He motioned to the monitors. "That's what that was today. Me collecting. I let her do the list. What could it matter? I mean random numbers. Who cares who picks them?" He shrugged his shoulders.

The silence in the room finally registered with Caruso. "What? She do something with the list? How can you mess up a random list? It's a bunch of numbers."

Right, David thought. Numbers you could manipulate to exclude any bottles of fake wine. Which she had apparently done. Caruso didn't know anything about the discovery of the bogus wines; he'd been locked in the bathroom.

"She have that big purse when she went to your place?" Gibbs asked.

"She always carried it. Said she had a change of underwear." That smirk again.

"She leave anything at your apartment?"

David hadn't seen that question coming. Where was Gibbs going?

"She gets me all hot and then changes her mind. Why would she leave anything?" Caruso asked with a puzzled frown.

David wondered also.

"I think this is a very smart woman. One who makes contingency plans. We saw that today. She was very careful, even though she believed the cameras were off. I'm thinking she had a reason to go to your place."

He let that hang.

"Ah," David said. "You think she left something incriminating at his place, to throw us off the track. She didn't stay because she didn't want to leave anything of herself behind."

Gibbs gave him the type of look you give a very good protégé.

"That. Or something she could use to blackmail him with." Everyone digested this new twist.

Gibbs leaned closer to Caruso. "You can't let her get away with that. You can't let her outsmart you. You have to show her. You must know something more that will help take her down. Think. All that time together. She must have let something slip. Something that will help us get her."

"Stupid bitch. Think she's so smart. She can't take on the FBI."

David smiled inside. Gibbs had him now. Gibbs was good. Had made it look easy. Heck, David himself wanted to come up with answers to help Gibbs.

"Wait, she did leave something. She took her bracelet off. Left it on the dresser. Said she'd get it next time."

Stolen bracelet probably. Something to tie him up. Caruso's job already was in jeopardy. He'd be lucky to end up in *Why Not Minot*, the FBI graveyard assignment in North Dakota.

"Probably left something he won't find, too," David said. "A planner would have more than one back-up plan. Something small, but valuable. Hidden where he wouldn't see it."

"I'll kill the bitch."

David shook his head. The guy was a moron. How he ever worked his way up the hierarchy was a mystery.

Caruso's mouth worked as he tried to take the statement back.

"Shut up. Just shut up," Tucker instructed him, "before I decide to forget we have a deal. A deal which does not cover your actions in this mess."

Caruso raised his chin and his mouth formed a tight line; he folded his arms across his chest. Anger and belligerence radiated off him, but he kept quiet.

A squad of agents arrived and Tucker put two on the command center; he sent two back to the office with Caruso and the two clerks. "They all write out statements. Caruso doesn't leave until I talk to him. No calls."

Tucker walked outside with Gibbs and the two detectives.

"Leach seduces Caruso and walks in and out like a free spirit and stuffs whatever she thinks she can sell into her purse. She has the monitors turned off, so no one can watch her. She do the wines?" He asked again.

Gibbs was nodding, but with a frown. "Inclined to think so. Too much of a coincidence to have two thieves here. I'd guess they have been working on the wines for some time, but they would have had to know what Dutch had in his cellar."

Tucker answered the unasked question. "Front page story. He spent a fortune at auction. Plus, an article in a wine magazine. Pictures of the house and the wines."

"Hmm. Then I think that means she definitely has an accomplice, the person counterfeiting the wines. I'd guess they used Fallern's warehouse to counterfeit Dutch's wine. Fallern saw an opportunity to cash in and made his own bogus wines to sell to Carlisle and some of his other customers. Leach or her partner, partner I think, killed Fallern, moved all the equipment and supplies out of the warehouse."

David nodded agreement and Gibbs continued.

"Leach brings the fake wines in her purse. Swaps them for the real ones and takes those out the same way. Fast forward to Saturday. Leach finds out she's not doing the inventory on the wines. She leaves incriminating evidence at Caruso's and does the random list, but creates a back-up with the buzzer in the door."

He paused. "Buzzer goes off; she moves fast. Locks everyone up. Gets out. She is quick. You saw the video. That was what? Ten minutes after the buzzer goes off; she has Caruso locked up and she is gone. She was buying herself time. Time to get out."

"Why didn't she want Caruso in her place?" David asked. "Something there that might clue him in? Her accomplice maybe?"

"Hah. He's a stupid slob who thinks with his dick," Scott said.

"Have to get in there and find out," Tucker replied. "We need an art expert for this one. Think Marty Martinson is available?" he asked Gibbs.

"He's tied up in Philly, but he can review your Cloud videos from there. I know someone local who might be able to help us out," Gibbs said slowly. "May Stratton. From the art thefts."

Tucker nodded. "She married Nick London, didn't she?"

"Yeah, we came down for her baby shower."

"Who are you talking about?" David asked.

Gibbs answered, "Marty is our art expert. May Stratton has an art degree; she helped the locals bust an art theft ring here and completed an inventory of the stolen art works. She could go in with the team when they serve the search warrant. But I don't want her looking at the videos until they are cleaned up." This last he addressed to Tucker.

Stratton was the woman David's buddy Sheriff Rogers had told him about when David had asked about Colin Gibbs.

Tucker agreed. "You get in touch with Ms. Stratton, ah, Mrs. London, and I'll get the warrants started. I want one for Caruso's place too; he'll give permission, but I'll get a warrant anyhow. I'm heading back to the office to do that. Hate to admit it, but I'm lost without my cell. You and Scott want in, Ramirez?"

"We'll tail Leach. Maybe she'll lead us to her partner. Or the stolen goods. Tucker, if you can document her switching the wines, that will tie her to the murder. High end collectibles and the rare wines are a big haul; they would explain why Fallern had to die. The timing works. He put the whole plan in jeopardy. Leach isn't the murderer, but she is most likely an accessory to murder."

They headed out, promising to keep each other updated. Ramirez let Scott drive; he picked up the car mic and called Polinski who was watching Leach. "We're on our way. She moving?"

"She's in a hurry. Packing things in her car. Getting ready to rabbit. We're watching from across the street. We have both exits covered. Dillon is out back; he put tape on her taillight. Make it easy to follow her in the dark."

"Good thinking. Twenty minutes." He hung up his mic. He leaned his head back and closed his eyes. "She's going to run. Thinks she bought herself a few hours by locking everyone up. Think she's calling her partner?"

"Yeah. For sure, she'll go after more pieces she can sell, probably stored where they make the wine. She'll go to their hideout."

"That's what I think. Would be nice to get the whole stash and the partner." He leaned forward and pulled out his cell, saw bars, keyed in Robin's number. No answer. He left a terse message. Scott was studiously avoiding eye contact. Easy, since he was driving. David picked up the mic and called in a wants and warrants on the Charger. Now Scott did look at him with a question. "Really?"

"Yes. I want to know who's driving the car Gibbs arrived in. Whoever it is, that's where he has Robin hidden. She's part of our case. We need to know her location."

"Just keep telling yourself that," Scott muttered.

The tag came back in moments with no wants, no warrants; registered to Doug Williamson.

"Why is that name familiar?" David asked aloud. "Hmm. The bartender at the hotel. I interviewed him. He was very protective, very concerned about Robin." Yeah. That was the vibe he got. Concerned? Or ready to move on her? Her staying with him; he didn't like it. It galled him. He didn't like the idea of her at the bartender's place.

This thing tonight? Wasn't about any kidnapping. She was in the wrong place at the wrong time and had gotten caught in the middle of a long-term con. His gut churned when he thought of her locked in the dark, not knowing what would happen, thinking she might be killed or kidnapped at any moment. He wanted to go to her, comfort her, smooth away the terror. He needed to see her, touch her, hold her. Determine for himself she was all right.

But first he had to arrest Leach.

"Your girl is okay," Scott told him gently.

"What do you mean? I don't have any girl."

"You hold onto that thought." Scott grunted. "She's not with the bartender."

"What makes you say that?"

"He was here. Driving. They could have put her up at the hotel. The bartender, the manager, both are friends. And, you said Gibbs knows those men guarding Patsy. They already have a team in place. Makes sense to put both women together."

The mic squawked. It was Polinski.

"She's moving. Went out the back. Dillon is on her. Traffic is heavy; we're two, three cars behind heading west, toward you on Radio. That cross on her taillight is the reason we haven't lost her. How far away are you?"

"Stalled at the light at Four Corners." He paused. "Heading east, now, on 41.

A few minutes later Dillon came up. "Turning north onto Commercial. Have to hang back, not much traffic here. Polinski, why don't you come around?"

"10-4."

David heard the sound of tires in the background.

"We'll take Davis to Airport," Scott said. Airport ran parallel to Commercial.

Another long few minutes, then Polinski said, "Can't get too close. She's the only vehicle."

"We're on Davis now, almost to Airport," David reported.

"She's turning left. Moving toward Airport. Too far away to see which road she turned on, but it may be Service Way Lane."

"On Airport," David radioed.

He listened to a short silence. Then, Pollinski said, "I'm passing Exchange."

The whole area was small businesses which either occupied their own buildings or leased units in industrial condominiums. The condos were similar to strip malls, but instead of separate shops, the buildings were divided into multiple units, each offering a small office and bathroom alongside a warehouse, or storage area, or work space. Some were long metal buildings lined with garage doors; others resembled upscale office buildings with the overhead doors in back. Many covered a whole block with entrances from both north and south. An assortment of businesses rented space: cabinet makers, car detailers, food suppliers, restaurant equipment and supplies, used books, anything and everything.

"Okay, we're nearing Exchange, paralleling you."

"Service Way Lane, she went down Service Way Lane."

Scott turned right at the red light and drove slowly down Service Way. David saw oncoming headlights. "There. There. A car turning south, just past the intersection." He pointed, speaking both into the mic and to Scott. "She's turning into one of those garage condo units. No one else coming. We're almost there." He spoke around the mic to Scott. "Drive by; we don't want to spook her." He looked down the alley as Scott drifted past. "One car, cross over taillight. About two thirds of the way down the building. I think there's about a dozen units. Looks like the alley could go all the way through to Exchange." He keyed the mic. "Dillon? Turn on Exchange, if you see her lights and this alley goes through, sit on it. Polinski, she turned onto the first lane east of the intersection; we're pulling into the next alley." Scott rolled into the next lane and made a three-point turn, facing out, headlights shining.

"Polinski, you should be able to see our lights."

"Be there in a minute." After a moment, he said, "Got you."

Scott cut the lights as Polinski made the turn.

David told him, "Head past us and check for a cut-through to Leach's complex. If you find one, block it."

Polinski drove past Scott. "No cut-through and our drive dead-ends."

Dillon reported, "Leach's lane does exit to Exchange. I'm here. Got it blocked."

Polinski returned to park beside Scott. Cut his lights. Exited his vehicle and walked to David's window. "What now? How are we going to play it?"

"We walk down there and see what we can see." He stepped out of the car and Scott pulled the shotgun from behind the seat. All three dashed across the front of the building. David peered around the corner and saw Leach's car parked with the lights off; he didn't hear the engine. A soft glow came from an office window. Suddenly, a car squealed around the corner. The three men dodged into the shadows as the car lit up the area and screeched to a halt beside Leach's vehicle. A man jumped out and ran into the building.

David edged around the corner and, staying close to the building, he eased his way down the alley with Scott and Polinski behind.

Loud voices were raised in argument and in a few more steps he could make out some words.

The first was a deep male voice. "…knew you were coming here. You're not taking anything."

An angry female voice replied.

David reached the office near Leach's car and took a quick look through the window. No one in the office, which was shadowy from light spilling in from the warehouse area. He tried the knob. It turned. He pushed the door open silently and slipped in. Scott and Polinski followed. It smelled…funny. A sharp, acidic odor. Then he recognized it. Vinegar. Stale wine.

He now heard both sides of the argument inside the warehouse. The female. Leach? "I told you. I'm not taking the fall. I'm not going to jail. They were looking at the wine. They'll know its fake. It won't take them long to realize I'm the only one who could have switched the bottles, and then they'll be coming for me. I'm not waiting. I want my half now. We've been over this. You keep the wines; I couldn't dispose of them anyhow."

David crept forward, careful not to bump anything.

The man spit out angry words. "They'd never have known it was you. They got no proof."

"They have enough reason to look at all those references and degrees you forged. They won't hold up under examination. You know that. They were good enough to get me hired because the contractor was in a bind and didn't check. Caruso didn't check either. I'm not hanging around for them to arrest me. I'm not going to jail. I'm getting out. It's over. I'm taking my share. You're in the clear. No one knows about you. You'd be smart to forget that last bottle and disappear too. I never got a chance to swap it. The sommelier never left the cellar. You can sell it to some other sucker."

"No. You don't take anything."

"We had a deal. I get half."

"You don't. You've screwed it up. Stupid bitch."

"I get my half and I'm gone. If they get me, I warn you, I'll give them you. I want my share."

The male voice said in a shocked tone, "What the hell? Where did you get a gun?"

Peeking through the warehouse door, David saw Leach pointing a gun at someone out of sight. He drew his own weapon, could sense Polinski and Scott follow suit.

The man's tone quickly became low and soothing. "Take it easy, Alice. God, you don't know anything about guns. You're liable to shoot me by accident. We'll talk. We can divide it up."

David inched forward. He could make out the man in the corner. He had his hands up, his palms raised in a calming motion. "Go ahead, take half. Whatever you want. The wines will be enough for me."

Scott moved to the other side of the doorway.

The man continued reasoning with Leach. "They can't prove anything. Merely that you got the job under false pretenses. They don't even know anything is missing. You were verifying what was there.

There's no record of the stuff you took. Calm down. They'll never know you switched the wines. Dutch could have done it. This is crazy. Put the gun down."

"No. I don't trust you," Leach said, her finger on the trigger.

David couldn't afford to wait. "Police!" he shouted. "Drop the weapon!"

The woman turned toward him. The gun moved to point in his direction.

David's turn to use a calming tone. "Put the gun down, Alice. It's all over. You don't want to shoot anyone."

For another five long seconds she did nothing.

"Come on Alice. Do it now. Before someone is hurt. It's over. You're only looking at theft. Less if you work with us. Pull the trigger and you have attempted murder. Or worse. No one's going anywhere. Put it down." He motioned toward the counter and held his breath.

She looked down at the gun as if seeing it for the first time. Lowered it to the countertop.

The man's voice filled the room. "She's crazy. She's crazy. She called me up and begged me to meet her here. She said I had to help her. When I got here she pulled a gun on me. You saw her. She was going to shoot me. She said she was going to kill me if I didn't help her."

Not quite the way David had heard it.

Polinski and Scott came in with weapons drawn.

"Put your hands behind your heads. Both of you," David ordered and motioned for Scott to cuff the man and pat him down, Polinski to do the same with Leach. He told Dillon to call for two squad cars to secure the premises.

David checked Leach's weapon, saw the safety was still on and handed it off to Dillon. All the while the guy complained, talking over his shoulder as Scott cuffed him and finished his pat down. "I didn't do anything. She was going to shoot me. She begged me to meet her here. I don't even know what this place is. She was going to kill me."

"And look what I found," Scott said as he reached under the guy's jacket and pulled a weapon out of his belt. A switchblade. Placed it on the counter along with the guy's phone. Pulled the billfold out of a back pocket. "Lewis Elliott of, um, Deerfield, Michigan. What are you doing in Naples, Mr. Elliott?"

"She was going to kill me. She had a gun. You idiots. Take these cuffs off me. It's her you should be questioning, not me."

Scott ignored the man's fury. "Someone will be talking to her, Mr. Elliott. I asked you a simple question. What are you doing in town?"

"I want my lawyer. I demand you get my lawyer. I'm not answering any questions."

Scott and David exchanged a look. "You can call him from downtown. Read them their rights."

"Mr. Elliott, why don't you go sit in the office with Sergeant Dillon?" David suggested, and Dillon took Elliott by the upper arm to lead him off. Sirens cut off outside the door.

"Ms. Leach, you are a suspect in a robbery and multiple kidnappings." Because that's what she'd done when she had locked Caruso in the bathroom, the two agents in the pantry, and Robin in the wine cellar. "Is there anything you want to say?"

"You shut up, Alice," Elliot yelled at her. "Don't say anything until we get a lawyer. You hear me?"

"How about it, Alice? You want to talk to us? He's saying this is all you."

She looked from David to where Elliott was still yelling at her from the doorway, then back to David. Undecided.

"Shut your stupid mouth, bitch," he hollered as Dillon dragged him out of the room.

That seemed to decide her. "I'll tell you everything. But I want a deal first."

David nodded. This was a woman who could think on her feet.

"You stupid bitch. They can't prove anything." Elliott struggled against Dillon. Officer Sanchez grabbed Elliott's other arm and together they manhandled him out of the building.

With Elliott gone, David relaxed and asked, "What can you tell us? We'll get you an attorney, but give me a hint. Because we know most everything already."

"Before I tell you stuff he did, I want a deal."

David shook his head regretfully. "What kind of stuff? We'll find it out anyhow."

"It will take you time. I can give it to you now. As soon as my attorney cuts a deal." She stopped, pursed her lips, came to a decision. "He shot someone. I think he shot someone."

"Who? When?"

"A week ago?" She motioned around the room. "His wine guy. I think he shot him."

The wine seller. "Okay. We can deal. Call your lawyer. I'll contact the DA."

He took her purse. "Phone in here?"

She hesitated.

"I'm just going to pull out your phone. Your purse will be processed and everything in it will be taken into evidence."

"Okay. Cell's in the side pocket."

He reached inside but didn't touch anything except the phone which he handed to her. Saw the items she'd stolen, plus a bottle of wine. He wanted to search the bag, check the wine, but decided he'd better wait until he had a warrant and the bag was processed. He handed the purse to Polinski to be tagged into evidence. "Take her downtown. Book both of them. Grand Larceny. Kidnapping. For now. Put him in a cell; put her in interrogation. Get them lawyers. We'll be down to talk to them."

Polinski walked her out.

Scott asked, "He going to be able to talk his way out?"

"Don't think so. We should be able to keep him locked up until she links him to Bobby Fallern. Then it will be murder. Fingerprint this place, maybe we can put him here before tonight." He motioned to the sink and empty wine bottles. "Looks like Fallern's secret room."

Two more squad cars arrived, and David ticked off a mental list of everything they had to do. Already had warrants for her; needed them for Elliott, cell phones, this place, who rented it, the files, and the computer. Vehicles. He pulled out his cell to start the process and put in a request to the DA.

Scott ran Elliott's tag and license and the car came back registered to Elliott in Michigan. "No local address. Maybe something in the office or on his cell. He'll probably use the Michigan address when we book him."

David nodded. "The weapon has to be Caruso's. He's one lucky SOB she didn't use it."

"Caruso's not your typical fibby. He's a screw up," Scott paused. "No pun intended. Can you believe he screwed Leach in that house? Never even checked her purse? Turned off the monitors." He shook his head. "Must have some high level pull to think he can get away with that."

"Leach sure knew how to keep him distracted. Doesn't look like her charms worked with Elliott."

They wandered around the warehouse waiting for a CSI team. The counter held multiple bottles of cheap jug red wine. And empty bottles. David nudged the pile of wine labels on the counter. Six different ones plus a stack of blank labels. He checked the garbage and found more. "I really wanted to search her purse. Not just peek inside."

"They'll do it when they book her," Scott said.

One wall with shelves held shipping boxes, all different sizes. Shelving on another wall held an assortment of objects. Vases, figurines, lamps, leather bound books. He bent over a tray of watches, not touching. Patek, Rolex, Hublot, Breitling. Geez, how many watches could a guy wear? All luxury watches. Another tray with some women's watches. Didn't know Dutch was married. Three, no four, trays of jewelry. Some hanging clothes.

"More here than they could have taken from Dutch's," Scott said. "It's a wonder anything was left in the house."

The back wall held a refrigerated cooler.

The warrants came through and they gloved up and searched the warehouse.

David opened the cooler and stepped in. It wasn't cold, merely chilled. Wine bottles. He whistled. "They have it temperature controlled."

And then he had a thought which brought a smile to his face. "Robin. Mrs. Garman. We need her here. To inventory these wines. And the FBI's art expert. We'll need her, too. Guess I'll give Gibbs a call and update him on our status."

Scott shook his head. "You got it bad, boy."

"What? We need them." It made sense. He wasn't doing it simply to see Robin, find out where she was. They really did need her to authenticate the wines.

Scott just grinned at him. "We do need both of them. But one of us has an ulterior motive."

"So, two birds." He raised one hand and with a shrug pulled out his cell with the other. He found the senior Gibbs's number and tapped it.

"Hmm. That's funny, went right to voicemail." He left a message explaining what he wanted and requested a reply.

CSI arrived, and he and Scott headed for Leach's. He wanted more information before he braced Elliott. It would be a long night. Not what he'd planned. He'd planned to see Robin as soon as he got off work. Tell her how he felt. Well, it wouldn't be happening tonight. Leach screwed that up. Now, with this warehouse, it might be days before he could apologize for what he'd said to her about Colin. He'd been jealous. He'd been an idiot. He'd admit it and explain. He snorted. Scott thought Caruso was stupid. Didn't come close to his own actions. At least she was safe. No one was trying to grab her. She'd been in the wrong place with too much knowledge. She'd been locked up at Dutch's because of the wines.

**

Robin saw Gibbs pat his pocket. It was the second time he'd done that in as many minutes. His cell, on vibrate. The guards were tense and alert, in 'protect and defend' mode again. But not evade. This time they were on the offensive. She was nervous with tension, wired. She and Patsy were huddled in the end suite by the bathroom door with instructions to get in the tub if shots were fired. If circumstances had been different she'd have found time to smile at the image. Both of them in the tub

Gibbs and Becca were by the door to the corridor, waiting. Jen was in the next suite at the door connecting to Patsy's room where Mary Lee and Reydar were with Daffy. There had been a brief meeting. Brief? Thirty seconds. Daffy laid out the plan. Ten seconds more for contingency plan B and the bathtub, though no one seemed to think they would need it. Apparently they had done this sort of thing before. Plan C, if something went wrong? The emergency exit.

The bad guys were here. Five of them.

She kept an eye on the monitor connected to the cameras in the hallway and inside Patsy's suites, the hotel cameras as well as the ones Daffy had set up. Patsy's suite was like Robin's, except different colors. Yellow and orange. Too bright. Another moment of peculiar levity. It was ludicrous that she was concerned about colors now.

Two men in yellow fireman's coats with helmets on their heads and the visors pulled low over their faces, one with the words Fire Chief printed in large letters on his back, the other with a name, Jones. The three other men wore jeans and white shirts. No masks this time. The fireman sprayed something onto the hotel surveillance camera, blinding it. Robin would have smiled again if the situation hadn't been so tense, because Daffy's cameras were still recording. That was the second time she'd found humor in this desperate situation. Something truly was wrong with her.

The fireman knocked on Patsy's door, the chief and a jean-clad goon stood beside him. The goon pulled a stocking over his head. Huh. Too late for that. The two other thugs hung by the elevator with a cart; they didn't bother with masks.

The monitor showed Daffy strip off his pants and muss his hair.

The fireman knocked again, holding a badge up to a peephole, blocking it. He kept his head down. "Sir, Naples Fire Department. We had a flame-out in the stairwell and need to access your room, sir."

"Coming," Daffy hollered through the door, pulling on a bathrobe, making sure everyone was set. He nodded to Mary Lee who pulled on a dark wig which wasn't intended to fool anyone for long, simply delay and confuse.

"We need to hurry here, sir," the fireman said.

Robin watched as Daffy set his gun on the counter and opened the door.

The three men pushed in, shoving Daffy back. He fell into one of the padded chairs. "What?" he said. "Fire in the stairwell? Are you evacuating us?" He started to stand.

"Sit," the chief ordered in a raspy voice, saw the gun on the counter and picked it up.

"Hey!" Daffy said. "That's my gun."

The chief held it by his side and scanned the empty room. "Where is she?" he asked.

"Who?"

The fireman opened the bathroom door, gave it a quick look, and moved into the bedroom.

Becca opened the door to the corridor and wailed, "I hate you! I hate you! How could you? How could you?"

The two men by the elevator turned toward her.

She dashed into the corridor and Ryan stepped out after her. "Honey, honey. Listen. It's all a mistake. It wasn't like that. Honey." He reached out an arm to calm her, but she evaded it and rushed toward the elevator.

"Don't come near me," she cried, tears streaming down her face. She swerved around the thugs and stepped inside, jabbing at the buttons.

One of the men grabbed the door. "You can't take this car." He reached for her arm. The other man smirked at Ryan who hurried toward her. "Honey. Please. I'm begging you. Don't leave."

Becca evaded the man, backing out of his reach. He stepped into the elevator and grabbed her arm. The other thug moved to block Ryan.

Becca kicked the man holding her in the knee and he collapsed with a yelp. The other man spun around at the sound and froze because Ryan was behind him with a gun to his head. "Federal Agents. Hands behind your head." The thug didn't hesitate. Ryan guarded as Becca handcuffed the man on the floor and patted him down and pulled a gun from his coat pocket which she put in her boot. Did the same with a knife she found in his pants pocket.

Ryan pushed his guy into the elevator with his buddy. "Down. On your knees."

Becca stepped over and used the flex cuffs on him. Searched him and retrieved another gun which she stuffed in her pocket. Then she cuffed both men's ankles. Ryan locked the elevator door open.

Robin and Patsy watched as Becca and Gibbs hurried to Patsy's suite. They took up positions flat on either side of the door. Becca peeked in.

The chief growled on the monitor, asked again, "Where is she?" The other fireman opened the closet doors.

"Nobody else is here," Daffy said, but he momentarily glanced toward the door connecting to the adjoining suite. A shadow moved past it.

The chief moved to the door, the firefighter flanking him. They stalked into the adjacent suite leaving the lone thug to guard Daffy.

Becca pushed the door open wide enough to slip inside with Ryan directly behind her.

Daffy asked, "What about this fire? Do we have time to pack?" Daffy added a nervous stutter. "How, how bad is it? Shouldn't we leave right now? Why are you checking the closets and the bathroom?" He kept the sentences strung together, his tone anxious and reached under the cushion.

"Mary, honey," he called in a high pitch.

The code words.

Four steps brought Ryan behind the goon standing over Daffy. "Police. Not a word. Turn around," he ordered.

Daffy was up, the gun he'd pulled from under the cushions trained on the thug.

The chief opened the bathroom door of the next suite. "Come out," he ordered with his gun raised.

Mary Lee turned around slowly to face him.

"You're not Patsy." He took a step backward.

The thug in the living room yelled a warning, but it was too late.

Mary Lee grabbed the chief's wrist, twisted it, and pulled him across her hip. Off balance, he tumbled down and over onto his back. She gave his arm one more twist and had the gun.

Reydar stepped out of the closet with his weapon trained on the fake fireman.

Both Becca and Ryan yelled, "FBI!"

"Stay down," Mary Lee ordered, putting the chief's gun in her waistband and pulling out her own.

The doors of the second elevator opened and Seldon and Doug charged into the corridor with the hotel's security people.

Then the cops were there and it was chaos for a few moments.

Robin and Patsy were ushered to the kitchen counter in Patsy's suite while the senior Gibbs explained the situation.

Everything was calm and under control by the time Ramirez and Scott arrived. Robin felt a small riff go through her when she heard him and her heart gave an extra beat. Part of her wanted to run to him. The more sensible part kept her where she was.

**

David could barely contain his fury. His teeth were clenched, as were his fists. Jesus. There was an attempt in the safe house? Five men? Jeeze. They were after Patsy. Five men had mounted an armed attack in the hotel? On the safe house? And Robin had been on the premises.

Not much had come over the radio, except no one was hurt. He'd gotten the full story on his cell. The bodyguards took down five men without a shot fired.

He and Scott exited the elevator to find two men wearing white shirts and black pants cuffed on the floor.

"You frisk them?" David asked the officers.

"Yeah. Mrs. Gibbs," he pointed at her, "did them first. They're clean."

David cast a questioning eye to Becca, frowning.

"I confiscated their weapons after Ryan and I took them down." She pulled a gun from her boot. "The .22 from that one." She pointed to him. "And this knife." She handed them over and pulled a small Colt from her pocket. "This from him." Like she did that sort of thing every day.

He ground his teeth and handed the weapons to his cops. "Log these in. You read them their rights?"

"Yes, sir."

"Take them downtown. Run them."

He turned. "Let's see what's inside." He strode into the suite.

A third man in a white shirt was on the floor and two firemen on the couch. All cuffed and still masked. Plus, a lot of other people. His men, hotel security, the bodyguards. Robin and Patsy sat at the kitchen counter and neither appeared anxious or concerned. He gave Robin a long look, wanting to grab her, ensure himself she was okay. She looked okay.

"Did you take the masks off those guys in the hall?" he asked his officer.

"No, they weren't wearing any."

Daffy added, "The firemen had their visors down. The other guy masked up when they came to my door after spraying the hotel camera in the corridor.

"They been searched?"

"Yeah. Weapons on the counter," Daffy said.

Three guns, two knives, brass knuckles.

Scott asked, "Sign out there says these rooms might be under surveillance. You have cameras running?"

Daffy nodded.

"Turn them off." It wasn't a request.

"Might be better to leave them on," Daffy said.

David frowned with annoyance at the suggestion.

"You might want to unmask these guys on tape," Daffy said.

"Yeah." David reined in his anger a notch. He wasn't thinking straight. "Do it. Let's get a look at them."

Scott pulled the mask off the guy in the white shirt. Moved to the fireman and raised the visor. "Well, well, well. My old friend, Billy Williams. He's local hired muscle. Fort Myers." He asked Williams, "Kidnapping is a little out of your league isn't it Billy?"

"Not saying anything. I want my lawyer."

"Of course you do," Scott said and moved to the chief. Pulled his helmet off.

"Oh my God," Patsy exclaimed. "It's Roger."

"Who?"

"The fire chief. He's Roger Swaine. He works for my father. Chief Financial Officer. He came here to write the check for the charity. I don't understand. Why would he want to abduct me?" Her voice held both disbelief and puzzlement.

"We'll have to ask him."

"I want my lawyer," Swaine said.

"Why am I not surprised. Get them all out of here." David motioned to his men. "Book them. Let them call their attorneys."

When the thugs were gone he said, "That explains how they got to you so easily, Patsy. Inside information." He looked around. "Someone tell me how this went down."

"I'll get coffee and snacks sent up," Seldon said and went to the house phone and David studied Daffy as he related the sequence of events. A simple report which, like Becca's, sounded like 'we do this all the time'.

"You expect me to believe you set up that plan and somehow, not only were you careless enough to answer the door without your weapon, you left it out for them to grab? How did that happen?"

"It was empty," Robin said.

David looked at her in surprise. Daffy too. She stopped short.

"And you know this, how?" David asked.

"Well, he emptied the bullets out before he put it there. I saw him." She stopped again. "On the monitor," she explained.

Daffy shrugged. "Left it there for someone to take. Felt they would be comfortable with my weapon and leave theirs holstered. Safer for us." He motioned to Jen and Mary Lee, Gibbs and his wife. "We've worked together before. Doing exactly this type of thing. The whole episode is recorded if you want to see."

David did and watched Daffy let the firemen in and Becca and Ryan distract the thugs in the corridor. "Like they did once before at a coin show," Daffy said. Story for another time David thought, as the replay continued. He was viewing a lot of replays lately.

"Huh." He was cooling off, getting himself under control. It was a well-planned and executed take down. Robin was safe and had never been in any danger. "Guess I was wrong. Good plan. Nice job."

He took a breath and said, "Agent Gibbs, I tried to call you."

Gibbs pulled out his cell, looked at it, and raised an eyebrow. "Two calls. Came in at the beginning of this whole incident. What did you have?"

David filled them in. "Scott and I thought we could use Robin to check the wines and your art expert for the other stuff. That's why I called." He hesitated, rubbed his jaw; it was half true. "It looks like we've solved the murder. Leach is willing to talk, implies it was Elliott, but wants a deal first. Her lawyer and someone from the District Attorney's office will work it out tomorrow."

"Oh, thank God," Robin said. "I can go home."

"No." Three people said at the same time and Robin looked at them in surprise.

"But you said you have the wine counterfeiters. And you have the kidnappers."

"You can't go home. Not tonight," Colin said. "We don't know if we have everyone. Until Leach talks, until Swaine or Williams talks, you stay here with Mary Lee and Jen."

"Oh." A different oh, this one filled with disappointment.

David moved toward her. "It will take time. Give us another day or two, honey." Had he just called her honey? Must have, because her attention was fixed on his face in surprise. He continued. "Be patient. Please?" he asked.

She searched his eyes and then looked past him again. "I'll do whatever Colin says."

He felt that jab, but she touched his hand to gentle the rebuff. "He's in charge of my protection."

David twisted his hand around and took hers, just to hold it. "Okay. But we need you at the warehouse in the morning to examine the wines, and I imagine the FBI will want your help." He checked with Gibbs.

"I am sure Agent Tucker will agree, yes. We'll need to see if your man has wines from Dutch's inventory, too, since we know some are missing."

Coffee and snacks arrived.

"Gibbs," Scott asked, "can you coordinate with Tucker? We still have to finish at Leach's tonight. We could meet with him tomorrow about ten at Leach's warehouse."

"I'll arrange it."

"I want to know where Robin is whenever she moves. Immediately." David said. He still held her hand. "None of this crap you had going tonight."

Colin's lips twitched. "We can do that."

David nodded once and squeezed her hand a moment longer than necessary, and then he and Scott grabbed coffee and sandwiches and took off.

Tuesday

When Robin arrived at Leach's storeroom with her bodyguards, the technicians were still fingerprinting, and David made the three of them glove up before entering. He led them through the office to the next room where Agent Tucker and Ryan Gibbs were talking with a woman.

"May!" Robin exclaimed in pleased recognition of the woman who created designer clothing from vintage fabrics at her shop on the Cougars Cove Dock. And May's face lit up when she saw Robin.

"Ryan told me you would be his wine expert. This is great. It's cool; we can be FBI consultants together." She stopped, an uncertain look on her face. "Maybe not the best of circumstances." They shared a hug. "Ryan was surprised when I said we knew each other."

"You're the best dress designer in town; everyone knows you. I knew you had a Master's Degree in fine art, but I hadn't heard you worked with the FBI."

"Back when I first came to Cougars Cove, I found some stolen paintings. It's when I met my husband. Ryan too. I'll have to tell you the story."

"Hey, May," Jen said. "We should all get together for lunch and shopping. You can tell Robin the tale and we can shop and eat."

"Great idea. Girls day out, a day off shopping. I could take a play day. We could …" But her attention was caught by something on the shelf, and she let go of Robin's hand to walk over and pick up a ring with an enormous stone which sparkled in the light.

"I know this ring and I know where it comes from." She held it out to Gibbs. "It belonged to Mademoiselle Domina and disappeared around the time of her death. It's worth a few million dollars on the open market, with provenance, which also was missing along with a bill of sale." The central stone was square with smaller diamonds on both sides set in a V-shape with more diamonds set in multiple bands. "It's unique; see, the center stone is a radiant-cut ten-caret diamond flanked with trillion shoulders and the split-band has these smaller diamonds. No mistaking it. I'll go through the files in the office here later once your guys are done looking through everything, see if I can find the provenance or a bill of sale."

Gibbs passed the ring to Tucker who passed it to Ramirez.

"It has a trillion diamonds?" he asked.

"No. Trillion is the name of the cut. Triangle-shaped stones."

The ring came back to May and she laid it in the tray on the shelf. "Guess these thieves didn't feel a need to lock anything up. I can't imagine leaving that ring sitting out in the open." She slid out the tray of men's watches. "These watches can be traced; each has an ID number. Might be paperwork for those also. The two Breitlings are very similar; I wouldn't expect one person to own both."

"I'll tell our CSI guys to look for any files on ownership." Scott headed into the office.

Robin began to sort through the papers sitting beside a printer on the counter and saw labels for a half dozen different high-end wines. Good labels. Good, but counterfeit. One was the champagne she'd found at Carlisle's, and she wasn't surprised to see the Domaine de la Romanee-Conti Grand Cru label. She ducked down and found the trash can full of imperfect earlier versions. Were they selling the wine? To people like Carlisle? Or swapping it out at Dutch's? She called up Dutch's inventory on her tablet. Yep, Dutch owned the wines. Half-cases and cases of each. Not any that were on the random list. She'd have to go back and check if Dutch's were real or fake.

Gallon jugs of cheap wine were arranged on a shelf under the counter. They contained wine the right color to fill the empty bottles on top of the counter which were the right shape for two of the labels. She made notes on her tablet and took pictures. Her guards wandered the room but kept an eye on her. David stayed close to her right elbow making her uncomfortable. So what else was new? He couldn't answer her calls or call her back but wouldn't give her space.

She turned away from the counter and opened the climate-controlled walk-in cooler. One shelf was covered with a cloth. "Can I move the cloth?" she asked the tech. He snapped pictures first and then gave her the go-ahead.

She rolled the cloth and caught her breath. Six bottles of 1787 Chateau d'Yquem. These would be the real thing; the ones stolen from Dutch's, swapped out for the fakes which were now in the cage. Six bottles at about one hundred eighty thousand dollars each. Close to a million dollars.

She remembered to exhale. The five missing 1907 Heidsieck champagnes were beside them. She couldn't help herself and reached out a gloved finger to stroke the weathered glass.

"I found the Heidsieck," she said, surprised by the reverence in her voice.

David was still beside her and the rest crowded in to look.

"This black glass," she said to David, touching it, not looking at him. "I think it's the same glass I saw in the warehouse when we found that man who was killed."

"What glass?"

"I saw broken black glass under the desk. When I thought I was going to be sick and put my head down. This is the same. This black glass—the fake bottle black glass. I'm sure."

He gave her a narrow look. "And you're just now telling me this?"

"No. I'm not just telling you now, Detective." Jerk. "I tried to call you when we first found the fake bottles, but the phones were dead and then the lights went out. And after that I forgot." She wasn't going to apologize. "I remembered last night and left a voice mail on your cell."

He pulled out his cell and scrolled through the calls. "Shit," he said under his breath.

Yeah. Idiot. She thought it, gave him a look which said it. "Which would explain why only five bottles were switched out. Not six." Robin said, thinking aloud. "The sixth bottle was broken when that man was murdered. I imagine it took time for them to find the right glass and then age it."

David said, "Leach had a black wine bottle in her purse when we booked her. I saw it. You'll have to tell us if it's the real thing or the fake."

Robin nodded. "That could make sense. Leach was really unhappy to see me, probably because she was planning to switch them out yesterday. I wasn't supposed to go into the cage, but I had time at the end of the day." She stopped.

David nodded. "I need to see those counterfeit bottles, and I need you to verify that the bottles in the cooler are the real thing."

"Oh, yeah, these are real," she whispered. Found her voice. "I'll need to check Dutch's inventory for those fake labels on the counter here, too.

Agent Tucker said, "I can run you over, quick. Won't need the bodyguards. I have agents there."

Jen gave Agent Tucker a smile. "We don't mind coming. We'll keep an eye on the agents, too. No charge." It was the same attitude they'd displayed when David had picked Robin up and suggested the two guards were superfluous in a building full of cops.

"She'll be safe at Dutch's." Tucker tried again with a frown.

Mary Lee said, "Will be, with us nearby."

"Okay, but no weapons."

"Our weapons stay with us; we stay with her."

When Tucker didn't respond, Jen added, "Where Robin goes, we go. Armed. If you want her, we're a package deal. Until you can tell us you have arrested everyone associated with the wine forgeries and the attempted kidnapping."

"Told you." David smirked at Tucker.

"Yeah, you did. Though it doesn't make any sense, with all the security we have." He shook his head and gave in.

So Robin found herself on her way back to Dutch's with Jen driving and Mary Lee in the shotgun position. David was with her in the back seat, and she sat as far from him as she could. Tucker and the crime scene team followed behind.

"Are you finding fingerprints?" she asked because the silence was making her uncomfortable. It took him some time to answer. "No. Leach and Lewis Elliott *gloved up* before touching anything. Elliott's claiming Leach called him and asked him to meet her at the warehouse, her warehouse. He insists he knows nothing about the thefts and is simply an innocent bystander. Unfortunately, we can't prove otherwise, because so far, we haven't found a single print. Everything is wiped clean, even the wine bottles and labels. No way to tie either of them to any of the stolen property. Or even, the warehouse itself."

**

This time at Dutch's she had to show ID which the agent compared to a list. He searched her bag; then put David and her bodyguards through the same process. All the while, Tucker nodded approval, smiled when his agents found the weapons and the permits.

Robin used the digital inventory to locate the wines and examined each bottle. It didn't take long; the labels were the same as the ones at the warehouse. She set the fakes on the counter, which made her think of another fake, David. It was sad. She'd thought they were in love and maybe she didn't expect marriage, hadn't really thought that far ahead, but she'd thought he loved her, that he was committed. Each time now when she saw him, she felt sad and foolish. Foolish for falling for his line. At least, after today, once she finished the inventory here and at Carlisle's, she'd be done with him. And, she was done with law enforcement. The thrill was gone. She was tired after a long day and a long night. She wanted to go home, to her own house, have a hot shower, laze in her comfortable rocker, enjoy her backyard, be alone. She'd look forward to that. Forget about David, go back to the wines.

"I'm guessing they didn't know what wines were in the collection, except for those in the news when Dutch bought them. They forged those labels ahead of time. Later, when they obtained access to the inventory, they selected these higher priced labels." She walked into the cage with the same sense of anticipation as yesterday.

Tucker said, following her, "Makes sense. I'll have one of my agents do some research on published articles. Got any more ideas?"

"I have some questions first. Wouldn't someone notice Leach was taking bottles out of the house?"

"You got a smart girl here, Ramirez. You want to tell her? I'm still too angry."

She looked from Tucker to David. What did he mean? David's girl? I'm not *his girl*.

"No one noticed," David said. "She carried a huge valise. It was organized to hold four bottles of wine in foam protector bags which were covered by a false bottom. She may have swapped three or four bottles a day. Maybe she made two trips a day. Swap two or three bottles in the morning, go out for lunch, drop the real bottles off at the warehouse, and pick up more fakes. She could have switched six or eight bottles a day." He stopped when he saw her shocked expression.

Tucker growled. "No one searched her, coming or going. My agent, Caruso, has been suspended without pay for two months and is going to lose his job. Even his connected uncle can't help him."

Huh. So, Tucker didn't like Caruso either.

David picked up the explanation. "On top of the wine compartment, foam sections were shaped to hold antiques and collectibles which Leach stole from upstairs. She put more packing on top of those and covered it all with her scarf and personal stuff. Simple, but clever."

"How did Leach know we were in the cage? Was she watching me? How could she do that?"

David told her. "She wasn't watching you. She had the door wired to alert her tablet if it were opened. I'm guessing she assumed you would notice the differences in the Heidsieck if you got a chance to look at them. She locked you in to buy herself time to get out of town. She was running when we caught up with her. She'll give us everything as soon as the lawyers work out the terms for a deal."

Robin nodded. "Then she really wasn't after me? Just anyone who came through the door?"

"No. Not just anyone. I'm thinking she panicked when the sommelier went in."

"She wasn't after me?" Robin asked again.

Tucker and David exchanged looks. Tucker shook his head. "No. But that's a guess. We still don't know who tried to run you down. Or who took two shots at you. We need to interview her and Elliott. I'd like you to keep your security until we have all our questions answered."

She laughed. "I don't think it's my decision to make. My security team seems to be in charge."

"Colin will say when," Jen agreed. "Not today; he wants her back at the safe house tonight."

"You mean where a woman was almost kidnapped last night? Seriously?" David interrupted in clear disbelief. "You're going back to the same place? How can you possibly think the hotel is safe?"

Mary Lee corrected him. "No. She'll go to a location where five armed men were taken down without a shot fired. To a location we have proven can be defended. But you didn't let me finish. Colin's open to her staying home. He'll decide later when we know more."

"Anyone after her will look for her at her house or in the hotel," he argued.

"Probably. But we'll be ready. Has Roger Swaine told you why he tried to grab Patsy?" Mary Lee changed the subject.

He shook his head in disgust. "All he's saying is 'lawyer'—and before you ask, the four tag-alongs know nothing. They're hired muscle. The fireman, Billy Williams, is one of Swaine's buddies from a gang he ran with in Fort Myers. Billy claims he doesn't know why Swaine was after Patsy. He simply went along for the ride. And the money. He doesn't think there was anyone behind Swaine." He motioned toward Tucker. "The FBI is following up on their history and on Swaine's background."

Robin wasn't happy at the thought of another night at the hotel; she was voting for home. The real danger was past. No one had been after her. The kidnappers had been after Patsy and they were in jail. The wine forgers were in jail. Though, a night in the hotel with this group could be fun. As long as no one invited David. She became aware he was staring at her and turned toward the bottles in the clear display cases.

She had never actually seen any of the rare and exotic wines, and she hadn't found any forged labels, but she had determined the ones in the warehouse cooler were authentic. The original provenance on the

Heidsieck had been stolen along with the bottles and replaced with reproductions. Fingerprints might help, she thought. Surely Dutch's would be on his own papers. She mentioned the thought to David thinking it might be a way of proving the papers at the warehouse were Dutch's.

She heard him mutter under his breath as he looked at his cell. She smiled a little when he cursed out loud, almost hoped the landline would be dead too, but no such luck.

"Good idea, Ms. Rogers. One of us should have thought of that," Tucker said.

She accepted the compliment. "I watch a lot of cop shows."

She pointed out the phony Heidsieck champagne, alongside the one real bottle and picked up one of the fakes.

It was David who saw the dried blood on the bottle. Saw the fingerprint in the dried blood.

The technician photographed it and uploaded the picture to the web for comparison. He scraped a small piece of the blood into an envelope.

"The blood could be Bobby Fallern's. And if we can be so lucky, the print could belong to Mr. Lewis Elliott of Deerfield, Michigan," David said. "When we finish here, we head to Carlisle's, be nice to find something we can tie to Elliott."

"Today?" she asked.

David nodded.

"I need to let Franks know. And I have a class to teach this afternoon."

"You don't have to do the whole inventory; just do what you did here."

"Still have to search the rest of the cellar." She stopped. "Wait a minute. I did see two of those labels on the purchase orders I entered into the inventory."

She pulled it up. "Here. Carlisle bought three cases last week." She showed David the form she had scanned in.

David checked with Tucker. "Did your guys already search at Carlisle's?"

Tucker pursed his lips, his eyes turned inward. "No. We took the cases and were waiting for Ms. Garman to complete her inventory." He turned to Robin. "Have you started that yet?"

David answered for her, "Yeah, she did, and she found some more fakes. Enough for a search warrant." He went to work on that, on the landline.

**

At Carlisle's, she matched all six of the labels. The bogus bottles were in the last stack, each in its own diamond rack. The techs took her prints. Jen's and Mary Lee's were already on file. Someone was sent to get Ian's. They all had handled bottles.

A call came for David notifying him Leach was ready to talk and Robin listened as he argued with Tucker over jurisdiction. The FBI wanted Leach because she had stolen from Federal property. David could keep Elliott; it was his fingerprint on the fake wine bottle and that proved Elliott touched the bottle at the time the blood was still wet. It was enough to hold him a few hours. DNA in the blood still wouldn't prove Elliott had shot Fallern, merely that he'd been nearby at a time Fallern was bleeding. Fingerprints on these bottles in Carlisle's cellar or on the paperwork would give David probable cause to arrest him. David needed Leach to implicate Elliott.

He left with instructions for Robin. "Call when you're done; I need the original documents, and you need to sign statements."

She considered saying something about his response to her calls when Mary Lee offered. "I'll call. And my cell will come up as *not provided*."

**

Two hours later, Ramirez and Tucker were still questioning Leach at FBI headquarters. Leach was happy to implicate Elliott and told them everything, but she had no hard evidence. Elliott had been working the wine scam with Fallern, selling the fakes to wine connoisseurs, wine buffs, self-proclaimed experts, marks. She did have a list of the buyers, which the FBI wanted. She hadn't been part of the scheme. When Elliott read about Dutch's wine cellar and heard the firm which had the government contract to complete the inventory had lost their art expert, he made big plans. He forged references and a résumé guaranteeing Leach would easily qualify for the position, and she had enough knowledge to sail through an interview. Her job was to switch out the rare wines and replace them with duplicates.

Once started, she couldn't stop talking. "The wines were Elliott's main objective, but he decided to take advantage of my position and grab any rare, top-quality items he could sell online collectibles: porcelains, figurines, sculptures, small paintings, jewelry. None of the pieces would be listed as stolen because I wouldn't enter them into inventory.

"But finding the black bottles was tougher than he had expected. He'd grumbled about it for weeks until he finally found six. Then, one day he came home from the warehouse livid.

"When I asked what was wrong he hit me and told me to shut up. He was furious. Screaming about a guy who had double-crossed him and how he had fixed him. Raving about some woman. Some bitch wine expert who had screwed everything up. He left in a rage."

Leach stopped and drank some water. "He was crazy. Waving a gun around. *He was going to fix her* he said. *Shut her up forever. Shoot her too.*"

David closed his eyes. He could see his fingers wrapped around Elliott's neck.

Leach continued. "The next day he rented the warehouse, the place where the cops found us, and two days later I read about that man Fallern. No one was supposed to get hurt, but a man selling fake wine was dead, and I know Elliott did it."

She drank more water. "I'm not sure, but I think he tried to run someone down, too. A woman, I think. He missed. And then he complained he couldn't get near her anymore; someone was always with her. He really bitched about it."

David walked to the one-way mirror. It was Elliott who had been trying to hurt Robin. Not Swaine. Swaine was trying to kidnap Patsy.

Robin was in the wrong place at the wrong time. But they still didn't have any hard facts or evidence.

He walked back to Leach. "Continue."

"When it came time to swap out the black bottles; he was missing the last one. I'd replaced five and wanted to just take the last bottle and its provenance. Let the FBI assume Dutch had bought fakes and had drunk the sixth bottle. I wasn't nervous about the fakes; they looked good, but the difference between them and the real thing was obvious. But Elliott was adamant. He finally finished the last one, and yesterday I was going to swap it out, but Garman came too early in the morning and then never left the area for lunch."

"How did you know Ms. Garman had entered the cage?" David asked even though he knew the answer.

"I booby trapped the door right after Stan told me about the sommelier. I wanted to know if anyone went into the cage; I wanted a warning, A head start." She looked down. Then back up. "One more day. One more day and we would have been okay. It's his fault," she said.

She blamed it all on Elliott. All his idea. She didn't want to do it. Any of it. But all he could see was the money they could make selling the stuff. When Robin found the fake bottles, Leach knew Elliott would take it out on her, because it's what he did when things went wrong. She wasn't going to let him beat her, and she didn't want to end up like Fallern.

Yes, Elliott was living with her. He'd been out when she went home to get her things. No, she didn't know for sure he killed Fallern. She hadn't known he owned a gun. But she did know where he might have hidden it. He had a secret panel in his car.

They took a break so David could send a team after it; the car was in impound.

Tucker was happy; he had what he needed, but David still didn't have Elliott wrapped up. He needed the damned gun. With Elliott's prints.

David checked his cell and saw an earlier message from Scott; Elliott was still proclaiming his innocence. *Leach was a crazy bitch*. His lawyer was demanding they let his client go.

A message from *not provided* twenty minutes ago. Robin was finished at Carlisle's. They would swing by Robin's house to pick up the file and come down to the station to sign statements. Which meant they should be arrive shortly. He texted back, *Done here; I'll wait for you.* Then he updated Tucker and headed back to the station.

He didn't believe anyone was after Robin, but he still felt uneasy. He didn't want her alone. No, he did want her alone. With him. How was he going to get through to her that he cared? It was like the fates were against him. Again, he hadn't responded to her call now and he hadn't checked his messages last night. Oh, he had an excuse. Following Leach, preventing a shooting, arresting Leach and Elliott. He and Scott had been making a quick walk through Leach's condo when her call came in about the wine. He'd ignored it; intending to get to it later. But later hadn't come; instead there had been the attempted kidnapping.

Last night he'd caught a couple of hours sleep and then went right back to work. Back to more interrogations. No one knew anything. Those who did know, weren't talking. And now he'd missed another call. He'd been busy. Screw it.

He met them at the door and settled them in the break room. "Leach confessed to everything. Elliott killed Fallern and tried to shoot Robin, then tried to run her down. After that, he couldn't get near her because Colin and then you ladies were protecting her. Leach says she never intended to harm anyone when she locked the doors; she was trying to gain time to escape."

And, most importantly. "The techs found Dutch's fingerprints on the letters of provenance in the files in the warehouse. Thank you for the suggestion. We'd have got there, but it would have taken longer."

He paused when Scott walked in, a smile on his face. "Ballistics just came in on the gun. It's the one used to kill Fallern and it's covered with Elliott's prints. And," he dragged that out. "Same weapon fired the bullets into Ms. Garman's vehicle."

"Yay." Robin jumped up and hugged Scott.

"Great." He didn't like her hugging Scott and gave him an angry scowl. "We have the murderer and the guy who tried to shoot you. As for the kidnappers. We don't have it all yet, but Patsy was the intended target. You were in the wrong place at the wrong time, Robin. Twice."

"What about the car thieves?" Mary Lee asked.

"Miami-Dade is still surveilling them. It's their investigation now, and, whatever happens, they'll take credit for the bust. I doubt if we'll even be mentioned."

"Carlisle? Was he involved?"

"No. FBI cleared him of everything but stupidity and greed."

"So no one is after me? I can go home? All this was a mistake?" She waved her arm around the room.

"No. You were in very real danger. From Elliott. And from Swaine, at the hotel and especially the other night at the wine auction." His gut clenched just thinking about it. He felt himself frown and cleared his face. He waited until she looked up at him. "Tucker said it was okay to tell you. He's fairly certain Swaine was on his own. You'll have to work things out with Colin, but as far as law enforcement is concerned, you're out of danger."

"Oh, good."

"Hey. I thought you were getting to like us," Mary Lee complained.

"I am, I am." Robin reached for her hand. "I do like you. I hope we can be friends. But I am happy to have my life back. Now I have to go teach my wine class and afterwards I'm going home and kicking back. Tell Colin. We'll get take out and open some wine." She'd already discussed the home option with Colin.

"Tucker's giving Ryan Gibbs a heads up, Colin probably knows," David said.

Jen stood. "Thank you, Detective. I know you didn't have to tell us and we appreciate it." She shook his hand. Mary Lee followed suite.

Robin looked at him long enough to do the same. "Thank you, Detective. For helping."

"I'll come by later with updates." Not a question.

"Sure." As if she had a choice.

He watched them leave, a small grin on his face. Then he saw Scott watching and growled, "What?"

"You've got it bad and you don't even know it."

David ignored the statement, because he was beginning to realize how bad he did have it.

David gave him a high five. "Let's arrest Elliott for theft. And murder."

And then he was going to be on Robin's doorstep.

**

There wasn't a parking spot in front of her bungalow; he had to park in front of the next house past the bulletproof SUV and Gibbs's rental. He smiled for the camera over the door and heard the security beep, and then the door was unlatched. Robin didn't look happy to see him; she backed away, waving him toward the kitchen as she reset the alarm. "We were just getting started."

The room was a flurry of activity. Her bodyguards were setting out paper plates and utensils, six places were set at the kitchen table, more on the counter. Colin and Daffy were opening Chinese food cartons and distributing chop sticks. The senior Gibbs manned the coffeemaker. Mrs. Gibbs served drinks, thrusting a beer into his hand. "Ryan's going to fill us in on the FBI's case," she told him. "Sit."

He gave Gibbs a questioning glance. "Only what Tucker has authorized for release. I imagine I have some newer information than you."

When they were all seated, David at the counter with Robin, Daffy in between them, and the cartons passed around, Gibbs began. "Patsy's original guards are back on duty; Daffy is back on vacation, and Reydar has returned home to his family."

"With a nice bonus for both of us," Daffy added, "which Penney will probably spend in the vintage shop. My wife," he explained to David.

"I know some great places to shop," Robin said.

Gibbs continued before they could sidetrack him. "Tucker is sure Swaine was working alone. He still isn't talking, but the agents are building a solid case. Swaine was in deep to his bookie and needed a quick payoff. It was all about the money; he needed money. Quickly. The DA is working with Swaine and the FBI, but the negotiations are going to take time."

He turned to David. "You have anything?"

"Not much. The men we picked up all have records and are low-level troublemakers." He forked a mess of lo mein; never had learned to operate chopsticks. He summarized what he had already told Robin. "Elliott's fingerprints on Dutch's provenance found in the warehouse tie him to the wine thefts. His fingerprint in Fallern's wet blood on the black wine bottle help tie him to the murder even though there is no way to determine when or where the blood got on the bottle, according to our DA. His weapon, which we found where Leach said it was hidden, has his fingerprints and only his prints, and it's the weapon which killed Fallern. It also matches the slugs we retrieved from Robin's car. We got him."

Colin nodded a few times. "That's it ladies. Robin is safe and you're out of work. But Becca will pay you through tomorrow. That right Mrs. Gibbs?" he asked with a sly smile.

"Two days more. We're going shopping tomorrow," she responded.

Jen jumped up. "Yippee. We're on our own in a great city and we are celebrating. All us girls, shopping tomorrow and lunch. Don't you worry Daffy, we won't let Penney spend more than you earned." She looked at Mary Lee, Becca, and Robin for agreement.

Mary Lee said, "I could do that. Call Penney right now and tell her. Robin, you should invite Patsy, tell her to meet us at ten at the Inn. I'll call May and have her take a day off. We'll make it our first girls' day out." The women made calls and the conversation turned to plans for the next day.

When the meal was over, everyone pitched in to clean up and Robin's house emptied out with everyone laughing goodnights and see you tomorrows. Robin held the door open for David, the last to leave.

"Thank you for stopping by, Detective."

"Look at me Robin."

She looked over his shoulder, toward the blue wall behind him. "You should leave."

"You have to give me a chance to explain."

"Nothing to explain," she said.

"We need to talk."

She shook her head.

"I need to talk, then. Give me chance, please." He was desperate. He had to convince her to listen. "Give me a chance."

She sighed and closed the door and looked straight at his tie. Her face was blank. "Talk."

He raised his hand, palm forward. "I didn't purposely not return your call. Scott and I were out all night following Leach, arresting her and Elliott, searching her condo. I was going to return your call as soon as we got a free minute. I'm sorry."

"I accept your apology," she said in a flat tone. "Goodnight." She reached for the door knob.

"No. Wait." She wasn't listening. He had to reach her, convince her. She had to listen. But she stood with her hand on the knob.

"Please. Can we sit down and talk? Give me ten minutes."

This time, she looked him straight in the eye and he saw indecision. She shrugged and led him into the living room, motioned him to sit. He didn't, because she stood, stiff, her arms folded under her breasts.

His mouth was dry, but he got the words out. "I want us to get back together."

Before he could continue, she spoke. "We've been through this before, David. You tell me you want us to be together and promise to call and then don't. This time you had an excuse. You seem to want me when you see me, then you walk away and a new day dawns, and you forget me."

He didn't, hadn't. He thought of her all the time. She was always there, smiling in his mind.

"I know it looks that way."

"Doesn't look that way, Detective. It is that way."

"No, it isn't." He stopped. "Yes, it looks that way to you. But I don't forget."

"You don't forget?" She considered him now, her head sideways, and then seemed to get it. "You don't forget," she said slowly, "you decide not to call."

He nodded.

"I don't understand. Why would you tell me this? How does it make anything better?"

"I didn't call, um, because I was afraid."

Her eyes narrowed in puzzlement. "You? Afraid of what?"

He spread his fingers. "You. Me. Us."

"There is no us."

"There is going to be."

"Now you say that. Tomorrow, you will change your mind."

That had been his pattern with her, but not anymore. He wasn't going to fight it. He was going to accept his feelings and give them a chance, follow them. "No. Not this time." He took her hands and looked her in the eye. Took a breath. "I'm not afraid this time. Not running this time. I want to take a chance on us. You and me. I think we can have a future together. I want to try. I would like to have you in my life. I think I need you in my life." He paused before continuing. She was listening.

"Other women?" He lifted a shoulder. "I could always walk away from them. No one got under my skin, like you. I think of you all the time. I see you when I close my eyes. I dream of you when I'm asleep. I reach for you. I need you. I need you." He took a breath. She was weakening.

"When I heard you were in the middle of that kidnapping last night, it was a shock to my heart. A jolt which finally reached my brain. I understood how much you mean to me. How much I don't want to lose you. I want there to be an us. I need there to be an us."

She backed up and he let her go. She collapsed in the chair and raised a hand to cover her eyes. "Oh, David."

He knelt in front of her, grabbing her other hand. "Please, give me another chance. Give us another chance."

She pulled her hand away from him. Twisted it with her own. "You can't do this to me. Why can't you leave me alone? We both know your rules. Never go with the same woman twice. Why break your rules for me?"

"I care for you. I want to be with you. I want us to try." He couldn't say the love word yet. Couldn't think it. Didn't dare promise it.

She rubbed her free hand up and down her face, her fingers covering her mouth. "Why?"

"Why what?"

"Why are you doing this to me? I could get over you if you would leave me alone. There are plenty of other women out there for you." She looked into his eyes, hers shiny with unshed tears.

"No. I don't want another woman. I can't get through a day, an hour, without thinking of you. Wanting you. Missing you. I want what we had before." Could she see his desperation? His sincerity?

She closed her eyes. A tear dripped down. "I can't do this, David. Go home."

He'd lost. He couldn't move. Dropped his head in defeat. Felt her soft hand on his cheek. Blinked in surprise.

"You make me weak. Tomorrow. If you still feel the same tomorrow. Call me. I'll decide tomorrow."

It took a minute for the words to register. He'd won. He stood, exhaled a breath he hadn't realized he was holding. "Thank you." He put his hands on her shoulders and leaned down to kiss her, but she pushed him away and stood.

"No. Not tonight. I'm tired. Go home. Please." She led the way to the door.

"I promise. I'll call." He touched her shoulder, his hand sliding down her arm and she turned and bumped into him. Raised her head. Her eyes searched his face, settled on his lips. She stood on her toes and kissed him. A kiss full of need and passion.

"Stay," she whispered. "Will you stay with me tonight? Only tonight. Not all night," she rushed on, before he could reply. "I know you can't do that, but will you stay as long as you can?"

He couldn't answer. Her plea was so hopeless it broke his heart. He lowered his head and claimed her mouth, stopping her words.

Wednesday

She woke slowly, luxuriating; her body felt good, alive. Maybe a little sore. A comfortable sore. She smiled and stretched, enjoying the moment. Reached out and felt emptiness. Her smile slipped. She rolled onto her side and reached to the edge of the bed. No obstruction. No David.

She didn't want to open her eyes and look. In fact, she squeezed them tighter and stuck her tongue between her teeth. Didn't let the moan escape her throat. Chided herself. What was her problem? She'd known this would happen, even as she had hoped it wouldn't. Heck, she'd given him permission to leave.

Grow up, she told herself. You're a big girl, playing an adult game. You knew the rules. Get over it, girl. You got one night. One more night. Almost night. So you didn't get everything you wanted; get over it. And, God, she did feel good.

His spot was still warm, he hadn't been gone long. She forced herself to peek. In the dim light of sunrise, light and shadows were cast over the bed. She didn't have to lean closer to catch his scent. It was all over the sheets. Herself. She groaned and lay back. His scent had been her tipping point last night. Part of it. His scent had weakened her, drawn her. And then she'd let him get too close and touch her. She'd been tired and weak, and the scent had reminded her of their night together. Partial night. His touch had speared through her body on a wave of lust, and she had grabbed the moment.

She let herself have another small smile. She wasn't sure how she felt about having an affair. Or a one-night stand? Physically, she felt good. Damn good. She took a survey of her body. Better than damn good. All over. Her heart? Her heart was okay. Not any worse than loving him and not having him. No worse than yesterday. Better, and her body was sated.

Her head? She studied the ceiling. She didn't feel used. More like a user; she felt a little twinge of guilt which brought a bigger smile. Using a man for sex. Good sex. Excellent sex. She was sure he didn't mind. She hadn't heard any complaints. Surely had none herself. Her lips quirked. They'd both gotten what they wanted. She stretched again. God, she felt good.

They hadn't made it to the bedroom the first time. Got as far as the couch. She closed her eyes on the memory. She'd fallen asleep and was awakened as he carried her to the bedroom, where they'd made love two more times.

Yep, she felt good. Making love to the man she loved was a whole lot better than yearning for him. Maybe this sex without commitment would be okay.

"What's going on in that head of yours?" David asked.

She sat up with a start, the covers falling and exposing her breasts. He stood in the doorway, leaning on the doorjamb. Had been. Now he approached the bed, his eyes locked on her chest.

"But you're gone," she spluttered.

"No. I'm here," he said, his eyes heavy with lust. "No way could I leave this." He reached out and caressed her, sending a shiver through her body.

The next time she woke, it was full daylight and she didn't have to open her eyes to look for him; she was spooned against his front, his arms tight around her. He snored softly. The man must be exhausted, she thought. She'd let him do all the work the last time. If she could, she'd whistle a tune, but she didn't know how. He was still here and it was daytime. He'd spent the night. She had a moment of sheer joy, but then her brain started.

Of course he was still here, dummy. He was locked in, a prisoner. That was why he was still here. The alarm was set.

No. Wait. She'd never set the alarm after Gibbs left. "I never set the alarm."

She must have said the last thought aloud, because the snoring stopped and he said, "Don't worry, I set it."

"What? When? How could you set it? You don't know the code."

"I did it when you fell asleep on the couch. You don't need the code to set it. And I do know the code."

"How could you?" She'd never shared it.

"I watched you clear it two times. I'm a cop. I observe."

She searched his face. "Why are you still here? You never spend the night. Gone by dawn."

"I'm here because this is where I want to be. With you." He leaned up on an elbow. "You've wormed your way under my skin, and now you're stuck with me." He stroked the edge of her face with a finger. "You're beautiful when you wake up."

She felt good. "I feel good. But I must be a mess."

"No. You look sexy with your hair all mussed. Like a woman well-satisfied." He reached across her face and tucked a strand behind her ear.

"I didn't expect you to stay all night."

His eyes hardened for a moment. "I told you last night you're important to me. I'll be spending a lot of nights with you. Waking with you in the morning." He kissed her softly. Backed off and rubbed a hand gently down her cheek. "I'll be around a lot. I'll be around a long time."

He brought her a cup of coffee in bed before he left for work, promising to call. He'd cleared and then set the alarm, it hadn't been an empty brag.

She hoped he would call, but he had a problem with follow through, so she prepared herself for disappointment; she'd be checking her phone all day. For a moment she considered staying home beside it and then immediately realized the idiocy of that. He'd call, or he wouldn't; he knew her cell number.

The phone rang as she was toweling her hair dry. Unknown. She grabbed it.

"Yes?"

"Hi."

"David?"

"I promised you I'd call. I was wrong when I said you were under my skin." He hesitated, and her heart stopped beating, but then he continued. "It's worse than that. You're inside my head. All the time. When I'm not with you, you're with me. I want us to work toward something. I know we can if you give me the chance."

Her heart started beating again. Was he suggesting a relationship?

"Will you have dinner with me tonight?" he asked.

Dinner? A date?

"Robin? You still there?" He sounded anxious.

"Yes. I'm still here." Her hand was trembling. She took a steadying breath and spoke weakly. "Yes, I'd love to have dinner with you tonight."

She heard his sigh of relief.

"I'll pick you up at seven. Wear something fancy. Dinner and dancing. Okay?"

"Yes. Seven. Fancy." It wasn't going to be just one night.

There was a long pause. He seemed to be having trouble with words. Afraid of saying the wrong thing?

"See you then." And he was gone.

She sat and clasped her hands in front, almost in prayer. It was happening. He was going to take her out. Take her to bed. She was going to have an affair, seize the moment. He couldn't hurt her any more than he already had. She'd already lost her heart and had it stomped. She had dealt with it and would again, but meanwhile, she was going to have fun. Enjoy it. Undies. She needed fancy undies. Matching. Vintage maybe. Good thing she was going shopping. Her new friends would laugh. Becca would give her an *I told you so,* look.

She stood, a little weak at the knees and wanted to jump in the air and clap her feet. Silly. Her cell rang where she'd left it on the nightstand. Unknown.

She touched the screen.

"Should have made that a breakfast date. Miss you already."

She couldn't stop her wide smile and the flush over her whole body surprised her. Me too, she wanted to say, but settled for. "I can't. Dinner?"

"Dinner. Got to go." And he was gone again.

Her heart was fluttering, and the silly grin wouldn't go away. She busied herself changing the sheets. Would he stay the whole night again? Didn't matter. This was sex, pure and simple; not love, lust. She could deal with it. Would deal with it. Grab her own share of pleasure.

But right now, she had a shopping play date. She had to pick Patsy up and they'd meet the other women at Cougars Cove Inn. She liked Patsy. They'd shared confidences and become friends during their time together in the hotel. For a rich socialite, Patsy was very down to earth. Mary Lee and Jen, too. Nice women. Friends, she hoped. And Becca. She was looking forward to meeting Daffy's Penney. Legs, he had called her with a promise to tell her the story behind the nickname. Another of Colin's aunts by marriage.

So many new people in her life. She sighed and hummed to herself on the way to her closet. And a new romance. Another buzz, this time a text: *It has to be supper? I don't know if I can wait. Lunch?*

She laughed, texted back: *Meeting with Jen, Mary Lee, Penney, and Becca to shop at Cougars Cove. I'm driving Patsy. We're doing lunch.*

Sounds like a hen party. Need a rooster?

Is he suggesting he join us? She sent back: *Seriously?*

No. Have fun. Tonight will be ours.

She held the phone a minute longer. Tonight. The shopping would keep her mind off tonight. Maybe.

She dressed casually and set out for the hotel, stuffing her cell between her thighs so she could feel if he texted again. She was smiling ear to ear when she pulled into the side lot where Patsy was waiting with a tall, skinny man. Mean looking. Oh, her bodyguard. Robin had forgotten about the security team. How would they like shopping with a cackle of women? The thought made her smile even broader. Her thigh vibrated, but the man already had the rear passenger door open. He pushed Patsy in and climbed in beside her.

"Don't you want to sit up front?" Robin asked. Jen or Mary Lee had always chosen the front seat. He gave her a curt shake of his head. She shrugged her shoulders, what did she know about bodyguards?

Patsy made the introductions. "Robin, this is Floyd Childer, my bodyguard. His partner, Wesley, is still a little under the weather from the food poisoning, so only Floyd will be coming with us today. You knew he'd be coming, right?"

She didn't want to admit she'd forgotten bodyguards were involved. "I guess I knew someone would be shopping with us. Are you looking forward to our trip, Mr. Childer?"

He grunted a response. "Which way are you going?" Not the friendly type of guard she was used to. Poor Patsy.

"South to Fifth Avenue, take it to 951, and head south to the Inn."

He leaned back in the seat and glanced out the window. Didn't search or check the way her own bodyguards had; their eyes always moving. He just glanced out casually. Oh, well.

"Patsy? Are you looking for anything in particular today?" Robin asked around her headrest, thinking about sexy underwear.

"I've heard about the wonderful local arts and crafts at the Cove; I want to buy something for my sister. How about you?"

Robin couldn't stop her smile. Wasn't going to say anything about underwear in front of grumpy. Shrugged a shoulder. "Got some things in mind."

"Did you sleep okay?" Patsy asked.

Huh? Robin gave her a quick look in the mirror. How could she know?

"Nightmares. Did you have nightmares?"

Oh, right. She'd told Patsy she expected to have nightmares after the hotel incident. "No. No nightmares." Not last night. Nor the night before. Because she hadn't personally been attacked? Because David hadn't verbally abused her? Something to think about. Another vibration against her leg, but she couldn't respond while driving.

"I didn't know you had a sister. Older or younger? Any other siblings?"

Patsy leaned forward around the headrest. Apparently family was the right topic as Patsy chatted about two brothers, older, and one sister, younger, until they approached the junction where Davis split off.

"Get in the left lane," Childer ordered.

"What?" Both women looked back at him.

"I said get in the left lane." He pulled Patsy back onto the seat and shoved forward by the headrest.

"That's the wrong direction," Robin said. "I need to go straight here and stay on the Trail." He must not know his way around town.

She turned around to look at him and he swung a gun into her face.

"Left lane, bitch, or you're dead."

She jerked the wheel and almost veered into the path of another car. Pulled back. Moved into the left lane. She grasped the wheel tighter with both hands to stop the shaking. The gun was huge, scary, but the animosity in his voice scared her more

"Take Davis," he growled.

She did, but said, "This, this takes us away from Cougars Cove."

"Keep going until I say different."

She glanced nervously in the mirror. Didn't want to look at the gun again. This couldn't be happening. They had the kidnapper.

He shoved Patsy, knocking her off the seat. "On the floor. Get down."

When she hesitated, he slapped her. "On the floor."

He seemed to hope Patsy would refuse, so he could strike her again. She wedged herself down.

Robin saw anger and contempt in his face and felt Patsy move to the floor, couldn't see her in the rearview.

Robin turned to him. "But you're her bodyguard," she said, trying to understand.

"Shut up. Turn around and drive. You try anything, Patsy gets a bullet in the belly. You get one in the head. No funny business." He waved the gun. "No one's going to get hurt, unless you do something stupid. Now drive."

She drove. Her hands were shaking, jerking. Her body felt oddly disconnected as if signals from her brain were being interrupted and sidetracked. What could she do? Her eyes darted to the sides. She was in traffic. Cause an accident? He still had the gun. She would pass a fire station. She could drive in there, but she was in the left lane and started to move to the right, but he tapped the side of her head with the gun.

"Stay where you are and drive."

She jerked spasmodically. Held the wheel tighter until her knuckles turned white. Concentrating on driving brought some calm, and she tried reasoning with him. "You can get out. Right now. Leave us. We'll never tell,"

Patsy was quick to back her up. "I'll pay you to let us go and forget this ever happened."

He ignored both statements, just sat back, looking around. "Take Alligator Alley. East. Pay the toll. No funny business. I'll shoot the toll collector first. Up to you. No reason for anyone to be hurt," he repeated.

She did as she was told and crossed 951. Didn't try to signal the friendly man who took her money and gave her change. Maybe she could attract the attention of a patrol car if she drove too fast. She pressed down on the gas pedal. But Floyd leaned forward.

"Don't speed. I'll be watching." He checked to make sure she slowed down and was holding at the speed limit. "Keep to the speed limit." He grabbed Patsy's purse, reached in, and pulled out her cell.

"You're going to take the next exit, and pull off onto the side of the road.

It seemed to take forever but it was only twenty minutes when she reached Route 29 to Immokalee. He nudged her again with the gun, motioning. She took the exit and stopped on the shoulder of 29 as he instructed.

"Turn off the engine and hand me the keys."

She did after first fumbling them.

"Now put your back to the door, hands in your lap, feet on the seat."

She stared at him with wide eyes. "Why?"

"I want you in a position where you can't make any sudden moves."

She was scared to and scared not to, so she did as she was told, shoving her cell under her thigh. In this position she could see Patsy on the floor.

He nodded once, leaned back to look down at Patsy. "You too. Back to the door." When he seemed satisfied with her position, he handed her a note. "You're going to read that while I film you. The gun will be pointing at you all the time and any false moves, someone gets shot. No reason for anyone to be hurt. Read it to me one time for practice," he ordered. "Make believe you're auditioning for a movie." He sounded pleased with himself, which Robin supposed he was.

After a couple of false starts Patsy managed a feeble sound. "You will transfer twenty-three million…" She stopped. Stared up at Childer in amazement, found her voice. "Twenty-three million dollars? Are you crazy? No one has that kind of money sitting around."

"Your daddy does. He wants you back, he pays my price." Calm and reasonable as if people did this every day. As if it made sense. "Keep reading."

She eyed him a moment longer and went back to the note. "You will transfer twenty-three million dollars to a numbered account if you want me back. You will be contacted with the account number and you will transfer the money immediately. These people know you have the funds available, and if the transaction is not made, they will kill me. If you call the police, they will kill me."

Floyd nodded and pointed Patsy's cell at her. "Good, now read it for the camera."

She did, in a quiet monotone. When she was done, he fiddled with the buttons on the phone. "Good girl. I'm sending this to the web, where it will be sent to your daddy in one hour. You'll be back home in a few hours and no one will even know you were missing, except your dad. Two women out shopping?" He made a face. "Shop till you drop, with a break for lunch. It will all be over before anyone even knows you're gone."

He smiled at Robin, an evil, wicked smile which chilled her insides. She almost mentioned they were meeting other people and then thought better of it. What would Jen and Mary Lee do when they were late? And they were late now. Would they wait? Call? She almost looked down. The cell was by her left hand, on vibrate and it had vibrated three or four more times while she was driving.

Childer was talking to her. "Give me your cell phone."

Oh, my God. "Um. Ah…." Before she could form words, he reached forward and grabbed her handbag, which he dumped out on the back seat. He sorted through her stuff, keeping an eye on her at the same time. Of course he didn't find her phone.

"It's, um, not in there," she said. She was still gripping the steering wheel. It seemed to give her strength.

She lowered her hand to her leg. Used two fingers and a thumb of her right hand on the cell. Gave him a quick glance. He wasn't looking at her. He was rummaging through her things again, as if he might have missed her phone. She fiddled with the buttons on the steering wheel.

"Where is it?" he demanded.

"My PHONE? Um. At, um, at home. SEE? It's not there. It was dead. I uh, I left it home to charge. In the charger."

She had to hide her cell. Not in her pocket. What would he do if he searched her and found it? Not in her waistband. It would show under her crop-top. She had to move it when he was distracted. Oh, God. Where? Maybe she could hide it in the crease under the seat-back.

She glanced at him again. He was doing something with Patsy's phone.

"Go over the bridge and head back down onto 75," he told her.

"But, that's going back the way we came, going west on 75. Back to Naples."

"You got it right, sweetheart. No one will be looking for us in Naples. They'll be looking for us in Miami. Exactly where the GPS in this cell will tell the cops we were headed. "Driving to the east coast to shop. I let it slip to the staff. Told them we were going to Sawgrass Mills Mall. It's all part of Mr. Swaine's original plan." He pulled the battery out of the cell. "Move."

Original plan? What did that mean? She twisted forward in her seat, put the car in drive, and joined the queue to get back on the highway. He was right. The cameras and toll taker would show them heading east. So would Patsy's cell. The cops wouldn't expect them to go back to Naples.

She reached for her cell again. There were three cars ahead of her waiting to enter the highway. Then two cars. One car left. She didn't dare look down. Glanced in the mirror again. She checked the car in front of her, her rearview again. He was taking the battery out of his own cell. She jammed her phone between her body and the seat back. Later she could push it further under, out of sight. She hoped.

"Move it." He waved the gun angrily motioning to the road, and she saw it was her turn and stepped on the gas, throwing him against the seat.

"Sorry. Sorry. I'm nervous," she wailed.

"Shut up and drive. No speeding."

A few moments later she took a breath and tried conversation. "But, Floyd, you're her bodyguard."

"Ah ha. Makes the job easier." He gave her a self-satisfied sneer. "Nobody is looking at her bodyguard."

"Why are you doing this? Why are you kidnapping us, Floyd?"

"It's too sweet a deal to pass up. Swaine's idea really. He planned it all out, step-by-step." Childer smirked, then scowled for a moment. "And then he botched it. But I planned to take over anyhow."

Patsy asked, "Why did he want to kidnap me? Daddy would have loaned him money."

"He needed a lot of money. His loan shark was threatening to send enforcers to break all his bones; gave him a little tune-up sample last week. In fact, it was the loan shark who suggested he get money from your father." Floyd leaned back self-satisfied and continued the story. "Swaine's from this area and has a lot of friends in Fort Myers; you coming here was a happy coincidence. All they had to do was grab you. Shoulda' worked perfectly." He shook his head in disgust.

"He hired my cousin who told me the whole plan. Swaine was going to poison me. He got me the job, and then he was going to take me out. But my cousin and me made our own plan. I let Wesley eat the contaminated food and pretended to be sick myself. They was supposed to grab you and take you to the safe house. Then my cousin and me would take over."

Robin risked another look in the mirror.

"Then those halfwits Swaine hired grabbed you. Twice. Idiots. And my cousin got shot. Swaine will pay for that." Floyd shook his head. "Stupid shit. Sent those idiots out to the beach and José shot my cousin.

Everyone knew José was gun happy. Only smart thing Swaine did was go after you himself and get caught, leaving you totally unprotected, except for me. I step in and walk off with his millions, and he goes down for kidnapping and murder." He gave them his sick smile again.

She was afraid she knew what his plans were for herself and Patsy. He'd never let them go.

"Why are we going back to Naples?" she asked. "Is someone waiting for us?"

"We're going back to Naples because I said so. And because Swaine rented a house there. We're going to wait there for the money transfer. And I'm goin' to make sure the cops know it's his plan. Now be quiet and drive."

She started to ask another question, but he cut her off. "Shut up."

Patsy spoke into the silence. "My father doesn't have that kind of money lying around. He can't get it in a few hours. It will take days."

"Swaine's his accountant. He says your father's ready to sign a big deal and has the funds available. Sitting there, waiting." He laughed. "Waiting for me."

A few minutes later he barked, "Take this exit. Turn north."

"North? Onto 951?"

"Yes."

A pause. "You want me to exit the turnpike? Onto 951?"

"Don't make me repeat myself, bitch. Exit onto 951 and go north."

She saw a traffic camera here, but would anybody even check it? She didn't know anything about how they worked. Did they take pictures of cars running the red light? She could run the red and hope.

The light was green. The next signal was green also.

About three miles later he said, "Take this right over the bridge. And then the first right again."

The estates. A nice residential area where homes were on two-and-a-half acre plots. "On 39th?"

"Yes. Now drive down one block and turn left."

"On 26th Lane?"

"Yeah." A pause. "Into this driveway."

She didn't dare repeat the number. "The brown mailbox. On the left?"

He nodded. He was leaning forward again. Eager. He jabbed her with the gun. "Turn."

She was afraid of what would happen at their destination, but she didn't have any choice. The drive curved around a stand of trees to a house hidden from the street. Floyd waved a remote and the garage door opened.

"Drive in."

She did and parked beside another car.

He lowered the roll-up door behind them.

"Mr. Childer, you can still let us go," Robin said.

"Shut up. Here's what we're going to do. You give me the car keys. Patsy gets out. I get out. You get out. We walk inside, Patsy first. You try anything, I put you down. I don't need you alive. You understand?" He smiled when he said it and she believed him.

She nodded her head. Her mouth was dry and her tongue wouldn't work and she couldn't find her voice. She understood how Patsy had felt reading the note. It was a different type of frightened than in the restroom. Who knew? Then it was as if electricity was racing through her veins. Now her brain was having trouble even communicating with her body. Closing her eyes, she made her limbs respond. She pushed the phone under the seatback and slid out.

He unlocked the door to the house and they filed into a small kitchen where he stopped them. "Take off your shoes and empty your pockets. Turn them inside out."

Robin looked at Patsy and both did as he instructed. When they were shoeless with their pockets hanging outside their clothes, he motioned them through a living room furnished in red and black leather with steel and glass tables, down a corridor to a bedroom. The door had a latch and padlock on the outside and the room was empty. No furniture. The windows were covered. A dark bathroom was straight ahead.

"Hurricane shutters," he said in a smug tone with barely restrained excitement. "Locked from the outside. You aren't going anywhere. Inside," he ordered.

Robin hesitated.

"I don't need you alive …" he warned again.

Anger was replacing her fear. Which was good. Also good: he hadn't killed them outright.

"You stay here until Daddy wires the money. I disappear. When I'm safe, I'll let Daddy know where you are. In six or eight hours this will all be over. I'll be out of the country and you'll be home with Daddy. You might go hungry, but you'll be alive. Meanwhile, you have a bathroom and air-conditioning. All the comforts of home." He sniggered. "And everyone thinks you're shopping in Miami with your new friend here."

Robin hoped he was wrong. She hoped people knew they were missing, were looking for them now. She and Patsy were supposed to meet with the Gibbs clan over an hour ago. They would be looking, wouldn't they? Robin's cell had been vibrating. David? He'd be worried, wouldn't he? When she didn't respond to his last text? Would he be looking?

But they couldn't wait. They had to depend on themselves to get out of here. Floyd wasn't going to let them leave alive. He closed the door and she heard the latch and padlock snap shut. As soon as they were alone, Robin hugged Patsy and whispered in her ear. "We don't know if he's listening. I have a plan. We're getting out of here. Don't say anything."

She broke off the hug. "I got to pee." She wished she had been brave enough to keep the cell, but then he would have found it when he made them empty their pockets.

**

Robin wasn't responding to his texts. One minute they were talking back and forth and then the next, silence. Granted, he had turned his phone off when he went to interview Swaine, but she had stopped responding even before then.

The interrogation hadn't gone anywhere. They'd all taken a crack at him. Agent Tucker first, then David, then Scott. David couldn't concentrate anyhow; he was distracted, wanting to check his cell. His distress didn't make any difference; Swaine wasn't talking. They'd wasted all night when he wouldn't talk except to say attorney, and now it was the attorney who wouldn't talk except to say *signed deal* in which Swaine would admit details, name partners. The attorney and the DA were dickering. Swaine wasn't talking.

Neither was Robin. No texts from her. Colin Gibbs was talking; he'd called David but left no message. Who cared? Nothing from Robin. She'd stopped texting. What had happened? He'd thought everything was going fine, but now she wasn't talking.

Scott interrupted his thoughts. "The DA has to make the decision on a deal and put it in writing. Swaine won't give us a hint. We don't really need anything from him. We caught him in the act. Details would be nice, but do we need them. Why make a deal?"

"Let the DA decide," David said, scrolling through his cell searching for a call.

Scott chided him. "What's wrong? Your girl playing hard to get?"

"Shut up." No texts from Robin. Two calls from Colin Gibbs, then two from Becca Gibbs. No messages. His cell rang while he was looking at it; Tucker's cell rang at the same time. Finally, Robin. But when he looked, he was disappointed, Becca Gibbs. Again. Disgusted, he almost shut it off but instead pushed talk.

"What?" he barked.

"Ramirez?"

"Speaking."

"Becca Gibbs. The kidnappers got Patsy."

"What?"

"They got Patsy. And Robin. Robin is with her."

"No." He closed his eyes a second. Flashed on her this morning, half covered. With a soft smile of satisfaction. They couldn't have Robin. How could they have Robin? He had the kidnapper in a cell.

"She went shopping with the girls," he said. Becca was wrong.

"Supposed to, but she never showed up. They were grabbed. Ryan is notifying Tucker. We haven't been able to reach either of you."

David looked at Tucker who was giving him the same look of disbelief. David put his phone on speaker. "Go ahead. I have you on speaker and I'm looking at Tucker. We have Swaine. What makes you think someone snatched Patsy?"

"Guy by the name of Floyd has them."

Tucker spoke, disgusted. "Floyd's the bodyguard. She should be with him."

"No. He snatched them."

"How do you know this?"

"Phone call. She called Colin. Robin called. More like her cell called. You need to put a trace on Robin's phone. Sounds like they're in a car. All I'm getting is road noises. Find out where she is. Patsy's cell, too. They're together. Wait. You can listen."

He heard voices on the other end; then he could make out Robin's faint voice.

"Take this exit. Turn north."

"Onto 951?"

"Yes."

A pause. "You want me to exit the turnpike? Onto 951?"

"Don't make me repeat myself. Exit onto 951 and go north."

Colin broke in. "They're at the 951/turnpike exchange."

In the silence of road sounds Colin explained what he knew. "Earlier in the call, Floyd bragged he snatched them. Said it was Swaine's plan. My dad and I are almost to you and I'll play it back when we get there; we recorded it."

When David heard Swaine's name, he wanted to go back to the interrogation room and slam the guy's head into the table. Multiple times. He actually turned in Swaine's direction but was stopped by a hand on his shoulder. Restraining and comforting at the same time. Scott.

David shrugged off the arm. Flexed his hands because he could still feel the impact of Swaine's head hitting the table. He breathed through his nose. Tried to unclench his teeth. Took a deep breath. Two. Nodded his thanks to Scott. "I'm okay." A lie.

They listened to the silence mixed with road noises coming through Colin's phone.

Then. "Take this right over the bridge. And then the first right again."

"On 39th?"

"Yes. Now drive down one block and turn left."

"On 26th Lane?"

"Yes." More road noises. "Into this driveway."

"On the left? The brown mailbox?"

"Turn." A pause. "Drive in."

Another pause. "Mr. Childer. You can still let us go." That was Robin. Good girl.

Childer said, "Here's what we are going to do. You give me the keys. Patsy gets out. I get out. You get out. We walk inside, Patsy first. You try anything, I put you down. I don't need you alive. You understand?"

David heard the engine turn off, and doors slam. Then complete silence.

He took another breath and asked the question foremost in his mind. "Why did she call you?" *Why didn't she call me?*

"I put my number on her speed dial when I was guarding her. Must have been all she could manage. Doesn't sound like anyone knows the cell is on."

"Bring that phone right to us."

"Just pulled into your lot."

David turned to Tucker. "What do you know about this Floyd Childer?"

"One of her bodyguards."

Colin and Ryan hurried in and over to the two detectives. Ryan Gibbs held out his cell. "This is what we recorded. From the beginning." He pushed a button.

"Move it."

Robin's voice, loud and clear. *"Sorry. Sorry."*

Robin again. *"But, Floyd, you're her bodyguard."*

David felt weak as he listened to the conversation. Floyd's brag was a kick in the gut. This rat bastard had Robin. David stood rigidly and listened to the whole tape. Silence followed the last word. He glanced around. The detectives in the squad room had listened and were waiting for direction. His direction.

He swallowed. "Listen up. We have a double kidnapping. Dillon, you and Polinski, I want everything you can find on Swaine and Floyd, um. Last name. What's his last name?"

"Childer, Floyd Childer," Tucker said.

"Floyd Childer and Roger Swaine. Rhonda, get SWAT and check on a chopper." He turned to a seated detective. "Warrants to trace the cells: Patsy Corson, Floyd Childer, Robin." He stumbled over her name. "Robin Garman. The father, Patsy's father. Corson."

"What else? What else?" he asked the room.

Tucker said, "One of us should call Mr. Corson. Use a personal cell. No law enforcement contacts. And we need more information from Swaine. How many more people he has here. If he has people watching Corson."

David looked at Colin's cell which remained silent.

The SWAT leader, Dennis Black, swept in with his usual air of calm competency, and David introduced him around. He shook hands with the senior Gibbs. "Met you on that art theft last year," he said with a nod of respect.

"I remember."

The rest of the SWAT team arrived. David gave them a quick briefing and replayed Robin's call and then handed Colin's phone to a technician to make copies.

Dillon broke in with information on Swaine. "Local boy. Some trouble as a teenager. Breaking and entering. Like we already know, he ran with a gang in Fort Myers, as did the three guys we caught in the restroom. The guy in the hospital, too. Don't have his connection to Childer yet, but we'll get it. We have a warrant for financials on Swaine and those should come in today."

Polinski added, "Nothing on Childer. A wannabe. Failed the military physical, flunked out of the police academy. Worked a couple low level guard jobs before Corson picked him up three months ago. A loser. How did he get a job as a bodyguard?"

"I'll get details from Corson," Tucker said.

A seated detective spoke. "Nothing on either Patsy Corson's or Chidler's phones. They must be turned off. We have Garman's phone north of I-75, near 951." He sent the GPS graphic to a monitor.

"Private home. Residential area." David noted. "Like Childer said."

"We'll set up at the restaurant near the corner at 951 and 39th Street." Black led his SWAT team out.

David was torn. He wanted to be with the SWAT team, but he had work here. SWAT needed more information before going into action.

Tucker said, "Gibbs should talk to Swaine,"

Scott shook his head. "We went at him for hours and didn't get anything. And the lawyer says he's not talking. What makes you think this guy can do anything?"

"It's what he does. He's the best we have. Anyone can get the answers, but only Gibbs will get them quick."

Scott looked at David who gave the go ahead, and Gibbs walked into the conference room as if he had all the time in the world, introduced himself to Swaine and his attorney, and sat down, placing a folder on the table.

The men watched through the one-way mirror.

"You have the signed deal?" the attorney asked Gibbs.

"No. I'm sorry. I'm not from the DA's office."

The attorney stood and leaned over the table, both hands flat against it. "I thought I made it clear; my client will not share any information without a signed agreement. Don't you guys talk to each other?"

"Yes, we do, Mr. Akorn. But we have new information and no longer need Mr. Swaine's assistance. I am only here as a courtesy to inform you, we will be filing additional charges."

"What new information? Where did you get it? What new charges?"

"You should sit down. We'll be here awhile, and you may as well be comfortable. Can I get you something to drink?"

The attorney frowned and sat. "No. We have nothing to say, without an agreement."

"I understand. I will do all the talking. Let me start by reviewing the current charges and then list the new ones. As to the attempted kidnapping, in Florida kidnapping is a first-degree felony and subject to life in prison. There is video evidence and multiple witnesses to the fact your client attempted to kidnap Ms. Corson."

Gibbs held up his hand when the attorney opened his mouth to talk. "Before you object to the video, Mr. Akorn, your client had no expectation of privacy in Ms. Corson's hotel room. A warning notice about the video surveillance was posted on the door."

"I'm sure we can have it excluded."

"There are still multiple witnesses. Your client is also considered responsible for any injuries occurring during an attempted kidnapping."

"There were no injuries."

"Not last night, but two men were shot on the beach during an earlier aborted attempt."

"Mr. Swaine knows nothing about that attempt. Not unless he receives immunity."

"The men we have in custody tell a different story."

"We dispute whatever they say. Men in jail will say anything. What did you promise them?"

"We promised them justice."

The attorney was silent.

"As to the new charges, those could include impeding a federal investigation, kidnapping, and murder."

"No one was murdered," Akorn said. "That man is going to recover."

"I repeat, murder and kidnapping."

Swaine glanced up, puzzled. "What? No one was kidnapped. No one was murdered. You were there last night. I recognize you. You know that."

"Yes, I was, and you are correct—about last night. I'm not talking about the crimes committed last night. I'm talking about this morning. I'm talking about the abduction of Ms. Corson." Gibbs waited a moment. "Unfortunately for you, your partner went through with the abduction early this morning, while we were waiting for you to talk to your attorney. Murder during an abduction is both a federal and a state crime."

David liked the way Gibbs phrased the lie.

Swaine stood, knocking over his chair. "What do you mean abduction? This morning? Are you crazy? I was here in your jail."

Akorn squeezed his client's shoulder. "Be quiet, Mr. Swaine. Don't say anything. Let me handle this. Quiet."

"But he said Patsy was kidnapped," Swaine bellowed.

"He said it, doesn't mean it happened. Sit down and let me handle this."

Swaine shoved his hand away. "I want to know." To Gibbs he demanded. "What do you mean?"

"Patsy Corson was kidnapped this morning."

Swaine's mouth worked. "But that's impossible."

"No. It happened. And a Thomas Barlow was killed during the commission of a felony."

That non-sequitur surprised a chuckle out of David. "This guy is good."

"Mr. Swaine, you neglected to mention part of your crew was still out there waiting to take Patsy. That makes you complicit in this morning's crime. If you had told us, maybe Patsy would be shopping with her friends right now. Maybe Mr. Barlow would still be alive."

"My client has nothing to say." Akorn put a restraining hand on Swaine. "Don't say anything."

Swaine pushed the hand off again. "You shut up. Just shut up. You can't even get me a deal, and now they're saying someone was murdered and it's my fault? Shut up. I can handle this." He spit that out, and Akorn backed off with a frown.

"You got my whole crew. All of it. Billy Williams hired them. They couldn't tell you anything. They don't know anything. There wasn't anyone else. You're crazy. We didn't kill anyone." He sat. "You can't pin this on me. My crew is in jail. I've been in jail." He threw his chin in the air.

The attorney got a word in. "My client is willing to trade some details for some leniency for the crimes he may have been involved in."

Gibbs ignored him. "You don't have a man watching Patsy's father?"

"No. Why would I need that? Patsy was going to call her father and have him transfer money. The whole thing would be over in an hour. I didn't need to watch Corson."

David let out a breath. Gibbs was getting them what they needed.

"Stop, Mr. Swaine. Don't say anything more." Akorn tried to calm his client. "This man needs to give you some proof there actually was a kidnapping."

Gibbs responded with a name. "Floyd Childer."

Swaine appeared puzzled for a moment. "Childer? What does Childer have to do with anything? He's some half-assed bodyguard. He doesn't know anything about—" Swaine stopped short. He seemed to realize what he'd said. His attorney squeezed his arm. "Uh, I mean, I don't know anything about Childer. He's Patsy's bodyguard."

David snorted. Gibbs was really playing the guy.

"Childer is saying different. Claims he works for you, Mr. Swaine, and followed your plan to kidnap Ms. Corson this morning. He snatched both Ms. Corson and her friend and took them to a house in the Estates. A house you rented, Mr. Swaine." All the truth.

Swaine dropped his head onto the table. Not as hard as David had envisioned slamming it. When he raised it, he said, "No way. He didn't know anything about, ah, what, ah, I might have been planning."

"Mr. Childer says this was all your idea. You made all the plans and hired him."

"I might have got him the job. Corson needed a Florida licensed guard." Swaine raised a shoulder. "I knew Childer from the old days. Recommended him. Knew he wouldn't be any trouble."

"Shit," Scott muttered. "How come we didn't know that?" He pulled out his cell.

"You recommended him?" Gibbs asked.

"Corson needed a guard. I knew Childer had a license. Figured if anything went wrong and the cops heard about the abduction, they'd look at him."

If anything went wrong? David almost bit his lip. Robin had almost been killed.

"We were only going to keep Patsy an hour. Two at the most. A wire transfer doesn't take long. Corson would never go public with the kidnapping. We'd, um, maybe threaten him if he did. No one was supposed to be hurt." The last sentence was almost a whine.

David swore. "He plans to grab her at a big rally and not expect someone to be hurt? He thinks no one will notice?"

"You arranged for both guards to be sick," Gibbs stated.

"Yeah. I didn't want anyone hurt. If the guards were sick, my men could just walk in and take Patsy. Didn't know Corson was calling in new guards."

"Childer says you told him to shoot anyone who got in the way." He paused a moment and gave Swaine a way out. "Don't answer yet. Here is the new deal. One of you will go down for capital murder. Florida has the death penalty. First one to give us the whole story gets a lighter sentence. Is Childer telling the truth?"

Swaine screamed, "No. No. He couldn't have told you that. He didn't know anything about the kidnapping. He can't know."

"Not only did he know, he put the plan into play. How else would we know about the house in the estates. The one you rented."

"They were only supposed to detain her. I didn't mean for anyone to be hurt. This is not the way it was supposed to happen. I had to have the money." Swaine was sobbing. "Childer? If Childer killed anyone, it had nothing to do with me. He couldn't have told you anything. He doesn't know."

Akorn stood. "A moment alone with my client. Please."

Gibbs nodded. "Three minutes." He picked up his file and left the room.

Four minutes later Swaine gave it all up.

Four long minutes, of pacing, checking his phone, not thinking about what could be happening to Robin. But Gibbs did it. Pulled it off. Without any signed agreement.

The attorney did all the talking.

"My client wants to help the police. He never intended to stand in their way. Mr. Swaine's idea was simply for Ms. Corson to go to this house he rented and stay there for a few hours until her father transferred the twenty-three million dollars into a numbered account. As soon as the transfer occurred, Ms. Corson could, um, ah, leave. She was never in any danger."

The attorney glossed over the kidnapping, making it seem like Patsy had accepted an invitation to view an open house.

David's fingers curled into claws. He could hear the noise Swaine's head would make when he slammed it against the table. Scott laid a hand on his shoulder. David had to straighten his fingers which were frozen into talons before he could wipe them over his face. This was what? The third? Fourth time Scott had calmed him?

"My client has no idea how Mr. Childer found out about his plans to um, detain Patsy or transfer the money. We'll give you the house address and he will answer all your questions. Mr. Swaine did not murder anyone and is not responsible for anything done while he was in jail."

And that was it. But they still didn't know if Childer was acting alone.

Scott and David headed for the Estates. Finally. Scott drove; David listened to Robin's recording three more times. Each time he heard the threat, he wanted to pull Childer through the phone and squeeze his neck, using his thumbs to crush his windpipe. His anger didn't ease off, but he had to get himself under control if he was to be of any help to anyone. He ran the tape through again.

Childer sounded sincere. *No one has to be hurt. I'll leave you here for your father to find.*

David didn't believe him. Kidnapping and murder would count against Childer only if he was caught. Killing the women would insure he wouldn't be caught. And, if he were caught, if they were dead, no one would be alive to identify him.

David's jaw ached; his palms were sweaty. No way to know what Childer was doing.

"Easy," Scott said. "He has to keep them alive. At least until he gets the payoff. That's a few hours away. He doesn't know we know."

Black radioed, "We're set up in the parking lot of the restaurant, out of sight, in back."

They pulled into the lot a few minutes later, parked, and exited their car. David was surprised when Colin and Ryan pulled in behind, but, after a slight hesitation, he nodded once, and they entered the command vehicle together.

Black frowned when he saw the two civilians, grimaced and said, "You stay inside." Gave Colin a speculative look; nodded toward the parking lot. "Your vehicle?" he asked. "We can use it. The GPS shows them in the third house; I want to see the front. Real time, not Google time. I want to send a man down that street, past that house, but all our vehicles are police issue."

Colin tossed the keys over. Black in turn tossed them without warning to a cop who caught them easily. "Marty, video the grounds and the neighboring properties," he told her. "Get us the number off the brown mailbox."

"Sure, Boss. Come on, Henderson," she said and they both left.

David knew her, hadn't recognized her in all the gear; SWAT wore dark clothes, vests, helmets with headsets. He needed to get his mind off what was happening to Robin and onto the task at hand. Pay attention.

Black pointed at a thin guy with close-cropped hair. "That guy there will pull the floor plan from County Building Review, and, Timmy," he pointed to a second guy, "is in contact right now with the chopper which is about to give us an aerial visual." Timmy was more solid than the thin blond and sported a pony tail which would have done Marty proud. "Once we know the entrances and exits, my people will pull the power and go in."

"How long?" David asked. The command center was open enough and the white walls should have added a feeling of roominess, but he still felt confined, trapped. Maybe it was all the people. More like he needed to be out doing something. Kicking in the door of the house.

"Half an hour, forty minutes. No more."

Not long. But a long time. "I want to go with you."

"You know I can't let you do that, Ramirez. But as soon as we clear the building, you can go in."

"But—"

"No. We know our job; let us do it. My team works with my team and only my team. You'll be in the way and mistakes can happen. Mistakes always mean someone gets hurt. We don't want any mistakes."

David knew that, but hell… These men were trained to work together, knew what to expect from each other. Robin was too precious to take such a chance. He'd be in their way. He hated it, but concentrated on his breathing, his fingers had curled into talons again.

"Tell me about the last two kidnap attempts," Black said. "I've heard the scuttlebutt. What happened? Did the women keep it together? Tell me about this woman who gave us all the directions? Anything I should know before we move?"

Yeah, he thought. She's beautiful and funny. She's warm and caring. I love her. All that went through his mind and he faltered at the last thought. Love?

He gave Black a succinct account, then said, "Both women are tough, smart. They won't get in your way." He didn't say, it's me who might not be able to function.

The monitor came to life with video of the street and houses, the driveways. The brown mailbox, number 3887, stood at the entrance of a long drive which wound around a stand of trees. The house was hidden. The next two drives led to small houses near the road. Marty made a U-turn and videoed across the street before she parked, blocking the dirt lane to 3887.

Someone put a Google map on the overhead. A dirt track ran behind the restaurant, paralleling 951, from 25th to 29th avenues. Trees on either side of the track would offer the SWAT team cover.

"Chopper video on monitor two. From the nose camera," Timmy said. "The camera is tied into the county appraisers' office."

David didn't hear the chopper, which meant Childer couldn't either.

The skinny guy continued. "We got the floor plan and the owner." The information appeared on the monitor.

"Contact him," Black said.

The plan showed the front door on the street side in the center of the building between two windows, the double garage door to the left. The side wall had a single door and a small window, then a high bathroom window about six feet off the ground, and a larger bedroom window. The back had three sliders opening onto a deck. The near side had two more bedroom windows, one bathroom window. No door on this side.

Black tapped the path on the Google map. "We go down here. Split up at the back corner. Surround the house. Marty and Henderson drive in from the street, blocking the drive. Gleason, Smith take the garage side door. Johnson, Duke, the living room slider; Ayers, you're with me at this bedroom slider. Pull the power. Go in together. Hit them from three directions."

Black looked at the chopper view and swore. "Damn. He has the hurricane shutters down. Louvered, so he can see out. We can't get through those. New plan. Marty and Henderson, stay with the car. Me and Ayers slip up to the front door with a ram. Gleason, Smith, Johnson, Duke on the garage side door. Duke, you pick the lock. When you're at the inner door, give the signal and we go through the two doors at the same time."

Black looked at David. "One man? In there?"

"Everything we've heard supports that, but we don't know," David said. "Childer could have picked up somebody. There could be more men in the house."

Black gave an abrupt nod. "We plan on more, anyhow." He turned to Timmy. "Warrants come through for the thermal camera, infrared? We need to locate everyone in the building."

"We got it. Chopper's sending it now."

They saw three hot shapes. One in the kitchen. Two in the back of the house in the master bedroom.

"Get some audio."

"Yes, Sir."

The chopper was well equipped thanks to confiscated drug money, old government equipment, and grants.

Nothing. No sound. Wasn't it working?

"No one's talking. Otherwise we'd pick it up. Okay. Gleason, Smith, you take point."

"I'm going with you," David said. He wasn't going to be left behind to cool his heels and pace this small area. He had to be near Robin. He raised his hands, palm out. "I'll stay back. But I need to be there." Not quite begging.

Black gave him a long look. "Grab a headset. Follow behind." He pointed toward David. "Stay out of the way. You don't go into the house until we have it cleared." He waited for agreement, then they set off down the path, stooping down when they reached the back corner of the property. Gleason set up the handheld infrared.

"One in the living room. Two people, looks like in the master bedroom. In the back. One of them is in the bathroom area. One near the bedroom door."

"What are they doing?"

"Hard to tell."

"Okay. Like we planned it. Not you Ramirez. Stay behind us. Stay outside. If you go running in there, you might cause someone to end up dead." He looked at David a moment to make sure he understood and turned back to his men. "Okay, lets head out. Smith, you—"

Black's words were drowned out by an earsplitting, horrific scream. A scream which rose and rose.

David could hear it inside his headphones. And outside. He thought it would never end, but ultimately it wavered and stopped. He was breathing through his mouth now. His fists clenched tightly, his nails digging into his palms. Ready to run for the house. Knowing he couldn't. Couldn't help.

Gleason said calmly, "Infrared shows two bodies in the master bedroom."

David stared helplessly at the house. Made a move toward it. Two bodies?

"One more body, moving toward the bedroom," Gleason added.

People he meant? Gleason meant people? Live people? Not dead bodies?

"Go. Go. Go," Black ordered in his mic. "Break in the doors."

A second shrill scream rent the air. Bloodcurdling. Heartrending. David understood what those words meant now. He felt as if the blood in his veins had stopped flowing, congealed; his heart stopped beating.

Robin.

The scream cut off sharply.

He froze in place.

The silence hung.

Then Ayers broke in the front door, yelling, "Police!"

Similar warnings sounded from the far side.

A dreadful silence followed.

David broke into a run. Stopped on the front stoop, heard the team move through the house as they cleared each room. Black and Ayers were blocking the hall, but he could see the heads of Gleason and Smith. Ayers moved forward a step. He reached out and grabbed a woman, propelling her around him and handing her off to Duke who had just charged in from the kitchen. Duke grabbed her to him protectively and, shielding her, ran with her out the front door.

All David could see was brown hair. Robin?

Once on the stoop Gleason let her go.

Patsy. Crying. "Robin. Robin. In there. Robin."

Oh, God. Oh, God. Robin. His heart dropped into his stomach. His breath stuck in his lungs. Time stopped. He was numb.

I never told you I love you.

He couldn't see down the hall. Too many men in the way. They were bracing a doorway.

Love you.

"Police!" Black yelled. This was followed by his shocked voice. "Son of a bitch." A pause. "Call a bus."

An ambulance? For Robin? She was still alive? He couldn't see. He dared to step inside and move down the hall. It felt like he was slogging through quicksand, like walking in a nightmare. He managed to put one foot in front of the other, afraid of what he would see. Men filled the doorway. He peered over a shoulder.

A body on the floor. He held his breath. Leaned forward, and got a full view.

A man. Groaning. Holding his arm to his chest. Rocking himself. Childer.

David exhaled. Robin. Where was she?

He searched the room. Black's back to him. Holding someone. He turned. Robin. Standing. One arm hanging by her side; her hand clutching something so tightly he could see the white knuckles from the doorway. A broken toilet tank cover?

Black spoke softly, moving his hand gently down her arm.

"It's okay. You can let it go," he said as he tried to loosen her fingers.

She glanced down at his hand on her arm and the broken lid locked in her fingers.

David unclenched his own fists.

"Oh," she whispered trancelike. "It was the only weapon we had. Patsy went into the bathroom and screamed. I yelled at Childer through the door. When he unlocked it and came in, I hit him in the stomach with it. That was as high as I could swing. He fell and raised his gun to shoot me and I smashed his arm. I think I broke it." She stopped, gulped, hiccupped, took a breath and looked guilty. "His arm I mean. The gun went flying. I yelled to Patsy to run and she ran past us out the door. Then you guys came in."

"You're not hurt?" David moved toward her. She shook her head. He unlocked her fingers and took the broken lid from her, passing it to Smith. He pulled her away from Black and wrapped her in his arms.

"Oh, baby." He brushed a kiss on her hair. Rubbed her back. Held her tightly to him.

Gleason walked over grinning. "Guy's arm is broken in two places. Couple of fingers smashed. Broken ribs too, maybe." He looked back at the kidnapper. "Nothing serious."

He passed an envelope to Black. "Airline tickets for tomorrow. Maybe he really was going to leave them alive."

"I didn't believe him," Robin said as if still in a trance. "I hit him because I thought he would kill us."

Johnson stepped in. "He was planning on killing you. Found a freshly dug hole in the backyard, about the right size for two bodies."

Ramirez paled. Black noticed. "Ramirez, why don't you go with the women back to the command center? Marty, you drive. Give the car back to Gibbs. I'll meet you up there. Want to have a word with Childer first, read him his rights."

**

Robin closed her eyes, practiced slow, relaxed breathing and clasped her hands in her lap. They were still apt to tremble if she didn't. It wouldn't be much longer. She hoped. All she wanted was to go home, shower, and collapse on her bed. She'd have a good long cry, too, probably in the shower. She'd been able to hold it together so far only because she didn't want to embarrass herself.

This part, sitting in the police station, telling her story over and over again, was almost as bad as the kidnapping. By God, couldn't these cops just let her go? How many times did she have to relive it? Three times, in what they called the command center. Four or five times here at the station. Agent Tucker, another agent, she never caught his name, then Tucker with David, then David with Scott. Like musical chairs.

Never David alone. He was angry, distant, detached, as if last night had never happened. As if he'd never held her tight in that house. She'd wanted to stay buried in his arms, but he'd set her aside. Now he wouldn't look at her. She couldn't stand it.

She felt a hand on her shoulder and when she looked up to see him staring at her, she lost it.

"No." She shook her head. "I will not tell the story one more time. I signed a statement and now I want to go home." She stopped. Her car was in an impound yard. "I want my car. I want to go home." The words didn't come out quite as forcefully as she wished, but at least she hadn't whined.

"I'm sure someone told you we're keeping your car a couple of days."

She felt herself about to throw a hissy fit, stomp her foot. She so did not want to be reduced to such childish behavior and pressed her lips tightly together.

"Calm down." He squeezed her shoulder. "I'll take you home and we'll arrange for a loaner."

She didn't want him to take her home. She didn't want to be in a car with him right now. He was too angry. Remote. Where was the man who had held her this morning before the sun rose fully? The one who had carried her from the kidnap house, kissing her hair, and murmuring soothing words. She wanted him to gather her in, comfort her, not treat her like some victim who needed a ride home.

"I'll get a cab. I want to go." She reached into her purse for her phone, remembered the police had taken that too and felt like bawling. But she wasn't going to in front of all these cops, in front of him.

"I need to borrow a phone."

"I'll take you home," he repeated, "and you can take my phone. Keep it until we're finished with yours."

"Yeah, that will work well when I'm called out to a murder scene which is exactly what I need." It wasn't a whine, more of a complaint.

"My personal phone."

So now she'd get his morning after women calling. She was not going there.

"Call me a cab. I don't need your phone."

"I said, I'll take you home."

He was determined, and she wasn't going to win this argument, she stood and headed for the door. He caught up with her and took her arm as if they were on a date, and she was too tired to fight him; she let him lead her to his car and open the passenger door. She stepped inside quickly. Her hands shook when she tried to buckle her seat belt. He knocked them away and did it for her; his hands shook, too. Then he shut the door and walked around to his side.

She kept her head down. She didn't want to see him. His scent filled the car and tears burned her eyes. She turned her face to the window, so he wouldn't be able to see them. Staring out unseeing, she took a deep breath. Three. She used a thumb and forefinger on the bridge of her nose surreptitiously wiping her tears, hoping it would look like a headache.

They rode in silence. It was not a comfortable silence. He apparently had nothing to say and she was afraid she would cry if she opened her mouth.

When he parked, she reached for the door handle, saying, "Don't bother coming around, I can manage the door." It came out as a hoarse croak. She reached for the door handle and for the first time looked up.

"This isn't my house," she blurted.

"It's mine. I don't want you alone."

He came around for her, helped her out and led her to the front door before she came to her senses and stopped. She shocked herself when she said, "But you never bring women home. You told me."

"You are not any woman."

"Right. You've treated me like a criminal all day."

"Come inside. We'll talk."

He unlocked the door and pulled her inside, took her to the kitchen and pushed her in front of a chair. "Sit."

She was so surprised, she did and watched as he opened a cupboard under the sink to pull out a bottle. He took two brandy glasses from an upper cupboard. Put one in front of her on the table and filled it. Then he sat across from her and poured a shot for himself. He gulped it in one swallow like a man in need and immediately poured another shot.

"Drink." He motioned to her glass.

"It's too early."

"Not for you. Any idiot can see you've reached the end of your rope. You're exhausted. You need some rest." He shook his head. "Never mind. Drink. Sip it."

She heard something in his voice and studied his face and saw barely controlled rage. His eyes were narrowed, his jaw clenched.

"What is it?"

"It's cognac. Sip it."

She reached for her glass and took a sip, not taking her eyes off him. It burned. She watched the muscles in his jaw relax.

"Another."

She did and felt the warmth spread through her chest. She looked around the kitchen, noticed no dirty dishes in the sink, clear counters except for the usual: coffee maker, toaster, knife set. She wondered idly if he cooked. Couldn't remember if he'd told her.

He sipped his drink. Motioned for her to take another. It seemed to be working on him at least. His lips were no longer a flat straight line; they had some shape. She didn't want to remember them on her.

"When was the last time you ate?"

She thought back. "Supper. Last night."

"No wonder you're falling down." He stood and opened the refrigerator and pulled out a container. "Leftover mac and cheese." After sticking it in the microwave, he turned and opened a drawer; took out a spoon and placed it in front of her.

She watched him, silently.

He was still angry, but not the spitting mad he had been. He took another small sip of his cognac.

When the microwave beeped, he set the bowl in front of her. "Eat," he ordered and sat across from her again.

Through gritted teeth he said, "I did not treat you like a criminal. I treated you like a witness. The same as I treated Patsy."

She didn't know how they had treated Patsy; they'd been kept separated.

"I treated you the way I had to treat you. Doing my job," he said between teeth still clenched, anger bleeding through.

"But I'm not Patsy." *I'm your lover.*

She looked into his eyes and felt a warm spot in her lower belly and a flush moving up her face. He did that to her. She hoped he would attribute it to the brandy. Confused, she spooned up a small bite of the mac and cheese. Tasted bacon. It was good. She took another bite. Now she felt a different warmth in her belly.

"I want you to stay here tonight, with me. You shouldn't be alone."

She shook her head. Not a smart idea. She thought of all the reasons not to. Actually, couldn't think of any. She blamed that on the brandy.

"You don't have to take care of me," she said. "I'm sure you have other things you need to do." Now, being too near to him didn't seem such a problem. She sighed. The brandy again.

He stood over her so quickly it startled her. She saw the fury on his face.

"If I'd let myself feel anything; I would have broken Childer in half. If I'd comforted you, if I'd touched you, I'd have taken you on the squad room floor. I had to stay detached. I thought you were dead." His voice hitched. He quickly recovered. "I thought I'd lost you. I'd barely found you and then I thought you were gone. Everything went dark when I heard that scream." He closed his eyes. When he opened them again, they were wet with unshed tears. "I thought I had lost you," he repeated.

He reached out and pulled her up, kissed her forehead, her cheek. He turned her head up. Touched her lips.

She pulled back. "You were cold, distant."

He rubbed his hands over her hair, down her back. Strong, warm, comforting hands.

"I told you. I was afraid if I touched you, I'd grab you and take you right there. God, Robin, I was scared you were dead. I love you. I'd only just realized I loved you and Childer had you. I thought he'd killed you."

She heard the word. Buried in the harangue. Her world stopped.

"Love me? You love me?"

"Yes. I love you." He kissed her gently and for the first time, he smiled.

"Now. Finish your mac and cheese. Then you take a shower and lie down." He raised a single finger. "Don't argue."

She looked in her bowl; she was hungry. And she was tired, dirty. It was what she'd planned to do anyhow. Why not do it here? *He loves me?*

She finished her food and stood. When she leaned over to pick up her bowl she stumbled. He caught her.

"It's the brandy," she said.

"Right." He gave her another kiss and led her to the bathroom off his bedroom. "Shower. You'll feel better." He turned the water on, tested it. "I'll bring you some clothes."

She stripped off her shorts and top, didn't want to ever wear them again, and stepped in the shower and let the warm water wash over her. The picked up the soap, it smelled of him, and she held it to her face and inhaled his scent. She rubbed it all over and used his shampoo on her hair. She washed away the grime and the remnants of the fear and the tension she'd felt in the police station and in the car. She had promised herself a good cry in the shower, but instead she laughed. He loved her.

She was bone tired and the warm water worked with the brandy and the food to calm her nerves. She could sleep. She found a clean t-shirt, his, and drawstring pants on the counter and he was waiting in the bedroom with the covers pulled down on the bed.

She crawled in. He climbed in beside her and curled her into him. "Sleep. We'll nap together." He was warm and comfortable where he'd pulled her close.

She was safe. In his arms. He kissed the back of her head and murmured, "I love you."

Loves me was her last thought; she was asleep as soon as her head reached the pillow.

She was locked in the dark room. He was out there. The monster. She knew he was coming. But some part of her knew what to do. "Go away!" she screamed. "You're not real." The ogre stopped, and light flooded the room. The monster dissolved.

Arms grabbed her. Held her. A voice in her ear. Soft comforting. "I have you, It's okay. You're safe. Wake up, honey. It's a dream."

David's voice. David's scent. David holding her.

"I'm okay," she croaked. "I'm okay." Safe in his arms. "I have nightmares. I had one after the mugging." She hiccupped. "Again after the convention, when Colin saved me."

She felt him stiffen when she mentioned the name. Jealous?

"Ryan Gibbs and Becca stayed with me that night," she explained. "Becca warmed milk. Gibbs, um, Ryan, sat with me. Like you're doing now."

She was okay, she had directed the nightmare. David had saved her. "I can warm milk."

She touched the tears on his face and remembered what Becca had said about letting Ryan warm milk.

"Warm milk will help." Another half hiccup. She nodded her head. Wiped her own eyes. "Can I watch? And maybe you can tell me again, you love me?"

"I love you."

Email the author at jaygeeheath@gmail.com

Visit her webpage at http://www.jaygeeheath.com/

Romantic Mystery
Right Dreams
by jay gee heath
cover design by Susan E. Jameson

Find at Amazon

She could deal with the pain. Knew how to work around it. Had worked through pain often enough before. It was the timing that sucked. These wounds were going to be career ending. Just great. Monday, she breaks up with her lover; Friday she kills her career. Hopefully, not herself too.

Romantic Mystery
Right Skills
by jay gee heath

When her husband returns after a ten-month disappearance, Cilla soon finds herself embroiled in a dangerous world of revenge, cyber espionage, and money laundering.

Mystery
Right Response
by jay gee heath

cover design by Susan E. Jameson

Ex-cop Becca Travis teams up with her FBI agent fiancé to solve a mysterious case involving multiple murders, drug running, and dirty bombs.

Romantic Mystery
Right Talents
by jay gee heath

Pregnant and alone, May starts over in the small coastal town of Cougars Cove where a stolen painting, an undercover investigation, and a promotional weekend give her a second chance at life and love.

The cat with attitude, T F Gato, tells humorous tales about his escapades with the wildlife and people in the Everglades. Includes eight delightful illustrations by Mia Mazza.

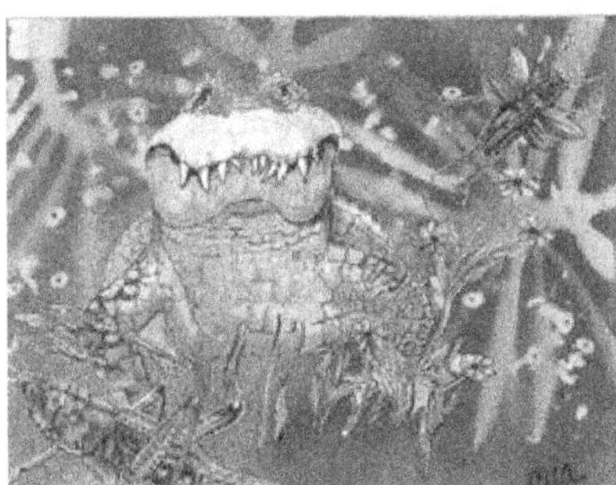